EAST *of the* ORTEGUAZA

The Story of an American Military Advisor and The Colombian Drug War

A Novel

Victor M. Roselló
Colonel, United States Army, Ret

ISBN: 1453691642
ISBN-13: 9781453691649

Published by Victor M. Roselló, Williamsburg, Virginia, USA.

Printed by CreateSpace 2010

Book cover design consultation courtesy of Stanley Erwin.

Front cover photo of Colombian Air Force UH-60 Blackhawk heli-copter courtesy of Santiago Castillo G., Bogotá, Colombia.

Back cover photo of Tres Esquinas courtesy of author.

CIA maps of Colombia, Base 803337AI (R00820) 1-08, courtesy of the University of Texas Libraries, University of Texas at Austin.

Modified maps of El Salvador based on UN map No. 3903 Rev. 3, May 2004, courtesy of the Department of Peacekeeping Operations, UN Cartographic Section.

Aerial photo of Tres Esquinas military base showing the aircraft runway and the Orteguaza River

★ ★ ★

DEDICATION

This book is dedicated to the residents of Leavenworth, Kansas and Williamsburg, Virginia. These two cities both figured prominently in the history of the United States of America. They also played major roles in this writing project. The first pages of this book were written in the city of Leavenworth, Kansas. As the first city of Kansas, Leavenworth is an appropriate origin for a novel due to its rich history and symbolism as a branch and starting point of the Santa Fe Trail in Kansas and the new age of American westward expansion. Similarly in importance, Williamsburg became the second capital of the British colony of Virginia (Jamestown was the first) and it symbolizes the earliest beginnings of our Nation from British colony to American republic. Williamsburg's rich history is an appropriate end point for the last page written and edited at Aromas Café on Prince George Street in Colonial Williamsburg. Fate brought me to these two wonderful locations and I am most grateful to the many people in both cities who inspired and encouraged me during this six year journey. Finally, and most important of all, this book is dedicated to the courageous men and women of the United States and Colombian Armed Forces who risk their lives daily in fulfillment of the many duties and activities described in this book with honor, humility, loyalty, selfless service, and quiet professionalism.

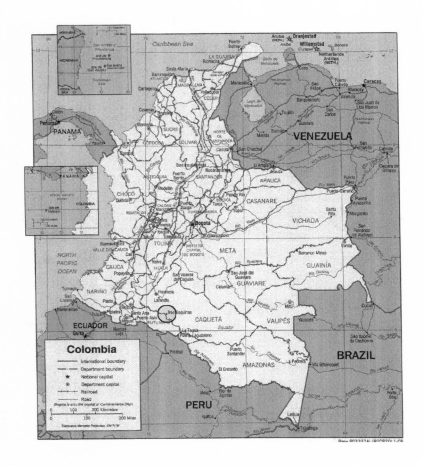

Colombia

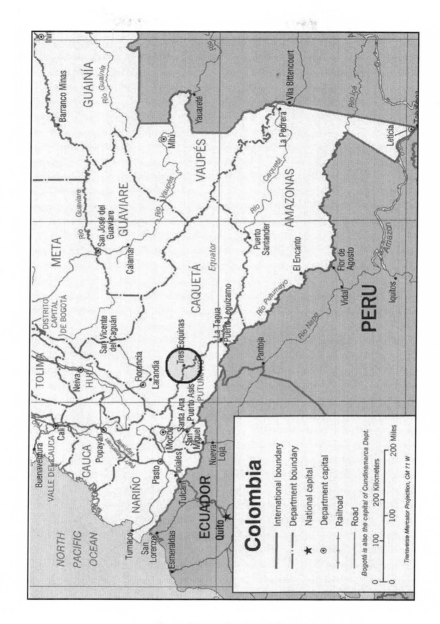

Southern Colombia

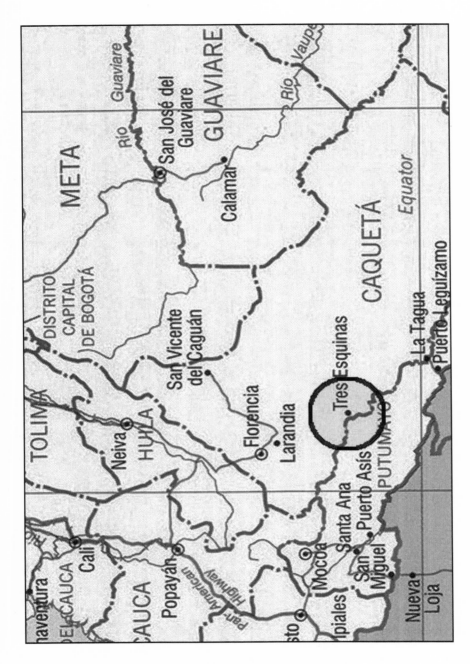

Caquetá Department

PREFACE

★ ★ ★

COLOMBIA: 2001

In 1999 the US and Colombian governments became active partners in countering illicit drug production and trafficking in Colombia. At the beginning of his four year term in 1998, Colombian president, Andrés Pastrana, agreed to allow the principle and most powerful guerrilla organization in his country, the *Fuerzas Armadas de Revolución Colombiana* or FARC, to establish a safe-haven. This safe-haven, a Demilitarized Zone, *Zona de Distensión,* or *Despeje*, as referred to by the Colombians, was a 40 thousand square kilometer zone of Colombian territory where the government and guerrillas began the deliberate and laborious process of attempting to negotiate an end to hostilities.

In conjunction with this peace initiative and to demonstrate its resolve, the US government contributed $1.3 billion dollars to help this country of 40 million more effectively combat the Colombian drug menace.

As part of its military contribution to this effort, the US Government provided new UH-60 Blackhawk helicopters along with other military equipment and support programs. It also began assigning American military advisors to the war ravaged country to assist in training fledgling counter-drug units under the umbrella plan, Plan Colombia. Approximately 200 American military advisors deployed to Colombia during this early period.

In early 1999 military advisors from the US Army's 7th Special Forces Group trained the newly activated 1st Counter-Narcotics Battalion or 1st BACNA in the Colombian base of Tolemaida near

Melgar, *Departamento,* Department or province, of Tolima. The 1st BACNA then moved to *Tres Esquinas* in Caquetá Department, a remote military base in southern Colombia near the Ecuadorian and Peruvian borders. Subsequently, two more battalions, the 2d and 3rd BACNA's, were trained and placed under a newly established 1st CN Brigade headquarters in Larandia, a military base near Florencia, and approximately 65 miles north of Tres Esquinas. The mission of these units was to destroy the drug-producing infrastructure deep in the jungles of southern Colombia.

Built in defense against Peru in 1932, the base of Tres Esquinas took on additional importance in February 2000 with establish-ment of *Fuerza de Tarea Conjunta del Sur*, or Joint Task Force-South, the Colombian Armed Forces joint command headquarters in southern Colombia responsible for military operations in sup-port of Plan Colombia. With as much as 70% of Colombian co-caine being produced in the southern Departments of Putumayo, Caquetá, and western Amazonas, Tres Esquinas was positioned at the heart of this hotly contested area of Colombia. This remote military base became the staging and launch point for helicopter-borne assaults, close air support missions, and waterborne naval operations by the 12,500 Colombian Armed Forces and National Police personnel assigned or under operational control of the JTF-South command.

To enhance Colombian military operations in Tres Esquinas, the US government created an entity capable of providing all-source military intelligence to the JTF-South commander. This entity was called the COJIC, the Colombian Joint Intelligence Center. Within the barbed wire perimeter fence around the base at Tres Esquinas and the chain link surrounding an olive drab canvas and tubular metal framed structure, US Army military in-telligence (MI) advisors helped develop a credible intelligence apparatus designed to support military counter-narcotics opera-tions. These military operations targeted and destroyed hundreds of cocaine producing and refining laboratories that dotted the Colombian countryside. This remote and isolated jungle base, accessible only by air or river, and 40 miles from the Ecuadorian and Peruvian borders with Colombia, is the main setting of this novel.

CHAPTER ONE

NARRATOR'S INTRODUCTION

One late Saturday afternoon while walking through the expanse of aisle ways of a popular retail department store, I made my way to the checkout counter that had the least number of shoppers standing in line. It was one of the those shopping moments…you know the kind…where you run into a store intending to buy just one thing and then you pick up those other things you've been meaning to buy. Upon checking off the handful of items that I carried…three fly fishing lures, a tippet line nipper, two ceramic candle holders, a car battery wrench, and a box of bran flakes cereal…the cashier inadvertently interrupted my mental daze.

"Thank you for shopping at Walmart, Mister Vallejo," the smiling cashier innocently said as she handed me back my credit card and sales receipt. Her voice jarred me back into the uncomfortable reality of the moment. As proper societal norms dictate, I responded with the ritualistic and socially correct, "You're very welcome."

Hello, my friends, I'm your narrator, retired US Army Colonel Ricardo J. Vallejo *pronounced Vah-yeh-ho*, but you can call me Rick. As your narrator, I will be guiding you on a journey to an exciting world that will be new to you. Throughout this journey, I will also be sharing some exciting and at times rather personal information with you.

I will begin by admitting something I'm most ashamed of because it really is quite trivial, almost childish. When I tell you, you will probably say that it is pure nonsense. But I have to get this off my chest. Please indulge me for a minute and by all means, try maintaining an open mind. Here goes…

As a recently retired Army career officer with thirty years of service, I still cringe every time I'm referred to as 'Mister.' Please, don't laugh. I know it is probably difficult for you to sympathize with me. After thirty years of holding a formal title of authority… Lieutenant… Captain… Major… Lieutenant Colonel…Colonel… the title of Mister has no significance or value to me. It's a put down. It's an empty title that has the same degree of importance as simply being called a 'man' or a 'woman.' Yes, I know it's an honorary title of respect and courtesy bestowed upon the senior members of society by its younger members. But it is a title and an honor simply earned for weathering life and just being a living and breathing part of it. Even worse, after serving in key and important leadership positions of authority and responsibility in our military, I have now been thrown into the vast ocean of a nameless and non-titled society. Yes, the transition from military to civilian life can be painful and quite difficult.

To lessen the pain, Congress could pass a law honoring all its retired military commissioned and noncommissioned officers with permanent ranks-for-life. Army warrant officers wouldn't get much benefit from this law since even in the Army they are addressed as "Mister" or "Miss"; unless, of course, they accepted the title of "Chief." I guess I could go back to college and earn a PhD or MD degree so that I could be referred to as *Doctor*. But after retiring late in life, it is probably not practical. An alternative might be to move to a Spanish-speaking country where the title, *Licenciado* or licensed individual is used. In many Spanish speaking countries Licenciado is an honorary title that is often bestowed on discharged military members, college graduates, college professors, or lawyers. Isn't that cool?…A title of honor for life.

I don't know if you are aware of this, but retired generals are still called generals after they retire. Why not extend this honor to all career military personnel? You see this formal recognition within military circles or when Fox or CNN want to reinforce the credibility of their military commentators. In my opinion this is unfair business practice. These No-Longer-Serving-On-Active-Duty-Civilian-Generals should be subject to the same abuse that the rest of us NLSOADC nobodies suffer within a society that could care less about formal military titles. But society should. Never mind, though. I'm digressing. I guess the Walmart episode is still fresh on my mind. I'll change subjects and get down to the business of this novel.

A good place to start the discussion is to tell you what motivated me to write this book in the first place. Well for starters, let me say that it's complicated. So, allow me to give you a little background.

While typing the first pages of my manuscript, I find myself frequently pausing to cherish the many wonderful memories… the images of battlefields afar…the landscapes…the great soldiers…all the events that are a product of service in the US Armed Forces for the majority of those who served. More importantly, much of my service occurred in Latin America. You see, I served with a corps of officers educated and trained by our Army to work in Latin America. Those duties took me on combat tours to El Salvador during its conflict years in the 1980's, the invasion of Panama in 1989, later to Colombia as a military advisor in the year 2001, and all the other countries of the region in between.

The beautiful mosaic of memories burned in my mind of my tours in Latin America will give me comfort throughout my fading life. The people, the lands, the foods, the languages, the traditions…leave me inspired…inspired by the music and poetry of diversity and multiculturalism.

If I get sentimental, understand I'm a romantic and sentimentalist at heart. I could have probably served our nation as an artist, musician, writer, or poet, as well as a soldier. But, I have no regrets. I chose the profession of arms and I brought my sensitive nature and a true love of life and soldiering to the profession. I will never be ashamed of this because the military is an organization of people…and people, regardless of their profession, share similar ideals, loves, and hates that bind them together as humans. All soldiers, young and old, should be treated with respect and dignity. As a leader I gave my soldiers that respect, dignity, and more. It's called living by the Army core values. These values should be lived and exercised, not just given lip service, as can happen in any organization plagued with politics, competition, or backstabbing. Anyway, I'm digressing again. Let's get back on track. The overarching reason for writing this book goes well beyond simply sharing some of those wonderful images and experiences that I still cherish and hold so dearly.

The world revolves, pages turn, and so do our lives. But a turn in the pages of my life took me from Latin America to the city of Leavenworth, Kansas. This is where this book was born.

Leavenworth, the "First City of Kansas," is not your typical place of origin of a book about an American military advisor and the Colombian drug war. At the same time it is the most appropriate, fitting, and symbolic place for a number of reasons.

The city hosts the oldest active military post west of the Mississippi River…Fort Leavenworth. At Fort Leavenworth young military field grade officers hone their mid-level management, leadership, and educational skills at the prestigious US Army Command and General Staff College. It is a place of serious study… reflection… and discussion of the art and science of fighting wars. The college's location, high on a bluff overlooking the Missouri River, symbolically represents the school's veneration as a true military center of higher learning.

Between 1987 and 1988, I underwent the "Leavenworth Experience," the term used for an officer attending the US Army's Command and General Staff College. Unlike the tumultuous years that were to follow, these years were relatively peaceful times in which the US Army had few living examples of participants of war among its younger field grade officers. Beyond the few prior enlisted student officers who served in Vietnam during the late 1960's and early '70's, and the one or two student officers who participated in the invasion of Grenada in 1983, no one in my graduating class had served in combat.

At the time of my attendance, the Salvadoran conflict in the 1980's was in full swing. Since I had just returned from service in El Salvador as a military advisor prior to attending CGSC, I was one of few who could proudly talk about and share recent wartime experiences with fellow CGSC classmates. At that time, El Salvador was the only war in town for the US Army. I was so inspired by this that I wrote and published my first professional article on El Salvador while serving in Fort Leavenworth.

Now my life has come full circle. The *Yin* is in balance with the *Yang*. Eighteen years after graduating from CGSC, I returned to Leavenworth, Kansas, in my new status of retired officer. My family and I settled down there to enjoy the peace and quiet that draw people to the natural beauty of small town rural America. It is only appropriate that I now write this book as an opportunity to capture and share my last experiences in the Army as a military advisor to the Colombian Army, just as I captured and shared my early experiences as a military advisor to the Salvadoran Army when I was first stationed here in the late '80's.

As I type, outside my window the oak, elm, maple, and sweet gum trees are in full autumn splendor…the vivid palette of bright red, yellow, and orange serves as a colorful inspiration. But I also know that this splendor is but a brief moment in time. I must take advantage of this inspiring moment while it briefly lasts.

Speaking of inspiring moments, let's discuss the book's title and subtitle. You probably think that I've been purposely avoiding addressing this topic, but, honestly, I just have so many things I want to share with you that I'm trying to say them all at once and probably doing an inadequate job of it.

As the book title states, *East of the Orteguaza* is the story of an American military advisor and the Colombian drug war. Although this book is a novel, its title is a geographic reference to an actual place in time…a military base that was at the center of the drug war, deep inside the jungles of southern Colombia…and a place where I lived and worked.

Tres Esquinas, pronounced Tres-Es-kee-nahs, is the name of this military base. In Spanish it means three corners, or the junction where two rivers, the Orteguaza, *pronounced Or-teh-goo-áh-zah*, and the Caquetá, *pronounced Kah-keh-táh*, flow together to create one main river. The Río Orteguaza is a tributary of the Río Caquetá and it runs parallel and west of the base…hence, the title*, East of the Orteguaza*.

Orteguaza is believed to be one of many names derived from the native indigenous groups of this Amazonian region, such as the *Tukano, Koreguaje,* or *Huitoto*. Historical research reveals that in 1635, Franciscan missionaries may have been the first to Hispanicize the name Orteguaza from the name of the *Oyoguaja* tribe of the Tukano Family. Still another conjecture is that Orteguaza originated from the native indigenous word *Ocoguaje*, which literally means "people of the water." Regardless of what historians and anthropologists know or don't know, it's still pretty fascinating in my opinion. Don't you agree?

But even more fascinating, Tres Esquinas is also a metaphor for life's intersections. Those many times we arrive at the forks in the road of our lives. Like the flowing rivers that intersect this geographical point, fate brought me to this place…a place that affected my life in those ways that life has a nasty habit of doing.

As I said before, this book is a novel and like many novels, the characters, places, and events of this story are inspired by real events. I think inspirations, perceptions, and appearances are distinctly different interpretations of reality. This book portrays my truth…my reality…not *the* truth. Don't we view life as a collection of reality, the perception of that reality, our dreams, and our fantasies? Are we not shaped by our perception of truth? Don't our perceptions of truth eventually become the reality that we portray in diaries or memoirs? As our memory fades, are our recollections of events tainted or flawed? Are recollections then no longer the real truth? This is why this book is a novel…based in part on facts…flawed by fading memories…and supplemented by fictional inspiration. Is this confusing? Not really…at least in my mind.

Allow me the liberty of digressing again to make a point. In my college undergraduate English classes I was fascinated by the study of modern drama and in particular, the *Avant Garde* theater movement which manifested its themes in the dramatic genre of Theater of the Absurd. I think I was drawn to this movement because the exaggerations depicted in many dramatic scenes symbolized the absurdities of life. One English professor in particular would always put this point of view in perspective. In his lectures he would say:

"One of the main themes of these literary works is the duality of appearance and reality. Things never appear the way they really are…and things are never really the way they appear."

"Why is reality depicted in such a confusing or exaggerated manner, you ask?" He would briefly pause and then answer his own question.

"Because the playwrights want to show us that life is not simple. It is complicated. It is complex. That is why the writer's interpretations of it are not readily understood. They purposely exaggerate to the point of absurdity to focus attention on the very same absurdities of life itself." And of course some of us just didn't get it.

It's very similar to viewing a piece of modern art and wondering why kindergarten children aren't allowed to display their works in modern art museums. You walk away seemingly more confused than informed. And of course, that is the message. Life is not orderly. It often does not lend itself to be labeled, packaged, categorized, or neatly boxed. We see life through the lens and the perspective of our narrow views...our prejudices... our own standards...or our ethnocentricities. We are not taught to be critical thinkers or to suspend judgment to learn and understand new ideas or concepts.

"Ahemmmm," the professor would continue.

"So, in life there are two realities. Reality as it is perceived by us or as it exists internally in our minds." Again he would pause for emphasis. "And reality as it exists externally in our surroundings. This external reality could be referred to as the absolute truth. Every event exists in its absolute form. Then it is filtered, tempered, molded, reshaped, or even distorted by our interpretations or perceptions. You will see this idea portrayed at its finest, when we study the 1950's Japanese play *Rashomon* by Kurosama Akira."

"Another important theme in this genre is the lack of communication between people. If someone greets you with, 'Hi, how are you?' regardless of how you really feel, you will usually respond with, 'Fine, thank you.' For a kind act, favor, or compliment, you may hear, 'Thank you,' at which time we automatically respond with, 'You are welcome.' If someone walking down the street trips or falls, the first question to them is, 'Are you okay?'"

"This is not communication. This is simply robotic action... society's verbal rituals. These are preset or ascribed expressions and phrases that we ritualistically use without giving much thought to their meaning or really caring if we're communicating or not. Sometimes when two people are talking, their verbal discourse is nothing more than an exchange of words and bumper stickers…words thrown back and forth without any real communication from the heart. When the heart speaks, then we have true communication. Many of the playwrights capitalized on this point in their plays by simply having their characters utter groans or outrageous noises instead of talking, since in their mind this is as good as the ritualistic non-communication that makes up much of what we say to each other."

Allow me to interrupt the professor with my own 'ahemmmm' since I've managed to again lead you astray. I guess I continue to draw from my past to explain the present and future.

"Thank you, professor."

"You're very welcome…"

Okay, enough of that. Let's just get to the bottom line, shall we? The main topic of this novel is a quiet war; a war so quiet that it rarely catches the attention of the news media. I want this novel to focus on the many and varied facets of US military advisory missions in support of allies in far away and obscure places.

Quiet wars have quiet heroes and those quiet heroes are American military advisors. In the case of this novel, advisors assigned to missions in the jungles, valleys, plains, and mountainous regions of Colombia helping the Colombian Armed Forces fight the drug war…the other war…the quiet war.

Quiet wars are generally shrouded in secrecy, as well as intrigue. Very little of what goes on in places like Colombia is shared with the general public…both within the US and Colombia. In fact very little of what goes on in these types of missions is known or understood by the general military population at large. Unlike post 9/11 events in Afghanistan and Iraq that capture many aspects of military dedication and commitment, this novel will attempt to provide a flavor for that other side that never sees the light of film crews, embedded reporters,

or microphones. This is not because this work is highly classified or covert. It's because we as a nation do very poorly in
showing the true character of our work abroad. We don't openly
reveal how our national purpose and interests are supported
overseas. Why can't we honor professional dedication everywhere, regardless of location? Are these wars illegal...illegiti-
mate...or unlawful? I don't think so.

Like US military support to El Salvador that for many years
was shrouded in total secrecy, US military support to Colombia
appears to be on a similar glide path. But there are good things
happening. Good things that reflect the heart and soul of our military. Why can't we share some of this good?

It may be because, unlike a Tom Clancy novel, quiet wars
translate to quiet events; sometimes exciting, but most times not.
But we can't expect life to always be what gifted fictional novelists
depict. Sometimes it is important to simply show it as it really is.
Like life itself, quiet wars are the details of the real, sometimes
mundane business of soldiers devoting their lives daily to pre-
serving our rights and freedoms through personal dedication and
commitment to duty.

Through the magic of a word processor I would like to share
these details with you. Give me the opportunity to tell you about
these events. In removing the veil that obscures these quiet wars,
I hope you will discover something that you may not have previously known.

But I'll dispense with all the drama. I'm rolling up my sleeves
and getting right to work. The keys on my word processor are going a mile a minute. We've already discussed the setting of this
book. So, let's get this story started, shall we?

First things first, though. My story won't begin in Colombia.
Before we get to Colombia, we will take a U-turn in time back to
the country of El Salvador...during another quiet war. After the

introductory and stage setting comments at the beginning of the next chapter, I will engage you in an exciting military operation. Let's take a look and see what's going on. Are you ready? Then let's begin…

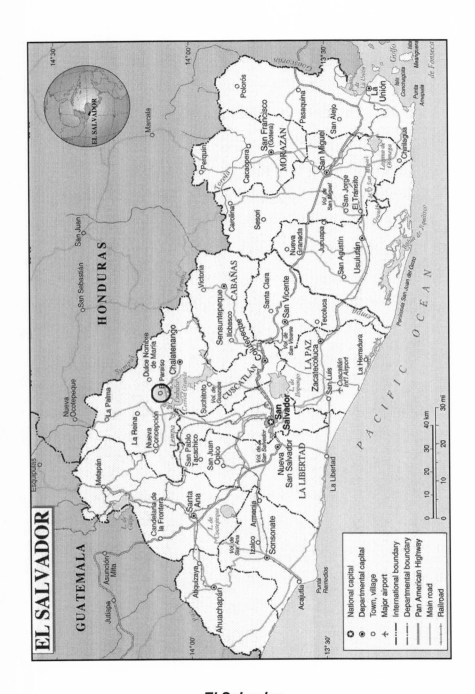

El Salvador

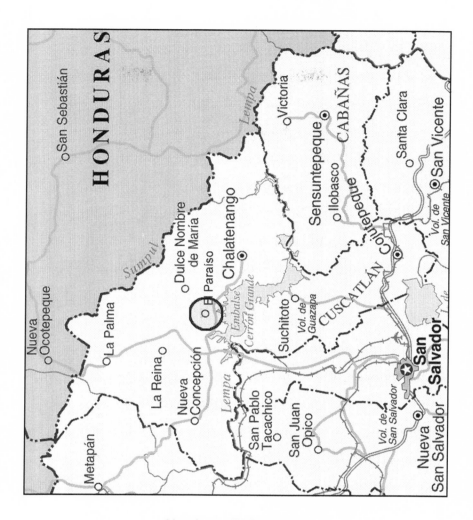

Northern El Salvador

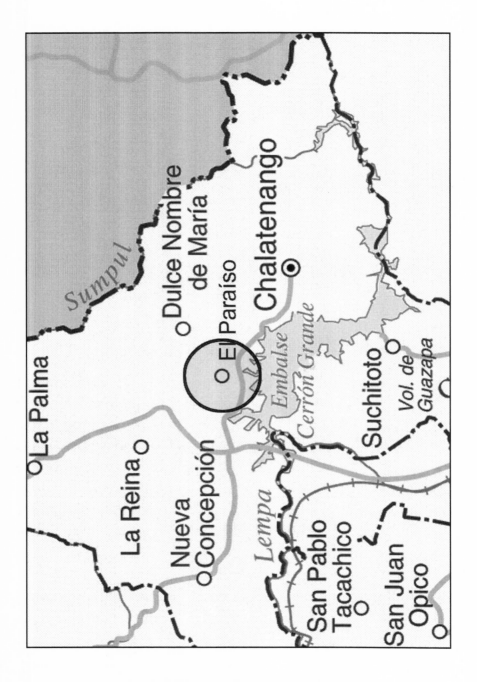

Chalatenango Department

CHAPTER TWO

★ ★ ★

SALVADORAN ECHOES

Mother, mother...there's too many of you crying...
Brother, brother, brother...there's far too many of
you dying...You know...we've got to find a way...
to bring some lovin' here today...

"What's Going On"
as recorded by Marvin Gaye

HEADQUARTERS, 4TH INFANTRY BRIGADE,
EL PARAISO, CHALATENANGO DEPARTMENT, EL SALVADOR
0130 HOURS, 31 MARCH 1987

Well, here we are in El Salvador, Central America's smallest country, but with people who have the biggest hearts in the region. As you surmise from the chapter descriptors, it is now 1987. To keep us chronologically on track, and you know how obsessed military people are with time and punctuality, I'll include a time and location in all the chapter headings so that you will know the time of day or night of each chapter. Very Tom Clancy-like, you know. If you can't read military or 24-Hour time, that's okay. I'll help you out. In this case it's quite early in the morning... 0130 hours...or 1:30 AM.

Then, let me create the mood for you. There will be lyrics from a song at the beginning of each chapter heading and at the end of the chapter. I think it is important to set the mood while we read and music is a very powerful medium for this. It can also bring to life moments and events of our past. Personally, I enjoy playing the piano for this very reason. I've played my entire life and it enriches me in many ways. Someday, I'll buy myself a brand new grand piano. When I die, may it be while playing the piano for there is nothing like ending life on a fine note.

So, ease yourself into the next scene. The soft and beautifully mesmerizing background music playing for you is Marvin Gaye's, *What's Going On.* Marvin Gaye's many inspiring lyrics and tunes during the 1960's and 1970's still reverberate today. *What's Going On* is a hauntingly beautiful anti-war tune that bridges time and space. It rings as true today as when it was first recorded and released during the Vietnam War era. Go on the web, find a copy of this song, and download it if you don't have a CD, cassette, or vinyl record of this beautiful number. If you like, play it as background music while reading this chapter. If you know it, sing or hum it to yourself.

Okay, *now* we are ready to start. As we key on the events that begin to unfold, we see a guerrilla commando secretly crawling toward an enemy military base. I will continue narrating for you and when appropriate, I will interject and guide using *Narrator's Notes* to clarify or gently move things along for you.

So, through the magic of modern technology, I've just rewound the VCR or DVD player of time and projected you back to 1987. While reading the next segment of this chapter, simply focus on this event as if it were real time. Remember, we will be looking at it through the eyes of the central figure of this chapter. Are you ready? Then let's see what's going on…

Luís Enrique Azriel, or *Comandante Quique, pronounced Kee-keh,* as his fellow guerrilla brethren called him, wiped the sweat from his eyes for what seemed like the 66th time since the beginning of the operation. The intense gaze of his light green eyes remained fixed to the front …focused on the demanding task at hand. He concentrated on his mission to help take his mind off the many scratches his already scarred body had received as he slowly crawled down the sharp volcanic rock strewn path of ingress. The fine black dirt caking on his perspiring body only added to the discomfort.

"Piece of cake," he thought in an attempt to distract himself... "just another dry run..." like the many that he had executed in the last six months from his training camp...deep inside the FPL or Popular Liberation Forces- controlled area between the border of northern Chalatenango Department, El Salvador, and Honduras. Although at this moment Quique was fighting reality, the fact remained that this was the real thing...finally.

Finally, after months of meticulous planning and preparation, Quique, the platoon leader of the highly specialized 1st Platoon, 1st Company of J-28 Group 1, FES, *Fuerzas Especiales Selectas*, was leading his men on a very specialized mission...his very first. This Select Special Forces group was from the FMLN, *Farbundo Martí* National Liberation Front, the umbrella organization for the five guerrilla groups engaged in combat and insurgent activities against the Salvadoran government. Tonight the FMLN was destined to make history as it delivered another surprise attack and drove another stake right into the heart of the enemy. Carrying a Heckler & Koch 9mm MP-5A3 submachine gun and a satchel charge filled with 800 grams of Trinitrotoluene, TNT, or reinforced Trotyl explosive strapped to his bare back, he slowly crawled toward the perimeter wire fence that surrounded the Salvadoran Army base of El Paraíso in Chalatenango Department.

From a secluded vantage point along the west side of the perimeter, he paused momentarily to listen for possible sounds from sentries guarding the highly secured army compound. If his unit were detected during this phase of the operation, the mission would be scrubbed. Absolute secrecy and surprise were the essential elements of success. But he smiled confidently in the twilight, knowing that the Salvadoran Army sentries on duty in the guard towers along this side of the compound were probably passed out...in deep sleep...some probably still hung over from all the Salvadoran *Tic Tac* distilled sugar cane *Aguardiente* they customarily drank on weekends or after duty hours to fight off boredom and isolation.

Reassured that all was proceeding according to plan, he continued to painstakingly crawl over the volcanic rock strewn lanes that he and his commandos had previously marked two nights ago during their reconnaissance mission. During that mission he and his team had carefully placed small wooden stakes along the approach routes leading straight to the base of the perimeter fence. They had also marked clear lanes through the mine field outside the perimeter. Attached to these stakes were small squares of aluminum foil that faced outward from the compound. As the bright moon peaked from behind the clouds, its beams reflected off the foil, clearly marking his lane.

This was but one of many ingenious ideas his group had adopted from their North Vietnamese allies during sapper commando training in North Vietnam. Everything, to include being barefooted, covered in black camouflaged paint, and wearing only black shorts, came right out of the North Vietnamese doctrinal manuals. This Spartan attire identified him as a member of the elite Special Forces of the FMLN. Countries that fought against foreign aggression like the heroic North Vietnamese people served as an inspiration and a guiding light to Quique and his comrades. The advanced specialized training they had received in Matanzas, Cuba last year only served to hone their already acquired combat skills and abilities.

When he reached the perimeter fence line, he paused again, and dusted off the face of his rubber banded wrist watch to read its faint luminous numbers. Apparently, Quique was running on pure high octane adrenaline, for he was 6 minutes ahead of the scheduled time to arrive at the perimeter fence.

He quietly waited, listening only to the chirping insects and his pounding heart. For an instant the thought of having an ice cold Salvadoran *Pilsner* beer right about now popped into his mind, but he quickly shook off the thought.

To the rear, six members of Team #1 of his platoon under the strict leadership of Team Leader, *Capitán* Danilo, followed behind him as they all prepared to move into their assault positions. The sixth man in this single file formation, *Compañero* Jairo, carried a Russian-made 85mm RPG-7 rocket-propelled grenade launcher. He would not enter the compound, but would remain at the fence entrance to provide direct supporting fire and keep the entry point secured.

About 25 meters to Quique's right and momentarily out of his field of vision, six other personnel from his Team #2, also from the 1st Platoon, under the solid leadership of Capitán Ezekiel simultaneously moved along a parallel lane. Because of the highly secret nature of this operation, radios were prohibited. In fact the entire operation would be executed according to strict time lines with no communicating between elements. This is where trust in the individual, trust in the mission, and trust in the National Liberation Front all came together. If the North Vietnamese Army and the Viet Cong had been able to do it this way, so could they. In fact it would be a victorious night...he could feel it...

US Army Special Forces Staff Sergeant Frederick Grogan tossed and turned in his bunk. He was having another sleepless night. His stomach churned from the second bout with amoebas in six months since being assigned as an advisor to the 4th Infantry Brigade in El Paraíso. It was obvious that the medication prescribed by the nurse in the medical clinic at the American Embassy in San Salvador had done little to lessen the discomfort. As a result he had spent the entire weekend either in bed or a short walking distance from a toilet.

"That blasted Salvadoran food," he said to himself. "If only I had stuck to my MRE, Meals Ready Eat." Instead, he ate about seven of the delicious Pupusas Revueltas with the suspect cultido…Probably, three more than he should have. They were good, but the cultido may have done him in.

Narrator's Note: Pupusas Revueltas are the melted cheese, refried bean, and pork rind stuffed tortillas that are incredibly delicious and are regarded the national dish of El Salvador. Cultido is a pickled cabbage side dish that Salvadorans enjoy eating with their pupusas. It is also customary to pour homemade tomato sauce on top of them. I don't blame SSG for stuffing himself with these. I get hungry just talking about them. But I'll be quiet for now…Back to the story…

"Well, it goes with the job," he weakly reaffirmed trying to convince himself that his present state of misery was worth it. Like the many hundreds of military advisors that served before him in distant places like Vietnam, doing the many things that would cement bonds of friendship between advisor and foreign military counterpart, SSG Grogan had done what was right to show solidarity, respect, and appreciation for a foreign culture. And now he was paying the price for having indulged in the precarious business of trying out the culinary delights of a foreign country.

Tomorrow, he would be fine, for he would visit the 4th Brigade medic and have him treat the problem. Salvadoran prescription medication always seemed to work better and faster than the US stuff. He wasn't quite sure why. It just did. Maybe they used European formulas or higher dosages of everything. Who cared? They worked.

Besides his stomach problems and to add to the misery, the air conditioner in his room was blowing warm air again. He should have picked up a new compressor the last time he was in the capital for the US Military Group Commander's monthly meeting at the American Embassy. Instead he continued to fix his air conditioner with Salvadoran rebuilt parts. Well, the USMILG would have another advisors' meeting in April. He would pick up the replacement parts then.

Since misery loves company, he thought about calling next door to his supervisor to see if he was awake, but decided against it since Major Rick Vallejo always slept soundly. Instead of calling him, he acted out the scene the way it would probably unfold. The short, thin, and wiry Puerto Rican with light brown almost yellow eyes would no doubt furrow his brow:

"Hey, Major Rick, are you awake? I got the shits and my air conditioner is out again."

Then the Major would probably shout back:

"Qué jodienda, Fred!!!! Let me sleep! What do you want me to do, hold your hand while you sit on the crapper?"

He would then most likely launch into one of his comical monologues:

"Oye, hermano, we're both lucky to have air conditioners, you know? When's the last time you went to the field with an air conditioner? Let me guess...Nunca...NEVER. During our last field training exercise in Camp Lejeune with the Marines, 7th SF Group, and the 82d Airborne, did we have air conditioners? Let me answer that for you also...NO. When we conducted our last airborne operation at Bragg, did you have an air conditioner in your M-1950 Weapons Case? Let me guess the answer again...NO. We're lucky our Salvadoran hosts installed these in our rooms, because if our Army wanted us to have air conditioners, then by God the Army would have issued those to us. So, stop your whining, suck it up, ruck up, and go back to sleep. As you know, on

Tuesday morning Colonel Rubio invites us to lead officer PT at 0700 hours. So, it is in your best interest to get plenty of rest."

...or maybe words to that effect.

Staring up at the ceiling of his hooch, SSG Grogan laughed to himself while playing out this fictitious dialogue over and over in his mind. Major Rick was quite a character. But you couldn't ask to work for a better guy. They had known each other from 7th SF Group and 82d Airborne Division days at Fort Bragg. Now, they were serving together as military advisors in the Salvadoran 4th Infantry Brigade at El Paraíso, a small isolated base west of the small town that bears its name, but which had no resemblance to the paradise its name proclaims. El Paraíso stood in the south central part of Chalatenango Department, one of thirteen departments or provinces in the war torn country of El Salvador and one of the most contested areas between the Salvadoran government and the FMLN. A curious name, the Front took its name from a popular Salvadoran Communist folk hero, Agustín Farabundo Martí, who was killed by government forces during a revolt in the 1930's. As Major Rick reminded him, the El Paraíso base was attacked once on 31 December 1983, resulting in an embarrassing set back for the Salvadoran Army's counterinsurgency effort. By 1987, the war was in its seventh year.

Then his thoughts wandered to his family...His lovely Panamanian wife, Selena, and the daughter and son that he had left behind in Fayetteville, North Carolina. He had last talked to them about a month ago when he managed to get a phone patch call through the American Embassy switch board in San Salvador. Being a member of the elite US Army Special Forces was always high adventure. It also put a strain on family life. In the time that he had served on this unaccompanied one year tour, SSG Grogan had never felt the pain of separation as much as tonight. The isolation, the distance from loved ones, and his state of health all worked together to synergistically create a gloom as heavy as the moist evening air. He continued to stare up at the ceiling hoping to doze off...

Quique easily pulled the strands of fence wire apart...easily done because during their previous reconnaissance mission, his sappers had surreptitiously cut holes in the fence with wire cutters and had spliced the fence back with fine black thread. This facilitated the work at hand during tonight's phase of the operation. In a matter of seconds, Quique pulled apart an opening large enough for all his team members to crawl through when it was time. And that time was fast approaching.

He tingled with excitement as H-Hour drew near. Glancing again at his digital watch, his eyes lit up as he saw the numbers count down, 0159 hours and 56, 57, 58, 59 seconds...

It was now 0200 hours.

Immediately and on schedule, mortar rounds from captured Salvadoran military 81mm mortars, firing from a few kilometers south of Highway 3E and along the lake shore of the *Embalse Cerrón Grande,* turned the base into a fiery inferno of death and destruction.

Precisely at the same time, Russian made 85mm RPG-7 rocket-propelled grenades from launchers firing from well concealed places in the high ground around the base unleashed Hell's fury. Buildings silhouetted from the blinding flashes of explosions and were simultaneously hit as the insurgent gun crews from the J-28 Weapons Support Group attempted to destroy all key facilities and basically every living thing inside the Salvadoran military compound.

In tandem and at full cyclic rate, two insurgent 7.62mm M60 machine guns, one on the hill directly east and overlooking the base and the other on a small hill just south, began raking the defenders with highly accurate and deadly cross fires. Gun barrels glowed fiery red in the night from maximum rate of fire…spewing bright red hot tracer rounds that arced down into the base… ricocheting off buildings, guard towers, and hitting surprised and dazed Salvadoran Army 4th Brigade soldiers.

While he marveled at the deadly fireworks display, Quique thought about the next part of his mission. His job was to ensure that the key points engaged by the weapons support group were destroyed and that no Salvadoran soldier lived to talk about this historic early morning attack.

He waited the assigned minutes. The supporting fires began to lift and shift away from his area as he motioned his men to begin entering the opening in the fence. With fatherly care, he tapped each one of them on the shoulder as they passed him. Once all team members were inside the wire, he gave Jairo, the RPG gunner, a thumb's up, looked up at the cloudy sky, made the sign of the cross, and entered the dark hole in the fence.

Quique knew that as he stepped inside, he was entering another dimension…a dimension that transported him from the relative security of the outer perimeter fence to a hellish world of slaughter and massacre.

The fence opening was the gate to *Dante's Inferno*. The acrid smell of burnt sulfur and nitroglycerin, created by the expended ammunition and exploded ordnance, irritated his eyes and burned his nasal cavities. His throat was dry and his mouth tasted of burnt rubber. His overwhelmed senses revolted at the visual display of horrific death and carnage. It was like nothing he had ever experienced before. His specialized training had not fully prepared him for the sound, taste, and smell of battle.

Hiding among the shadows of scrub brush, he paused for a moment along with the rest of Team #1 to regain his composure and to prepare his mind before proceeding to the next set of tasks. Through the thick smoke hanging over the battleground, he made out the dark forms of Capitán Ezekiel and the members of Team #2 off to his right. He quietly counted:

"Uno……dos……tres…." But where were the fourth and fifth commandos?

Precious seconds ticked by.

Had they been captured?

With relief he saw the remaining team members moving through the wire, apparently victims of a minor delay in their execution of the fence line penetration. The sixth member of Team #2 was the RPG gunner who, like Team #1, would remain at the perimeter fence entry point. So far, everything was proceeding according to plan. Their attack would now begin.

Like a choreographed *Danse Macabre*, Quique's men began their *Mephisto Waltz* of death. They dispersed to hit their pre-assigned targets. Quique had already assumed a semi-crouched position as he pulled his MP-5A3 around his body by the carrying strap and gripped the submachine gun's hand grip...right index finger loosely curled around the trigger. He then gave the thirty round magazine clip a quick upward slap with his left hand to ensure it was still seated; unhooked the satchel charge from around his body; and stealthily jogged toward the nearby barracks buildings that housed dazed 4th Brigade soldiers. Judging by the thick dark smoke rising from the roof of his designated target, it appeared to have taken a direct mortar hit. He checked the front door to ensure that it was unlocked and pulled the detonation cord fuse cap. As soon as the cord fuse began hissing, Quique tossed the bag into the dark interior. From the barracks and according to plan, he ran toward the next location, the designated interim rallying point.

Although Quique certainly should have anticipated it, the night turned into day as three of the six satchel charges exploded within seconds of each other, closely followed by the slow ripple of explosions four, five, and six...each explosion corresponding to his charge and that of the other five team members. Based on the number of explosions, all members delivered their charges in their designated areas. The concussions from the blasts made his ears ring and temporarily disoriented him.

From the other side of the compound came the explosions from two of the five satchel charges from Team #2. This concerned and temporarily distracted him. It would not be until much later that Quique would learn that prior to delivering their ordnance, three members of that team, including its leader, Capitán Ezekiel, were killed by defending Salvadoran Army soldiers.

He then prepared for the next phase of the mission which was to cover the escape routes of any soldiers that survived the satchel charges in the barracks, headquarters building, the command bunker, the communications antennas, and the supply and ammunition storage areas.

While he silently waited from his rallying point well to the east of the now burning buildings, he spotted two dark forms staggering out of the command bunker. He fired and hit both, apparently killing the two soldiers.

The staccato fire from the guerrilla machine guns could still be heard engaging defending enemy soldiers over in the area of the 2d Platoon. Apparently, enemy resistance in that part of the compound was heavy. He hoped that his fellow officer, Comandante Rubén, the 2d Platoon Leader responsible for providing security and supporting fires within the compound, was fairing well.

As each commando of Team #1 completed covering designated buildings and escape routes, they began assembling around Quique at their rallying point. He conducted a quick head count. All personnel were accounted for and no one had been killed or wounded.

The next phase of the complex operation was to move further east towards the soccer and track field where they planned to ambush any Gringo advisors assigned to the 4th Brigade who may have survived the mortars or satchel charges. FES intelligence indicated that three Americans worked in the compound, but it was not known if any were there that morning because they traveled to and from the capital quite frequently. In any event an informant in the 4th Brigade reported that the escape and evasion plan of the Americans was to run toward the soccer field where they would wait for helicopter evacuation back to San Salvador. If everything proceeded as planned, tonight three Gringo advisors would be among the many dead Salvadoran Army soldiers.

The six commandos took up designated ambush positions on the wooded area overlooking the soccer field in anticipation of the arrival of the unsuspecting American advisors.

They waited and waited for several minutes, but still no one arrived. They had precious few minutes to waste.

"*Hijo de Puta*!!!" Quique muttered…This could be good news or bad news. They could already be dead or they may not be here at all.

As he started to rise from his prone position to scrub this portion of the mission, a running shadow caught his attention.

Ahhh…we may have at least one Gringo advisor, he surmised.

Zeroing on the moving figure, Quique fired a three round burst. The figure fell down the steps leading down to the soccer field. The individual appeared to be dead on contact.

Quique carefully made his way over to the fallen figure and leaned over to check him. The cloth name tags on the dead advisor's bloodied uniform shirt read, "GROGAN" and "U.S. ARMY."

"*Berraco!!!*" Quique said under his breath. "I have bagged my first American advisor." Quique then ripped the advisor's identification tags from his neck and placed these inside his ammunition pouch. "As proof," he thought to himself.

Suddenly, without warning and from the direction of the far side of the soccer field, a rifle round hit Quique on the right shoulder with so much force that it spun him around.

He shouted out in pain while applying direct pressure on the shoulder wound that was now bleeding heavily.

There should have been no resistance of any sort at this point of the operation. The mortars and machinegun teams should have eliminated all Salvadoran military resistance by now.

But he knew that the point was irrelevant. He was hit, but fortunately for him, not seriously.

"Danilo," he shouted to the 1st Team Leader, "Eliminate that sniper."

"Sí, Comandante. Listo."

Capitán Danilo and two of his men carefully moved toward the last known point of enemy fire. Suddenly, a rifle round hit *Compañero* Chamba and knocked him to the ground, leaving him dead on the spot.

A split second later, another shot sounded as Danilo grabbed his left thigh. He too fell to the ground in pain from his bullet wound.

"This is an ambush! There must be more than one!" he yelled to Quique. Bullets continued to whiz by their heads or kicked up the dirt around them.

"Carajo!!!" Quique angrily shouted. "We don't have much time. The covering fire from our mortars will begin in..." he glanced at his watch..."six minutes. We have to begin our withdrawal now. Lay down a base of fire and let's get out of here."

Team member Estéban came to Quique and Danilo's aid, while the other two team members, Abel and Pablo, fired bursts from their MP-5A3s wildly in the general direction of the incoming rifle rounds, not really knowing where to shoot.

With great difficulty, Quique and Danilo staggered back past the now burning main barracks buildings while still receiving fire from the unknown assailants.

They finally reached the wire perimeter fence and their exit point. Jairo waved them through as he stood guard with his RPG in the ready.

Escaping into the relative security of the night as cleanly as they entered a mere forty-five minutes prior, the team headed toward their objective rallying point to assess damages and conduct a roll call.

Quique was ecstatic. He had done it...a successful mission as an FES platoon leader, a prize war wound, and the death of an American advisor. What a victorious night for him and his comrades.

He looked back at the burning buildings and devastation. Glancing at his watch one last time before leaving, he thought to himself, "The covering fires from the FES mortars should begin landing...just about ...NOW."

Father, father...We don't need to escalate...You see, war is not the answer... For only love can conquer hate...You know we've got to find a way...To bring some lovin'here today...

Marvin Gaye

CHAPTER THREE

PTSD

Purple haze... all in my brain... Lately things just don't seem the same...Actin' funny, but I don't know why...'Scuse me while I kiss the sky...

Purple haze all in my eyes, uhh...Don't know if it's day or night...You got me blowin', blowin' my mind...Is it tomorrow, or just the end of time?

"Purple Haze"
as recorded by Jimmi Hendrix

HEADQUARTERS, JOINT TASK FORCE-SOUTH,
TRES ESQUINAS, CAQUETA DEPARTMENT, COLOMBIA
0345 HOURS, 30 JUNE 2001

I bolted from my bunk as I heard the sounds of the explosions of the incoming mortar rounds...light gray Army T-shirt and shorts drenched in sweat. Fear consumed my body with uncontrollable shaking. Peering through the darkness of the small room, I slowly regained my senses. My watch showed that it was 0345 hours. I sat down on a folding chair and lowered my head into my hands. Slowly...slowly...my mind was returning to the reality of the moment. The only sounds came from the loud drone of the air conditioner and my pounding heart. There was no mortar fire here. I was now in Tres Esquinas, Colombia.

Wow, that one was more vivid than the last two. The nightmares from El Paraíso 1987 had begun again.

★ ★★

Dear reader, I apologize for missing my cue. Sorry for not getting back to you sooner, but I thought I could just let things play out by themselves. With all the loose and un-collated pages of this manuscript, I find it difficult to remember where to interject myself. Please pardon the indiscretion. Just give me a minute and I will get back to the scene you just read. First let's talk music…

The background music is the great Jimmi Hendrix. His song *Purple Haze,* a 1960's classic, captures a little bit of my mental confusion at the moment. The hard pounding and pulsating rock beat provides appropriate background music to my serious dilemma. You'll understand why shortly. Get a copy of this psychedelic rock classic and play it loud…like it was meant to be played.

From the chapter heading you can see that we have fast-forwarded from 1987 to 2001. We are no longer in El Salvador, but in Colombia. 0345 hours means?…Yes, of course…3:45 in the morning. This is not difficult. It just takes a little getting used to. It only gets tricky when you get to 1:00 PM which is 1300 hours. 2:00 PM is 1400 hours. 3:00 PM is 1500 hours…you get the idea. What's 7:00 PM? 1900 hours.

You know, I think the older I get, the more cynical I've become. I'm not sure why. Maybe I expect the same degree of commitment and purpose from others that I demand of myself. With this kind of attitude it's no wonder that one gets so frustrated and disappointed with life. I guess we have to be less judgmental, more tolerant, and more accepting of others. The problem is that I find that this leads to living our lives with more stress. It's stressful to live a life when we are the yielding ones at the intersections of life, while others are the inconsiderate speeders that drive through and abuse, hurt, or take advantage. But I digress again. Well, maybe for just a little bit more…

Then there's the unseen and invisible nature of stress itself. What is stress? Where does it come from? After all, isn't it just our reaction to something external that actually causes the stress in the first place? But I'm babbling....

Speaking of stress, I think I told you in the previous chapter that I was at El Paraíso, El Salvador the night it was attacked. I lost many Salvadoran Army friends that fateful morning and also lost my dear partner, SSG Grogan. And it's my fault. You know why? You will start to see.

Allow the following scene to play out. We're still in Colombia, but the scene has shifted to Bogotá... just for a brief moment and then I'll get you back again to Tres Esquinas. Please read on...

"It's PTSD...Post Traumatic Stress Disorder," the military psychologist told me.

"Give it a little time, it will eventually subside."

"Well, the fact of the matter is that it hasn't subsided. It seems to have begun again since my arrival to Colombia. Doc, what do you think triggers these nightmares...these flashbacks from El Paraíso?"

"Rick, anything that your mind associates with that traumatic event...be it explosions, smoke, a weapon firing, and the like, can trigger it.

"But why does it only happen in my sleep?"

"I think that during the day you are very much in control of your thoughts and feelings. You're more strong-willed then most. During the course of the week...your mind accumulates sensory images from your work and retains them. While you're asleep, you no longer control your conscious self...your strong will is no longer in charge. So now the mind instinctively tries to free itself of emotional damage. It's the mind's way of attempting to purge and heal itself. Quite frankly, if you want to rid yourself of these flashbacks and nightmares, you will eventually have to disassociate yourself from all things that are military."

"Now that's the dumbest thing I've ever heard you say, Doc. How the heck am I to do that, when I'm staying in the Army until I retire at 30 or beyond?"

"You're going to have to decide between your career and your mental health."

"Well, that's easy…my career."

"You're career goes or it stays?"

"Doc, I'm staying. Okay? I swear you military shrinks. If you were civilian doctors you would be either out of work, underpaid, or would never have patients," I joked with my old friend from 82d Airborne Division days.

"Well, I've got you and you've got me and you have another appointment in five months, laughed Colonel "Doc" Bateman. My schedule has me making the embassy milk run again in about the November time frame. If you are still here, I'll e-mail you with a date and time for you to meet me in Bogotá. Otherwise, make an appointment to see me up at USSOUTHCOM headquarters in Miami when you finish your tour at Tres Esquinas."

Narrator's Note: Have I managed to confuse you? I hope not. What's important is that we are back in Tres Esquinas. Remember life is chaotic .Chaos is part of change. Life is in constant change. My life at this time was in a state of chaos. So, your confusion may be similar to mine. But, if I've managed to lose you in these quick opening scenes, don't worry. Just keep reading. It will sort itself out…Trust me. Back to the scene…

I picked up the camouflaged poncho liner I used as a blanket. It had slid off the bed and lay on top of my black canvas jungle boots which were next to the bunk. I got back into my bunk and propped my head up against the cool metal wall. The vivid images of that terrible night of El Paraíso in March 1987 ran through my mind... again... probably for the millionth time. It was always the same internal debate...the constant replaying of the same "what ifs" and "if only I had..."

If only I had waited for SSG Fred Grogan. No, if I had, we would have both died together on the steps leading down to the soccer field. But still, Fred must have been wondering where I was the entire time. That was not right. That is the part that still makes me feel guilty. There was a third military advisor, or more correctly, a CIA advisor. But Tom Kennedy was back in the States dealing with a family emergency. Otherwise, he would probably have been a victim too.

Why did I leave my hooch ahead of Fred without letting him know? I had to face the cold hard reality again. I panicked. Yep, I totally lost it. I left my hooch in sheer terror...sheer fright...pure and naked fear had gripped my throat...its icy hand controlled me. Fear would not permit me to scream or talk. I had left as if I were suffocating...my breathing passages…totally restricted.

I remember that the noise from the mortar explosions made me jump out of my bunk. I quickly speed -laced my boots, grabbed my 5.56 mm Colt CAR-15 carbine, web harness with ammo pouches, and bolted out the door in a flash. Both Fred and I had agreed to always sleep in our green Vietnam era fatigues. When the big attack came, we had joked, we sure as hell were not going into combat in our Fruit of the Loom's or BVD's. Michael Jordan can make money doing commercials in his underwear, but not hard core soldiers. Hahahahaha… This always got a laugh from Fred.

It is said that the most extreme reaction to fear is flight. And that I did. I ran out the door of my hooch like I was running the 400 meter dash in a track meet. I ran through the curtain of mortar fire as if trying to escape the flames and maddening noise of Hell, itself. I don't even remember if I was shot at by any of the enemy commandos on the compound. As fast as I ran, I would have been a difficult target to hit. In the cloud of fear, I was oblivious to my immediate surroundings.

I finally reached the soccer field that was our designated rallying point and hid behind some wood planks covered by a dry rotted canvas tarp at the far end of the field, the spot Fred and I were to occupy.

How long was I there? I still can't remember. It seemed like a life time. My screwed up mind at that moment could only think of one thing...to get away from the death and chaos of the 4th Brigade compound. In my confused state I mistakenly thought that an evacuation helicopter would be arriving and would magically lift me to safety. When you are consumed by fear, it is difficult to think clearly and rationally. In my case I was not thinking at all.

Eventually, I got the nerve to look up toward the steps leading down to the soccer field. Petrified, I watched as a small group of enemy commandos wearing black shorts and covered in black paint assumed prone positions near the steps. Before I could comprehend, I saw Fred running down the steps and being hit. I watched him stumble and fall...apparently dying instantly.

An enemy commando moved toward Fred and bent over him, like a deer hunter inspecting his fallen prey.

And then it happened. At that precise moment something unexplainable clicked in my mind. Extreme fear instantly gave way to pure anger and hate. I had just witnessed the murder of my operations/intelligence NCO and the killer was standing over him, obviously relishing the moment. Taking aim with my CAR-15 carbine, I fired at the commando and the other dark forms that were with him. Years of military training kicked in resulting in a memorized series of actions in which I took aim and fired...over and over again...I could not stop until I had killed them all...until I avenged the murder of SSG Grogan.

I saw the group of commandos fleeing the scene. I followed them while periodically stopping to fire. Only the fact that my magazine clips eventually emptied suspended the revenging shooting spree.

I reached the spot where SSG Grogan was lying motionless on the ground. Before I could check for vital signs, there came the dreaded WHUMP...WHUMP...WHUMP known to all soldiers as the sounds of incoming mortar rounds leaving their tubes in rapid succession. The hail of the mortar barrage illuminated the night with explosions and ear splitting noise and confusion. One round hit near me and everything went black. That was the last I remembered. When I awoke, I was recovering from concussion and shrapnel wounds at Gorgas US Army Hospital in Panama. Some heavy pieces of shrapnel had also been removed from my right foot.

While recovering, the memories were at first very vague. Eventually, over the years they would become very clear... crystal clear. The sounds, the sights, that all consuming and overwhelming feeling of fear...all came back to me in a constant stream of vivid images...the confusion...the firing...the smoke... the explosions...the acrid smell of exploded ordnance...burning buildings...perspiration...cold and clammy hands...the pounding heart...the overwhelming sense of desperation. Thankfully, no one will ever know how I reacted to my first taste of combat...only my tormented soul and my guilty conscience.

31 March 1987 was a dark day for the US and Salvadoran Armies. After the FMLN commandos departed and the smoke cleared from El Paraíso, 69 Salvadoran soldiers were dead, approximately 79 wounded, and the United States Army lost its first military advisor in ground combat in support of the Salvadoran

conflict. The FMLN lost only eight commandos during that daring raid. I contributed to the enemy body count.

I instinctively know that it is my tour in Colombia that triggered the flashbacks from El Paraíso. What part of my tour triggered these? I'll explain.

The Colombian Army suffered a major military setback early in my deployment to Tres Esquinas. In fact I had only been there for about two weeks. On the evening of 15 June 2001 and continuing into 16 June 2001, the Colombian 49th Jungle Battalion operating from the small military base of Coreguaje, just north of the Colombian Navy South headquarters base at Puerto Leguízamo, was attacked by approximately 500 FARC combatants of the Southern Bloc. This surprise attack resulted in 30 Colombian military personnel killed in action (KIA).

Colombian military intelligence believes this attack was the combined action of the FARC 14th and 48th Fronts. It is also believed that the Juan José Rondón Mobile Column led the attack. It is highly unusual for this FARC special operations element to come out of the Eastern Bloc sector and into the Southern Bloc area of responsibility. Its involvement indicates that the operation involved a high level coordinated plan by the FARC Secretariat.

The set back was bad news for the Colombian military. What affected me most were the daily reviews of the post operations reports. Listening to the grisly details of combat casualties must have triggered my own thoughts about what happened at El Paraíso in 1987. This resurgence of mental anguish was directly related to my present job as senior American intelligence advisor at Joint Task Force-South. I guess that Doc Bateman was right. I would eventually have to choose between what I loved doing in the Army and my mental peace of mind. Clearly, I had already made that decision. I had chosen my future course of action.

How did I get to Tres Esquinas? Let's rewind these chapters of my life and restart the tape from the beginning. Everything will start to fall into place. I hope to see you in the next chapter…

Purple haze…all in my eyes, uhh…Don't know if… it's day or night…You got me blowin, blowin my mind…Is it tomorrow, or just the end of time?

Jimmi Hendrix

CHAPTER FOUR

ASSIGNMENT: COLOMBIA

You say yes...I say no...you say stop...and I say go, go, go...oh...no. You say good-bye...and I say hello. Hello, hello...I don't know why you say goodbye, I say hello.

"Hello Goodbye"
as recorded by The Beatles

HEADQUARTERS, UNITED STATES ARMY SOUTH (USARSO)
FORT BUCHANAN, PUERTO RICO
1430 HOURS, 4 MAY 2001

Ah, yes...the immortal and timeless music of the Beatles. Like most from the Baby Boomer generation, their music influenced my life. These guys where on the charts week after week, year after year. So upon hearing a Beatles' number, I can usually tell you where I was at a particular moment in time during my teen age and young adult period. Think about the power music has over our lives. How beautiful that a song can trigger our memory and push images and events spontaneously up from the recesses of our mind. This whole association of places and times by the mere hearing of a song is fabulous. Let's see... Oh, I was in high school when that song came out. In fact I played this song in a rock band. Seriously, but, hey, we don't have time for that now. In fact, I will no longer take up time by pointing out the songs at the beginnings and endings of each chapter. I'll let you enjoy the musical selections. You can figure it all out. Let's get back to the story...

★ ★ ★

"Rick, I need a big favor from you," said US Army Major General Angel Valencia as soon as I walked into his office at US Army South Headquarters, USARSO in Fort Buchanan, Puerto Rico.

My muscles tightened. When a General Officer prefaces a statement with the words, "I need a big favor from you," it usually means he is asking you to do something either totally out of character, involving hardship, or beyond reason. Otherwise, he would just tell you to do it minus the prefacing remark.

Regardless, I answered as politely as I could, "Yes, sir, what can I do for you?"

"You've been to Tres Esquinas, Colombia before and understand the requirements for advisory support down there."

"Yes, sir," I said holding my breath.

"I need you to go to Tres Esquinas for an indefinite amount of time. You're a regionally experienced officer and I need someone I can count on. I don't have a replacement for Colonel Nieves down at the Colombian Joint Intelligence Center, and he has to return to his unit in Fort Benning. We've already extended him twice. I'd like you to be his backfill until we can find someone else."

I swallowed hard. "General Valencia, sir, I would be happy to go."

Narrator's Note: Professional military officers are made up of tough stuff. Accepting responsibility and being team players are part of those traits. But if Satan kept a logbook and annotated every time an Army officer said the words, 'I will be happy to do it,' Hell would be full of highly motivated, well intentioned, can do... but lying officers. Just my opinion...

"Thanks, Rick. I knew I could count on you."

"Was there ever any doubt?" I thought to myself.

"Rick, you'll report by the end of this month. I figure Mr. Phil Denzel should be able to hold things down for you while you're away. Don't you?"

"Yes sir, he's a capable and responsible individual. That's why I selected him as my deputy. I fully trust him to do what's right and to keep the mission and the organization always at the forefront."

"Excellent...well, let Ruthie know that she can count on Ethel and me to provide her and the kids with support while you're gone."

"Thanks, sir. I appreciate that."

"Okay, *hermano,* I'll let you go. You have a lot of preparations to make prior to departing."

General Valencia then gave me the customary Hispanic *abrazo* or man hug.

"Yes, sir, I'm looking forward to the opportunity."

Scribble...scribble...and another entry in Satan's log...

And that's all there is to it, dear readers. Just like that...in a matter of seconds my whole life changed. Why do the events in life that have the most enduring impact start with so little fanfare? Ahhhh...but that's what makes military duty so enjoyable and challenging...all rolled up together into one big, gigantic ball of dun, pain, hardship, sacrifice, action, fun, and excitement. Yes, I still miss it...Just as many times as I complained about it. What a paradox...a duality of extremes...classic antithesis. Is this why many military service members end up all screwed up in the head? I don't mean crazy or loco screwed up, just screwed up from dealing with all the hot-cold, love-hate, happy-sad, good-bad, easy-tough, boredom-fear, and the like. It's no wonder we're not quite sure what to do with our lives after leaving service as a result of this constant exposure to life's dualities.

Well, let's get back on track. I was actually proud of myself for not stepping into the middle of dialogues...well, not that much anyway. Since I'm already talking, allow me to continue to describe this next scene. Better yet, I'll just tell you what was on my mind at the time.

The fact of the matter is that I had been to Colombia on numerous occasions, usually for only two to three days at a time. I always made it a point to visit my Colombian military counterparts at the D2 and E2 offices in Bogotá once a quarter. That's the Colombian equivalent of our J2 and G2 intelligence directorates... D2 or Department Two...and E2 or *Ejército* (Army) Two. Two is the designated staff number for the intelligence office. Three is operations and four is supply and logistics. One is personnel. I also made it a point to check in with the US Military Group Commander and other Embassy Country Team staff members to get feedback from them on our military progress in Colombia. As the G2, Director of Intelligence, for United States Army South (USARSO), I oversaw a training program in which my personnel provided the Colombian Army with numerous seminar hours of counter-narcotics intelligence training. At this very moment, one of my NCOs served as a senior intelligence analyst in support of the COJIC in Tres Esquinas.

Bogotá, the capital of Colombia is a far cry from Tres Esquinas. As a truly modern metropolis and cosmopolitan city, duty in the capital is fun and exciting...in every sense of the word. It has luxurious hotels, fine restaurants, and an active night life. At 8000 feet above sea level, its climate is quite pleasant.

On the other hand, Tres Esquinas is the pits. At sea level, it is a hot, humid, ugly, desolate, and isolated jungle base. To get there, you fly out from Bogotá on a small aircraft over turbulent, usually cloud shrouded and craggy mountain peaks with ominous sounding names like *Cerro Nevado, Cerro Pacande, or Cerro Purgatorio.* For me, if there was ever a place in the world that I detested, it had to be TQ. TQ is the military code name for Tres Esquinas. TQ makes Fort Polk, Louisiana look like Las Vegas in comparison. And now I had "volunteered" to serve there for an indefinite amount of time. I should have my head examined. Well, come to think of it, I had, but for other reasons that I've already discussed.

Fortunately, I had my guiding light. I always tried to live my career according to the motto of the Army's 1st Infantry Division: *No mission too difficult. No sacrifice too great. Duty first.* I never served in the "Big Red One," but my Operations NCO in Korea had...back when I was a First Lieutenant. It was he who inspired me to live by these words. These words provided me with the inspiration and dedication I felt were important to being a professional military officer. I was always committed to the Army above self, family, and friends. I never shied away from the hard jobs and pursued them with the passion and dedication that distinguishes a professional career military officer.

I apologize for walking you through the next scenes, but they are also an important dynamic in a soldier's life. Be it spouse, parents, grandparents, in-laws, significant other, uncle, aunt, school teacher, principal, or friend...there is always someone in our lives impacted by military duty as much, if not more, than us. Behind every soldier there is a relative or friend who shares the same, if not more, degree of pain from separation, combat deployment, injury, or death.

You know, the more I think about it, the more I realize that we soldiers are cruel to our family members and friends. I mean which is more stressful? Going on a dangerous mission or sitting at home wondering about a loved one going on a dangerous mission? The not knowing part must drive one crazy. How many times did I go on a midnight combat parachute jump at Fort Bragg while my family stayed at home wondering whether I would be another statistic? It is tough and they always rose to the occasion.

"ONE MINUTE," I shouted over the howling rush of air and noise from the engines of a USAF C-130 or C-141 transport aircraft in flight while holding up my right index finger. Straddling the open door of an aircraft in flight is nuts. The howling and swirling air coming in through the two opened exit doors added to the calamity, confusion, mayhem, and controlled chaos inside the aircraft. Yet, this is what US Army paratroopers and jumpmasters do for a living. I visually confirmed my terrain reference points and informed the line of tired, sweaty, nervous, anxious, but eager paratroopers standing in front of me that they would exit this aircraft while in flight and dangle their precious bodies from silk, cord, and canvas on a moonless night to be delivered to an unknown spot on the ground about the size of their boots. Yes, this is nuts. Did I say this already? But I really can't stress it enough. This is what we did about three to four times a month while serving in the 82d Airborne Division.

At the thirty second mark from jump time, I would signal the first jumper to take his position at the door, as the Safety, the soldier helping me work the aircraft door and serving as my assistant, secured the jumper's static line. We all stared at the red light on the edge of the opened door for the signal from the aircraft's pilot to begin exiting paratroopers. The red light would turn off for a second as the green light below it illuminated with a chilling and eerie glow. Then it was off to the races as jumpers exited their respective doors all under the careful supervision of the jumpmaster team. At this point you eyed each jumper while keeping a watchful check on the green light. Once it turned red, the jump sequence stopped and no more jumpers were allowed to safely exit the aircraft.

Stopping the jumpers from exiting once the red light turned back on was a lot tougher than it sounds because jumping is such an adrenaline rush. We had heard stories of Jumpmasters being accidentally pushed out of the aircraft by overly eager jumpers because they had blocked the exit door. Combat parachute jumping is a massive emotional high…and jumpers are on it…eyes focused on the jumper ahead…edging toward the open door…three jumpers left…two jumpers left…then it's your turn…To be stopped at the last second is cruel mental punishment for that jumper who would have to wait again for his next turn to jump. That meant that he would have to experience all these emotional extremes again. The aircraft would fly around again to make another one, two, or three passes, ensuring everyone got out. It's important that this be done efficiently, because the two Jumpmasters on board cannot exit the aircraft until the last jumper is out. Eventually, my turn came to exit the door and I would then worry about all the potential malfunctions associated with combat parachuting like being dragged behind the aircraft by one's static line; colliding with another jumper in the air; getting twisted suspension lines; having air stolen from one's parachute; having a partial parachute malfunction; dealing with a tree or water landing, breaking a leg, arm, hip, or collar bone upon landing; or, heaven forbid, having a total main chute malfunction with no time to deploy the reserve chute. This makes for a stressful and nerve racking set of events. But as Colonel Guy V. Henry of the 3rd Cavalry Regiment said to his men during the Battle of the Rosebud in 1876 after being shot through the eye, knocked off his horse, and trampled by Sioux Indian warriors, "It is nothing. For this we are soldiers." I guess the modern rendition of this might be, "It is nothing for this we are airborne soldiers."

★ ★ ★

"Ricky…Colombia? And for how long? You say it's an open ended deployment? Tell me it isn't true."

The conversation went back and forth and my wife, Ruthie, was still having a hard time dealing with the news of the deployment to Colombia.

"Ricky, what about the boys? They still need their father around the house."

"Look, Ruthie. I'm just going to fill in until USARSO can find someone for a longer period. It shouldn't be a long deployment."

Although Ruthie was use to deployments, having lived through two straight Christmas' in a row without me at home, she seemed to be having trouble adjusting to this one.

"Ricky, you're getting too old for this. Field advisor duty is a young man's sport. You'll be hitting your 30 year retirement in what…three more years? Besides, it's dangerous in Colombia. People get killed there all the time."

"Ruthie, it's the right thing to do. You know Latin America is my life and I've always been committed to the region. I'm also committed to helping my foreign counterparts become better professional intelligence officers. I don't like this assignment anymore than you do, but it's the right thing to do."

"Ricky, for you it's always the right thing to do."

I remained quiet for I knew I could not argue this point with her.

"How soon do you deploy?"

"By the end of this month."

"In two weeks?"

"Yeah…something like that."

"Who will be left in charge of G2 operations in your absence?"

"Phil Denzel is the Deputy G2. He will have to run things for a while."

"And your scheduled trips to the region for the rest of the year?"

"Well, obviously the section will continue to support our commitments without my presence. The teams are well trained. They can handle it."

★ ★ ★

"Colonel, you are authorized to draw one pair of jungle boots and three new Battle Dress Uniforms," shouted the elderly gentleman with white hair from behind the counter at the Central Issue Facility, where I was drawing extra field equipment for my deployment. I guess he was hard of hearing or just used to yelling loudly to soldiers drawing field gear.

"That's great...thanks. I can use some new BDU's and boots."

"You're taking your Kevlar helmet with you, are you not?"

"Yes, I'm taking my ballistics helmet."

"You're also authorized a body armor vest. Do you want one?"

"Well...I don't know...those things are heavy...yeah, sure. You never know when you might need one."

"Your hand receipt indicates that you haven't drawn any tent equipment or sleeping bag.

Would you like any of these?"

"No, I'll be sleeping indoors."

"Extra ammo pouches...canteens?"

"No, thanks."

"Okay. Then sign here and you'll be on your way."

"Thanks for the support, sir. It's always a pleasure dealing with professionals."

"You're very welcome, Colonel. You be safe, you here?"

"I'll do my best," I said with a big smile.

★ ★ ★

"Let's see...looks like you have all your shots..." Doctor Sánchez said as he reviewed my medical record at the Troop Medical Clinic.

"Hmmmm...you suffered a broken heal bone in 1991...Was that on a jump?

"Yeah...my chute collapsed at 100 feet...similar to falling ten stories without a parachute. My body bounced twice from the impact. It was the first time I left the drop zone in a field ambulance. Those young medics drove so fast, I thought I was going to die in a traffic accident, rather than from the jump injury," I laughed.

Doctor Sánchez looked up from my medical record, not amused.

"Does it still bother you...I mean the injury?"

"Sometimes...the hardware...a plate and five screws...rubs against my ankle...and I can't walk normally. Other than that, it's okay in light of the fact that I pulverized my heel bone on that jump."

"I assume you never jumped again after that accident?"

"Actually, Doc, I jumped forty-five more times after the accident."

"Please don't take this the wrong way, but you guys ought to have your heads examined."

"Yes, I've been told that before," I said laughing. "It goes with the job."

"Yes, of course," Doc Sánchez said unconvincingly as he closed the medical record on his desk.

"Now remember, Colonel. Take one malaria prophylaxis capsule daily. Start the first one 72 hours before you deploy to Colombia," Doctor Sánchez reiterated. "Then take one daily while there, and then continue to take them 30 days after you return from your deployment. I can't stress this enough."

"Roger, Doc. Got it. Does it have any side effects?"

"Very minor ones…You may experience a little stomach irritation at first, but that usually goes away after the first two or three days. There is a noticeable reddening of the face…almost as if you had been outside in the sun too long. But don't worry. That's normal."

My pet peeve has always been how casually medical doctors talk about side effects.

To me anything that altered body functions was of concern. But in terms of the dangerous effects from malaria, it was a trade-off…one effect for the other.

"Any questions, Colonel?"

"No, Doc. I got it. Thanks."

"Colonel, good luck and be safe. Colombia can get a little nasty at times."

"Yes, I know. I'll do my best. Thanks again."

"Colonel, sign and date right at the bottom," the young legal advisor told me.

As I looked up from the power of attorney form, it struck me how good looking this young Specialist was. Her blue eyes and red hair were captivating.

"Is your will up to date?" she asked, interrupting my day dream.

"Yes, it is."

"Good, sir. Then that is all you need from us."

I was not ready to go, just yet.

"Out of curiosity, are you a Virgo?"

Specialist Thompson looked at me for a second…one of those surprised whimsical looks…you know the arched eyebrow… tilting her head…She responded,

"Yes, as a matter of fact, I am. How did you know?"

"Just a hunch," I answered.

"Well, I don't really believe in astrology."

"I know…most people don't. But I think we are still fascinated by it. I'm fascinated by the fact that I'm usually able to guess a person's birth sign, usually after having spoken to them or observing them briefly. I've read the subject in enough detail to be able to identify the basic characteristics of each sign. Then you have to be able to factor the two additional influences of the effects of the Moon sign and the ascendant or rising planet. If there is no validity to it, figure the odds of my guessing your sign from twelve possible choices."

"Yes, you're probably right about that. It is interesting."

"It is very interesting. Did you know that there is a scientific basis behind the use of astrology? Supposedly it was invented by the Babylonians who used it to calculate their agricultural cycles. That is why Aries is the first sign of the zodiac, even though it begins on the 23d of March. That's when their farming cycle began. The twelve astrological signs are named after the constellations they observed in the night skies every thirty days. Leo the lion, Scorpio the scorpion, and the like are actual names of constellations. There is an astronomical basis for it."

"That's fascinating. But how does this equate to peoples' personalities."

"Ah, yes…good question. The Babylonians kept records of the births of all their children and assigned the constellation or astrological sign to each child. Over time they observed that as they grew up, their children exhibited observable patterns of behavior based on their birth signs. This then became the basis for our use of astrology to determine the personalities of people today."

"Wow, that's neat. I didn't realize that there is a scientific or historical basis for astrology."

"Most people don't because they wrongly assume that astrology is just a parlor trick. I find it interesting and will continue to employ it in my life to assess the personalities of my supervisors and co-workers alike. While many people think its rubbish, I'll just continue to be armed with more information about them. Hahahahaha...I usually know more about them then they do about themselves."

"Wow, Sir, that's scary stuff."

"I don't consider it scary. I consider it the applicability of knowledge in the unseen or unknown areas of life. Let me see if I'm correct. I'll also guess that you're tidy and very structured in your life. You are probably an art major or someone who appreciates the arts too."

"Sir, how do you know that?"

"I've observed how much care you've taken in getting my paperwork together. You seem to take pride and extra care in what you prepare. That's just a hunch based on observing you. I learned that from being a student of body language."

"Wow, that's fascinating. I am an English major. I received my bachelor's degree from the University of Texas in Austin. The Army trained me later to be a legal assistant."

"That's great. Congratulations. I will also tell you that I studied Physiognomy...that's the ancient Chinese art of reading faces. You have some very interesting facial features that tell me a lot about your personality. I would describe those to you, but sometimes I embarrass people when I tell them personal things, such as their attitude toward sex."

"You can also read that?" Specialist Thompson blushed.

"Actually, I can, but I don't know how accurate it really is. Most people won't admit if I'm right or not. Anyway, it makes for an interesting day at the airport as I read peoples faces while waiting for a flight."

"Wow that's very interesting. Does Military Intelligence teach you that?"

"No, it's just something I've always been fascinated with. My view is that life is much more than just the casual daily activities we engage in. MI would never discuss these kinds of things with its officers because we would be branded as being a bunch of witch doctors, voodoo worshippers, or the like. We have enough problems with our credibility without adding to the ridicule factor.

"Sir, can you describe my husband for me?"

"Well, since I don't know him, I will need his birth date. Do you know that?"

"Yes, he was born on September 5th 1979. I believe that makes him a Virgo also."

"Yes, that's correct. Although that indicates compatibility, we would still have to determine his Moon sign since it affects his emotional make-up. I can find that out for you by checking some charts. I can check that for you also if you're interested."

"No, Sir. You have a lot of things to do before your trip. But I really appreciate it."

"Let me tell you a real-life story. It happened to me while serving as G2 of the 82d Airborne Division. One day the Chief of Staff called me into his office. We were two weeks away from a field training exercise against the 10th Mountain Division. He told me that the G5 wanted to develop a psychological operations campaign against the three commanders from the 10th that would be serving as aggressor or opposing force battalion commanders. He gave me their names and tasked me to prepare personality profiles of each so that the G5 could get to work. I then returned to my office and discussed the matter with my operations officer because he once served in the 10th. 'No problem,' he told me. 'I'll have the information for you in thirty minutes.' He returned an hour later and told me, 'Zero luck, Sir. My contacts in the 10th Mountain have been given the gag order not to release any information regarding their people involved in the exercise.' So, what did I do? I walked over to the G1 administrative offices and met with the G1 himself. I told him, 'John, I need a favor. I need the birth dates of these three commanders from the 10th. Can you help me out?' 'Sure,' he said.

'Give me a minute.' He walked out and shortly returned with the information.' 'Here…put it to good use," he winked at me. I then prepared a personality profile based on the astrological signs of these three guys and took it over to the Chief of Staff.

He read it and asked me, "Rick, where did you get this information?"

"Sir, I got it from a unique source." I prayed that he wouldn't push the issue.

"Why?" I asked.

"This information is much too personal and detailed. I've known one of these guys my entire career and only his wife would know the kind of details you've provided me here."

"Well, sir, you tasked me and I wanted to ensure you got the very best product."

"Thanks, I'll take out some of the more personal stuff out and give it to the G5."

"And that is how my knowledge of astrology saved the day. Crazy, isn't it?"

"I wouldn't say crazy, sir. I would say that it is crazy not to use this knowledge as a resource."

"Precisely my point… Use all available resources to compliment what you have already obtained through other means. Someday when MI grows up, they'll consider these additional resources in their OSINT program…Open Source Intelligence."

"Great stuff. sir, I have another customer to tend to now. Thank you for sharing that information with me. It's really fascinating."

"Not at all. Please keep the information about astrology and the development of the personality profiles of those three officers close hold. There are too many close minded persons in my branch where that information could get me in trouble."

"Don't worry, sir, I understand where you're coming from. Your secret is safe. Have a safe deployment and I hope to see you when you get back."

"Thanks, Specialist Thompson. You have a great day."

"Papa, why are you going away and leaving us?" asked my 4-year old son, Eric. This was about the tenth time in the last hour he'd asked. My older 15-year old son quietly looked on.

"Because the Army wants me to go."

"Well, why don't you tell the big bad Army that you don't want to go?"

"It's not that easy, Eric," my older son piped in. Believe me." Ricardo Jr. had been through this countless times in his life as an Army brat...the label given to kids in an Army family.

"That's right, Eric. It's much bigger than both of us," I sheepishly added.

"Will you be home for Christmas?"

"I plan to be here. Yes."

"That's good. Christmas isn't the same without you here. Will you call us?"

"Every chance I get."

"You won't lose our number will you?"

"No, I promise. I won't lose our telephone number."

"That's good. Losing a telephone number wouldn't be a good thing."

"Yes, I know," I said while giving Eric a big hug and a kiss.

"That's good. Thank you, Papa."

And so it goes my dear readers...the ritual of a deployment. But hey, let's get moving. We have a job to do. Next stop... Bogotá, Colombia!!!

I say high...you say low...you say why...and I say I don't know...oh...no. You say goodbye and I say hello...hello, hello...I don't know why you say goodbye, I say hello. Hello, hello...I don't know why you say goodbye, I say hello.

The Beatles

CHAPTER FIVE

AMERICAN EMBASSY, BOGOTA

All my bags are packed, I'm ready to go... I'm standing here, outside your door...I hate to wake you up to say good bye. But the dawn is breakin', it's early morn, the taxi's waitin' he's blowin' his horn...already I'm so lonesome I could die...

"Leaving on a Jet Plane"
as recorded by Peter, Paul, and Mary

IN BOUND FLIGHT, EL DORADO AIRPORT, SANTA FE DE BOGOTA, DISTRITO FEDERAL DE BOGOTA, COLOMBIA, 1930 HOURS, 21 MAY2001

The venerable sounds of Peter, Paul, and Mary played in my headset as Miami-based American Airlines Flight 915 gradually descended from its cruising altitude of 31,000 feet. The twinkling lights from the many small country houses below along the Río Magdalena valley signified that the aircraft was approaching its destination. Gazing out the window, I was struck by the familiar contrasts of the Colombian countryside. It's amazing that such a lovely country with so much natural beauty, natural resources, and wonderful people, has been caught in the middle of the longest running and bloodiest insurgency in Latin America. Particularly tragic is that the so-called insurgent organizations that created this unrest and instability have degenerated into nothing more than a lucrative and profit making business...its leaders fill their pockets with millions of dollars from the illegal drug business. The faceless bands of young guerrillas join its ranks for upward social and economic mobility. Staring at the peace and tranquility below, I shook my head in disbelief.

My thoughts were suddenly interrupted by the heavy southern accented voice of the pilot, informing all passengers and crew to prepare for landing.

Minutes later, I held my breath in anticipation of the welcome bump as the Boeing 757's landing gear made smooth contact with the runway of El Dorado International Airport, Bogotá, Colombia.

I readied myself for the next series of events as the airliner taxied to the terminal.

Let's see...immigration and custom forms...official passport with visa...navy blue blazer and carry-on bags in hand. I should be meeting Major Luis Alvarado, the USARSO Liaison Officer in Bogotá, at the entrance to the immigration processing area.

Exiting the airliner and walking down the long tunneled passageway, I stopped twice to switch my carry-on bags from one hand to the other.

At the customs and immigration station, I looked for, but did not see, the liaison officer. Standing in line, some well-dressed passengers, looked me over from top to bottom...looking rather cool themselves. In fact, everyone in line seemed to be eyeing everyone else suspiciously. At this airport, like no other I've visited in Latin America, there always seemed to be a prevailing quiet paranoia that reflected the current state of affairs within this war torn country.

During my first visit to Colombia, I remember suspiciously eying the other passengers, while asking myself how many of the well-dressed passengers in line were narco-traffickers, guerrillas, or guerrilla supporters profiting from the drug war. After making frequent visits to the country, I knew that most were simply war wearied and innocent Colombians returning to their country after visiting relatives in Miami or Los Angeles. The condition of mistrust is simply the paranoia that exists in a country subjected to so much violence and terrorism.

After about twenty minutes of waiting in line, my turn to move through immigrations came up. If Major Alvarado had been there to greet me, we would have breezed through in seconds using the diplomatic passport line. Getting American military personnel in and out of the airport quickly is a privilege and a security safeguard that the American Ambassador obtained from host nation officials. However, this was not the case this evening.

I handed my documents to a young uniformed airport police official who nonchalantly reviewed them.

"*Buenas noches* and welcome back to Colombia, *Señor* Vallejo," greeted the official in Spanish. He could tell from the previous visas and stamps on my official passport that this was not my first visit.

"Buenas noches," I respond with a big I-hope-everything-is-in-order smile.

"And what is the purpose of your visit?" he asked.

"*Embajada Americana.*"

"*Ah...Sí...claro...Embajada Americana. Y su oficio?*"

"*Militar.*"

"*Su rango?*"

"*Coronel.*"

"And where is your Embassy escort officer?"

"He is apparently delayed," I answered, already accustomed to the normal immigrations questions.

With a shrug, the immigrations official stamped my passport and handed it back.

"Have a pleasant stay in Colombia, Coronel."

"*Gracias.*"

I made my way to the baggage claim area while keeping an eye out for Major Alvarado. The baggage carousel was already turning and full of bags as I edged my way to a clear spot along its axis of movement.

From behind, someone tapped me on the shoulder. It was Major Alvarado, dressed in a dark blue blazer, light gray slacks, a buttoned-down light yellow shirt, and a blue and gold regimental striped tie.

He was a young officer…not tall…probably 33 or so years old. I think he was originally from New York, but couldn't remember. Despite the environment, his dark hair was closely cut and he had that military presence about him. He immediately apologized for not arriving on time, but he had been delayed due to a last minute tasking from the US Military Group, USMILGP, Bogotá Commander, Colonel Kent Bernardo.

"You know we have another congressional delegation coming in a few weeks and our coordination meeting tonight went over-time." he stated, apologetically.

"No problem, hermano." I placed my hand on his shoulder. "Those things happen. I'm just glad to see you again."

"Thanks, Colonel. I trust you had an uneventful flight?"

"Yes…absolutely. The folks at American Airlines always do a great job."

"That's good. Colonel, how many bags do you have?"

"I have a large black roll away suitcase and a duffel bag full of uniforms and equipment."

"Okay. I see a military duffel bag coming up. Is that it, you think?"

"Yes, that's it and behind it appears to be my suitcase. Figure the odds."

With both bags in tow, I handed the airport police official my customs declaration form and we exited the baggage claim area.

Outside, we walked through the usual gauntlet of enthusiastic well-wishers who eagerly eyed each passenger searching for friends or relatives from the flight. Taxi drivers asked if we needed transportation.

Out in the parking lot, I took a deep breath. The cool evening Bogotá air was a sharp contrast to the tropical heat and humidity from my headquarters in Puerto Rico.

"Ahhh...it's great to be back in Bogotá," I said to anyone who really cared to listen.

An evening arrival at El Dorado always came at a time when the hustle and bustle of the Bogotá traffic was beginning to wind down somewhat.

We placed the luggage into the rear cargo area and then boarded the beige colored armored American Embassy van.

"Colonel Vallejo, this is Darío, my driver this evening."

"*Hola,* Darío. *Cómo estás?*"

"Bien, señor. Welcome back to Bogotá."

"*Gracias.* It's always a pleasure coming back here."

The van departed the busy airport and headed east along *Avenida Eldorado.* Apparently, Bogotá's lighter evening traffic didn't register with Darío because he drove as if the accelerator was stuck to the floor board or we were being chased by an imaginary assailant.

I looked at Major Alvarado who read my mind.

"New driving requirements," he said. "The threat level is elevated this week."

"Oh, okay. If the guerrillas don't get us, our anti-terrorist procedures will." I joked.

"Yes, something like that," Major Alvarado laughed.

For the most part the ride was quiet as I peered out the window...taking in all the sights of one of Latin America's most colorful cities.

"Out of curiosity, where will I be staying prior to departing for TQ?"

"Oh, I guess you didn't get my e-mail. Since you will be in the capital for only one day of in- processing, the USMILGP commander has given you permission to stay at the Embassy Suites Hotel."

Hotel accommodations for all US military personnel were always arranged by the USMILGP, since that office monitors announcements of heightened threats or off limits areas in the city for visiting military personnel.

"That's fantastic," I said with a big grin. "God bless, Kent Bernardo."

The USMILGP commander and I were old buddies that had served together in El Salvador.

"You know, Major Alvarado. Of all the great places to stay in Bogotá, and I've stayed in a few…the Embassy Suites hotel is my favorite for a number of reasons. The hotel has a friendly staff, particularly the two young ladies that work at reception who are old friends; There is always a fresh pot of Colombian *Sello Rojo* coffee brewing in the lobby at all hours; the management allows me to play the grand piano that sits in the lobby after the bar closes; they offer a dynamite complimentary breakfast, and last but not least…"

"You can't beat the complimentary cocktails during their Happy Hour from 5 to 7 pm," volunteered Major Alvarado, anticipating my response.

"Obviously, you know what I mean."

"Yes, sir, I do, but unfortunately, Happy Hour is over. If I were you, I would order a few cold *Club Colombia's* because you may not see any for a while where you're going."

"Actually, I prefer the taste of *Águila* beer, but I understand where you're coming from."

By the time the embassy driver turned right off of *Carrera 7*, I began to recognize some of the familiar landmarks leading to the hotel.

We drew to the front of the hotel on *Calle 70* and were met by the hotel's energetic bellboys.

One of them recognized me as I got out of the vehicle.

"*Bienvenido de nuevo a nuestro hotel, Coronel Vallejo.*"

"*Gracias,* Freddy. I immediately recognized the boyish-looking dark haired man who eagerly took my bag from my hand.

"It's always a pleasure to be back among my friends and to be welcomed at this hotel," I reiterated in Spanish.

As we entered the hotel lobby, Major Alvarado directed the bellboys to the back of the van to bring in the remaining luggage.

At the reception desk I was greeted by a familiar and friendly sight.

"Coronel, what a pleasure to have you back with us," said Eva, the receptionist, who couldn't contain her genuine enthusiasm. She was short, petite, and just a lovely looking lady in her dark blue business suit.

"Well, I'm back here again to support our combined efforts to bring peace to your beautiful country and to strengthen the democratic process," I said imitating a high ranking US official. "Plus, I wanted to check up on you to ensure that your French boyfriend is not taking advantage of you again," I added jokingly.

"Aiiii...Coronel. You never lose your sense of humor. But actually, Jean Pierre and I recently got back together again."

"It doesn't surprise me. If he were smart, he would marry you...By the way, where is your side kick, María?"

Before Eva could answer, a short dark haired lady came out of the back office with a big bright smile on her face.

"Coronel, you can't seem to stay away from Colombia very long."

"Yes, María, I'm sure your husband must complain about the same thing," I kidded with her.

"Rafael isn't the jealous type. He will be getting off work pretty soon to pick me up around 11:30 tonight. Would you like to say hello to him?"

"I'd love to, but I'm afraid that I have a few things to prepare this evening and have a long day tomorrow at the Embassy. Please pass on my regards to him."

"I'll do that, Coronel. Maybe you will have time to entertain us on the piano tonight?"

"That would be nice, María. Thanks for the invitation. But we'll see. As a minimum, I'll stop by for a cup of Sello Rojo."

Like I had told Major Alvarado, I always enjoyed the warm and friendly welcome from the hotel staff.

"Colonel Vallejo, I don't mean to interrupt, but do you want to check out your room before joining me downstairs?" asked Major Alvarado.

"Yes, give me a few minutes to do that and to also wash my face. We'll have a cold one at the bar afterwards. I'll buy."

"Okay, sir. I'll be waiting here for you."

"A Club Colombia and an Águila, real cold, *por favor*," I told Bartolomé, the bartender.

"A pleasure, Coronel."

"Well, what's the scoop, Major Alvarado?"

"Sir, here's your schedule," he said, handing me a red folder.

"I will pick you up in the same van tomorrow at 0800 hours. You are scheduled to do all your in-processing in civilian coat and tie with the USMILGP in the morning. Then you will have an office call with the USMILGP commander at 1000 hours...chat with the Chief of Station at 1100 hours, and if she is available, with Ambassador Masterson at 1130 hours. If she is not available, you will meet with the Deputy Chargé of Mission, Ms. Tara Vore."

Major Alvarado stopped talking as our beers were poured into glasses. We quickly brought glasses up to toast.

"To life, liberty, and the pursuit of happiness," I said toasting to the national purpose of the United States.

"To life, liberty, and the pursuit of happiness," Major Alvarado repeated.

"Ahhhhhhh...that hit the proverbial spot."

"I couldn't agree with you more, Colonel." He paused for a second to collect his thoughts and to look over his note book.

"We currently have you on a standby flight to TQ tomorrow at 1330 hours from the Eddie Cabal ramp at El Dorado Airport. So, you'll need to bring your bags with you tomorrow. All we could get was the Casa C-212 cargo flight for you. The Agency is scheduled to fly their Beechcraft King Air to TQ the following day. If the C-212 is a no go, because of excess cargo, we'll try to get you out to TQ with them the following morning. We've coordinated with your hotel to hold your room just in case. Any questions, sir?"

"No, sounds like the typical flight shuffling to TQ. Doesn't look as if we have many airlines competing for that flight route," I laughed. Between you and me, I would prefer to fly to TQ on the Agency's bird than in the old flying bucket C-212."

"Yes, sir, I know. But that's the best we can do this week."

"Believe me. I understand fully. Thanks for coordinating the schedule and the office calls for me. I'm looking forward to meeting the Ambassador. When is Colonel Nieves scheduled to depart TQ?"

"Sir, if you fly out tomorrow, you'll have one full day with him. Otherwise, if you fly out later, you may only have a few minutes with him...and that will be in passing as you get off the plane and he boards it. However, SFC Contreras will be with you for about four days of overlap."

I thought about this for a minute. When the 7th Special Forces Group personnel had completed their training of the 1st Colombian

Counter-Drug Battalion in TQ and had departed the base, there were now only three US military advisors in TQ. Colonel Jorge Nieves was the current senior US Army operations and intelligence advisor that I would replace. SFC Hector Contreras from USARSO provided intelligence analysis advisory support to the intelligence directorate, but he would be leaving. SFC Juan Tirado, another US Army NCO, was responsible for force protection engineer upgrades. And as far as I knew, that was it. Once SFC Contreras left, there would be only two US military advisors at TQ.

"Sir, anything else?"

"No, I think I'm okay for now...See you bright and early tomorrow?"

"Yes, Sir, I'll be here. Oh, before I forget, please bring your uniform and boots in a garment bag, so that you can easily change into it at the Embassy after the interviews. I'll see you tomorrow."

We both got up from our chairs. Major Alvarado headed for the hotel door, while I walked over to the small table with a coffee pot in the lobby. After the glass of Águila beer, the cup of Colombian Sello Rojo coffee provided my taste buds with still another flavorful sensation. I then walked over to the old, but stately grand piano near the bar area and played a quick score from the Beatles: *Yesterday*, *Something*, *Strawberry Fields Forever*, and *She Loves You*. As usual Eva and María, who were still on duty, applauded from behind the reception desk. I laughed as I closed the keyboard cover, got up from the piano, and bowed. I then took the elevator up to my room. From the room I called the hotel operator to get the AT&T access number to call home to let Ruthie and the kids know that I had arrived safely. After the call I plopped on the bed still fully clothed and fell asleep with the sobs of my family still on my mind.

★ ★ ★

The next morning and right on time Major Alvarado walked into the lobby where I sat reading the *El Tiempo* newspaper. I had decided to wear a dark gray business suit with a light blue shirt and a maroon colored tie. I folded the paper as I got up to greet him.

"Sir, how was your first night?" he asked.

"Slept like a baby."

"Have you already had breakfast?"

"Oh, absolutely. The complimentary breakfast here is outstanding."

"Sir, and I assume you've already checked out?"

"Yes, and I confirmed that they will hold a room for me, just in case. I'm ready to go."

We walked out together as the energetic bellboy, Julio, carted my bags over to the parked van in front of the hotel. Darío, the driver greeted me. And with little fanfare, we were quickly off to the American Embassy. I sat quietly in the van, contemplating the busy scenes of a city and its people starting another new day. We made good time and before long we were at the security check point of the Embassy. The security guard asked for identifications while another guard ran a mirror underneath the van. The engine compartment was also inspected. Once the security personnel had completed their checks, we drove in through a heavy iron gate and into a large parking lot.

"Colonel, I'll leave your bags in the van. Once you complete your meetings, we'll have lunch in the cafeteria, you can change into BDU's, and then will head out to the airport. Please remember to bring your garment bag with you."

"Great. Sounds like a good plan. Where will I link up with you?"

"I'll be in the USMILGP office the entire time."

"Okay…great."

We walked into the large and massive stone building and over to Marine Post 1 to show identifications and to get my visitor's pass. Once security procedures were completed, we headed to the USMILGP office, my first stop of the day. The USMILGP office is the coordination center for all foreign military assistance and training in country. In Colombia this office was particularly busy and central to support of Plan Colombia. From inside the American Embassy this office tracked the presence of all military advisors in country, the status of training initiatives in support of the host country, and the acquisition and delivery of equipment for their use. As part of this important operation, my first order of business was in-processing with this office. This began with the customary security briefing.

"Colonel, read this entire form and sign and date. Then read each of the attached security threat updates and ensure that you read and sign each one. Ensure you provide the dates of your last range qualification with your M9 Beretta pistol and when you were last human rights certified. Once you complete everything let me know."

"Got it, Sergeant."

The USMILGP security NCO, SFC Albert Alphonse, did not smile a single time during his orientation. I figured this was because he took his job seriously. Or maybe he was bored. Through my years in the Army, I had met many people who took their jobs so seriously, they separated their lives and personality from their duties. Sad, I thought. In fact for a moment he reminded me of being back at Fort Bragg, North Carolina. On occasion, while getting my mail at the post office, young, muscular, and long haired individuals would pass me in the hallway without even saying good morning, good afternoon, or even recognizing my presence, despite the fact I was in uniform and clearly displaying my rank insignia. This was always a dead give away that these individuals were members of the elite Delta Force. They were so elite, they figured they were not part of the bigger Army establishment so they did not have to abide by its rules, regulations, or courtesies. I'm sorry guys, but attitudes like that blow covers. Remember, your job is to blend in, not stand out as aberrations.

Once I finished reading and signing the paperwork, I returned the packet to Sergeant Alphonse. He looked at the clock and said, "Sir, you are scheduled to meet with Colonel Bernardo at 1000 hours. He is currently at the morning country team meeting with the Ambassador and they are already running quite late."

"Yes, I know. I'll wait at this desk here if nobody minds."

"Yes, that won't be a problem. I'll let you know when he arrives."

While I waited, I took advantage of the time to call back to my headquarters and see how things were going. I gave my secretary some instructions on some projects I had been working on and also talked to Mr. Denzel about other issues. Once my telephone coordination was completed, I settled down to reading the latest edition of the Colombian magazine, *Semana*.

Sometime later, I lost track of time, my concentration was interrupted by Kent Bernardo's arrival.

"Rick, how are you?" the tall, thin, and red headed USMILGP Commander walked in flashing his characteristically bright smile. He was dressed in his usual worn out camouflaged fatigues. Kent was not much on appearance. While everyone else wore the light weight jungle boots, he still wore his US Army basic issue black leather boots.

"Kent, my friend, it's good to see you again. How's the family?"

"Everyone's doing well...we really like it here. I'm even considering retiring here."

"Retiring here...what do you mean? I told you last time we talked that you were going to get your star out of this tour," I said.

"I don't believe it. Come on, let's go into my office."

I followed Kent. He immediately went to his computer, checked his e-mail, got on the telephone, talked to his driver in Spanish, pulled a paper out of his inbox, signed it, then walked around his desk…all within a matter of minutes.

"I see you're still working a mile a minute," I commented. "How do you manage to keep your sanity?"

"Oh, it's not that bad, once you get used to it. I like the idea of working hard in support of our Colombian allies."

"You told me the same when we were supporting the Salvadorans in the 1980's"

"Yeah, I know. This kind of work is in my blood. I can't get enough of it."

"I know what you mean." I reflected. It seemed that we always started our conversations the same way.

"So, what's you're latest update for me?"

"Well, Rick…since our last talk, everything is moving at warp speed for us in support of Plan Colombia. Operations at TQ have been proceeding at a good clip and USSOUTHCOM continues to support the advisory effort in the COJIC. General Montalvo has maintained a steady stream of operations and his units are destroying coca base labs at a good rate. This month they also found and destroyed two HCL labs. That's quite an accomplishment. I attribute this to better intelligence being developed by the personnel at the COJIC. But of course, there is always room for improvement. Anything you can do to improve upon that should reflect itself in more successes on the battlefield."

"Well, I will certainly give it my best. But it sounds as if they are at quite a high level already. We may be talking about some simple fine tuning."

"I really can't tell you much more than that. Take time to assess their procedures and see what you can do."

"Can do…I look forward to the challenge," I stated affirmatively.

"Great...Rick a lot of people here are looking forward to your presence at TQ. I know the Ambassador in particular is under a lot of pressure by Congress to produce. Funding for Plan Colombia directly depends on measurable results. We need to rollup drug labs. We need to destroy illicit coca fields. We need to kill or capture the drug leadership. In short, this menace and threat have got to be shut down. The only doubter of your skills is the Chief of Station. Dirk Jones is a cynic who trusts no one but his own people. He's a dye in the wool operator who thinks the Agency is God's gift to solving the problems of the world...including those in Colombia. My recommendation is to listen to what he has to say, take notes, and don't argue with him. After all, regardless of what uniform you wear, the Chief of Station is the senior intelligence officer in country. He is overall responsible for all intelligence activities and Tres Esquinas is no exception."

"Tell me something new," I said. "Remember the fist fights and turf wars in El Salvador between US military advisors and the Agency's operators? Nothing changes. Interagency competition will always plague our actions in small wars. I don't know that we can ever change service and agency cultural attitudes."

"There's no use even trying. This stuff has been around since Jesus was a corporal and neither you nor I or our entire Army can do anything about it."

"Well, at least its fun complaining about it," I said.

"Yeah, 'til you turn blue...if that's your idea of fun."

"No, not at all...but anyway...what time before the appointment?"

"Like about now. Let's start heading in that direction. His office is nearby."

A short walk and Kent rang the buzzer in the secure Agency office. We were immediately buzzed inside. There, the receptionist greeted us with little enthusiasm,

"Mr. Jones will see you shortly. Can I offer you gentlemen some coffee?" said the very prim young lady without looking up. She was probably in her mid-thirties, well dressed, blond hair in a bun, wore glasses, uptight, and personified most Agency administrative employees that I had known in the past. The administrative personnel of the Agency always treated non-Agency people with suspicion or like the enemy. It was something like, "You're not one of us, so I can't trust you" type of behavior. After you got to know them, they behaved like normal people, but the first encounters were usually a series of icy stares. On the other hand the Agency's field operators were pretty relaxed and easy-going. I guess it was because these guys and gals lived, breathed, and depended on developing contacts and relation-ships, so they were more into the people business.

"Kent, how are you?" the mustached Dirk Jones walked out of his office and greeted us. He was a very tall and physical fit man with broad shoulders. He appeared to be in his early 50's and the kind of guy that you wouldn't want to anger. His large bushy moustache went very well with his bravado.

"Dirk, I'm doing well. I want you to meet Colonel Rick Vallejo who is on his way to TQ."

"Ah, yes…Colonel Vallejo…we've being looking forward to your arrival. How's life treating you?" he asked while extending his large hand out to greet me.

"Sir, things are going well for us at USARSO. We are always busy with support to the region, as you know."

"Great. Why don't you gentlemen come into my office. I have an important matter to discuss with you."

As we walked, I looked at Kent who only gave me a shoulder shrug in return.

"Can I get you gentlemen some coffee?"

"No. thank you," Kent and I answered at the same time.

"Well, okay...here's the real deal, guys. One of our employees, Mr. Stan Luna, will be working with you in TQ. He is a seasoned operator and will be engaged in working our side of the intelligence community. He's a good man, I've known him for years, and he will fill a hole that we, the community, have not been able to cover appropriately. He will be joining you this week. Questions?"

I looked at Kent who signaled me to go ahead.

"Mr. Jones, how does Mr. Luna fit into the chain of command? I mean who's in charge of him?" I asked.

"You are overall in charge of all US personnel at TQ, including Stan. I look to you in particular to provide him with force protection support. However, he answers to me directly for any operational mission requirements. His activities should not interfere with yours because his focus is entirely different from yours. Am I making sense?" Dirk asked.

I thought for a moment and briefly had a flashback from El Salvador. The Agency habitually liked to operate under the umbrella of a US military mission because if anything went wrong, they could play their "plausible deniability" card when things went sour. Typically the senior US military representative got stuck holding the proverbial bag of feces when this happened. In El Salvador it was not unusual for agents to refer to themselves by military rank even though many of them had never served in the armed forces. In this way the rank structure provided a certain guise of operating as part of a bigger military operation that allowed them to blend in with the rest of the poor uniformed guys. But I knew this and realized that it was simply the price of doing business with the Agency.

"No, I have no questions. I look forward to working with Mr. Luna."

"You'll like Stan. He's an easy going guy and a family man. That's really all I needed to discuss with you. You've pretty much received your marching orders from USSOUTHOCOM, who really covers the day to day administrative and military assistance support at TQ. If you ever need anything from us, please feel free to work through Stan. Oh, do you have transportation to TQ?"

Kent spoke up. "We have Rick scheduled to fly this afternoon on the Casa-212. But if that flight scrubs because of other competing priorities, I have him on stand by for tomorrow morning's King Air."

"Okay, well you're welcome to use it. It usually flies only supply and logistics. We usually have plenty of space and unlike the Casa, it's also pressurized. Stan will be on it for the flight to TQ tomorrow."

"Thanks, I said, but we're trying to beat a deadline so that I can have at least a one day over lap with Colonel Nieves who I'm replacing."

"Well, the offer stands. That's all I have gentlemen. Thank you for your time."

As Kent and I walked out the door together, he hesitated for a moment, but decided against commenting. "Let's talk in my office," he said.

Back inside the USMILGP office, Mrs. Linda García, the USMILGP secretary looked up at us.

"Colonel Bernardo, the Ambassador's secretary just called. They've had some schedule changes and would like to meet with Colonel Vallejo now."

"Okay, then let's go. That's the one person I don't like to keep waiting," joked Kent.

We took the elevator up a floor or two, I never kept track, and walked into a spacious sitting area. The first thing that caught my eye was a large three dimensional-like painting...one of those that has a lot of metal relief built into its surface. The receptionist, an older lady, nicely dressed, welcomed us very politely and enthusiastically, and genuinely appeared to feel that way.

"Good morning gentlemen, the Ambassador is waiting to see you. You may walk right in to her office."

As we moved in direction of the ambassador's office, Ambassador Pam Masterson, a very distinguished looking and attractive blonde lady wearing a red blazer suit and skirt, came out of her office to greet us. She was probably in her late 50's. Her dark eyes were very penetrating.

"Colonel Bernardo, good to see you…what's it been…less than an hour since I last saw you at my staff meeting?" she laughed. I immediately liked her.

"Seems like more time than that," Kent laughed. Ambassador Masterson, this is…"

"Why, Colonel Vallejo, of course. How are you?"

"Fine, ma'am, thank you." I noticed there was another woman in her office.

"Colonel Vallejo, have you met my Deputy Chargé of Mission, Ms. Tara Vore?"

"No, but I've heard of her. How are you Ma'am?"

"Please call me Tara," she said with a pleasant smile. She was a tall brunette with a very deliberate and powerful presence who seemed to be all business. She wore a dark blue and white pinstripe woman's business suit and I estimated she was in her late 40's. She had a certain matter of fact quality and an air of self confidence about her that was quite impressive.

"Well, are you all set for your stay in Tres Esquinas?" the Ambassador asked.

"Yes, ma'am. I'm rarin' to go."

"Good. I have high expectations of you…and so does everyone else here. Plan Colombia is alive and well. We just need to keep the momentum in our favor.

"Mrs. Ambassador, Rick and I served together in El Salvador during the height of the conflict," said Kent.

"Oh, splendid," the Ambassador beamed.

"Yes, ma'am, those of us who served there feel that the advisory effort contributed greatly to professionalize the Salvadoran Army and ultimately setting the conditions for peace to prevail. I think military advisors will make a big difference here in Colombia too."

The Ambassador and her Chargé briefly raised their eyebrows as they exchanged glances.

"Colonel Vallejo, I must caution you of one thing," said the Ambassador. "Members of Congress do not like to use the term, 'advisors' because it is negatively connected with the Vietnam advisory effort and the unfortunate negativity associated with that conflict. There's a lot of pressure to not escalate this war like we did in Vietnam."

"I understand, ma'am," I responded. "What do you prefer we call ourselves?"

"Until Congress answers that question for us, the Chargé and I prefer to simply refer to you as, 'Little Helpers.' We figure that is as benign a title as any we can come up with for now."

We all laughed.

"Got it, ma'am...and I understand the sensitivities. Although, you know we can't stop the Colombians from calling us *Asesores*."

"Welcome to the world of politics, Colonel Vallejo," the Ambassador smiled.

"Sometimes I feel that I spend more time fighting the political battle with Congress than I do helping the Colombians fight their drug war."

She paused for a second.

"Do you know General Manuel Montalvo?"

"Yes, we've met on various occasions during my visits to Tres Esquinas. Personnel from my staff are supporting him with the latest imagery exploitation equipment and software. They routinely fly in and out of Tres Esquinas."

"Yes, I knew USSOUTHCOM had been managing the intelligence support effort there. I didn't know that it was your people involved."

"Well, technically we are all one and the same. But, yes, those personnel come from USARSO headquarters."

"Good. Then you are a known entity with General Montalvo. That will help tremendously in the transition from the people side of things. He is really very pro-USA and is working very closely with us on Plan Colombia. Basically, his headquarters is at the center of the military element of the Plan. His successes will directly reflect on us and the tremendous commitment that our Administration has made in support of the drug war here in Colombia. You are still yet another piece of what I hope will be continuing success."

"Yes, ma'am, I will not disappoint you or your staff."

"I know you won't, Colonel Vallejo. I just want you to know just how important everything we do here is. You are now a part of this evolving story. Well, I don't have anything else for you. When do you fly to Tres Esquinas?"

I looked at my watch. "In about another two hours…if my flight goes as scheduled."

"Well good luck to you. And please know that my entire staff and I are here to support you in whatever way we can."

"Thank you, ma'am, and you know that I'll do my very best."

With that Kent and I shook hands with the two distinguished ladies and we left the office.

I walked out with a good feeling knowing that the American Embassy was in the hands of a very capable, competent, and impressive lady. I didn't realize until then that everything we were doing in Colombia had so much visibility. I promised myself that I would not let anyone down.

Back in Kent's office we resumed our discussion.

"Kent, what was it you wanted to tell me after our visit with the Chief of Station?"

"Oh, no, it was just an afterthought. While Dirk was telling you about the chain of command lash up between you and Mr. Luna, I remembered the one episode we had in 3rd Brigade headquarters in San Miguel, El Salvador between our military advisors and the Agency."

"Was that the incident when the results of the UN Truth Commission were leaked to the Salvadoran Armed Forces by a CIA agent and the USMILGP got blamed for it?" I asked.

"Exactly. That is another case of when the shadow rank structure is used to provide plausible deniability. During that incident the CIA agent in San Miguel leaked the news and it made it all the way to the Salvadoran Presidential Palace. Then the Agency turned around and said it was a US military advisor that had leaked it. How in the world would we have access to that kind of information? Anyway, watch yourself in TQ. And always watch your back. It's not quite as bad here as it was in El Salvador, but you never know. Hey, I've got to get you to the airport. Let's stop at the Embassy cafeteria downstairs for a quick lunch and then my driver and Major Alvarado will escort you to the airport."

"Do you mind if I change into BDU's in your office before departing the Embassy?"

"Yeah, go ahead…we have time."

I got my uniform from my garment bag and changed in Kent's office. Then we walked the short distance to the main floor cafeteria. Despite the hustle, bustle, and noise in the cafeteria, we ate lunch in silence as I collected my thoughts. The farewells and the trip to the airport were one big blur. Half way there Major Alvarado got the call that the CASA flight was overloaded and they would not be taking any passengers. We headed back to the Embassy where I changed back to civilian attire. Major Alvarado's driver drove me back to my hotel where I napped and watched TV the rest of the day and evening. Although I'm sure I had something to eat, I don't remember what I had for dinner that night. The next morning after the same morning pick up ritual, I was headed back to the airport to catch the Agency's flight to TQ.

> *So kiss me and smile for me...tell me that you'll wait for me...hold me like you'll never let me go...Cause I'm leavin' on a jet plane, don't know when I'll be back again...Oh babe, I hate to go...*
>
> *Peter, Paul, and Mary*

CHAPTER SIX

TRES ESQUINAS

No more will my green sea go turn a deeper blue...I could not foresee this thing happening to you...If I look hard enough into the settin' sun... My love will laugh with me before the mornin' comes...

"Paint it, Black"
as recorded by The Rolling Stones

HEADQUARTERS, JOINT TASK FORCE-SOUTH,
TRES ESQUINAS, CAQUETA DEPARTMENT, COLOMBIA,
1115 HOURS, 23 MAY 2001

It was a radiantly beautiful and sunshine splashed day as our small twin engine plane sat on the end of the runway of El Dorado International Airport...its two engines revving up for take off. Staring out the right window, I saw a large American Airlines 757 dwarfing us as it taxied to move in behind.

Let me share another secret with you. I'm not fond of air travel, especially in a war torn country. So, in anticipation, my mind goes into its usual mental gyrations. It is interesting how when an airplane is preparing to take off, we come to grips with the significance of the event...or in some cases, life itself in our own personal way. It can feel like a new beginning of some sort... the excitement that travel to a new place creates. Or it can simply be the joy of returning back home or to the place where our flight originated. To some people, it may be the novelty or fear they feel right before an airplane takes off. If you look at the passengers in an airliner, you will see a drama unfolding. Couples will hold hands at the moment of take off out of fear or wanting to affirm their love for each other. Some passengers make the sign of the cross. Others close their eyes in deep thought or prayer. Others stare out the window. Still others yawn, not out of lack of sleep or hunger, but due to oxygen deprivation. The business executives and frequent flyers simply continue to read their copies of the *Wall Street Journal* or the *New York Times*. As the noise from the engines increased, I fell somewhere in the middle of all of these categories. I was sure of one thing, however. I knew that this new adventure unfolding would definitely change my life. My head lurched to the rear as the pilot released the brakes and we sped down the runway for take off.

I could see the back of the pilot's head through the open cabin door. Stan Luna and I were the sole passengers inside the cabin of this small aircraft. Within minutes, Stan was already nodding off and would soon fall asleep. For these CIA guys, this was just another day in the office. Stan was a Hispanic American, maybe Cal-Mex, I can't remember, in his early 60's, gray haired, tanned complexion, and about medium height and build. He had a grandfather figure side to him that was quite disarming. In just a short period of time that I had talked to Stan while waiting for our flight, I found him to be very well balanced and even tempered. He and I saw eye-to-eye on a lot of things and I decided that we were going to work hard on making our time at TQ a professional and pleasurable experience. Behind me the cargo stow area was overfilled with hard plastic carrying cases of equipment and card board boxes with provisions. These CIA shuttle flights are the backbone of US logistics support to its agents in the TQ area and elsewhere in country. Without this vehicle, travel and provisioning of field personnel out "in the sticks" was very difficult, if next to impossible.

Out my right window, there was nothing to see. The sun I last saw in Bogotá was gone…blotted out by thick dark clouds of rain that were my only company until less than an hour later when the airplane began descending.

Stan started to stir; he looked out the window…then his watch…and went back to sleep. I removed a topographic map of Colombia from my backpack to take my mind off the flight. It soon fell to my lap as I dozed off to sleep for the last part of the flight.

The voice of John, the CIA contract pilot, came over the intercom and interrupted my peaceful interlude with the words, "We are ten minutes from landing at TQ."

Outside my window the dark clouds had scattered enough to give me a view of the endless emerald canopy of forest and jungle. What a contrast to the high mountains around Bogotá. I was hypnotized by nature's splendor and the vastness of the region. I simply stared out in amazement. I knew that I shouldn't be amazed, but I was. Every time I saw it. And I've seen this endless panorama many times. This is at the heart of what makes the drug war so difficult to win. Simply looking at the expanse of inhospitable territory and it should become perfectly clear.

While on final approach to TQ, a latte coffee-colored ribbon cut through the verdant landscape. The Río Orteguaza flowed along the west bank of TQ on its way to merging and becoming one with the Río Caquetá. As I told you in an earlier chapter, TQ is strategically positioned on this crossway point.

Our airplane steeply banked to the left and then to the right as John flew through the dark rain clouds attempting to line his plane up with the concrete runway at TQ. Along with the COJIC and the Amazon Over the Horizon Radar system being constructed at the site, the 7,000 foot runway at TQ was of strategic importance to this small out of the way base. I shuddered as I thought of the fact that this remote jungle outpost would be my home for God knew how long.

The landing, though, was smooth. John was one of the best and it showed. We taxied to a point near the large olive green canvas building that was the COJIC. Outside on the parking ramp, I saw an entourage of uniformed individuals that was obviously my welcome committee. They were all dressed in a mix of green camouflaged battle dress uniforms. I patiently waited for John to shut the engines off. Thinking back on it, I was really in no hurry to get off the airplane. He got up from his seat and walked back to open the rear main exit door on the left of the aircraft. A twist of the handle and it slowly hinged down. He nodded to signal me that it was okay for us to get up. I reluctantly left my seat and walked back stopping to avoid hitting my head on the top of the door. Stan followed me.

The blast of hot and humid tropical air almost took my breath away. Jungle air has to be experienced to be appreciated. It is not like a sauna, but more like a Turkish bath, if you can appreciate the difference…sort of like breathing steam or vapor suspended in the air. The key point is that you would not go into either one of these fully clothed, but of course, we did…in military uniforms. Rather than the smell of Eucalyptus, the smell of rotting wood was overpowering. I wondered if the dead souls entering Hell felt the same way. I stepped out of the aircraft hearing the words, "Welcome to the Hell hole," somewhere in my mind.

It is not difficult to describe TQ. In fact it's very easy. It is nothing more than a 7,000 ft concrete runway surrounded by small houses, barracks, office buildings, and the COJIC. The runway at the center of the base is the life line in and out of this place. With the exception of limited travel along the Río Orteguaza that runs by the base, loss of this runway would virtually cut us off from the outside world.

Parked in various spaces adjacent the main runway was the main means to repel attacks and to provide close air support for units in contact. A menacing-looking olive drab twin turbo prop Colombian Air Force AC-47 *Fantasma* gunship sat silently nearby. Depending on the variant in support of the base that month, its armament was three 12.7mm or .50 caliber side mounted machineguns or a multi-barrel 7.62mm mini-gun, capable of firing up to 6,000 rounds per minute. Sitting close to it was an olive drab UH-1N *Arpia* helicopter gunship or sometimes a Bell 212 *Rapaz* armed helicopter, configured with a mini-gun, or side rack mounted 7.62 mm machineguns. That day on the south apron sat two multi gray single engine Embraer AT-27 *Tucano* aircraft. At other times there might be the much improved A-29B Super Tucano with two 12.7mm or .50 caliber machineguns, a wing mounted 20 mm cannon pod, two 500 pound bombs, four 250 pound bombs, and its distinctive nose painted shark mouth. By the way, these aircraft were assigned to GASUR or the Air Group South headquartered in Tres Esquinas. Remember that JTF-South was a joint and multi-service command.

Around all this armament and facilities were a series of trenches, fighting positions, bunkers, observation towers, triple strand concertina barbed wire, and mines. That's it. If I said more it would detract from my pessimistic view of this place. But I will include more details as the story unfolds. For now, let's get back to my arrival at TQ.

At the bottom of the steps of the plane, my dark mood changed as I saw some familiar faces. The first to speak was US Army Colonel Jaime Nieves, the officer I was replacing. He was a tall and tanned Hispanic who wore wrinkled and faded camouflaged BDU's.

"Welcome back to Tres Esquinas, Rick. We've been anxiously awaiting your arrival. General Montalvo apologizes, but he could not be here to personally greet you so he sent his intelligence officer, Colonel Ismael Gutiérrez in his place."

"Thanks…it's great to be here." I could sense Satan making another log entry under my name in his journal. The tall, brown eyed Colombian officer with a short military style haircut standing next to COL Nieves stuck out his hand.

"Coronel, welcome back to Tres Esquinas," he said in Spanish. How was your flight?"

"Mi Coronel, what a pleasure to see you again. The flight was uneventful," I answered in Spanish. I had met Colombian Army COL Gutiérrez during my previous one day visits to TQ. I was genuinely happy to see a good Colombian friend again. I then introduced Stan to COL Gutiérrez.

"Mi Coronel, this is Stan Luna. He will be working with you and providing additional intelligence support. He works for Mr. Dirk Jones from the Embassy."

"Bienvenido a Tres Esquinas, Señor Stan. We are always happy to have additional support," said COL Gutiérrez.

"Thank you, Coronel. I will be meeting with you at your convenience to tell you about what I can do for you," answered Stan.

"Good...how about after you get settled into your quarters at the White House?" *The White House was the contract rental house that the CIA maintained in TQ for its operators.*

"Better yet, can I invite you and your assistants over this evening for some snacks and some Johnny Walker Black Label? We can discuss the time later." Like any good CIA operator, Stan was well trained in the finer art of persuasion and wasted no time establishing this fact.

"Yes, that will be fine," COL Gutiérrez said.

Present also was US military Sergeant First Class Héctor Contreras, my senior intelligence analyst and rep from USARSO. I shook his hand and patted him on the back.

"SFC Contreras, I understand you'll be staying with me for a few days to accomplish our hand over of responsibilities, and then you're leaving?"

"Yes, sir...That's the plan. Colonel Nieves is leaving with John back to Bogotá today. I will leave on Tuesday of next week when

John returns. That should give us enough time to get you read in to the situation and procedures here."

"Okay, I guess that will work. I'm not comfortable with the short time programmed for battle hand over, but at the same time I don't blame you for wanting to leave as soon as possible. TQ is no vacation spot."

SFC Contreras looked at COL Nieves who smiled, and resumed the conversation.

"I've got my pick-up truck here. SFC Contreras will load your bags and Stan's as well as any equipment and provisions John brought for us."

John, the pilot, had already unstrapped the equipment onboard and was handing boxes to two Colombian Army enlisted men that were helping to unload the plane. He looked up from his work and asked, "COL Nieves, besides you, who am I flying back to Bogotá with me?"

"Well, I've got a *Cabo Segundo* Meléndez who's going on emergency leave…death in the family, I understand… and *Sargento* Romero who has scheduled dental surgery."

"Okay…well let's get them on board quickly. I want to leave right away. The clouds gathering look somewhat ominous. I don't want to get stuck here in the middle of a strong storm."

This is something else I had to look forward to while at TQ… the daily rains or storms that highlight the rainy season. I looked at the small pools of standing water that had already saturated the ground around us from an earlier rain. The only semi-dry area was the runway itself as steam rose from its surface.

The two Colombian passengers helped each other carry their bags into the plane. John loaded these into the back cargo hold that was previously empty.

"Well, my friend. Good luck," COL Nieves broke the silence. "Sorry that I have to run, but I got extended here well beyond my initial commitment. My unit is screaming for my return."

"I understand. I was briefed on your situation. Besides, you've provided more than your share of support. Maybe we'll run into each other again down the road. Take care and the best of luck to you."

"Thanks, Rick…It's not that bad here. It'll grow on you."

"I'm sure it will," I answered feeling as if I were talking to a prison warden.

As Colonel Nieves entered the plane, I turned to SFC Contreras who had already loaded my gear in the back of his pick-up truck. "Sir, whenever you're ready."

"Yes, of course. I'm ready." I felt like running back to the airplane since it was my last link to civilization and a way out of this wretched hole. I had no choice.

"Okay…Let's go."

All three of us, SFC Contreras, Stan, and I, walked a short distance over a muddy and graveled flight parking apron to the mud splattered silver Ford Ranger pick-up truck. I glanced at my already muddied boots. SFC Contreras read my mind.

"Sir, don't worry about the boots. It's impossible to keep them clean here. No one will say anything."

"Right," I glumly answered.

After dropping Stan off at his three bedroom CIA rental house, we drove the short distance to the aluminum prefab trailer-like facilities that were our barracks. A single-room hooch would be my only place of privacy while at TQ. As SFC Contreras searched for the key to my hooch he said:

"Sir, what I recommend you do is get your gear unpacked and your uniforms and things organized. Then we can inventory your survival issue items. The officer's club or casino, as they call it here, serves dinner at 1830 hrs. I can pick you up, if you want to eat. If not, I know you've had a long day, so you may want to opt for some rest. Either way I will pick you up tomorrow morning at 0730 hours…just prior to the 0740 hours morning update for

General Montalvo. I will pick you up here and escort you to the COJIC. Later we will meet all the key players on the staff."

"That sounds like a reasonable plan, but I will pass on dinner," I answered, still half in a daze. As I reflected on this, I heard the drone of John's airplane revving up. I watched him take off from the open door of my hooch and followed the plane until it was a mere speck in the cloudy Colombian sky. I felt as if a part of me… perhaps my only way out of this place…had left on that airplane this memorable day.

We inventoried all my survival gear. This equipment was required by the USMILGP for all its deployed field advisors. I now had an assigned 9 mm Beretta M9 pistol with five clips of ammo and a 5.56 mm Colt M4 assault rifle with nine 30 round magazines of ammo. In my large military rucksack were boxes of more ammo, packets of emergency MREs, Meals Ready to Eat, a lensatic compass, various scale maps, a GPS, a UHF radio like the one's used by downed pilots, a strobe light and infrared light chemlights for viewing by pilots wearing night vision goggles or NVGs, regular chemlights in various colors, and a poncho with liner. With these items in a rucksack, plus my flack vest, a Kevlar ballistic helmet, and a load bearing equipment harness, we were suppose to be able to withstand either an attack from the FARC or an Escape and Evasion (E&E) from TQ if the situation warranted. A Global Star SATCOM phone was an additional asset. TQ was so isolated that it had no cellular phone coverage.

"Sir, I recommend that you experiment with this phone until you understand how it works. It takes a little practice getting use to it. As an experiment try calling USMILGP Bogotá or USARSO in Fort Buchanan. Keep in mind that you have to be outdoors to establish a satellite link. Do not use this system except in emergencies because the cost per call is astronomical. If you ever have to E&E, ensure that you have this phone with you." SFC Contreras paused while I fiddled with the satellite phone.

"Here are the keys to the silver Ford Ranger pick up truck. It is for your use. I will pick you up tomorrow in the second pick-up truck, a maroon Chevy Luv."

When SFC Contreras was satisfied that I had everything inventoried, he left for the evening. I don't remember what I snacked on from my own provisions that night. I do remember lying down on my small bunk and staring up at the mold and rust stains on the ceiling panels, but not for long. A slowly moving mist of slumber began to gently envelope my mind. I did not resist this warm and alluring sensation and my eyes closed.

Despite my dispirited disposition the day before, I awoke the next morning with zeal and enthusiasm. I felt like myself again. A quick shower and shave restored my vigor. I decided not to let the isolation and conditions of TQ get to me. I was determined to make a good and positive first impression.

My breakfast was simple...a few Keebler saltine crackers with Kraft Cheese Whiz and a glass of bottled water with powdered orange-flavored Tang. As I popped a multi-vitamin and the malaria capsule, I heard a knock on the door. SFC Contreras was right on time. I grabbed my patrol cap and stepped out to greet him at the door.

"Sir, how was your first night in TQ?"

"Great...I slept like a baby...can't complain."

As per our SOP, standard operating procedures, I wore the LBE, load bearing equipment harness that held my pistol magazine clips in magazine pouches, regular rifle ammo pouches, and a canvas holster for my pistol. Additionally, I carried a map case for two hand held Motorola Saber radios. The map case was a green canvas pouch used by soldiers for carrying maps and documents in the field. I conveniently carried this slung over my shoulder. I liked it because I could easily access my maps, notebooks, pens, and other personal items. It was the same map case that I carried when on the airborne operation into Torrijos International Airport during the invasion of Panama in 1989. It also had enough space to carry the two portable push to talk hand-held radios. One radio was for communications with the other advisors on station. The other one was to communicate on the internal Colombian Army TQ net.

SFC Contreras did the best he could to drive his Chevy pick up around the large muddy water-filled potholes capable of swallowing an entire truck along the equally muddy road to the COJIC. From an improvised parking lot, we walked to the COJIC in time to make the 0740 hours Commander's morning update briefing or *Programa* as the Colombians called it. As I think I told you before in a previous chapter, the COJIC was a huge one story olive drab canvas and tubular steel building that was the nerve center for all planning and coordination for Joint Task Force-South, the Colombian Armed Forces headquarters for Plan Colombia. The JTF-South Commander, Brigadier General Manuel Montalvo, worked on one side of the COJIC along with his staff. On the other side of the large partitioned wall was the intelligence analysis area where US military intelligence advisors worked from cubicles alongside their Colombian counterparts. A large 300 KW generator located nearby provided power for all electronic equipment and air conditioners. The building was actually quite a spacious and comfortable working environment. I saw this as the lone positive among the list of negatives at TQ.

This daily update briefing took place inside a concrete and sand-bagged reinforced bunker next to the COJIC. It was nothing more than a small room with metal folding chairs facing a large table with radios from where the JTF Commander communicated with his units during the updates. Attending the update briefing would become a twice daily 6 day a week ritual for me from now on. Besides the 0740 hours morning briefing, I would also attend another update at 1940 hours. Having to attend briefings is a royal pain in the butt, but these briefings also served the purpose of keeping the staff informed on the developments of the many counter-narcotics operations taking place in the area of operations. They also kept me informed. As you can probably imagine, one of my jobs was to keep the American Embassy up to date on the progress being made on the military side of Plan Colombia. The daily update briefings along with the reports put out by the T3 Operations and T2 Intelligence directors would serve this purpose. Although I had responsibility to serve as a reporter for the Ambassador, my primary job was to assist and advise the Colombian intelligence section. That's really the bread and butter of my advisory support. Soon, however, I would learn that to this simple job description I would add a number of duties that were not as apparent on the first take. Dear friends, I will explain those to you a little later in another chapter dedicated just to this. SFC Contreras and I found two empty chairs in the middle of the room.

My thoughts were interrupted when someone called the room to attention. Brigadier General Montalvo walked in and was met by Colonel Gilberto de la Barca, the JTF-South Chief of Staff, who rendered the customary report and greeting. Salutes were exchanged and General Montalvo ordered everyone to be seated. He slowly scanned the room looking at everyone. General Montalvo was a tall and very imposing person. His no-nonsense bearing dominated his physique. Military closely cropped hair, dark eyes, and a unique sternness rounded out his appearance. His BDU uniform was pressed and his boots were spit shined polished or as Colombians called it, polished *A La Americana*. He stopped scanning the room when he saw me and a smile came to his face.

"Coronel Vallejo, welcome to Tres Esquinas," he said in Spanish. I'm told that you will be staying with us for a little longer than your usual one day visits."

"Yes, General," I answered in Spanish. Looks as if we'll be working together for awhile."

"Very good," he said. "And let me add that your presence is yet another indicator of your country's commitment to us. Your presence and support are indicators of your country's confidence in our operations. Again, I welcome you."

I nodded in agreement as I said, "Gracias, mi General."

The meeting proceeded with each staff officer providing General Montalvo with a quick update of their respective areas. The T2 and T3 took up the majority of the briefing. Then General Montalvo proceeded to call all his subordinate commanders for their updates by radio. About 30 minutes later we were through.

My first priority that morning was to follow SFC Contreras around as he walked through the various areas. I knew most of the personnel from my previous visits, but the office calls were done as a courtesy to our hosts. Later and when I had more time to myself, my priority would be to begin assessing the level of military intelligence expertise by the T2 analysts in the COJIC. The T2 or Task Force 2 was the intelligence staff element responsible for intelligence. I would do this in combination with applying the Intelligence Cycle. This was the template intelligence professionals used to assess how the intelligence functions at an organization worked. The intelligence cycle simply stipulates the steps involved in the generation of intelligence. Those steps are: Planning, Directing, Collecting, Analyzing, Producing, and Disseminating intelligence. Any inefficiency detected at each step would indicate problems with the process.

With SFC Contreras accompanying me, I spent the greater part of the day talking to the Colombian intelligence analysts that conducted the tedious day-to-day intelligence support to the JTF-South mission. That mission was to disrupt and destroy the cocaine producing capabilities in the southern departments of Colombia. For the most part this required piecing together intelligence obtained from HUMINT (human intelligence) sources, IMINT (imagery intelligence) from airborne imagery platforms (surveillance aircraft), and SIGINT (signals intelligence). Analysts would then develop target folders for the combat commanders to use in support of the drug eradication missions. These target folders included narratives, descriptions, locations with map coordinates, and even copies of aerial imagery to enhance the commander's ability to visualize the target and to interdict cocaine movement corridors, supply and logistics centers, coca base labs, and HCL or crystallization labs. HCL labs, an abbreviation for the hydrochloric acid used in the cocaine refinement process, were considered the grand prize in these operations for they were usually the largest, most sophisticated, and most expensive in the drug production cycle. They were basically large chemical labs that processed the coca base into refined and export quality cocaine. The most numerous targets were the coca base labs, hundreds of wood and tin shanties in which coca leaves were processed into coca paste or the base product for refined cocaine. In the period I was deployed to Tres Esquinas, the COJIC would find and destroy hundreds of these small labs. They seemed to be as common as trees in a jungle.

In addition to directing the intelligence effort on the drug infrastructure, the T2 also focused his effort on HPT or high payoff targets. These included guerrilla base camps and the locations of the guerrilla leadership of the FARC. During these early years of Plan Colombia, our Congress prohibited support to combating the guerrilla insurgency. What I mean by this is that the drug war was treated separately from the insurgency. Technically, we were prohibited from conducting counterinsurgency operations against the FARC. However, knowing that the FARC was intimately connected to the drug movement, we could not target one and not the other. As far as we in the field were concerned, the FARC and its leadership were fair game.

Why the disparity? Over time the FARC had transformed from being an insurgent organization that provided security to the drug cartels, to directly involving its personnel in the production and transport of cocaine. Insurgents that finance their war with monies obtained from drug production can generally sustain themselves indefinitely as long as the millions and millions of dollars from drug revenue continue to fill the coffers of the movement. This had metamorphosed from an insurgent movement to a multimillion dollar business enterprise. Money served as a strong motivator, not just for the FARC leadership, but for the FARC foot soldiers that were better paid than their Colombian military enlisted counterparts.

I was quite pleased with the effort being made to develop intelligence in the COJIC, but I was also displeased by the lack of HUMINT. This came as no surprise since the southern departments of Colombia had long been FARC sanctuaries free of Colombian government presence. Trying to establish HUMINT operations and sources in this part of Colombia presented a serious challenge to the military. As a result, they relied heavily on technically acquired intelligence, particularly from airborne imagery and signals intercept. For now I had to make due with what we had and focused my advice to improving the quality of intelligence derived from these sources.

We at USARSO had invested time, money, and effort in improving the quality of the Colombian imagery intelligence effort. Mobile Training Teams from my organization spent weeks and months instructing intelligence analysts on the latest equipment that enhanced this effort. The US Army had developed new digital map production technologies and imagery gathering systems that were in much demand in this war. When you realize that much of southern Colombian jungle had not been mapped, you begin to understand the challenge that this posed for military units attempting to conduct operations in the green vastness of

Amazonian jungle. This is why I had decided that my organization could make its biggest contribution to the war effort by focusing our effort on the imagery and mapping part of the intelligence advisory mission.

Day in and day out I met with the personnel of the COJIC. I reviewed target folders, looked over aerial photos, and generally tried to stay engaged in the intelligence effort. I relied heavily on the deputy T2, Major Norberto Cano, a young, bright, and take charge of the situation kind of officer, to fill me in on the FARC order of battle. No matter what my level of expertise or years of experience as an intelligence professional, every war was different and so was the enemy. I came to respect the young major for his intelligence assessments and thorough understanding of the FARC.

One advantage that I did have over the intelligence analysts was that I was the outsider that provided a more objective view of intelligence estimates. The young analysts seemed to appreciate this perspective. Sometimes I wasn't quite sure how the more senior members of the organization viewed my presence. In this business this does matter and it was important to me. Still, I had a job to do and I fulfilled my obligations to the best of my ability.

I mentioned earlier that I had the responsibility of keeping the American ambassador informed of daily successes of the JTF through a daily written report. To do this, I would confer with the T3 Operations officer, LTC Arturo Montañéz, who would show me the morning reports from the units in the field deployed on drug interdiction and eradication missions.

A typical daily written situation report might look something like this:

1. During the third day of Operation Meteor, Company A (Antelope), 2d BACNA reported 6 enemy killed in action (EKIA) and 3 friendly wounded in action (FWIA).

2. Company C (Canada), 3d BACNA reported 2 EKIA.

3. 4 coca base labs were destroyed.

4. The following items were confiscated and destroyed:

    a. 9500 kilograms of cement

    b. 50 kilograms of caustic soda

    c. 770 gallons of gasoline

    d. Eight 50 gallon drums of gasoline soaked coca leaf

    e. 180 bags of lose coca leaf

    f. One balance scale

    g. One press

    h. Two weed eaters

    i. One fumigator

I would type reports similar to this every morning and send them via e-mail to the USMILGP operations officer over a secure communications link using an LST-5 SATCOM radio, a lap top computer, and one of two SATCOM antennas. Some days these reports were multi-paged. Other times they were simply one page in length. Over time it became one of my more tedious chores, but never-the-less I suspected that this was one of the ways that the Embassy kept a running score card on the success of the military portion of Plan Colombia.

The problem with captured equipment and coca base counts is that we did not really know what impact our effort was having on the entire drug production system. The analogy of killing ants and destroying ant hills serves a useful purpose. You may kill many of them, but the fact is that you can't kill them all. They just keep coming back. Secondly, you don't really know what their starting number is. If in one month you report killing 1,000 ants, for example, what impact did this really have on the other 15 thousand that you didn't get? And then, of course, there's the question of how quick they regenerate new members in the various colonies. Is simply killing or capturing a real marker of success? Or should we adopt another means of gauging success?

I thought about this many times and finally convinced myself that we had to believe that eventually this effort would generate some returns. Keeping the FARC leadership on its toes or moving to avoid capture had to be valuable in the long run. Maybe they would eventually realize that they just couldn't continue to be on the run all their lives. Maybe we would eventually find and kill the queen ant of a colony. The war on drugs anchors its success on many maybes: maybe this…maybe that…maybe these…maybe those…

But despite my frustrations and sometimes pessimistic outlooks, the war marched on. During 2001 TQ continued to figure prominently in the Colombian drug war. Every week, sometimes twice a week, scores of UH-1N helicopters landed on the grassy fields adjacent TQ's runway to pick up or drop off Colombian combat personnel. These combat operations were designed to provide surprise, as troops from TQ or nearby Larandia would swoop down on unsuspecting drug producers and FARC security personnel. JTF-South had the bad guys on the run with no let up.

Whenever I could, I would walk over to the ramp side just to watch the air assault staging portion of these operations unfold. The best I could do was simply to watch since American military advisors were prohibited by the Embassy to engage in combat operations with the Colombian Armed Forces. So, I would watch as soldiers and National Policemen huddled at designated points along the runway waiting to be picked up by the helicopters. Then a group of UH-1 or UH-60 helicopters…sometimes ten… sometimes 15 would fly in a file formation and set down near the awaiting 'stick' of combat personnel. In the meantime, two UH-1 helicopter gun ships would circle overhead providing over watch around these multi-ship formations. I must say that regardless of age or time in service I was always impressed by these operations. I suppose they are the US Army's version of US Navy carrier landings and takeoffs...lot's of noise...lot's of expensive equipment...and plenty of excitement.

My one consolation in all these operations is that intelligence assessments and target folders developed in the COJIC figured prominently and were at the center of the many drug bases targeted in the Putumayo and Caquetá areas. General Montalvo kept a tally on how well we were doing and used this information in his presentation to VIP's. One thing for sure, though. Drug processing labs got hit hard with numerous drug personnel being killed or captured, and drug labs with tons of cocaine, precursor chemicals, and equipment destroyed. This I did know.

> *I look inside myself and see my heart is black...I see my red door and it has been painted black...Maybe then I'll fade away and not have to face the facts...It's not easy facin' up when your whole world is black...*
>
> *The Rolling Stones*

CHAPTER SEVEN

LIFE AS A MILITARY ADVISOR

I am he as you are he as you are me and we are all together...See how they run like pigs from a gun see how they fly...I'm crying...

Sitting on a bench...waiting for the bus to come. Corporation t-shirts, stupid bloody Tuesday... you've been a naughty boy...you let your hair grow long. I am eating eggs...they are eating eggs...I'm John Lennon...goo goo ga joob.

"I am the Walrus"
as recorded by The Beatles

HEADQUARTERS, JOINT TASK FORCE-SOUTH,
TRES ESQUINAS, CAQUETA DEPARTMENT, COLOMBIA
1000 HOURS, 5 JULY 2001

A month passed and I still missed not having SFC Contreras around. He left the following Tuesday after my arrival to TQ and was now back at USARSO. I learned that he took a short vacation and visited his family in New Jersey. In the meantime, I could only focus on the mission and my tasks as an advisor.

Do you want to know what life was like as an advisor? Providing examples is probably an easy way to cover this topic. Just for kicks, I will refer to these as the Essential Elements of Advisory Duty. These elements are: Time, Additional Duties, Going Native, Language, Language, Language, Expert with a Plan, Stay in your Lane, and Have Fun.

Element #1: Time. When you are in a combat environment, every day is like the 1993 movie *Ground Hog Day*. The alarm clock sounds, you go through the morning ritual of getting prepared, you report to work, you get back from work, you go through the evening ritual of preparing for bed, and you go to bed…over and over and over again.

"Well that's not so different from the average 9 to 5 schedule of the American worker," you say. Well, yes and no. There is one basic difference. The typical American job includes weekends. You have weekends. Weekends provide variety in our lives. They break up the work week. They provide a needed break.

Can you imagine a world where there are no weekends? Then deploy into a combat zone with a soldier. The work week goes on and on with no real distinction between the beginning and end of the week. Pretty soon you lose your sense of time.

If you work everyday, does it matter if it is Monday or Friday? Why should it? The next day is another work day regardless. This, my friends, is the one major distinction. I think most soldiers in a combat zone feel this effect. It really is not just something akin to military advisors. We in the military all share this phenomenon when in a combat zone.

So, understanding that you are a prisoner of time, you can fight it, as Bill Murray, the main character in the movie *Ground Hog Day* did at first, or you can maximize the experience to gain from it, as he ultimately did. That is when we can focus on making real contributions to the advisory mission. That is where real job satisfaction and a sense of contributing to something bigger than us may be experienced.

Element #2: Additional Duties. Additional duties are those actions and activities that lie outside of what we consider our principal duty. So, what is the principal duty of a military advisor? To advise, right? Well, what does that really mean? Are you going to shadow your counterparts wherever they go? Will you stand in the back of the room every time there is an important meeting? Will you work with the personnel of the unit and try to coach and mentor them? Will you be a visible entity within the organization or will you be absent from important events? Will you opt to stay in your office and be consulted? Where do you see yourself in this process? Where should you place yourself to maximize this effort? These are all questions that you should answer in order to maximize your contributions to the advisory effort and to maximize your presence with your counterparts.

But, let's talk about what those additional duties are. They will come in two forms: those activities that no one is doing that you decide to take on yourself and those activities that your hosts and counterparts will ask you to do. While at Tres Esquinas, I can't even remember what all those were. But I will try to capture some to give you a flavor for these duties.

An example of an additional duty you may take on yourself is security officer. When you are out in the sticks, you develop the awareness for the need for security. You start to become your own security officer because you don't trust the system to do its job. This does not mean that you take on those responsibilities. It means that you keep an eye on this area and you start thinking like a security officer because it could affect your health and welfare. In the meantime you spend more time with that officer responsible for security so that you can assist or train him to do his job more efficiently.

Real story…at TQ one day a Colombian junior officer informed me that a US Government contractor for a major construction project on site was using his influence to illegally bring prostitutes on to the base byway of the weekly supply flights supporting his contract. I was curious, so one day I watched the operation take place. As the old Soviet Antonov cargo plane landed, two large extended cab Chevy pick-up trucks drove in and parked near the off load ramp. When the aircraft loading ramp dropped, four young girls in blue jeans were the first ones off the plane. They walked directly into the open doors of the pick-up trucks which then left the area and headed to the construction project site, no questions asked.

My major concern with this activity of course was that these girls posed a potential security threat to the base. They were being recruited from Neiva Department, which was known for having a large FARC presence. It appeared that base security was also part of the problem because its members were frequently invited to the parties hosted at the construction site. This is how the young ladies were getting on base past the security officer responsible for checking off names of onboard personnel. To make a long story short, after a few phone calls and an investigation by the American Embassy, the illicit morale and welfare operation terminated.

I know what you're probably thinking. Why didn't the Colombian chain of command know about this and if they did, why didn't they do something about it? Frankly, I don't know, but if I were to venture a guess, I would have to speculate…speculate, mind you, because I never knew. I think that perhaps the chain of command had to know, but did not assess the risk to the base to the same degree as the Americans. Plus the morale and welfare benefits outweighed the risks for them.

Prudish Americans over reacting, you say? We will never know, but I think we did the right thing. In this kind of war, you just cant' afford to let your guard down. It's just too risky, overall, and the consequences could be deadly.

Another example of an additional duty is the supply and logistics officer. You may decide to make random checks of the supply room to verify accountability and safeguarding of supplies. Again, this does not mean you take on this duty. It means that you keep an eye on this area for the benefit of the organization. Spend some time with this officer to help you verify how efficiently this is being done. For those of you that served as company or battalion commanders, this may sound familiar because as you know a good commander conducts routine unannounced inspections of all primary areas: the motor pool, the dining facility, the arms room, the protective mask room, the supply room, and on and on. Why do you do this? Because it is important for the commander to see for himself how the personnel within his organization are performing their duties. Doing this will prevent many headaches in the long run. Although as an advisor you are not the commander, you are suppose to be working to professionalize your counterparts. In my opinion, professionalizing, again another general expression, covers a multitude of areas and disciplines At least that's how I saw it.

Let me provide still yet another example of this. During my first week in TQ I decided to visit the base clinic. I figured if assigned US military personnel ever needed medical treatment, I wanted to know what shape this important facility was in.

Upon entering the main office I was accosted by the tall and energetic senior medical officer, Capitán Nicky Jiménez, who everyone called Capitán Nicky. Male sexism, you say, not addressing her by her last name? Perhaps…Uh, probably, yes… Yeah, most definitely.

"Coronel, what a pleasure to meet you," she said in Spanish. "I had heard from Colonel Nieves that you would be replacing him. Would you like to see our facility?"

"Yes, of course, if you have the time," I answered in Spanish.

"*Por su puesto,* Coronel. But of course I have time."

As we walked around the facility, I was struck by how clean and ascetic everything was. Not being a medical professional, I assumed that this was an important and positive step. Everything seemed to be in order. One thing that I did note was that on the night stand by each of the ward beds was a large quart-size bottle of iodine. I don't exactly know why, but I still shudder at the image of having wounds washed in iodine.

CPT Nicky broke my moment of introspection.

"Coronel, this is our X-ray room. We have a reliable X-ray machine, but I have one problem. The frames for the X-rays film have been damaged by jungle mold and as you can see they are not useable." CPT Nicky held up one of these for me to inspect. Again I was no X-ray technician, but I knew we had a problem.

"How many of these do you need?" I asked.

"I could use two 14x17 and one 10x12. They are Kodak X-Omatic cassettes."

I pulled out my small and frayed green pocket notebook and noted this information.

"Nicky, I assume you have gone through your own military medical channels and have not gotten support on this matter?"

"Yes, of course, Coronel. But our medical supply system is very slow to respond."

"Well, I can't promise you anything, but I will request support from USMILGP and maybe they can help. These things don't appear to be too expensive."

"No, they are not. Thank you, Coronel that will be a big help."

Just for the record and in case I forget to address this issue later in the story, about two months later the USMILGP came through and provided the necessary X-ray frames. I suspect I was supported on this matter because American soldiers in TQ could presumably depend on this medical facility for care and treatment in the event of a medical emergency.

During the remainder of the tour of the medical facility, I noted the fact that the Colombian medical system could not supply sufficient quantities of malaria pills for their soldiers assigned to TQ. So, as a result, it was customary for soldiers on guard duty to catch malaria and, according to Nicky, they all caught malaria. I really felt sorry for the plight of the common Colombian soldier when I remembered that my own medical system had provided me with plentiful supplies of malaria pills. Anyway, such was my first visit to the medical facility. Again, to use this as an example, it is in the best interests of the advisor to take the time to visit important facilities and operations that are part of the support system.

Sometimes, you don't exactly get it right all the time. A case in point was our primary water source at TQ. Water was pumped into the base through a hose that sucked water in from the Río Orteguaza. This hose funneled river water into a series of water tanks in which chemicals were added to the holding tank. Again I'm not a water filtration expert, but soon became one. That was the night that my force protection NCO, SFC Juan Tirado, explained this to me.

SFC Tirado had arrived at TQ a month before me. He was on a 179 day or six month deployment. As the force protection NCO and a combat engineer, his job was to help the Colombians beef up their base defense positions. On this night he would provide other skills.

"Sir, I'm at the water pump station," he told me over the radio. "The main pump is broken and no water is coming in."

"Roger, I'll be right there," I said.

With flashlights we inspected the facility and the problem did appear to be the main pump.

"SFC Tirado, isn't anyone on the Colombian staff responsible for this?

"Yes, the T4, but they won't be able to get any experts to look at it until next week out of Larandia."

"And where did you learn about water filtration?"

"I've had a little experience working on my parent's farm in Puerto Rico," he said. God bless the diversity of our Army, I thought to myself.

We spent the next hour inspecting the entire system with no luck. Finally, SFC Tirado got an idea.

"You know, sir, there is one more possibility." He walked over to the river bank and waded into the waste deep brown flowing waters. He then pulled what appeared to be the water intake unit out of the water and removed its filter.

"I think I found the problem," he said excitedly. As he spoke, he began pulling old leaves and other debris from the filter.

"Yup, this is the problem. The intake filter is clogged and it probably tripped one of the circuit breakers. I bet if we reset it, it will work. Let me make sure I get all this junk debris out first."

Minutes later, we walked back to the main water unit and looked for the main circuit breaker box. It was located on the backside of the equipment room. Sure enough, he was right. A quick flick of the circuit breaker that was in the off position, and we heard the sound of running water flowing into the settling tank.

"Success, my friend," I told SFC Tirado. "You've saved the day."

"At least for now," he replied. He would save the day on many more occasions.

But he was right about that. Living as an advisor is a day to day event. But I didn't tell you that we advisors used the water from the base strictly for showering. I know that doesn't sound very inviting, but we just didn't have enough available water bottles for drinking and bathing. But more on that later…

One day the worst of our fears came to light. After communications equipment, power generators are the life blood of the COJIC. The base ran on a 450 KW generator that was run and maintained by the Colombian Air Force base commander. The COJIC and our barracks ran on a separate 300 KW generator that was maintained by the US Army Corps of Engineers. We advisors also provided diesel fuel for this generator. When the 300 KW generator went down for maintenance, a 200 KW back up generator kicked in supplying auxillary power to the COJIC. Unfortunately, this was not enough to power both the COJIC and our barracks rooms. Why am I telling you this? Because as Murphy's Law proclaims, if something can go wrong, it will. And it did.

One day the 300 KW main power generator that provided electricity to the COJIC and our sleeping quarters broke down. It was our responsibility to maintain the COJIC operational. SFC Tirado inspected the generators weekly and one day he reported that the main unit had begun to leak oil heavily. We contacted our engineer counterpart and he informed us that a repair team would arrive from Florencia by air, about 70 miles away, when transportation was available.

To make a long story short, the civilian maintenance personnel from Florencia did finally arrive a week later, but not until we went without main power for a week. Somehow SFC Tirado rigged two small back up 25 KW generators from the Agency to provide electricity for our sleeping quarters and the COJIC operated with the smaller 200 KW back up generator. Moral of the story...preventive maintenance checks and services are important wherever you are and probably even more so when you are stuck out in the middle of nowhere. Secondly, it's important to have a backup power generation plan in the event that the main unit goes out.

I apologize for hitting you with all these, but all these stories just seem to keep popping in my head. The following is somewhat amusing. It deals with still another additional duty. This was the Arrival and Departure Control Officer.

Because of the absence of roads to TQ, as well as being surrounded by the FARC, we received all our supplies by air. Being notified of arriving flights was usually a hit and miss proposition. Most of the time we would hear the drone of an arriving flight just as it touched down on the runway. When it did arrive, Stan, SFC Tirado, or I would drive one of our two pick up trucks to meet the aircraft. The Agency bird was not a problem because it operated on a regular schedule. And if it was the Agency bird, it usually dropped off food and refreshments for Stan to use for his hosting of social events in his home. At other times replacement parts for radios and intercept equipment came in. It really didn't matter because our job was to load the pick up truck and make delivery of the items as required. Meanwhile, the Agency was nice enough to allow our hosts to fly personnel on emergency leave back to Bogotá. So, as the plane sat on the runway, Major Eduardo Espinoza, our Colombian Air Force flight coordination officer, would have Colombian military personnel standing by in hopes that they could ride back on the plane. He was responsible for lining passengers up on whatever platform was available. I saw numerous personnel with dental appointments, deaths in the family, or routine leaves go out on those flights. I always felt that despite the potential security risks involved in transporting "uncleared" (from a security perspective) foreign nationals on a government aircraft, the benefits of our support to the host country's military were worth the risk. Even General Montalvo frequently used this service to attend meetings in Bogotá. Again this is an example of weighing the benefits with the risks and making a decision to support a bigger cause. Yes, I know that our Colombian hosts probably did a similar cost benefit analysis with the party girls transported from Neiva, but in my mind this is somewhat different. What decision would you make in this case? Would you agree with our decision? Just curious…

The transportation scheduling service of this additional duty was the easy part, however. It was the unexpected flights that caught us totally unprepared. A great example was the unexpected Sunday afternoon (our only partial day off to rest) arrival of a commercial aircraft. The old Soviet two prop Antonov landed that day and on board were about 1800 bottles of water for us advisors. Divide 1800 bottles by 12 bottles per case and that will tell you how much off loading we did. What does it come out to?... 150 cases? Wait...it gets better.

I got the call from the tower that afternoon. Upon arrival with SFC Tirado, the Colombian crew informed me that I had to remove all the cases of water bottles in 15 minutes because they had other deliveries to make that day. Since it would take that long just to get host country backup support, we decided to immediately attack the task at hand. Okay, now do the math. 150 cases of water bottles needed to be offloaded by two people in 15 minutes. So, 10 cases had to be offloaded every minute out of the aircraft to beat the flight schedule. I know this doesn't seem like a big deal, but understand how important bottled water was for us, not having an alternative potable water source. Dressed in Bermuda shorts, t-shirts, and flip-flops, SFC Tirado and I began throwing cases off the back ramp of the plane by hand as fast as we could. Complicating the problem was that we had to throw the cases over bundles of concertina wire sitting on a large cargo pallet. On occasion a poorly thrown case would land on top of the bundles and would puncture the plastic bottles. When the pick up truck was full, SFC Tirado drove over to our supply hooch, while I continued to off load our cargo. Soaked and tired as dogs, we completed our task just in time for the crew to get back on board and fire up their engines. Days later, I was informed by the USMILGP logistics officer that the pallet of bottles had been sitting at Apiay AFB, Meta Department, waiting for an available commercial flight to transport them to TQ. For that reason they themselves did not know when the water would arrive. I guess that if it had been another item of supply, we would have had a reason to complain. But being that it was our bottled water, a real commodity in TQ, we did not mind. It would have just been nice to know when the aircraft was arriving, and aircraft would continue to arrive unexpectedly.

Another of my favorite stories was the Saturday afternoon I was contacted by the TQ control tower.

"Halcón, there's an American C-130 cargo aircraft inbound in about ten minutes. We will park it on the south ramp."

"Thanks, tower, I'm on my way." I replied.

So, as usual, I dropped whatever I was in the middle of… it didn't matter if it was lunch, a shower, sleep, a good book, a meeting with my counterparts, etc…and I drove my silver pick-up truck to the south apron.

Sure enough, a camouflaged patterned C-130 with subdued USAF markings landed and taxied to the parking apron with all four engines at almost full throttle.

While it dropped its back loading ramp, I walked with much difficulty toward it, holding my camouflage field cap in my hand to keep it from blowing away. In my mind I can still feel the hot air from the prop blast and my uniform flapping and beating my body unmercifully. As I approached the ramp, a crew member wearing headphones who I figured was the Air Force load master, held her hand up for me to stop. What was most striking was not that she was a woman, but that she was dressed in Bermuda shorts and a Hawaiian shirt. From where I stood I could also tell that other crew members were also in similar civilian attire. Then two olive drab military Humvees were driven down the ramp and parked a little ways beyond the aircraft. Engines still at almost full throttle, the back ramp closed and the aircraft began to taxi. Once at the end of the runway it took off. All this happened in a matter of minutes. I walked over to the Hummers wondering what the next step was in this whirlwind operation. I figured I should call the American Embassy to get an answer. So, I drove to the COJIC and got on the land line.

"Those vehicles have been donated to the Colombian Army by the State Department," the USMILGP operations officer informed me.

"Is this part of Plan Colombia funding?" I inquired.

"Yes, something like that. There is another delivery of two more inbound in about a week."

"Could you give me a heads up of when they are inbound so that I don't have to go through any more anal gymnastics?"

"I'll try, but sometimes we don't know ourselves when the aircraft are inbound."

"Well, that's great. Besides, I have another beef. What's with the Vietnam war-style hot landing zone supply mission with all four engines running almost at full throttle?" I asked.

"Many of these flights are supported by the Air Guard or Reserves and they think you guys down in TQ are under constant threat of attack. It's just their way of executing force protection measures."

"Well, their force protection measures just about ripped my uniform off with the prop blast. And oh by the way, that crew looked like a scene from the 1970's and '80's TV series *M*A*S*H*... Bermuda shorts...Hawaiian shirts...and flip-flops."

"Oh, really, well I'll make sure we inform their parent unit. Do you know where they were from? Oh, why am I asking you? I should know. Let me look at my arrival information...here...hold on..."

"It may have been the Washington, Utah, or Nevada State Air Guard...somewhere in the northwest, but I can't remember right now," I jumped in.

"Roger, anything else?" Major Ed Caine, the Operations Officer, now appeared to be in a hurry.

"Actually, yes, the most important thing...what do I do with the Hummers?"

"Just let General Montalvo know that they arrived. I believe he was told by the Ambassador that he was getting those."

"Okay, Ed, thanks for filling me in. I'll take care of it. Nothing further...Out."

So I think you get the picture.

Next be prepared for requests from your own counterparts in the supported Army. "Coronel, can you help me get a tourist visa to the States?...Coronel, can you get me on the next flight to Bogotá?...Coronel, can we have some of your bottled water? Coronel can you translate this English word into Spanish for me? Coronel, can you supply us a copy of the technical manual for the 60 mm mortar? Coronel, can you get me a scope for my M4 rifle?...Coronel, Coronel...Coronel." Bottom line, it's not that this was so much a pain for us, it's just that you had to decide which you could accomplish and which you had no power to accomplish. So, be ready to assist as best as you can and always be on the lookout for the unexpected (easier said than done).

Element #3: Going Native. The element that we refer to as "going native" is the most controversial of all advisory functions. I believe the term dates back to the memoirs of British Major T.E Lawrence, the famed *Lawrence of Arabia*. In his case he opted for the native dress and customs of the local tribes he supported and stopped looking like a British officer.

This is a central question for the advisor to ponder: How much of the native customs and rituals do you choose to make your own in order to blend in or to be more socially accepted by your counterparts? Special Operations soldiers are exempt from answering this question because when operating behind enemy lines or whatever the modern equivalent to that is today, they are required to dress like their counterparts simply to blend in for their own security.

For the rest of the conventional flag saluting Army the question stands. Do you stay rooted to your role as a representative of the US Army and maintain your standards of conduct of your own organization? Or should you opt for a balance?

I believe in the latter. It's my opinion that you look for the reasonable in between. By all means, try to copy some of your counterpart's social customs as a courtesy to them and to show that you are genuinely interested in accepting their culture. However, ensure you do not compromise your position as a representative of the US Army. This means that you stay committed to US Army values.

This also means that you always wear your uniform *completely*, just as you have your entire career. For some reason and I can't explain why, when advisors operate in support of a foreign army, the first thing they tend to discard is their head gear. You see it all the time. Advisors start walking around hatless. Even general officers do this. It's an interesting phenomenon that I have observed many, many times. I guess we tend to think that this somehow makes us more informal. Or maybe we begin to mimic our counterparts who many times do not wear their headgear. So, remember, don't compromise your own army's values and standards. In short, be professional and conduct yourself as such.

Element #4: Language, Language, Language. There is no greater contribution to the advisory effort than to learn your counterpart's language, and to learn it well. Strive to be fluent. There is so much that a language communicates that cannot be entirely captured by an interpreter…the nuances…the inflections of words…and their meanings. Speaking fluently in the native tongue should be every advisor's goal throughout the tour. Spend as much of your free time studying to perfect your language skills.

There is also an interesting aspect to fluency. Even though I was a fluent native Spanish speaker, I learned that all countries have their own country-specific phrases and expressions that are unique to them and their people. Learning these can be quite fun and will open many doors of opportunity for you and your counterparts. I still remember the roundtables in college when students from various Latin American countries would share the different words and expressions used in their native countries. These sessions were always laughter-filled events, but it taught me that fluency is a relative term that allows you to communicate the most basic of grammatical terms and general vocabulary. The rest can only be filled in through travel, association, and experience.

Element #5: Expert with a Plan. I know that the term "expert" is a relative term that is freely thrown around, particularly in the academic and in the media world, but I use the term here in the sense of knowing your job skills better than anyone else around you. This is probably by far the most important aspect of being an advisor. If you are to advise your counterparts on how to better fulfill their duties, then you had better know what you are talking about. Never forget that you are in a sense, a tutor. You are filling in the education and training gaps that cannot be otherwise provided because of time or resources for the host nation.

Where this duty can get away from you is when there is no master training plan in the advisory mission. What I mean by this is that there may be no centrally orchestrated effort to guide the advisor. There are many ways to do this: the higher headquarters of the advisory mission may issue or brief the basic mission essential tasks that the host nation must achieve. This is a start. Then a plan to achieve the basic skills associated with those essential tasks should be developed. Then annual, quarterly, or monthly training guidance should be developed. This way the advisor has a road map to guide his effort along. Otherwise, what you will find is that the effort will be left to the individual advisor to discern and this may lead to an inconsistency in focus. Some individual advisors may not even be capable of accessing the situation to the degree necessary to effectively provide support. A year later all that their presence accomplished was that they were there, but unfortunately that's it. No added value was the unfortunate outcome of their tour.

During the advisory years in El Salvador, intelligence advisors taught classes as part of training courses that were routinely scheduled. Students were tested on their newly acquired skills and records were kept by the USMILGP to determine at what intervals new or refresher training was required. This is what I mean by having a formal system established to provide consistency and continuity of effort and perhaps most important of all, to provide the individual advisor with a master plan and guidance to fulfill his duties. Otherwise the effort would be akin to running a school with no standards of performance, established curriculum, blocks of instruction, or focus of effort for the teachers. The results should be obvious.

Colombia is a little bit different. Beyond the training and organizing of the Counter-Narcotics Brigade and its subordinate battalions, the US Army assisted a much better trained and seasoned army that had achieved certain higher levels of training and expertise. They had also spent about 40 years of dealing with insurgency. Our job is to guide our counterparts along and assist them in areas where they are lacking in expertise.

One area of support was in the area of imagery interpretation. Our mission brought military and civilian technicians to TQ with advanced hardware and software systems providing greater capability to support with better maps and imagery.

As I pointed out in the previous chapter, my primary mission-related daily duties revolved around the monitoring of the intelligence analysis and collection management systems to ensure we were maximizing capabilities. This was a constant and never ending process of deliberating with analysts to ascertain the basis for intelligence estimates and forecasts. This is the bread and butter of an intelligence operation and is probably the most difficult to do right all the time. Most people don't realize that intelligence estimates are based on piecing sometimes many, more often sometimes few parts, and assessing what they mean. The written products forecasting events are sometimes nothing more than assessments that are developed based on best guess analysis. It is an art and being good at it requires many years of working the same target or country. I was in no way an expert on Colombia, but I did understand the intelligence cycle. So I tried to combine my basic skills with a desire to become more target knowledge-able. I relied heavily on the expertise of those Colombian military analysts who watched and understood FARC behavior, actions, and movement patterns. Acquiring this knowledge takes many years of watching the target. That is where true expertise devel-ops. So-called 'experts' are able to discern the truth after having watched their adversary day in and day out for years.

My passion, however, was signals intercept. As an electronic warfare trained officer, I was always intrigued with the world of communication's intercept. This is why I spent many hours at the signals intercept station, listening to FARC communications and developing assessments with the intercept operations of poten-tial FARC intentions. It was a pretty high speed operation with dedicated intercept operators, a wide array of antennas, and numerous radios that constantly scanned the airways and made a significant contribution to the war effort.

What I discovered over the years is that there is really no established or standard way to assist and advise your counter-parts. Many times requesting to sit down with your counterparts and discussing issues is useful. Other times simply talking with the section personnel and sharing your views is the way to go. When absolutely necessary, request a classroom and then pro-vide a short block of instruction, if you think something needs to be taught because things are really messed up. I think the bot-tom line is that the advising part of the mission must be promoted in a positive way. Keep in mind that counterparts will rarely ask directly for an opinion. But if I saw something that needed atten-tion, or something I had a strong opinion on, I took the time to call that person aside and discuss the matter. You will be doing the mission and the individual a great service. The main purpose of an advisory mission is to not only impart our service doctrine, but also to share some of our service culture, work ethic, and standards.

Element #6: Stay in Your Lane. What is the single most frustrating part of being and advisor? Probably it's having a coun-terpart that doesn't take your advice into consideration. What is the single most important factor that may lead to killing the advi-sor/counterpart relationship? Probably it is our positive, can do, 'no mission too difficult,' and type-A personality. You don't know how many times I wish I could take back the countless shouting matches I had with counterparts. Looking back on these episodes they were unnecessary, counter-productive, and probably set my professional relationships with my counterparts back light years. Face it. Our job is to advise. The host nation's job is to execute. Sounds easy enough, doesn't it? But this is the most difficult part to live up to. It is so easy to want to take over the operation…to lead, to initiate…and to execute. But this is precisely what limits the advisory effort and takes initiative away from counterparts. Even T.E. Lawrence said that it is better to have your counterpart do things half way right than to have you do all things for them. Only through making mistakes and by doing things themselves will counterparts begin to appreciate your role in helping them. Also don't forget that after we've departed, your counterparts will still be fighting their war. Their projection of time is long term while we generally only project in terms of a one year assignment. We are track and field coaches attempting to train sprinters, when in fact we need coaches trained in long distance running. After we depart, other advisors arrive and perhaps, others, and others…all bringing with them their sprinter coaching techniques. This leads to tremendous frustration for everyone and does not provide any useful expenditure of energy. I recommend that we spend more time reflecting on this single issue because it is central to establishing a healthy working environment in the organization and in accomplishing our mission objectives.

Element #7: Have Fun. Ok, I know there are some of you reading this who will strongly disagree with me on this last point because you associate fun with not being serious or professional. Well, I got to tell you that I disagree. When you're having fun, it shows in your enthusiasm and even your motivation. A little humor goes a long way toward putting things in perspective in the grand scheme of things. I think that like everything in life, we must strike a balance in our own lives. Balance light heartedness with seriousness and I truly feel everything will work itself out. Humor and laughter are also great stress relievers and a great way to purge ourselves of the stresses of advisory duty...and yes, advising is full of daily stresses. If you let these build up over time, then like an inflating balloon, something's got to give and you will explode...one way or another. So, take time to vent with humor.

True story...and I hope you appreciate the humor. Through the course of my tour, I established professional friendships with many Colombian military personnel. However, my favorite was Major Eduardo Espinoza, the Colombian Air Force officer who I told you lined up military personnel for transportation back to Bogotá. Eduardo was a genuinely jovial individual who spoke English. Whenever he saw me, we would joke about life at TQ, which we both hated...usually a blend of English and Spanish or something in between.

One day Eduardo told me a secret. He said he had fallen in love with...actually, it translated more to having the 'hots' for...

one of the CIA contract pilots, Marta. Marta flew during the weeks that John, the primary contract pilot, was off. Once Eduardo figured out Marta's flight schedule, he would wait for her at ramp side hoping to talk to her while he boarded Colombian military passengers on her aircraft. The times I saw him talking to her, it didn't look like she was particularly interested in him, but he seemed to think otherwise.

Anyway, one day she landed and I drove my pick up truck to load radio equipment we had been expecting for the intercept site. When I arrived, the short dark haired and dashing Marta was sitting on the floor inside her aircraft in front of the rear main exit door waiting for us to arrive. She had on her aviator sunglasses and was wearing khaki slacks, a white long sleeve shirt with the sleeves rolled up, and some brown leather clogs. Funny, I thought to myself. I didn't know one could fly an airplane in clogs. I figured this was a good time to strike up a conversation with her.

"Marta, how are you doing today?" I inquired.

"I'm doing great. I have just one more stop to make today before returning to Bogotá and the weather is great for flying for once."

"Well that's good to hear. Tell me something. Those clogs look nice on you. How do you fly in them?"

"Thanks for the compliment, but I just slip them off while flying. It's not hard at all," she said.

"Sounds like you really enjoy your job. How is it overall? I asked.

"It's the best job in the world. In six months I earn what would normally take me a year to make. Six months on, six months off. Can't beat it."

"How did you get into flying?" We had a little time because Eduardo was still rounding up some of his passengers and hadn't arrived.

"I was a US Army aviator flying C-12's and when I got out, I signed up with the Agency as a contract pilot."

"Wow, that's impressive. Just out of curiosity, what's the most exciting thing about flying for you?"

"I would have to say the knowledge that I'm flying over guerrilla-held territory all the time. It's a real turn on."

"Oh?" I answered somewhat surprised.

"Yes, especially when I take off from places like TQ...you know brakes on...engines powering up...plane rocking back and forth...just raring to go, like a horse in the starting gate...yeah, it doesn't get any better."

"It doesn't, huh?"

"Nope...it's pure ecstasy...a total turn on."

"I see...well, uh...cool...that's...uh...nice to know." I wasn't quite sure how much further to take this conversation.

Marta grinned at me. I think she was just teasing me.

About that time Eduardo showed up with four Colombian enlisted men needing a ride back to Bogotá. He briefly chatted with Marta in English, but it was short lived because she needed to take off quickly in order to make her next pick up at Puerto Leguízamo. I waited around for him to finish the boarding process. Once everyone was onboard, he helped her close the rear exit door. Then we both waited to watch her take off. Eduardo, like a little kid, waved at her as she flew down the runway past us.

Walking back to my pick up truck, I listened to him telling me all the places he would take Marta if he could get a date with her in Bogotá. So, as we got on board the truck, I knew it was time to mess with him.

"Eduardo, do you know what Marta told me before you showed up?"

"No, what?" He had that look of someone expecting to hear something special.

"Well, I asked her what excited her the most when she flew and you know what she said?" I was really milking the moment.

"No, tell me…what?"

I stopped the pick up truck so as to not miss anything. "Well, she said that when she is at the end of the runway ready for take off, she gets so turned on, her panties start getting wet." I almost ruined things by breaking out laughing.

Eduardo's eyes got as big as saucers. "Seriously? She told you this?"

"Yep, as sure as I'm sitting here."

"*Dios mio!*…I knew she was a hot one!"

"Oh, she's hot alright…even more so during those take-offs. Next time you talk to her, ask her to tell you about her take offs. She may surprise you with more things she feels when she flies. Especially if it's a long flight…" By then, I couldn't keep it in anymore, and I broke out laughing.

At that point, Eduardo figured it out. "Coronel, you're pushing my leg, right?"

"Hahahaha…" I was laughing hysterically. "Eduardo, yes, I'm pulling your leg, but it's not totally made up. She did say that she gets excited when the plane takes off. It's just not as moving an experience as I described…hahahaha."

"Ok, my friend. You owe me." Eduardo was laughing along by then. I drove the pick up to the parking area, dropped him off at the COJIC, and went to the intercept site with the cargo bed full of radios. He waived and laughed as he walked over to his office in the COJIC. I laughed all the way to the intercept site. I'm still laughing as I type this. If I offended any readers, then I apologize, but you should have seen the look on his face…Oh, man… priceless.

Anyway, to summarize, humor is an important ingredient. You wouldn't believe how much stress I burned off from laughing along with Eduardo that day.

Well, I wanted to share a few of my thoughts regarding those areas that advisors can have an impact. Countries and cultures are different, so there is no cookie cutter approach to this whole business. However, human nature has much in common, and it is in that area where I think those things common to all people and armies may apply. Good luck and don't forget to have a good time.

> *Sitting in an English garden waiting for the sun. If the sun don't come, you get wet from sitting in the English rain. I am eating eggs...they are eating eggs...I am John Lennon...Goo goo ga joob. Expert singers, choking smokers... don't you think the joker laughs at you? See how they snort, like pigs in a sty, see how they snide...I'm crying.*
>
> *The Beatles*

CHAPTER EIGHT

THE FARC

You say you want a revolution...well...you know...
we all want to change the world. You tell me
that it's evolution...well...you know...we all want
to change the world...But when you talk about
destruction... Don't you know that you can count
me out...Don't you know it's gonna be all right...
all right...all right.

"Revolution"
as recorded by The Beatles

ZONA DE DESPEJE
LA MACARENA, META DEPARTMENT, COLOMBIA
0300 HOURS, 2 JUNE 2001

Dear friend, one commonly established belief among military professionals is that the enemy gets a vote. What this means is that regardless of your plans and intentions as to how you think the enemy will behave or react to your operations, he still gets to decide for himself how he thinks he should act. So is the case here. Weeks before I arrived at TQ, the FARC had been making plans and mapping out where to conduct attacks. Although this chapter is out of chronological sequence, I felt that it comes at a convenient juncture to break away from the many descriptions and discussions on what was happening in TQ. Besides, in time and space, this is about the time we learned about what you are about to read here. Makes sense? So, let's spice things up a bit by eavesdropping on the enemy while the advisory effort continues in TQ. Let's be a fly on the wall. Shall we? Then let's do it…

Comandante Jorge Briceño Suárez, known by his alias, *Mono Jojoy, pronounced Mo-no-Ho-hoy,* one of the senior military commanders of the FARC, arrived in the small town of La Macarena early that evening to make preparations for *Tirofijo's* later arrival on the morning of the 2d of June. Mono Jojoy was a large rotund man of fair complexion and a dark moustache…hence the name "mono"…a Colombian expression meaning a light or fair skinned individual.

Narrator's Note: This should not be confused with the common Spanish word meaning "monkey"…or "cute"…at least in this case. But, I'm digressing. Please continue…

Anyway, dressed in a camouflaged uniform with a white t-shirt showing, Mono always wore a black beret with a silver star in honor of Che Guevara, who to him would always be the patron saint of Latin American revolutionaries. On this occasion he carried a 9mm Beretta M9 semiautomatic pistol in the olive drab canvas holster on his right side.

At around 0300 hours, Manuel Marulanda Vélez, alias Tirofijo, *pronounced Tee-ro-fee-ho,* or 'Sure Shot,' and his entourage of security and staff arrived in their convoy of armored SUV's. They had been on muddy and sometimes non-existing roads that night from vicinity the village of Los Pozos, San Vicente del Caguán, only about 20 miles away. It was there that he and other FARC personnel had negotiated with Colombian government officials earlier in the day. Tirofijo rode in the second SUV, a flat gray and mud splattered Chevy Blazer, one of many of an extensive fleet of SUV's that he regularly rotated for use in and out of operations areas.

When his vehicle pulled up, he immediately got out without fanfare or protocol. Following his SUV's headlight beams, he slowly walked in direction of the welcoming committee, comprised of Mono Jojoy and Milton de Jesús, the *Bloque Sur* or Southern Bloc commander. Tirofijo vigorously shook Mono Jojoy's hand and gave him a friendly embrace...he was also dressed in camouflage fatigues... wearing his trademark military cap with raised bill. A yellow towel, used for swatting mosquitoes, was draped over his right shoulder. On his left shoulder he wore an armband with the yellow, blue, and red colors of the Colombian flag, probably from his meetings with Colombian government officials. A machete hung from his left hip. His sagging eyes looked tired and the almost grandfather appearance defied the fact that he was the leader of the most powerful guerrilla organization in Colombia... and perhaps even the richest in the world.

He turned to look at Milton de Jesus, who held his outstretched hand expecting a handshake. None was forthcoming as Tirofijo's friendly demeanor quickly changed.

"Happy Birthday, *Jefe*," said Milton in Spanish with as big a smile as the corners of his mouth would permit. "What has it been...sixteen days since you celebrated your 73d birthday earlier this month?"

"Don't remind me, Milton," Tirofijo answered, not amused. "Every year I feel my age a little more and I believe I'm finally starting to feel every bit of my 73 years."

"Jefe, you could fool us. The word in the field is that you can still outwork most of your younger cadre," said Milton jokingly trying to warm up an already chilly reception.

"Well, I don't know about that...but enough of this. Let's dispense with the small talk. Jorge, show me where I will be staying and have my personal items brought there. I want to get a few hours sleep before beginning our conference at 9:00 AM sharp. I'll have breakfast at 7:30 AM. Make it *Ajiaco Bogotano* and *Chocolate Santafereño."*

"Sí, señor. Don't worry, we'll take care of that. We have a little *Puchero Boyacense* and a couple of *Tamales Santafereños* left over from dinner last night, if you would like that now," Mono Jojoy added as he signaled one of his deputy's toward him.

Tirofijo added, "No, thank you. We ate prior to leaving Los Pozos. But don't forget my bottle of Chivas Regal for tonight...no... on a second thought make it *Johnny Walker Blue Label*...I feel pretty good about our negotiations with the government."

"*Por su puesto*, of course, señor," said Mono Jojoy with a big grin.

Narrator's Note: Colombian cuisine is a varied fare of different regional specialties combined with traditional recipes. Ajiaco Bogotana is the popular Colombian shredded chicken and broth soup. Chocolate Santafereño is the tasty hot chocolate drink accompanied with a slice of white cheese. The Puchero is a plate of mixed meats and vegetables served with rice on the side. Boyacense translates to being from the Boyacá region of Colombia. Tamales are a very popular recipe in just about every country in the Latin American world. 'Santafereños' refers to being from Santa Fe de Bogotá, the capital. Mmmmmmm...I'm getting hungry just talking about all this food. Oh, you'll notice that I didn't bother pronouncing these for you...Too much work. Let's get back to the story before we miss everything...

Tiburón could not believe it. He had been in the small some-times dusty, sometimes muddy town of La Macarena, inside the secure area of El Despeje or Demilitarized Zone since the 28th of May following the order to meet here by the FARC Secretariat on the 22d of May. Still the FARC Secretariat had not come up with a future military strategy. Equally surprising to him was that despite all the pressure from the Secretariat, Comandante Milton de Jesús could not come up with any reasonable plan on how to best utilize resources within his own Southern Block area of responsibility. Also perplexed was Tiburón's old friend and second most important figure from the Southern Bloc attending the conference, José Benito Cabrera Cuevas, alias Fabián Ramírez, the *Cabecilla*, *pronounced kah-beh-see-yah*, or head of the 14th *Cuadrilla* or Front, *pronounced kwah-dree-yah*.

During a break prior to the start of this morning's meeting from what had now turned into a week-long conference, Tiburón smoked a Cuban *Cohiba* cigar...a *Robusto*...his favorite. The shade from the large *Caoba* tree behind the school that served as their conference site provided comfortable shade from the early morning sun.

Then something caught his attention. Three individuals in civilian attire walked a short distance from him and sat down in the shade of a flat black Ford SUV. Judging by the reactions of the other two, the oldest one, white-haired in his fifties and wearing khaki pants and a black T-shirt, appeared to be telling a joke. The other two, in their late thirties and wearing dark pants and plaid shirts, laughed along with him. Both of the younger ones had dark black hair...one was clean shaven, while the other one sported a nicely trimmed beard. What had caught Tiburón's attention was that they looked *Gringo*. He swore that they spoke English, but with an accent that was rather foreign to him.

"Fabián," he turned to his partner. "Who are those three characters over there? I've never seen them before."

Fabián looked over to where Tiburón pointed.

"Oh, those three? IRA."

"IRA?"

"*Sí, tú sabes*...El Irish Republican Army."

"So, what brings the IRA to El Despeje?"

"I'm told that they are experts on car bombs and urban mortars. They are providing some of our cadre with demolitions and explosives training."

"Is that a fact?" Since when does the IRA advise us?"

"Since our international branch in Europe established contact and liaison with freedom fighter organizations. I also heard that the IRA is receiving a little cocaine profit in exchange for their expertise."

"You're kidding, right?"

"No, hermano. I'm serious. There have been at least fifteen of those jokers in and out of El Despeje since early 1999...Would you like to meet them?"

"No, my English is not that good."

"That's alright. The one with the beard speaks fluent Spanish. Come on."

The two walked toward the three IRA members who were still sitting and laughing by the SUV. When they recognized Fabián, they got to their feet and greeted him like an old friend.

"Niall Connolly, I'd like you to meet a friend," Fabian said in Spanish. "His name is Tiburón."

"The shark, huh? I've wrestled a few of those in my day... hahaha. Well, is it yourself?" asked Connolly in heavily accented Spanish as he extended his hand. He was the one with short black hair and a nicely trimmed beard. A black jacket complimented a blue striped shirt and black pants. In his mid-30's, he was the youngest of the three.

"*Hola, igualmente*," answered back Tiburón, shaking his hand, but still feeling somewhat uncomfortable around the foreigners.

"Tiburón," continued Connolly in Spanish and still having a hard time keeping from laughing over his alias. "I'd like you to meet me two old friends from the Old Country. This is James Monaghan."

"How's the form, lad?" asked Monaghan in English as Tiburón shook the hand of the older 50 year old fellow with the white hair. He was dressed in a black and white plaid shirt, khaki pants, and also wore a black jacket. A black t-shirt could be seen underneath his plaid shirt.

"And this is Martin McCauley."

"Anything strange, lad?" asked McCauley also in English," the shorter of the three, he was 38 years old, clean shaven, and had black hair. He wore dark pants and a brown jacket that hid the shirt underneath.

Tiburón mumbled back not knowing quite how to answer.

"Em, like, what do you do, Tiburón?…Hang out at Sea World?" Connolly asked this time not hiding his amusement.

"I'm the Deputy Cabecilla of the Teófilo Forero Mobile Column" answered Tiburón sternly.

"Yerra, I've heard of you guys. If my memory serves me right, Teófilo Forrero was the leader of the Colombian Communist Party when he was assassinated in the 1990's. Your group has quite a reputation, even in Northern Ireland. Special Ops, right?" he asked in Spanish.

"Yes, it pays the rent," Tiburón said forcing a slight smile.

"Em, look at me lad. Look at old Monaghan there. We've been doing this all our lives. Luck of the Irish, you know. Although I miss me ole lady in Gleanageary, Dublin, I wouldn't trade my work for the world. The same with me buddies. Me old friend, James, still has family in Donegal in Northern Ireland and Martin is from Lurgan, Armagh."

"Yes, I know exactly what you mean. It's hard to get it out of your system...especially when you are committed to a lifetime cause. Do you travel much within Latin America?" asked Tiburón, now a bit more interested and feeling more at ease.

"As a matter of fact, we just finished an assignment in Cuba. I'm the Sinn Fein regional representative to Cuba. Speaking of which, I have some Havana's that I got from our friend Fidel. They have his logo on them. You can have them. I still prefer fags to these."

Tiburón accepted the two cigars that Connolly gave him as he put his own cigar out.

"Beautiful island...Cuba is...you know? Too bad about all the poverty. But we are really enjoying our first visit to Colombia even more. Wonderful country you have here...especially your ladies. Bagorra, are they beautiful! Wouldn't mind taking one or two for a ride. Me wanker could use a little lift...hahaha."

"Yes...we are rather proud of our country... and our ladies." said Tiburón proudly, not quite understanding the crude Irish humor.

"I don't blame you. Maybe someday Colombia will be all yours.... hahaha...I mean the FARCs, you know." Connolly had a wry laugh.

Before Tiburón could comment, the school bell rang signaling the start of the day's conference.

"Well, back to our conference," said Fabián, as they all shook hands again.

"Em, like, grade school be in session for the FARC," said Connolly sarcastically and in English as the other two Irishmen joined in the laughter.

"Nice meeting you, lad," he said to Tiburón. "We will be leaving La Macarena in a few weeks. Two of our comrades will be staying back. You may run into them...John Francis Johnston and James Edward Walker...Old country types. You'll like them. Cheers, lads. Ireland forever."

When they walked beyond earshot, Tiburón was the first to comment.

"You know. I didn't appreciate the sarcasm and ridicule. If we ever cross paths, I cut their *huevos* off."

"Tiburón, you're being too hard on them. They're probably just blowing off some steam. This is probably rest and recreation for them. Besides, they're involved in a dirty business…Irish terrorists, you know," said Fabián.

"Yes, but there are terrorists and then there are terrorists. We are not terrorists. We are freedom fighters, fighting for a cause within our native country. They on the other hand…going around selling their expertise like mercenaries…well, it's different."

They both walked in silence through the entrance of the JFK Elementary School and departed company as each headed for their assigned seats. Tiburón walked over and sat down next to his boss.

"*Paisa*, why don't we suggest that our unit be used to head a surprise attack against an important strategic target in the Putumayo? I'm itching for some action," he told the cabecilla of the Teófilo Forero mobile column, Hermides Buitrago, alias Oscar or El Paisa.

"*Oye…*Tiburón," responded Paisa, brotherly in nature. "We have to let the leadership decide that. Even though we are attached to the Southern Bloc, the Teófilo Forero remains a strategic asset of the Secretariat. It is they who always decide how to employ us."

"Well, I wish they would agree on something or another before we all turn into a bunch of over-weight old men getting soft around the belly from partaking of all the luxuries in El Despeje. I never thought that I would ever complain about having Johnny Walker Black available every night."

"Just a little more patience, Tiburón. We'll get a decision soon."

For Tiburón the instructions were perfectly clear. In early February of this year Manuel Marulanda, Tirofijo, had ordered the Southern Bloc to stop Plan Colombia's successes in Putumayo and Caquetá Departments.

"I want results!" Tirofijo had ordered. "Hit the Colombian Army and hit it hard. Plan Colombia is developing too much momentum and getting far too much positive press coverage. It's time to stop this progress in its tracks."

February, March, and April rolled by and the Southern Bloc had still not conducted any major offensive operations.

On the 22d of May 2001, Tirofijo ordered all cabecillas from the Southern Bloc to join him in El Despeje on the 28th of May for a conference to discuss matters at hand.

Immediately, cabecillas from all areas of the Southern Bloc began arriving at La Macarena in El Despeje for the big powwow.

Tirofijo's entrance into the small and run down JFK elementary school was the signal for everyone in the large classroom serving as a conference room to be quiet. There were two dilapidated wooden tables forming a "T"-shape configuration in the center of the conference area with metal folding chairs around them. Six black and white aerial photographs and assorted maps of Colombia were tacked on to the walls. Sitting at the smaller table that crossed the "T" were the members of the Secretariat, the highest governing body of the FARC organization. At the longer table forming the base of the "T" sat the Cabecillas of the Southern Bloc. The Southern Bloc had responsibility for some of the southern provinces or departments and included some of the most inhospitable and impassable terrain in Colombia. It also had the most important FARC supply and logistics routes from Peru and Ecuador and the largest coca growing and production capabilities in all the country. It was a critical part of the FARC's financial infrastructure. The FARC could not allow Plan Colombia to disrupt the status quo of the FARC in this remote area of the country. Due to a lack of government presence, the FARC had ruled here for decades. It would not surrender its control of this area so vital to survival of the cocaine business...at least without a fight.

The classroom was hot and the air was oppressively stale and stifling. The cigarette and cigar smoke added to the suffocating and claustrophobic feelings. Perspiration poured down Tiburón's back. Even for someone that was use to extreme climatic conditions and hardened from intense training, Tiburón found it difficult to concentrate. He looked up from his notebook computer where he had typed in the names of the key individuals seated at the table all dressed in camouflaged fatigues. In numerical order by Front were the cabecillas and their staffs: Ovideo Matallana (2d Front), Jairo Humberto Cortés, alias Jorge Hugo or J.H. (3rd Front), Wilfredo Castañeda, alias Euclides (13th Front), Fabián Ramirez, (14th Front) and the second most important figure in the Southern Bloc, José Ceballos, alias Mocho César (15th Front), Jorge Humberto Caballero, alias Roblado (32d Front), Floresmiro Burbano, alias Martín Corena (48th Front), Hermes Capera Quezada , alias Héctor Ramírez (49th Front), and Angel Gabriel Lozada García, alias Edgar Tovar (64th Front). Milton de Jesús, the Southern Front commander sat across from Tiburón.

Conspicuously absent was Franklin Smith of the 61st Front. Rumor had it that he was bothered by a war related injury or was not able to attend due to Colombian Army operations—not uncommon in a war of this nature. Also absent was Mocho Diego, the cabecilla from the recently created Amazonas Front. Tiburón had only heard of him and had never met him.

El Paisa sat to the right of Tiburón.

At the head table were some of the camouflaged uniformed members of the FARC Secretariat. Tirofijo sat in the center. On his right was Mono Jojoy. On his left and sporting gray hair and beard was the spectacled Raúl Reyes, FARC spokesperson for the negotiations with the Colombian government. To the left of

Reyes was Alfonso Cano, the political head of the Secretariat, and rumor had it, possibly next in line to replace Tirofijo.

Cano was a strange sight indeed. Referred to in the ranks as "*El Hombre Lobo,*" his heavy black beard and curly hair made him look every bit like the popular 1950's movie personality, "The Wolfman." Glasses topped off this already wild, wooly, but professor-like appearance. Rounding out the Secretariat representation at the head table was the black bearded and long haired Timoleón Jiménez, wearing a small flat hunter's hat with ear flaps up. On the opposite end from him was the moustached Efraín Guzmán, alias El Cucho and Uriah Cuellar, the commander of the Juan José Rondón Mobile Column, the FARC secretariat's strategic unit.

Tirofijo nodded to Mono Jojoy to begin the briefing. Mono Jojoy got up from his chair and stood in front of one of the large maps on the wall behind him.

"Señores," he commenced in Spanish, "the Secretariat has reached a decision based on excellent intelligence of the area of Puerto Leguízamo."

He used a laser pointer to point to a spot on the map along the Colombian and Peruvian border.

"As you all know, Puerto Leguízamo is the headquarters of the naval component of Joint Task Force-South. The patrol boats from this headquarters base have been disrupting our logistics on the Río Putumayo between, Peru, Ecuador, and Colombia. To the north of Puerto Leguízamo is a unit we have our sights on. This is the 49th Jungle Battalion. It is located just north of Puerto Leguízamo near Coreguaje."

Everyone in the room focused on the bright red spot from the laser pointer as he circled the area.

"We have been observing this unit's movements over the course of a month. This unit conducts its patrols along the same route, at the same time, and sets up its security positions at the same locations every night. We will deliver a surprise attack against this unit in hopes of drawing naval infantry units from Puerto Leguízamo to set the conditions for our attack of the main base. We are not interested in taking out the base itself, but the patrol boats sitting in their berths."

Mono Jojoy paused and looked around the room to get a sensing from the assembled commanders. No one spoke.

"The main attack in this sector will be led by the Juan José Rondón Mobile Column from the Eastern Bloc and will be supported by elements of the 14th and 48th Fronts of the Southern Bloc."

This last sentence from Mono Jojoy created a stir as the cabecillas talked in hushed tones among themselves. Milton de Jesús and Martín Corena looked at each other and rolled their eyes.

Then Milton de Jesús stood up. "Mono, why is the Rondón column coming out of the Eastern Front to lead an attack in our sector?"

"The Rondón column is coming into your sector…"

"Let me answer that question, Jorge," Tirofijo interrupted Mono Jojoy.

"Comandante de Jesús, the Rondón column is coming out of the Eastern Bloc to lead an attack in your sector to show you, Señor Comandante, how to execute an offensive operation of important and strategic magnitude. I have given you every opportunity to plan offensive actions in the south. And yet you have not followed through with my directive. Before joining my staff, Comandante Jorge Briceño commanded the Eastern Bloc successfully and led it to many victorious offensive actions. In his opinion...and I agree... the Rondón column can lead this attack, along with your 14th and 48th Fronts providing supporting personnel. Does that answer your question, Comandante?"

"Sí...Sí, señor. It is very clear," stammered the Southern Bloc commander.

"Following this meeting," Tirofijo continued, "I want you, Fabián Ramírez, Martín Corena, and Uriah Cuellar, who will lead the attack, to immediately begin planning for this operation here in La Macarena. I will give you only a few days to complete this planning. You must work quickly for I want to execute the attack on the early morning of the 15th or 16th of June."

Again the room filled with the crescendo of loud whispers.

"But, señor...that is impossible. It is already the beginning of June. I cannot mobilize my personnel and resources in that short amount of time."

"Do it, Milton, or I will find a new Cabecilla for the Southern Bloc that can. I have come this close..." Tirofijo raised his right hand and made a diminutive sign with his thumb and index finger... "to firing you. So, I'm putting you on notice...that's final."

There was nothing more for Milton de Jesús to say. He sat down.

"Continue, Jorge," Tirofijo motioned to Mono Jojoy, clearly upset.

"Sí, Comandante." Mono Jojoy walked over to another map and resumed his briefing.

"The attack vicinity of Puerto Legíizamo will be the first phase of a campaign to counter future advances by Plan Colombia. This campaign is designated, *Campaña Para Restauración de Nuestra Soberanía Nacional Jaime Pardo Leal*...Campaign for the Restoration of Our National Sovereignty –Jaime Pardo Leal. It is named in honor of our slain hero and FARC political candidate to the 1986 presidential elections, *Licenciado* Jaime Pardo Leal." He paused for a few seconds.

"The second phase will be much more complicated and ambitious...and will take much more detailed planning. In this phase we want to attack one of the two most important strategic targets in our area."

The bright red spot from Mono Jojoy's laser pointer moved to locations north on the map.

"The first is Tres Esquinas, the headquarters of the JTF-South and the military center of gravity of Plan Colombia for planning and operations. The second is Larandia, the base camp of the Counter Narcotics Brigade and the brigade's twenty-one UH-1 helicopters."

Mono Jojoy again paused for the murmuring and whispering in the room to subside.

"Señores, I know what you're thinking. But not everything is quite like you imagine. Of course it would be nice to attack and eliminate these bases important to the success of Plan Colombia once and for all. But that takes entirely too many resources and manpower. What we want to do is disrupt the important activities or operations that take place at these bases. We want to conduct precision strikes…using special operations…sabotage… against key operational nodes within the perimeter wires of these bases. Let me use one example. Larandia has three key targets of interest to us. The first are the helicopters that sit on the helipads there. The second are the headquarters and barracks complex of the Counter Narcotics Brigade. The third are the supporting facilities for the main aircraft runway. Each of these is an important supporting node for the Colombian Army to prosecute Plan Colombia. Take any of these out and you put the brakes on future operations. This is what we're after. Señores, planning for this Phase II will begin tomorrow. The Teófilo Forero Mobile Column has been designated the lead executing unit which will also be supported by designated fronts from the Southern Bloc that we will further identify during the session this afternoon after lunch."

With big grins on their faces, El Paisa and Tiburón turned toward each other and beamed with pleasure.

"Following what we assume will be successful Phase I operations in and around Puerto Leguízamo, Comandante Marulanda wants to be prepared to execute Phase II as early as September of this year. This will be a major effort that will involve many of the Southern Bloc Fronts. Most of you will have a piece of the action. Few will remain idle. We well all share in the victory of destroying Plan Colombia and defending our national sovereignty from foreign *gringo* intervention."

The cabecillas all jumped to their feet with resounding applause, jubilation, and cheering. The chanting of *Colombia será nuestra…Colombia será nuestra…*Colombia will be ours… grew to a crescendo. Everyone, including the members of the head table were on their feet. Tiburón had never seen such a display of jubilation from the usually somber leadership. Maybe this campaign would be a good thing to raise the slumping morale of the Southern Bloc.

Tirofijo was the only person still seated. He stood up and with the upward and downward movement of his outstretched arms, signaled everyone to quiet down.

"Señores, I share your jubilation. But the real work begins today. Following my leave of this room, Jorge Briceño will be in charge of establishing the planning committees for this campaign. You are all under his authority and command. Is that clearly understood?"

Tirofijo's gaze scanned the faces of each of the commanders and finally made eye contact with Milton de Jesús. Milton purposely turned his gaze away and looked down at the floor.

"*Bueno,* that is all. Jorge, son tuyos. *They are yours.*"

With that Tirofijo, followed by the other members of the Secretariat minus Mono Jojoy, exited the room. The planning for Campaign – Jaime Pardo Leal had begun.

Narrator's Note: And so a fly on the wall we were. Pretty serious stuff these FARC guys were planning. Mono Jojoy outlined the plans for two attacks. The first attack against the Colombian Army's 49th Jungle Battalion in Coreguaje did in fact take place on the 15th and 16th of June 2001…or approximately two weeks after this meeting. This surprise attack also occurred shortly after I arrived in TQ. It is the attack I discussed in Chapter 3 (PTSD) and that was giving me flashbacks from El Paraíso, El Salvador. Remember? If not, please feel free to go back to Chapter 3 and read this part again. What I didn't know at the time was where and when the second attack would take place. Dear friends, as you read on, you will start to see the indicators as we did at TQ on how all this planning would eventually manifest itself. Let's get on to the next chapter…

> **You say you got a real solution…Well, you know, we'd all love to see the plan…You ask me for a contribution…well, you know, we're doing what we can. But when you want money for people with minds that hate…All I can tell is brother you have to wait. Don't you know it's gonna be all right…all right…all right.**
>
> **The Beatles**

CHAPTER NINE

AC-47 FANTASMA

Listen children, to a story...that was written long ago...'bout a kingdom on a mountain...and the valley-folk below...On the mountain was a treasure...buried deep beneath the stone...and the valley-people swore...they've have it for their very own...

Go ahead and hate your neighbor, go ahead and cheat a friend...Do it in the name of Heaven, you can justify it in the end...There won't be any trumpets blowing, come the judgment day...On the bloody morning after....One tin soldier rides away.

"One Tin Soldier"
as recorded by Coven

HEADQUARTERS, JOINT TASK FORCE-SOUTH
TRES ESQUINAS, CAQUETA DEPARTMENT, COLOMBIA
0900 HOURS, 29 JULY 2001

Sunday constituted the only official free day for the JTF staff and COJIC personnel in Tres Esquinas. This included the US advisors assigned to support the operation. That meant no mandatory JTF Commander's update briefings at 0740 or 1940 hours. And for me, it was laundry day, kick-back-and-read-a-book-day, or watch some television on satellite TV.

Regardless of the day of the week, I always stopped by the COJIC to check in with the T2 duty personnel to learn if anything had occurred in the operations area overnight. As in all wars, the enemy does not respect weekends or time off, so it is always important that the advisor stay informed daily on activities.

Today, though, I felt a little laid back. I decided that I needed to "let my hair down." So I made an exception to my personal dress code for visiting the COJIC and put on some khaki dress shorts, a black Callaway or Taylor Made golf shirt, don't recall which, and some Sperry Top-Sider deck shoes without socks. Just doing this made me feel as if it was a real day off. Still I attached the holstered 9mm pistol to the carrying strap of my document bag and placed the two hand held radios inside the webbed bag.

The Chevy Ranger pick-up truck drive to the COJIC was the usual dodging of large muddy water-filled, man eating potholes. I parked in "my" parking spot and stepped out of the vehicle, being extra careful not to step in the standing water outside the driver's side door. I slung the document bag over my shoulder and walked toward the COJIC main entrance.

I noticed that the security guard at the security entrance was new, so I showed him my security pass.

"Buenos Días"...then I added…"*Asesor.*"

The guard acknowledged and waived me through.

Inside, Capitán Dominguez was the senior T2 officer on duty. He looked up from his chair behind his work desk and stood up to greet me.

"*Qué novedades,* Capitán? What's new?"

"Coronel, buenos días. It was a relatively quiet night. The 1st and 3rd CD Battalions are operating south of Puerto Asis and they reported destroying five drug labs last night. We should be getting a complete inventory on these labs by noon today. None of these were crystallization labs, unfortunately."

"Well, that's the way it goes. Intelligence was not too specific on the location of the big HCL lab in the area, but there's no question that it's there. Finding it is another story. It's too bad we didn't have an informant along on this operation. It would sure help to be able to walk right up to it."

"Well, the battalions have time. They're not scheduled to leave the area for another week."

"Bien...Gracias, Capitán. If anyone asks for me, I will be at the intercept site for about the next 45 minutes. I'd like to know what, if anything, they've been tracking. I'll be monitoring my own hand held radios continuously."

"Listo, Coronel. Have a good rest of the day."

The slow drive to the intercept site took me past the big 450 KW generator on my left that provided powered the entire installation minus the COJIC and our barracks.

Then on my right, I passed the Dining Facility or Casino, as the Colombians called it, where breakfast was probably just finishing up. Weeks before I had decided to forgo breakfast and have bread or crackers with Kraft Cheez Whiz in my room. Okay, okay, it wasn't always crackers and cheese. I did alternate this with dry breakfast cereal from time to time. But I hoped that small jar of cheese spread would hold up for a few more weeks before I could order some more from someone flying back to Bogotá. I did get some deviled ham and Vienna sausage at the base commissary and that helped provide some variety. However, this morning I would complete the morning rounds before returning to my hooch for breakfast. I always lived by the Army Ranger proverb that I learned while undergoing the physically and mentally demanding course in my earlier years as an officer, "Gentlemen, eating is never a priority when there is mission-related work to be done." The phrase had stuck with me my entire career and was a guiding light when duty called.

On my left was the tennis court where I kept getting trounced by my Colombian counterparts. Oh, well, I thought. I hadn't played tennis since being out of college. Let the Colombians feel good about beating me. I'll tell you more about this in a later chapter.

I smiled to myself.

On the right was the inclined concrete boat ramp for the port operations of TQ. I stopped for a moment to allow two security guard soldiers walking toward their barracks to jump into the back of the pick-up truck.

Regardless of their rank or country, I never hesitated to help fellow soldiers in time of need. Some days on this drive I would stop three or four times to pick up and drop off soldiers and civilians needing rides. Transportation in TQ was a privilege that only a few personnel had. Although not for ulterior motives, I always felt that anything that we advisors could do to help win hearts and minds was worth the effort.

After rounding the end of the concrete runway, the soldiers in the back slapped the top of the cab signaling me that it was time to be dropped off.

I stopped the vehicle to let them off and as I drove away the two soldiers waved in gratitude.

On my right was the massive Amazon Over-The-Horizon-Radar dome that looked like a large white golf ball at the top of a tower. If there were ever a lucrative target and a reason for the FARC to attack TQ, this one would place in the top two along with the COJIC. The work at the project appeared to be moving on schedule.

The slow drive past the small arms firing range and down the muddy road was always a challenge as the pick up truck slipped and slid from one side of the road to the other. The daily rains never helped maintain suitable road conditions. Reaching the top of the small hill and turning left on the muddy road, the monitoring station came into view. I parked the truck parallel to the small wooden fence that ran around the small wooden building. Who would ever guess that this small house was an important military intelligence collection site? I laughed to myself as I answered my own question. Probably the sight of the antenna farm of HF and

VHF inverted-V's, doublets, long wires, and small beams might have been a tip off. Who were we trying to fool?

Inside the building Sargento Segundo Juan Losada stood in front of a suite of VHF and HF radios. Since he was on duty, he was in Colombian Army green fatigues. Next to him four radios automatically scanned the airwaves for FARC communications. He was but one of two weekend shift personnel on duty to monitor communications. So focused was he on his work that he didn't see me enter the room.

While bending over to check the frequency of one of his radios, SGT Losada looked up.

"Coronel, I didn't see you come in," he said in Spanish.

"You looked so wrapped up in your work, I didn't want to disturb your concentration."

"Coronel, I 'm never too busy to recognize a colonel advisor," he laughed.

"Well, I never disturb a genius at work...Did you get the battery connectors for the airborne radio suite?"

"I got them yesterday and I just finished installing them this morning. I think that we are now ready to power the intercept equipment up and I have the new connectors that will allow us to hook up our coaxial cables to the outside antenna of the *Fantasma.*"

"*Fantástico*. If you're ready, I can take you over to the aircraft parking area now and we can work on installing the suite to see if everything is operational."

"Muy bien, Coronel. I'll just need some help carrying the equipment suite and battery over to your pick up truck. Let me get *Cabo Segundo* Sánchez over here to help us and then I'll transfer the mission over to him until I get back. He had just returned from breakfast before you entered and is washing up."

"Let's do it, Sargento. I'm excited with the prospect. Get Corporal Sánchez while I get the truck ready."

I went out to the truck to move the spare tire and manual gas pump so as to make space in the cargo bed. I used the manual pump to draw gasoline from the 55 gallon drums that stored the fuel for our pick up trucks. About the time I finished, SGT Losada and CPL Sánchez were carrying the equipment out of the monitoring station. They carefully placed the bulky equipment into the back of the pick up truck. This radio rack mounted the airborne suite to be used on board the AC-47 Fantasma or phantom, the twin engine converted cargo plane that provided close air support with its twin .50 caliber machineguns. This rack was a needed improvement to the hand held radio normally used by the onboard radio intercept operator. General Montalvo had directed that an intercept operator accompany every AC-47 mission. The rack of radios would permit better quality and improved reception. The little hand held Yaesu radio that the operators were using on previous monitoring missions wasn't cutting it and I knew that the poor sensitivity of this small radio and its built in antenna wasn't allowing us to complete our assigned mission. The new suite of radios would change all this.

"Corporal Sánchez, you are in charge of the mission until we get back," SGT Losada told him.

"Don't worry. I'll keep things under control. If things get too busy for me, I'll get a couple of off duty personnel to help me."

In addition to being a monitoring station, the building conveniently served as a small barracks for the personnel assigned to the intercept mission. That way there was always someone available to help with the mission during surge operations. SGT Losada hopped into the back cargo bed to hold on to the radio rack.

Slipping and sliding from side to side, I slowly drove the Chevy back over the numerous ruts and water-filled mud holes on the road. Because of concern of damage to the radios, it seemed as if I felt every single bump along the way back to the flight line.

When we reached our destination, I told the guard what we were doing and drove the pick-up near the parked AC-47 Fantasma. Once parked, we carried the radio suite and placed it at the foot of the open door on the left side of the aircraft. The crew chief, Técnico Segundo Tomás Morales was onboard and was busy strapping everything down.

"Técnico Morales, we need to carry this equipment on board to test it."

"*Sí, claro, sin problema,*" he answered. The crew chief had seen me and the intercept boys working before onboard the AC-47.

SGT Losada and I labored to lift the rack up the high door opening of the AC-47. Once we got the radio rack on board, we carried it over to the front of the aircraft to be strapped next to some canvas drop seats across from an inboard air to ground radio rack. The portable lithium battery would get connected to the auxiliary power plug of the radio and then the coaxial cable from the radio set would be connected to the antenna input connector for the onboard air-to-ground radio system. This way the radio intercept operator could now benefit from the external UHF antenna fin on the front belly of the aircraft, thereby maximizing his ability to collect by improving reception.

While SGT Losada and I were busy strapping in the rack and connecting the wires and cables, we had not noticed what was going on onboard the aircraft.

Suddenly, the port engine of the AC-47 came to life.

Surprised by this, I looked up at the crew chief and asked what was going on. I had to yell to be heard over the noise from the revving engine.

The crew chief pulled his head phones off and yelled in Spanish, "*Rutina,* just routine. You have time to finish what you're doing."

Satisfied that the crew was simply conducting routine maintenance, SGT Losada and I went back to testing our radio equipment and hook ups.

Then the starboard engine came to life. I again looked up at the crew chief, who motioned me with the same "not to worry" wave.

After the second engine came to life, both engines were revved at close to full RPM and the aircraft started rocking back and forth. I looked at SGT Losada, who returned my same look of surprise. Then the crew chief suddenly closed the cabin door and the aircraft began to taxi.

Due to the aircraft's movement, I had to carefully walk back to the rear of the aircraft trying to keep my balance and to keep from falling. The crew chief was strapping himself into the drop seat across from the three .50 caliber machineguns.

Because of the loud noise of the engines, I had to yell to be heard, "What's going on? I thought you said this was routine?"

"It is," answered the crew chief. "We are responding to a routine request for air support. I thought you were part of our intercept support."

"You've got to be kidding! I'm not authorized to go on a combat mission with you. If the Ambassador finds out she'll kick me out of country so fast, Colombia will experience a sonic boom."

The crew chief looked at me and got on his mike to alert the pilot. By then the AC-47 had gathered speed and seconds later lifted off on its close air support mission. I had no choice but to strap myself in to the nearest seat.

Once the aircraft reached altitude, the pilot walked out of the cockpit.

"Técnico Morales said there was a problem. What was he talking about?" he asked smiling and in almost perfect English. Colombian Air Force pilots are mostly trained at US military facilities and speak relatively good English. "By the way, it's a pleasure having the senior American advisor with us. I'm Major Miguel Sanz. Everyone calls me Major Mike," he added.

Not wanting to tell him of the sticky political problem I was now in, I could only answer, "No, not a problem, Major Mike…Just a case of miscommunication. Thanks for letting me come along. It's a real honor and pleasure to accompany you on this flight," I said lying beyond belief.

"I also need to tell you that we'll be over the support area in about 30 minutes. It's a short flight. So, in about 25 minutes when we get near our target, you'll have to disconnect your intercept equipment so that we can use our air to ground radio to communicate with the unit requesting support."

"I understand," I said. Unfortunately, this was one of the disadvantages of relying on the aircraft's external antenna. We would only have about 25 minutes available to conduct our intercept support mission.

I walked over and sat next to SGT Losada who had his headphones on and was already at work monitoring. My stomach started feeling a little queasy. My olfactory nerve was overwhelmed by the smell of hydraulic oil, gun oil from the three .50 caliber machineguns, and the hot cabin temperature. I never faired well on military flights. If I had known I was going up, I would have popped two Dramamine's to avoid getting air sick. As many times as I had conducted airborne operations with the 82d Airborne, the taking of Dramamine was always part of the ritual. Still feeling my head spinning, I sat down and adjusted my headphones.

"*Algo?* Anything?" I managed to yell to SGT Losada.

SGT Losada shook his head while motioning a thumbs-down.

Darn it, I thought to myself. All this work for nothing … I plugged my headphones into the second radio and set it on automatic scan. Together we sat in silence hoping to hear something of importance.

Minutes passed. I looked at my watch and calculated that we only had about two minutes left before disconnecting our antenna.

Suddenly, SGT Losada grabbed the left headphone cup and signaled me.

"I've got something on VHF…144.5 Mhz."

I took my headphone jack and plugged it into the second auxiliary input of SGT Losada's radio. The communications was loud and in the clear, devoid of any code number groups.

"I have the phantom in sight and he is flying very low," the voice over the radio repeated in Spanish to an unknown station. "We will engage as soon as he over flies our position."

I pulled my headphones off and ran toward the open cockpit door. I grabbed the pilot's shoulder who took off his headphones in surprise.

"Turn and pull up immediately. The FARC's about to shoot us down."

The sudden thrust and pull up of the nose of the AC-47 knocked me down on the deck. I tried to get up, but the G-forces were too much. I was flat on my back for a moment.

Once the aircraft had leveled, I slowly got up rubbing my right shoulder where I had hit the corner of the air-to-ground radio rack. I stuck my head back into the cockpit.

"What was that all about?" the pilot asked.

"We intercepted a communication that referenced having a fantasma in their sights. We figure the FARC set up an air ambush for us after having gotten wind that we were inbound."

"Can you give us more details?" Captain Efraín Vázquez, the copilot, asked.

"We'll try, but we will have to go beyond our time using your external antenna."

"Go ahead. We'll go around one more time at higher altitude while you ascertain what the threat may be."

I gave the copilot a thumbs-up and went back to our monitoring position.

SGT Losada was busy copying information.

I remained quiet while the young sergeant worked away. SGT Losada then pulled his headphones off.

"Coronel, it was us they were talking about. Apparently, a FARC column attacked a company of the 2d BACNA with the intention of withdrawing while a second column set up an air ambush against us. The last communication stated that the FARC element involved…a column from the 48th Front…was ordered to quickly abandon the area. It sounds as if they've terminated their attack."

"Good information, hermano…nice job. I'll tell the crew."

I walked back to the cockpit and informed the pilot and copilot of the news.

They talked between themselves. After a brief exchange over their microphones, the copilot got up from his seat and went back into the cabin.

"The pilot wants to contact Antelope Company, 2d BACNA who requested the air support. We'll need to use our air-to-ground radio."

"I understand," I said as I unplugged the intercept radio cable from the panel of the radio and plugged the aircraft's antenna cable into the radio.

The copilot got on the radio and talked briefly with the unit on the ground. He then keyed the microphone on his headset and talked to the pilot. Nodding his head in agreement, he took his headset off.

"The pilot and the unit agree that we cancel the fire support mission. The unit from 2d BACNA is no longer in contact, but is in hot pursuit of the FARC element. Since it's a daytime mission we would waste our time trying to spot a retreating enemy in this thick jungle. I've informed the pilot and we are heading back. You can reconnect your equipment back to the antenna. That was good work on your part."

"Thanks, but it was Sargento Losada who got the intercept."

I smiled and gave SGT Losada a pat on the back as I strapped myself into the drop seat next to him.

On the flight back to TQ, both of us continued to monitor our respective radios. Finally, the sudden bump from the landing gear touching the runway was the only warning that we were back in TQ. The AC-47 slowly taxied back to its parking area and the engines cut off. SGT Losada and I talked to the pilots and got their permission to leave the intercept equipment onboard. After a brief exchange of jokes and laughing with the crew, SGT Losada and I left the aircraft. If anyone had been observing, they would have seen SGT Losada dressed in green camouflaged fatigues accompanied by an American military advisor dressed in khaki shorts, a golf shirt, and topsiders, happily walking over to the pick-up truck, obviously jubilant over something. I realized that now I looked like a scene from the TV series, M*A*S*H and it briefly reminded me of the time I saw the C-130 crew in Hawaiian shirts...hahahaha...how things come around. Most importantly, we had validated the use of our equipment onboard the AC-47 for intercept force protection. And if anyone ever asks you, I never went on an AC-47 close air support mission with the Colombian Air Force on a Sunday morning.

> *So, the people of the valley...sent a message up the hill...asking for the buried treasure...tons of gold for which they'd kill. Came an answer from the kingdom...with our brothers we will share... all the secrets of our mountain...all the riches buried there.*

Now the valley cried with anger...mount your horses...draw your swords...and they killed the mountain-people...so they won their just reward. Now they stood beside the treasure, on the mountain, dark and red...turned the stone and looked beneath it..."Peace on Earth" was all it said.

Go ahead and hate your neighbor, go ahead and cheat a friend...Do it in the name of Heaven, you can justify it in the end...There won't be any trumpets blowing, come the judgment day...On the bloody morning after....One tin soldier rides away.

Coven

CHAPTER TEN

CODEL AND COCAINE

If you wanna hang out you've got to take her out...cocaine. If you wanna get down, down on the ground...cocaine. She don't lie, she don't lie, she don't lie...cocaine.

When your day is done and you wanna run... cocaine. If you got bad news, you wanna kick them blues...cocaine. She don't lie, she don't lie, she don't lie...cocaine.

"Cocaine"
as recorded by Eric Clapton

HEADQUARTERS, JOINT TASK FORCE-SOUTH
TRES ESQUINAS, CAQUETA DEPARTMENT, COLOMBIA
1300 HOURS, 6 AUGUST 2001

When you are at the center of attention of the drug war, then you can expect to get a lot of attention. Such was the case with TQ. In the time that I was there we had three US VIP visits, including one CODEL or congressional delegation. One visit was by an Under Secretary of the Defense official along with his entourage who turned out to be a royal pain in the derriere. The other visit was from General Thomas Mace, the Commander of the United States Southern Command (USSOUTHCOM), accompanied by an Under Secretary of State and his staff, and lastly, the American Ambassador and members of her country team. Everyone wanted to know how effectively the drug war was being waged and what the US was getting in return for its investment in Colombia.

Today, however, we were hosting the fourth and most important group to visit us: US Senator Moe Readerman and a cast of thousands…or so, it seemed, accompanied by various general officers and, of course, the American Ambassador. It made for a high octane dog and pony show briefing.

Based on what I saw and experienced I think these visits serve a useful purpose… for the VIP. After all, is there a better way to get first hand experience of what is going on than to visit places like TQ? But we must ask another obvious question too. Can a person reasonably expect to fully learn the truth in a half day visit? What truth they get is what is presented to them in a series of briefings and demonstrations. It would be time better spent for these VIPs to leave their congressional staffers at the site for one, two, or three weeks so they could gauge for themselves what was really going on.

The other side of the coin is the usefulness of these trips for the host. In our case I knew that these visits were important political events for the JTF-South Commander. For this reason he stopped his operations to prepare for the VIP's. A US congressional delegation was a high powered event and the success of US congressional support to Colombia could rest in congressmen's perceptions…positive or negative. So a lot was riding on presenting the absolutely best side of operational success. Much was at stake for the hosting commander. Plus General Montalvo was a ham. He relished any opportunity to show off his organization.

As I stood on the parking apron along with the entire JTF-South staff, General Montalvo adjusted his pistol belt again and reviewed his briefing notes. I could tell that he was pumped up for this visit and was genuinely interested in ensuring that everything went as planned. His nervous agitation was a dead give away of his present mood.

"*Mi General, no se preocupe*…Don't worry, sir, you'll do great," I told him.

"I know, but a lot rides on the success of this visit." He must have read my mind. "Everything has to proceed like clockwork," he responded in Spanish. General Montalvo had been around the block enough times and understood the politics of VIP visits. If the Colombian Army Commander, General Dora, were to get wind that the visit was all hosed up, it would not go well for the JTF-South Commander. Besides supporting our national counter-drug policy, the general had to demonstrate in an afternoon that it was succeeding. This is probably what had him on edge at this moment.

Prior to setting up our VIP receiving line along the tarmac, the control tower operator notified us that the delegation aircraft was about ten minutes out from landing. We immediately walked over to the parking apron and began assembling. As I gazed out north of the runway I spotted a speck in the distance.

"There they are, General," I pointed in direction of the aircraft.

"It's show time, folks," General Montalvo said in English to his staff while imitating Roy Scheider in the 1979 movie, *All that Jazz*.

We all lined up shoulder to shoulder. Because I was the senior US Army advisor at TQ, General Montalvo gave me the privilege of standing next to him in line.

"These are your politicians, not mine," he winked. "You have to look good too."

"Believe me, General, these guys see so many soldiers on these visits that they'll forget my name by the time they're headed home."

He nodded and winked to indicate that he knew what I meant.

On the tarmac, we had formed what in essence would become a receiving line for the VIPs. I gave my uniform a quick look over. Out of nervous habit, I tugged down on my BDU shirt and adjusted my own pistol belt to ensure that it was square on my waist.

At that moment out of the north, a flat gray USAF MC-130 slowly approached. Within seconds it made a smooth landing and passed by us on the concrete runway. I guess I had already been stranded in TQ so long that seeing the USAF logo on the aircraft actually registered a note of pride and emotion for me. It stopped at the south end of the runway and slowly taxied back to our location.

No sooner did the pilot cut the four engines when the front portside door swung open. A senior USAF staff officer was the first to descend and waited at the foot of the steps. Senator Readerman was the first VIP to exit the aircraft followed by Ambassador Masterson. The senator was fair skinned with white hair. He wore a light blue long sleeved shirt and khaki pants. Mrs. Ambassador sported black dress slacks, a white sweater-like blouse, and a pink unstructured business coat. They all seemed to be in good spirits as they walked over to greet us. General Mace, USSOUTHCOM commander, followed closely behind. General Montalvo left our formation and walked over to the aircraft. He was the first to speak.

"Senator Readerman, welcome to Tres Esquinas. It is both a pleasure and an honor to have you visit us," he said in heavily accented and broken English while extending his hand of greeting to the senator. This is probably what he was rehearsing and was fidgeting about earlier.

"Gracias, General. I am honored at this opportunity," Senator Readerman replied while vigorously shaking the General's hand. Together, they walked toward us. While walking next to the senator, Ambassador Masterson addressed the senator:

"Senator, this is Army Colonel Rick Vallejo. He is our senior military advis… errr… trainer at Tres Esquinas."

"Colonel Vallejo, thanks for what you're doing for our country. We are very appreciative of you sacrifices."

"Thank you Mr. Senator. It's an honor to be here and to participate in your hosting."

A few handshakes later, I peeled off from the reception group and joined BG Montalvo and the senator. My translating duties were being handled by the senator's personal interpreter, so I simply walked behind them in preparation for General Montalvo's briefing inside the COJIC.

"Hey, sir, how are you doing?" The voice behind me sounded familiar. I turned around and I was floored. It was LTC Pedro Báez, a fellow MI officer who had worked with me in El Salvador, many years back.

"Pete, I didn't know you were part of this group. How are you doing?"

"I'm doing great. I'm part of the delegation from USSOUTHCOM J2 and guess what? I've been authorized to stay here with you for about three weeks. It looks like I will be replacing you sometime after the end of your tour. It just makes too much sense to conduct a smoother overlap between the departing and arriving officer."

"Well, that makes entirely too much sense to me too," I said. "We will talk later after the show is over."

The entourage entered the cool confines of the COJIC and assembled on the metal folding chairs in the briefing area. I stood next to General Montalvo and in front of the briefing screen to translate his presentation. Although General Montalvo understood English and could speak a little bit, he did not feel comfortable presenting his pitch in English. That to me was understandable and a smart decision.

Senator Readerman sat in the front row with Ambassador Masterson next to him. General Montalvo cleared his throat and began his presentation in Spanish pausing for me to translate.

"Senator Readerman, Ambassador Masterson, General Mace…and distinguished friends of the Colombian Armed Forces. It is indeed an honor for me to host your visit. The presentation I will provide will serve to give you an idea of the successes we are having in fighting the drug menace here in Tres Esquinas." General Montalvo paused for my translation as he looked among the seated delegates. I could tell from the twinkle in his eyes that he was in his element.

"The mission of JTF-South is to plan, coordinate, and execute joint operations in support of the eradication of narco-trafficking under the legal procedures and mandates stipulated by Colombian national law. Since officially standing up in February 2000, JTF-South and its primary combat elements, the Counter-Narcotics Battalions of the 1st Counter-Narcotics Brigade, have achieved numerous successes in combating narco-terrorism. I must stress that our mission is to eradicate the narcotics infrastructure in our area of operations. We do not engage in counterinsurgency operations."

Prior to looking right into Senator Readerman's eyes, General Montalvo gave me a side-ways glance. As I mentioned before, our Congress was in hot debate over this issue and still made a distinction between funding counter-narcotics versus counter-insurgency. This distinction was irrelevant to the Colombians since to them, and accurately so, the insurgents were also narco-traffickers. Fighting one aspect of this criminal activity without fighting the other is like a major city declaring war on bank robbers and car thieves and not muggers, rapists, and murderers. It was a legal technicality that hindered the effectiveness of the fight. Although he disagreed with this view, General Montalvo understood its sensitivity.

"Next slide, please. Our sector of responsibility includes the three departments of Putumayo, Caquetá, and western Amazonas. The FARC's Southern Bloc has an estimated strength of 3750 personnel in this area. 1500 of these are in Putumayo Department and 2250 personnel operate in Caquetá Department. The slide shows the break out of these combatants by Front. The Fronts in our area are the 2d, 3rd, 14th, 15th, 32d, 48th, 49th, and 61st Fronts. These Fronts are quite active in supporting the drug war and make huge profits from it. Next slide."

"This slide shows the routes used by the guerrillas to transport precursor chemicals, weapons, and ammunition from Ecuador to Colombia. These routes are a Ho Chi Minh trail-like web of combined jungle trails, roads, and rivers. The use of Ecuador as a supply base, as well as safe haven for the FARC, continues to affect our ability to more effectively counter the threat. We are working together with the Ecuadorian Armed Forces to get their cooperation in helping us seal those borders, but thus far, we have had only limited success. As you can probably imagine, sealing jungle routes is an impossible task unless you devote all your personnel and resources to that task. We just don't have that luxury. Next slide."

In the course of the next hour, General Montalvo gave his detailed perspective of many of the characteristics of prosecuting the drug war. He interwove anecdotes of his experiences from the field into the presentation. He showed slides with direct texts of intercepted FARC communications in which the operators coordinated drug buys, transport of drugs, and overall drug operations. To his credit, General Montalvo displayed a positive and upbeat attitude about the progress being made. He is the kind of commander that you want leading the charge against the unpleasant and unsavory nature of countering drugs. From the looks on their faces, it appeared that the VIPs were pleased with JTF-South's progress in support of Plan Colombia.

"This next slide is a summary of our military successes to date. So far this year alone, we have destroyed 452 coca base labs, 21 HCL labs, 2850 kilograms of refined cocaine, and have eradicated 34,775 hectares of coca plants. We have also destroyed 42 enemy base camps, killed 142 narco-terrorists, and captured 361. As you can see, we have been quite busy here in Tres Esquinas in prosecuting the drug war. With your moral support, and of course, your generous funding, we will eventually win this war. If we stay true to the effort, God will grant victory for our perseverance. This concludes my presentation. We are running a little behind schedule and I have much more to show you. Senator, do you have any questions?"

Although I'm sure we could have spent the rest of the day engaging General Montalvo in a question and answer period, the delegation took his cue on keeping the agenda moving, so they opted to leave the COJIC and move on to the next presentation. We loaded trucks and vehicles and headed over to the boat ramp for a demonstration of the river-fighting capabilities of the Naval-South element.

I had already voiced my opinion to the USMILGP Commander about this, but I was voted down. This next part of the tour had the delegates actually getting on board the 22 foot Piranha speed boats and riding up and down the river. To me it was very much like a Disney World water ride and a waste of time and resources. For some reason the Ambassador saw it as the most important part of the tour. I have to admit that getting in a small motor boat with machineguns and speeding up and down a jungle river will get your attention. Maybe the Ambassador felt that after the day was done, most delegates would forget everything they've heard that day, but certainly would never forget their jungle river boat ride.

After getting out of the transport vehicles, I escorted Senator Readerman to the first of the awaiting Piranhas. Unfortunately, we had to walk down a steep embankment to get to our boat. So, I walked ahead of the Senator and extended my hand to assist him in walking down to his boat. I reached for his hand

and managed to get the Senator into his boat and proceeded to do the same for all the VIPs that followed him. Finally, after they were all onboard their respective boats, I crowded into the last boat and joined the river tour. We sped up and down the river.

Throughout the demonstration I kept my eyes on the far bank knowing that everything across the river was enemy territory. If the FARC was observing us, they would be at odds trying to figure out what this display of boating was all about. What a sight we must have been. Finally, after what seemed like an eternity, the boats returned to their mooring areas and we boarded our trucks again. We then moved to our last, and what I considered, the most interesting of all demonstrations—a mock up of a jungle cocaine drug lab.

We walked over to the coca base lab which stood adjacent to the COJIC. It was a run down-looking wooden plank building that had been constructed to look like a typical jungle coca base production facility.

General Montalvo and I were at the head of the formation of VIPs.

"Señoras y señores," he announced in Spanish, "Major Alberto Andrade, my assistant operations officer, will now take you through a tour of a typical jungle drug lab and will explain the processing procedures that are involved in making cocaine." I took a moment to translate this to our guests. I nodded to Major Andrade who began the presentation.

"Buenos días, distinguished guests," he said in Spanish. What you see here is a representation of a typical jungle coca base lab. Today, we will walk you through, step by step, on how coca paste is produced." He paused for me to translate this portion of his briefing. In the course of the next thirty minutes of presentation, we alternated between his Spanish presentation and my English translations.

"First of all let me begin by saying that this small dilapidated one room shack represents a typical jungle drug lab for the production of coca paste. Coca paste is the first step in the process of refining cocaine. As you can appreciate, this small shack can be easily hidden in the vastness of a jungle. However, one key point links these small wooden buildings together…That is the need to be located near a source of plentiful water, such as a lake, stream, or river, because water is an important ingredient in this process."

"Up on the high ground to your right is one our soldiers dressed like a FARC guerrilla security guard. This is also something that you will find at these labs. These guards provide both security to the personnel working inside the lab and also advance warning of the approach of our Army." Major Andrade again paused for me.

"The small bushes with bright green leaves that you see growing here are actual coca bushes. These coca bushes represent the first stage in the coca production process which is the cultivation stage. The process of picking the coca leaves from the plants represents the second stage. This is the harvesting stage. My demonstrator is showing you how this is done. Basically, he pulls or scrapes the leaves off the branches and places them in a large burlap bag. This process of pulling or scraping the leaves is where we get the name for the laborers who pull the coca leaves from the branches. They are called *Raspachines*. It comes from the Spanish word *raspar* or to scrape. I should add at this point that although we are demonstrating the process by which the coca leaves are pulled off the branches, keep in mind that in reality these coca bushes may actually be miles away from the drug lab. This makes it easier to avoid detection. Coca harvesters simply transport their bags of coca leaves to the nearest drug lab for processing. Any questions so far?"

I translated this portion of the briefing and paused to see if anyone in the delegation had questions. Getting none, I nodded to Major Andrade.

"One hectare, or approximately 2.5 acres of cultivated land produces 1000 kilograms of coca leaf. A kilogram is approximately two pounds. Those 1000 kilos of coca leaf will produce 1.6 kilos of coca base. So, it takes about 2000 lbs of coca leaves to produce about 3 lbs of coca base. That's a lot of coca leaves, but these are quite plentiful. The coca plant is harvested every 60 days. It averages three to six harvests a year. The coca plant grows in any climate condition without special care or treatment. It is very easy to grow and maintain."

"Next, the Raspachin carries his full bag of coca leaves to the drug lab where the next stage, the coca base production begins. The bag of coca leaves is emptied into a large wooden trough or platform typically called the dance floor. In a minute you will see why it has this name. As I said previously, coca base labs require 1000 kilos of coca leaves to produce 1.6 kilos of coca paste. Think of these amounts in relation to a bag of coffee. Here in Colombia a standard bag of coffee is half a kilogram or about one pound of coffee. Once the coca leaves are in the trough, the lab personnel then use a weed eater to cut up the leaves into finer particles. This is done to enhance and speed up the process of breaking down the coca leaf and thereby extracting more of its natural leaf narcotics chemicals. Rather than expose you to the noise and dust from the weed eater, my demonstrator already has a bag of mulched coca leaf prepared. He will pour the bag of mulched coca leaves back into the trough simulating the weed eating product."

The demonstrator completed this action then began pouring water and a white powder to the mound of fine coca leaves in the trough.

"What my demonstrator is now doing is adding water and powdered calcium hydroxide or slaked lime to the leaves. This is the first step in preparing the coca leaves. Then powdered cement is added. This also gives body to the powdery leaves. He combines this slaked lime, cement, and water by stepping on the leaves to mix everything together, almost like the traditional way of pressing grapes. This is why the trough is called the dance floor. Depending on the size of the coca production, this process may involve more than one 'dancer.' The dancers will usually do this for about fifteen minutes. Lab workers even urinate in the coca leaf powder to achieve the same effect as the water. During this process the fine coca leaves begin turning into a wet mulch or paste. Sulfuric acid is then added to begin the breakdown of the coca leaf. After another fifteen minutes, this coca leaf mulch is placed inside a 55 gallon container filled with gasoline. The coca leaf mulch will sit in the container for twelve hours. During this period the coca leaf mulch releases its narcotic chemicals into the gasoline. After twelve hours, liquid ammonia solvent is added to the gasoline mixture. Twelve minutes later the gasoline is drained or siphoned from the 55 gallon container. The coca mulch is no longer of use and is discarded. The gasoline is now of most value because it has leached and now holds the narcotic quality that will be further refined."

Major Andrade again paused to allow me the time for a much needed translation. He continued. The audience was spellbound.

"In the next step, my demonstrator will take a sample from narcotics gasoline that we prepared last night and will mix it with Drano powder that contains sodium hydroxide, aluminum, sodium nitrate, and sodium chloride. This white chemical powder now absorbs the narcotics from the gasoline. It turns into a white floury dough-like substance which is further mixed with sulfuric acid. The coca paste is allowed to dry under a sun lamp or a microwave oven. The paste is then placed in a wooden mold in the form of a small block. This small bock of coca base or coca paste is wrapped in cellophane and is then shipped off to the crystallization or HCL lab which constitutes the next stage in the coca refinement process. The HCL lab will turn this block of coca base into pure cocaine powder."

Major Andrade again paused and resumed after I finished translating.

"We've demonstrated these procedures to you, but what does this all mean in the grand scheme of things? As I informed earlier in the presentation, one hectare of coca leaf producing land is harvested every 60 days. It in turn produces 1.6 kilos of coca base. These 1.6 kilos of coca base or paste will be converted to 1.4 kilos of pure cocaine. This means that based on six harvests a year one hectare of coca leaves will produce 8.4 kilos of pure cocaine. We calculate that we have approximately 75,000 hectares of cultivated coca plant fields in the JTF-South area of jurisdiction, encompassing primarily the departments of Putumayo and Caquetá. Based on this ratio of 1 hectare of coca leaves producing 1.6 kilos of coca base as the figure I'm using, 75,000 hectares of coca plants will produce 120,000 kilos of coca base. Multiply this times six harvests and it will yield 720,000 kilograms or 720 tons of coca base a year. These 720 tons of coca base will be refined to produce 645,000 kilos or 645 tons of pure refined cocaine. As you can appreciate, these numbers are staggering."

I translated these figures, which fortunately I had previously written down. Major Andrade paused for a minute to allow the information to sink in as he waited for the whispering and murmuring to subside.

"Ladies and gentlemen, this completes my presentation. What are your questions?"

After translating Major Andrade's comments, five or six hands shot up indicating interest in the topic. Senator Readerman asked the first question in English.

"Major Andrade, thank you for a very illuminating and informative presentation. I am captivated by this information. Although I know that it was not covered in your presentation, can you briefly talk us through the steps of the coca paste refinement process that occurs in the HCL lab?"

Major Andrade understood enough English to jump on the question without translation.

"Gracias, Señor Senador for that excellent question," he responded in Spanish. "It will be an honor for me to answer it." Major Andrade had obviously been coached on laying it on thick with the distinguished guests.

"Briefly, in the crystallization or HCL lab, the coca paste is removed from its cellophane wrapper and mixed with acetone solvent...nail polish remover, if you will. It is then further combined with carbonates and the resulting wet powdery substance is filtered. The resulting liquid is heated for forty minutes and is mixed with ethyl acetate and hydrochloric acid...hence the name HCL lab or *Cristalizadero*. The remaining chemicals are further filtered and heated in a microwave oven for fifteen minutes. The results are crystals of refined and pure cocaine."

"Thank you. That is quite an eye opener," Senator Readerman said turning around and directing his comments to the delegation. "It's not difficult to understand why cocaine users develop nose bleeds from snorting cocaine. Can you imagine putting Drano, nail polish remover, slaked lime, gasoline, cement, sulfuric and hydrochloric acids up your nose?"

"And urine," one of his aides added.

"Yes, and urine," the senator laughed. He had an easy going style and a great sense of humor. I found myself genuinely liking the man.

"What's worse is that people inject themselves with all those chemicals. I mean sulfuric acid alone...that's what's found in car batteries." He shook his head in disbelief. He then turned to one of his staff assistants.

"Marcy, please make a note. When we get back, I want to meet with our national drug czar to begin an information campaign...TV commercials... radio... the internet...newspaper articles... whatever ...to educate the American people on what cocaine is really made of. It's obvious from this presentation that in addition to the narcotics effects of the drug on the nervous system, the chemicals in cocaine have a devastating effect on the body. Basically, cocaine users are injecting themselves with caustic and acidic poisons that are destroying their vital organs. I mean who in their right mind would put liquid Drano or nail polish remover into their bodies? And yet, that is precisely what they are doing without knowledge. What a tragedy to our nation. Major Andrade, thank you. You have provided us a great service. The information you've shared with us may eventually be heard within all American households through the power of television and the internet, if I can get our national drug program to create commercials that include this information. We in the US Senate recognize that the consumption of cocaine by Americans is one of the problems in the world of supply and demand. One of our jobs is to better educate the American population on the dangers of illegal drugs. I am confident that the information you have provided will make a difference. Does anyone else have a question for our young major here?"

Someone's hand shot up. It was a staff assistant.

"Major Andrade, how much money is being made off of all this? I mean how much money does the campesino make at the coca base lab...the HCL lab...and the final price on the street?"

"Thank you for that question, señor," Major Andrade responded in Spanish. "I will provide you with some estimates. The coca leaf grower is paid $1 to $4 for a kilogram, weight-wise, of coca leaves transported to the coca base lab. As I said earlier, since half a kilogram is about one pound, then 1 kilogram is two lbs. The base coca lab personnel are paid from $100 to $400 for a kilogram or kilo of coca base produced. Again to help you visualize the quantities, think of that kilo block of coca base as a two pound bag of coffee. The intermediate agent or transporter of that valuable kilo of coca base will receive approximately $800 to $1200 just for taking it to the *Cristalizadero* or HCL lab. The producer at the HCL lab gets paid $3,000 to $10,000 for producing a kilo of pure cocaine from that kilo of coca base. By the time that kilo of cocaine hits the streets of New York City or Los Angeles it will command a price from $25,000 to $35,000."

"Thank you very much. That is very interesting information," the staff officer replied.

"You're most welcome, sir. I think we have time for one more question," Major Andrade said after getting the kill sign from General Montalvo. A lady's hand went up.

"Major Andrade, how expensive is it to produce a kilo of coca base? I mean you demonstrated that there are quite a few chemicals used in this process. It certainly isn't cheap."

"Yes, thank you for that question, señora."

"I don't have all the figures on hand, but I do know that cement and gasoline are two of the most widely used precursor items. One kilo of coca base will require three bags of cement at a cost of about $30 and 150 gallons of gasoline will cost them about $260. Add an additional $110 for other sundry chemicals and supplies and you get a total of about $400 to produce a kilo of coca base. I know this is about what the base lab personnel are paid for producing a kilo of coca base. For this reason they or members of their operation are usually also paid for transporting the coca base to the HCL lab. It's not cheap, but then again the profit margin is phenomenal. Ladies and gentlemen, thank you for your interest in our mission. I hope that you have learned something today about the dirty business of coca production. Have a safe flight back to the US."

With that Major Andrade turned the tour back to General Montalvo who asked that everyone join him in a round of applause for Major Andrade's presentation. He then led the group out of the small enclosure of the drug lab back to the ramp of the parked aircraft. General Montalvo and the Ambassador exchanged words and he then came toward me.

"The Ambassador has requested that we accompany her and the delegates to Puerto Asís, the next stop in their tour."

"But General, from Puerto Asís they will fly directly back to Bogotá. How will we return to Tres Esquinas?"

"Not a problem. I will have my personal UH-1D and a UH-1helicopter gunship waiting for us at the Puerto Asís airport. After the tour we will fly over to 1st CD Brigade forward command post in Santana and get a briefing from the CD Brigade Commander. Then we will fly back to Tres Esquinas. I understand that LTC Pete Báez will be staying with us at TQ. He can accompany us too."

"Let's do it then, General."

We three and two of General Montalvo's staff officers got on board the USAF MC-130 and rejoined the delegation. The flight to Puerto Asís, a small river town 93 miles west of TQ, was uneventful and we landed at the city airport there after less than thirty minutes.

The rest of the tour went off as scheduled. From the small airport at Puerto Asís, the delegates were driven to a hearts of palm production facility to demonstrate one of the alternative cultivation initiatives being financed by USAID. This topic fascinates me because I think with some investment, alternative crop production makes sense and provides the coca farmer with a real alternative to the big money paid for coca growing and harvesting. Many countries in the region are searching for ways to create more industry in rural areas. For example, on a trip to Honduras I learned how the government is doing more to expand the growing and harvesting of cashews. This is an example of a lucrative product. The cashew nut grows outside and on the bottom of the *marañon* fruit. The fruit is harvested as juice and pulp and is a popular flavor in natural fruit ice creams in Central and South America. I certainly ate my share of fruity ice cream when assigned to El Salvador. The cashew nut is removed from the bottom of the fruit and is roasted and packaged for export. In the United States we pay a higher price for cashews than say, peanuts. Many Honduran farmers benefit from our willingness to pay top dollars for cashews.

With help from USAID, the Honduran government was also looking at ways at expanding the production of orchids in agronomical laboratories. One small laboratory can produce hundreds of healthy and blemish-free orchids for export and sale to the US. The top price that orchids command in the floral market makes this a lucrative business for any government. Stores like Walmart already benefit from contracts with Honduran producers. A country like Colombia that already leads the world in the production and export of cut roses for florists, could expand its market with the production of orchids. It's unfortunate that more money, effort, and interest did not go into looking for these great alternatives, because they were certainly out there.

This hearts of palm facility in particular was most impressive. Although not as well known or popular in the States, hearts of palm or *palmito* is widely used in salads throughout the Latin American region. It comes from a small palm tree and is extracted from its stalk. In the Southern Cone of South America, for example, palmito is a salad staple in meals. It is a delicious product that tastes like artichoke hearts. We were allowed to sample some of the various canned and jarred products from the production facility. The palmito is delicious and was like manna for me. With my limited diet at TQ, I could have eaten an entire case of palmito right there on the spot. It probably would not have looked cool, however.

With the tour being over, we headed back to the airport where the delegates boarded their MC-130. General Montalvo and I waved as they lifted off from the airport runway. His two helicopters sat on the runway apron with their engines now cranking up. As the characteristically loud whine that accompanies the slow start up of a helicopter continued, General Montalvo, Pete, the T2, T3, and I strapped ourselves into the canvas seats in the cabin. General Montalvo grabbed a headset and mike and began to talk to the two aviators that would fly us to Santana. Within minutes we lifted off and began a true nap of the earth flight that brushed the tree tops. We were accompanied by the UH-1 gunship that sported a swivel mounted 6 barrel 7.62 mm mini-gun and some rack mounted machineguns. We dipped and rose, hard banked left and hard banked right. These guys seemed to really know their jobs, although I'm not sure how much of this moving and scooting my stomach could take.

Fortunately for me, the flight to the small town of Santana was short. We landed in an open area near the operations building just outside the town and were met by the 1st CD Brigade Commander, Colonel Jorge Castillo. Before leaving the helicopter, I briefly talked to the aviators flying us. Both were contractors hired by the Colombian government. One was a former aviator from El Salvador who flew in the war there and the other was Peruvian. Small world, I thought.

COL Jorge Castillo was an impressive officer. He was tall, thin, and dark skinned. But beyond that there was a certain something quality about him that I have always admired in some officers. It is usually described as a calm and unassuming presence that surrounds the individual. He always spoke slowly and almost in measured words. When General Montalvo asked him a question,

Jorge would pause and think it through. I don't remember him ever answering a question immediately. It's as if he analyzed what was being asked and reflected on it to provide the most complete answer. Personally, I felt that this is why he was a fine field commander. His poise and composure under stress must have been a comfort and inspiration to his men.

As we walked from the helicopter, Jorge immediately began briefing General Montalvo on the highlights of his operation. The 1st CD Brigade had two battalions in the field and both were busy finding and destroying coca base labs. The real mission was to find an HCL lab that was known to be operating in the area. From what I was able to determine, this time the brigade counted on an informant to lead them to the location of this HCL lab. Many of the Colombian Army's successes can be attributed to the role of informants in leading the units in the field to the sites of these coca processing facilities. This will always be a prime source of information, as long as there is a way of ascertaining the validity and trust of the individual source. So far, informants provided a necessary advantage to other forms of intelligence. Personally, I wish more people would step forward in this process. But money…and plenty of it…was needed to reward informants. Our CIA provided some of it…but not enough…according to General Montalvo. It could certainly lead to bringing the drug war to a speedier end.

A small dilapidated white stucco building served as the headquarters for the CD Brigade. Santana was not a large compound. From the outside of the building I could see the adjacent streets where the people of the town moved to and from their daily activities. In my estimation the base seemed vulnerable to attack, but I guess I looked at things from a much broader US perspective. I don't know. I tried to push the concerns out of my mind so that I could concentrate on COL Castillo's' briefing.

"General, when we first arrived," COL Castillo briefed General Montalvo in Spanish," we immediately had success. At this location just south of us, the 1st Battalion found and destroyed five coca base labs on the first day. They continued to average two a day, but since yesterday, have not had further success. The 2d Battalion operating to the north…he pointed to the map affixed to an easel with his laser pointer…had an initial fire fight and discovered a small FARC base camp. They killed three guerrillas and captured one. He is a mid-level leader and is currently being interrogated back in Bogotá. So far, though, the 1st Battalion has not found the HCL lab. I guess our intelligence was not all that great." I fidgeted with my notepad upon hearing this, but I had little input on this operation. The intelligence analysts at TQ had told me that General Montalvo launched this operation based on very close hold intelligence…meaning that it was not shared with anyone other than the 1st CD Brigade Commander. I did not have a problem with that because I had seen this time and time again in El Salvador. Commanders typically maintain their own personal information sources. At times this can be frustrating because while intelligence personnel are working with one set of data, the Commander may in fact have direct eyes on information of the target and may simply be using his intelligence section to confirm or deny what he already knows. You know what? The heck with it. Let's just go and bag the bad guys and their nasty drug making stuff. As far as I'm concerned, the host nation should rely on whatever works for them.

As I contemplated this, General Montalvo got up from his folding metal chair.

"Coronel, read my lips", he said to COL Castillo in Spanish. "I want base labs…I want that HCL facility…I want guerrilla base camps…I want body counts…If a unit makes contact, I want them to stay in contact…don't let the enemy get away. Do you understand? God concedes victory to those that persevere."

With that, he gave Jorge a fatherly slap on the back. The general had great confidence in his commander. General Montalvo was just the type of leader that kept pressure on his field commanders and pushed them to the limit to produce results. He never let up on them.

And with that we walked back to the two UH-1 helicopters as their turbine engines began to whine and main rotor blades slowly turned. Fortunately, our flight back to TQ was uneventful.

If your thing is gone and you wanna ride on... cocaine. Don't forget this fact...you can't get it back...cocaine. She don't lie, she don't lie, she don't lie...cocaine.

Eric Clapton

CHAPTER ELEVEN

REMINESCING ABOUT MILITARY LIFE

Don't you understand, what I'm trying to say? Can't you see the fears that I'm feeling today? If the button is pushed, there's no running away... There'll be no one to save with the world in a grave...Take a look around you boy...It's bound to scare you, boy...And you'll tell me over and over and over again my friend...Ah, you don't believe we're on the eve of destruction.

"Eve of Destruction"
as recorded by Barry McGuire

HEADQUARTERS, JOINT TASK FORCE-SOUTH
TRES ESQUINAS, CAQUETA DEPARTMENT, COLOMBIA
2030 HOURS, 8 AUGUST 2001

Pete shadowed me around daily as we inquired and had chats with the COJIC intelligence analysts. We quizzed them and had long discussions about the basis for the development of intelligence hypotheses, conjectures, and assessments. Working together with him was like being in El Salvador again. We both understood the importance of our work, its gravity and, certainly, the seriousness of the war.

Upon the completion of the 1940 hours evening update briefing, we walked over to the "American" side of the COJIC... our cubicle work sites. Picking up a two week-old copy of the Colombian newspaper *El Tiempo* from a discarded stack on a table, I totally immersed myself into its content. Similarly,

Pete unzipped the outside pocket of his black backpack and pulled out a three day old copy of the *El Espectador* newspaper that he had bought during his brief stop-over in Bogotá. For awhile we both read totally lost in thought.

Finally, Pete interrupted the silence.

"So, how do you like Colombia? I mean, how does it compare with our advisory effort in El Salvador?" he asked.

"It's a lot the same and at the same time, it's very different," I answered, not looking up and still engaged in a story about rising coffee prices on the world market.

"How are they the same or different?" Pete continued to query.

Realizing that trying to read the newspaper was becoming a distraction in itself, I folded the newspaper and put it down on my desk.

"The challenge here is bigger. Colombia is the size of the combined states of Texas, Oklahoma and New Mexico. El Salvador is the size of Massachusetts. You could drop El Sal in the middle of Caquetá or Putumayo departments and it would not touch the departmental boundaries. This country is huge. There are a lot more places for the bad guys to hide."

I paused and collected my thoughts for a moment.

"Then you have to cope with the threat. From a historical standpoint I honestly feel the FMLN had legitimate grievances against the Salvadoran government. It was an insurgent movement that was rooted on the political and social disparities that existed in El Sal in the 1970's and 1980's. There was no political opposition because it was being exterminated by the ultra-right wing members of the government and the military. Quite frankly, I don't blame the leadership of the FMLN for taking up arms. Yeah, you had a few Communists that were in it for the wrong reasons, but in general the Salvadoran civil war was based on the need of the population to express itself freely and democratically. Those conditions did not exist in El Salvador in the early 1980's. That, in my opinion, is what created the insurgent explosion that rocked that country for over ten years of war. Fortunately, the election of Napoleón Duarte of the Christian Democrat Party ushered in a new era that created the conditions for change. By 1986 or 1987, a new democratic *Glasnost* emerged that established the basis for a true democracy for that country. By 1988 when Alfredo Cristiani from the National Republican Alliance party became president, the conditions were in place for a peaceful settlement to the conflict. Cristiani simply opened the door wider and brought the whole process home."

I paused again for a second, surprised that I had remembered my Salvadoran political history as well as I had. I continued.

"Colombia is more complicated. Here we are dealing with the primary guerrilla group, the FARC. This organization is nothing more than an organized crime syndicate. While the FMLN depended on Danny Ortega and the Sandinistas in Nicaragua, as well as Fidel Castro and his goons in Cuba to bankroll their war, the FARC generates millions of dollars from the sale of cocaine. These guys probably generate more money than some governments in Latin America. The roots of insurgency that originated more than forty years ago have been tainted by the drive for wealth. To win this war, we will have to dismantle the profit-making apparatus that funds everything: The coca leaf, coca paste, and refined cocaine production infrastructure is the engine and source of power for this guerrilla movement. That is the center of gravity that needs to be targeted and ultimately destroyed. As you can see, the dynamics at play here are very different and more challenging than what we faced in El Salvador."

"What about the advisory effort here?" What are we doing the same or different?"

"Well, we have some US Army advisors in the capital within the COCFA, the Colombian Armed Forces Operations Center. But not nearly as many as we had in the Salvadoran EMCFA, the

Salvadoran joint command headquarters. Remember when we worked there and even had our own office to prepare reports?" I answered.

"Oh, I remember like it was yesterday," Pete said with a big nostalgic sigh.

"In addition to that we have advisors out in the sticks in places like TQ...But again not to the same extent as in El Sal. I mean... you remember...we had two to three guys assigned to each of the six Salvadoran infantry brigades, as well as to some military detachments. Here in Colombia I don't see the same systematic approach in the assignment of advisory personnel. Maybe that will change with time. I hear that the Ambassador is trying to get the numbers of advisors up to about 300-400, or so."

"Wow...that would put it at about our numbers in El Sal. Do you remember the joke there? We had a congressionally set limit of fifty-five permanent advisors, but at any given time we had close to 250 other advisors that were there TDY on temporary duty," Pete laughed.

"Yes, I remember that. It was a shell game. But it goes to show you that in these kinds of wars, it takes a definite commitment of personnel, but in generally small numbers to generate results. I mean when you really analyze it...What's 200 advisors? It is peanuts...chump change. Compare that to the thousands that served or were deployed to Vietnam, Grenada, Panama, Somalia, or Bosnia. I'd rather attack the problem with 200 or 300 than to have to commit 20 or 30,000 later when all hell breaks lose."

"Yeah...you won't get any argument from me. Sometimes it seems that politics get in the way of long term vision, direction, or just plain common sense."

"I agree. I also see more involvement from other agencies than what we experienced in El Sal. For example the US State Department and their Narcotics Affairs Section operates here. So does DEA and FBI. Of course we have a different war here. There is more attention paid to the criminal element at work here. As a result more advice and assistance are given to the Colombian National Police."

"Is that the only difference?"

"Well, there is a cultural incongruence at work that I can't really put my finger on. I hate to say it, but even though we're both Hispanic, I feel there's a little resentment at our presence. What I mean by that is that El Sal was a poor country. Salvadorans genuinely wanted and depended on US military assistance to help fight the war. You could sense it in the conversations with counterparts…just in the way they expressed genuine gratitude. I don't get that same "wanted" feeling from the Colombian military. But I mean that's okay. Colombia is a much richer country in natural resources, industry, and commerce. Their military has also had more combat experience than most armed forces in Latin America. Certainly, they've been fighting counterinsurgency warfare more than we have. And historically, our own military involvement with the Colombian military may not have been as great as with El Sal, perhaps. Sometimes I think the Colombians tolerate us only because we're a part of Plan Colombia and everything associated with that in terms of money, military hardware, and modern technology."

"For example, take Colonel Sordo, the Colombian Air Force officer who serves as the TQ deputy commander. I mean this guy's been riding me since the day I arrived here. He's always in my face about one thing or another. In addition to just being a big fat, obnoxious jerk, he probably voices his attitude, while others just keep it in. I don't mean to imply that they are all anti-American as he clearly is, but I think there's some resentment at play here in general."

"Doesn't that affect your support to your counterparts? I mean, if I had to support someone with an attitude like this Colonel Sordo, it would be all over. I would cold cock that guy so hard, he would be out for a week. They would have to move his fat ass on a military pallet onboard one of their C-130's."

"Yes, and you would be gone in a heart beat, too. The Embassy wouldn't tolerate that kind of behavior. We have to be cool about things like this and continue to support despite personality conflicts. It's just like in our own military."

"I know…I know…I'm just letting off steam." Pete recanted.

"I'd be lying to you if I said that it doesn't affect me. But at the same time I have to always behave professionally. I focus on the big picture of why we're here and try not to let flagrant assholes get to me. Look, he is really just an anomaly. Despite what I've said, I think most of these guys really appreciate our support and our presence. I think they understand that for us, this is a real stink hole to work in. Despite that, we leave our families behind to spend time together in this crappy place and share their misery and isolation. We work together in helping them deal with the drug war. I mean this war is our problem too. I think they appreciate all that."

"You're right, Rick. I'm just letting my emotions get to me."

"You…letting you're emotions get to you? I don't believe it. That's too Hispanic of you," I joked.

"Hey, be careful and watch who you're calling Hispanic. I'm not just Hispanic. I'm a product of a rich Tex-Mex-American heritage. It is a proud family tradition. *Viva la Raza*," Pete said in his best imitation of a strong Mexican accent.

We both laughed for a minute. Then we were quiet again. An occasional cackle of laughter resurrected.

"Pete, we've shared some good times together. The images from our tours in El Salvador seem like yesterday. What wonderful memories. Remember eating burgers at *Biggest* or fried chicken at *Pollo Campero* across from the *Estado Mayor?* Man that has got to be the best tasting fried chicken in the world!!" I said.

"Yeah, but how about the natural fruit ice creams at *Pops?* Oh, man what I wouldn't give for one of their natural *Guayaba, Marañon,* or *Guanábana* flavored cones. God, those were good!"

"Good? They were out of this world! My family and I went back to visit my wife's family in El Sal a few years ago. I sat down at *Pops* and ordered six cones…one right after the other. My Mother-in-law must have thought I was crazy. I just couldn't get enough of them. I guess I was trying to catch up from all the years that had passed since I had last had Pops ice cream. Who can ever forget the taste of their pistachio ice cream? What was it they called it when they dipped the ice cream cone in that melted chocolate?"

"Oh you must mean cappuccino-style."

"Yeah…cappuccino-style…Man was that great!" I mentally savored the delicious flavor from these images.

"Did you ever eat pizza at *Pizza Boom*?"

"Oh, yeah, all the time, I answered. "I use to order my cheese pizza with jalapeños and that Salvadoran herb…Let's see what was it…? Oh yeah…*loroco.*

"I use to order my cheese pupusas with loroco. Man, those were awesome," Pete said.

"Yes, that was great food. I also remember you had quite a string of girls you dated," I added.

"Oh, yes. Those Salvadoran ladies are beautiful. Do you remember when I went to the USMILGP Commander's welcome party escorted by three girls?" Pete laughed.

"Yep…What were you thinking, man? I remember that went over like a turd in the punch bowl with the USMILGP commander's wife. Did she ever talk to you after that incident?"

"Yes, she did, although she never brought it up in conversation. I was just trying to prove to the other advisors that I was Da Man," Pete laughed.

"You, Da Man, all right. Not a smart one, but you, Da Man… no question about that." I laughed some more.

The conversation died down as we reflected on those wonderful images from another period and another war. Then Pete broke the silence again.

"How do you feel about women in the Army?"

"Huh?…Boy, that one came clear out of the blue. Oh, I don't know. I think that they should be given every opportunity to serve their country…and they are doing that quite admirably."

"Thank you, Mr. Politically Correct, for that answer." Pete kidded. "Now tell me how you really feel."

"I truly believe that, Pete. Our profession is a wonderful place for women to serve and grow professionally. But it has its limits and it has its downsides. I'm just saying that based on gut feeling. On the one hand an integrated military simply reflects the realities of the American work place. Women are part of the work force in business and in the private and public sector. I see military service the same."

"But you and I know that the military is not your typical American work place. One thing is to work in an office together and then go home to your own house or apartment. Another is to go to war where you may be sharing the same tent or crawling in the mud together," Pete replied.

"Well, that's a separate issue all together. Now we're talking about whether they should serve in combat as infantry or Special Forces personnel. I say that if they are qualified, then why not? In modern warfare, they will live and die anyway, regardless of position, so why not let them die serving their country as combatants? After all, are we not all soldiers?…trained to fight and to shoot our weapons?"

"Yeah, but I think it's more complicated than that. Can you see yourself sharing the same fox hole or trench with a woman?" Wouldn't sexual urges come into play that could detract from the combat mission? I see that as the real distracting element that we just can't blow off." Pete would not back off.

"Well, I do too...but you know...so what? Women serve in the FARC and I don't see the senior leadership making a big deal of it. Women served with the FMLN in El Sal and some even rose to the rank of commander. Women have been well integrated into the ranks of guerrilla organizations around the world and, apparently, quite effectively. Why shouldn't they share in the defense of a real cause, just like the men? My view is that we should give them a chance." I paused for a second and continued.

"Look, I remember during a night combat equipment jump with the 82d, the soldier sitting next to me on the C-130 was a female MP. She had a Squad Automatic Weapon in her M-1950 weapons case and was probably carrying close to 150 lbs in her rucksack. That lady was also about 6 foot 2 and could probably carry me on her back. After we jumped, I saw her on the drop zone, double timing with her rucksack on and carrying that SAW, as if it were nothing. Don't tell me that a hard-as-nails lady like that can't be a combat soldier. Look at the many women that have been the ultimate champions on the CBS TV reality show *Survivor*. The weakest sex may be a relative term that has lost all meaning in today's world of marathons, team sports competitions, race car driving, professional golf, and the like."

Pete thought for a moment and then countered using a different attack plan. "Do you remember ruck marching in the 82d?... 12 miles in 3 hours carrying canteens full of water, load bearing equipment, weapons, helmet, and a 35 lb. rucksack?"

"Of course, who can ever forget those miserable moments?"

"Well, do you remember your reenlistment rates during that time?" Pete asked.

"Yes, I remember that many of my more qualified female linguists...some of the best and brightest...refused to re-up because they couldn't stand the ruck marches."

Pete went on the attack. "So, generally speaking, your young female soldiers could not meet the Division's standard for ruck marching, right?"

"It's a little more complicated than that. Many of the short and petite females could not meet the standard. Many who were taller and stronger made the standard. In fact I thought about this particular Division standard often. Let's look at it from a purely physical perspective. I know the Division Commander, MG Irons, refused to compromise on this issue. He said a standard is a standard. But let's examine this issue a little closer. He was 6'4", and probably weighed about 200 lbs. Meanwhile, many of my more petite women soldiers may have been 5' tall and weighed 100 lbs. Do you understand where I'm coming from?"

"No, I don't. The Division Commander had it right…a standard is a standard." Pete retorted.

"Well, my friend, I'm here to tell you that that is in contradiction to US Army policy regarding physical standards. In the Army annual Physical Fitness Test we have separate standards for men and women. Right? The Army recognizes that women may not have the same upper body strength as a man, for example. So, how do we impose one physical standard on the entire organization? Here's the real issue. For a MG Irons who is 6'4" and weighs 200 lbs, carrying a 35 lb. rucksack for 12 miles is like carrying a bag lunch in his fanny pack. The weight is insignificant. For a 5' woman weighing 100 lbs, she is carrying more than 1/3 her body weight. I feel this is unjust. This is like creating a Division standard that says everyone in the Division will be able to crawl into a small packing box regardless of their height. In this case the short people have an advantage over the tall ones. But can you force the tall ones to crawl into a space that only short people can crawl into? The answer is no. But yet we impose these kinds of standards on our young talent pool. Are you with me so far?"

"Yes, I follow. Go on," said Pete.

"If I were king for a day, I would create a new standard. Remember how in Ranger school we crossed-loaded all the heavy equipment that soldiers carried on patrol? The big guys carried the crew served weapons, radios, and extra water, while the small guys carried less? Well, let's establish a similar standard for ruck marching. I'll call it the 1/3 rule for lack of a better name. With this rule a 200 lb soldier would carry about a 65 or 66 lb. rucksack. If you weighed 250 lbs, you would carry a 75 or 76 lb. rucksack. Now everyone, including the Division Commander, would have a real appreciation of what these young ladies are going through. I think that it would cause the leadership to rethink their standards. As a minimum, it would certainly spread the pain a little bit more so that those endowed with height or weight might reconsider the impact of so called standards. Don't take this to mean that we shouldn't have standards. We do. But when you talk of physical standards, we have to apply a little common sense. What do you think?"

"I have to admit that I agree. The good ole boys have to ensure that they don't do things that on the surface make sense only to those that have physical prowess."

Pete reflected on this issue a little more. His silence did not last long.

"What about the sexual urge thing? How would you deal with that?"

"I gather you're asking me how attractive women soldiers are viewed by the majority of the male soldiers?" I asked.

"Yes, of course."

"Easy...If she's ugly...It's not an issue," I laughed.

"And if she's not? What if she looks like Rachel Hunter or Cindy Crawford?" Pete refused to give in on his views in this discussion.

"Yeah, that's the part that I'm still not sure how I really feel. Is it Specialist Rachel Hunter's fault that she's attractive or is it

Lieutenant Dickie Long, her platoon leader's fault that he's got the hots for her?"

"Well, of course, it is Lieutenant Long's fault. But that still doesn't solve our problem. Men will be boys…and women will be girls. The social animal rule is always in effect," Pete countered.

"And what is the social animal rule?" I asked.

"The social animal rule states that men are like dogs. They're territorial and possessive. When a female dog walks in on the scene, all the male dogs will be sniffing her and trying to get her attention. I've seen the same phenomenon manifest itself numerous times in real life. Soon you have a disruptive environment in that the male dogs, that is to say, the males in that section or office, are all competing for the lady's attention. Jealousies arise. Even the other men that aren't in the competition will still feel jealousy for whomever she favors. I've seen it develop into fights and loss of friendships. That's where I feel it's a dangerous precedent."

I pondered this issue for a moment for I had seen tension built up in scenarios similar to what Pete described.

"Well, we have to accept the fact that it's a social problem, not exclusively a military problem. Based on that logic, no woman would ever serve in the work place because they would be a disruptive influence to the peace of mind of the males. So if we barred them from the work place, we would then become like a fundamentalist Islamic society. We are a country that prides itself on basic freedoms in life, liberty, and the pursuit of happiness. Imagine how absurd it would be if we proceeded along this path."

"Okay, I agree with you. This discussion ends in a stalemate, although I'll rethink my logic and strategy next time," Pete laughed. "What else do you want to talk about?"

"What do you mean what else do I want to talk about? You're the one that's always asking the controversial questions," I said jokingly.

"Hey, I just thought about something we can talk about."

"What's that?"

"Do you think the US will ever be attacked?"

"It's interesting that you should ask that. I remember that at a Commander's conference in Fort Belvoir, Virginia back in 1997, the featured speaker was a futurist. This is a guy who is paid to predict the future using scientific analysis. After his interesting account of his view of the future...I mean anyone who can get up and talk about the future with so much authority makes for an interesting listen... I raised my hand. I said, 'Sir, thank you for your interesting portrayal. I see a surprise strategic attack on the US as the worst case scenario for the intelligence community. Don't you see that possibility in our future?' You know how he answered? He said that with our strategic satellite surveillance systems and worldwide intelligence, it was impossible to carry out a surprise attack on the US. I thought for a moment and then told him that many years ago I had read a futuristic book that predicted that US technology would eventually invent a totally bullet proof vest that would give our soldiers almost virtually total invulnerability on the battlefield. He answered that the laws of physics would never permit a totally bullet proof vest. After that comment I sat down. I totally disagreed with this guy and feel that a futurist cannot discount any possibilities. Anyone who is that sure about the future is dangerous and should not be allowed to practice his profession. I don't know. It's just that no man has a monopoly on predicting the future. How about you? What are your thoughts on this subject?"

"I agree with you too. I think that with the reductions in military end strength following our success in the Gulf War in 1991, our country is more vulnerable to attack today then it was during the Cold War. I have this uneasy feeling about our future also. I also agree that this so called futurist needs to get a job selling used cars where he can lie with authority and get paid for it," he joked.

"I'm so interested in this topic that I wrote a futuristic research paper while attending the US Army War College in 1996. I used popular prophecies like those from Nostradamus and the Bible to predict potential future outcomes for the US. Based on these accounts I concluded two things. The US will go to war with China and the US Army will be heavily involved in domestic disaster relief operations because of future cataclysmic natural disasters."

"Wow…that's pretty heavy. Do you think this will occur in the year 2010?"

"I don't know that it will be 2010. I used that date because it was the popular catch phrase at the time. You know all the reports coming out about Army 2010 or Army 2020. Like I said before, no one has a monopoly on knowledge of future events."

Pete got quiet for a minute as he pondered what we just discussed. I looked at my watch and realized that time had flown by very quickly.

"Pete, I think I'll call it a night. I'm going back to my room to get a snack. Can I offer you a sandwich with cheese spread?"

"No…thanks. I don't know how you eat those things without getting tired of them. I'll watch some TV, drink a beer, and eat a bag of Doritos."

"You've got Doritos?" My eyes lit up like a little boy.

"Yes, I brought them with me from the Embassy commissary store. I'll give you a bag."

"That would be great. Thanks. Can I get them from you now?"

"Sure…let's go. We've done enough damage for one night of conversation.

With that we left the COJIC and called it a night.

Yeah, my blood's so mad, fells like coagulatin'…I'm sitting here, just contemplatin'…I can't twist the truth, it knows no regulation…handful of senators don't pass legislation…and marches alone can't bring integration...when human respect is just too frustratin'...and you tell me over and over and over again my friend...ah, you don't believe we're on the eve of destruction.

Barry McGuire

★ ★ ★

CHAPTER TWELVE

CLAUSEWITZ ON GENERALSHIP

People moving out...People moving in...why, because of the color of their skin...run, run, run, but you sho' can't hide. An eye for an eye...a tooth for a tooth...vote for me, and I'll set you free...Rap on brother, rap on. Well the only person talkin' bout love they brother is the preacher...and it seems...nobody is interested in learnin' but the teacher...Segregation, determination, demonstration, integration, aggravation, humiliation, obligation or our nation...Ball of confusion...that's what the world is today.

**"Ball of Confusion"
as recorded by The Temptations**

**OFFICERS CLUB,
TRES ESQUINAS, CAQUETA DEPARTMENT, COLOMBIA
2015 HOURS, 16 August 2001**

"Rick...are you going to pop on the Brigadier General's promotion list?" Pete asked one evening as we sat on the rear deck of the Officers Club, jungle boots propped up on the old rusted metal picnic tables. In front of us the muddy waters of the Río Orteguaza slowly flowed southward. The 1940 hours update briefing had ended early that evening.

"The BG list...? Why?" I asked.

"Oh, I don't know...just curious, I guess."

"I never hold my breath about something as political as that," I shot back. The topic of promotion to general is a sore subject with most MI colonels.

"Well, let me ask you this," said Pete again while pausing to pop open his *Costeña* beer.

"Realistically, what do you think your chances are of ever making BG?"

"You know, I really don't know…Probably between slim to none."

"Why do you say that…? I mean…I've known you for a long time. You're as capable as any of those guys serving as general officer today."

"Well, it's not an issue of being capable. Everybody is capable. What I mean is that there are so many qualified guys and gals in MI Branch that it's really a crapshoot. There are certainly many more officers who are a lot smarter than me. Plus, I've probably burned a few bridges along the way. And I don't have the smarts to be a general officer." I paused for a moment while continuing to ponder the question.

"Pete, you and I both know that MI Branch is the third largest officer branch in the Army. We have as many colonels as Field Artillery Branch, for example. But how many colonels get picked up for BG from MI every year?

"On a good year…probably two…on the average maybe one," Pete responded.

"Right…And how many get picked up from Field Artillery?"

"On a good year…probably around eight…on a bad year… probably three," Pete fired back.

"See, that's the problem…too many MI colonels…probably between 150 and 200 competing for only one BG position every year. You do the math."

"Well, okay. Let's try a different approach," continued Pete.

"If you could serve in any position in the Army today what would it be and why?"

"Well, obviously, the J2 Director of Intelligence at USSOUTHCOM in Miami."

Narrator's Note: The J2 is the senior US military intelligence officer for the Latin American and Caribbean regions and held the rank of Brigadier General on the USSOUTHCOM staff. Wait a minute. What am I doing? I am the narrator... and I am Rick. Oops, sorry about that. Man, I need a beer. Oh, I'm already having one. Never mind...Let's just get back to the dialogue...

"Rumor has it that BG Don Turdgess is leaving that position next year, so that will mean that the next MI officer selected to BG will occupy his position. That leaves me out."

"Well, what do you think are the qualifications for that job?"

Again I pondered the question as I took a slow sip from my own can of Costeña beer.

"God, this is nasty stuff. I wish I could get Club Colombia or Águila beer here in TQ....What are the qualifications for that job? As an MI officer or as a Latin American Foreign Area Officer?"

"Either."

"Well, obviously, I'd have to say from a FAO perspective... regional experience...yes, certainly regional expertise."

"And what might that be? Pete continued to drill me.

"Well, a trained and qualified 48B Latin American Foreign Area Officer knows the region and has probably established contacts within Latin America. I've been a FAO for twenty of my twenty five years in service."

"Okay, that's good. You are a trained specialist in the Latin American and Caribbean region."

"I think language is important too. I'm a fluent native Spanish speaker and I test my language proficiency through the Defense

Language Aptitude Test every year as required to maintain certification. Plus, I have worked as an interpreter at executive levels."

"You mean, like interpreting for General Montalvo and the Congressional Delegation?"

"Yes, that's a good recent example of many throughout my career."

"Do you really think having fluency in Spanish is necessary to be the J2?" asked Pete.

"Let me answer that two ways. First, non-language speakers in our Army will tell you that it isn't necessary...It's just nice to have. However, language speakers, like you and me, would say that it is essential to establishing honest and enduring relations with our foreign counterparts. Knowing and speaking in a native tongue has a bonding effect on a relationship. A Chilean General once said that US officers who are responsible for the Latin American region and who don't speak the language have no clout. According to him, they are perceived to have no interest in their jobs or do not care what is really going on in their area. They are looked upon as being insincere, disinterested, unconcerned, or...in some cases even mistrusted by their Latin American counterparts. But like I said, non-speakers would never agree with that statement. But he said it, not me. Unfortunately, in the US, ethnocentrism is a ruling factor."

"Well, I agree with you 100%," said Pete.

"Let me also add that I have working level fluency in Brazilian-Portuguese."

"You studied that in grad school, right?"

"Yes, that was part of my education at the University of Chicago."

Pete whistled.

"You're one of the Chicago Boys?" he laughed.

"Not exactly. That was the name given by Chile to their graduates from the renowned U of C School of Economics.

But I did earn my Master of Arts degree in Latin American and Caribbean Area Studies there."

"That is a tremendous qualifier. Out of curiosity, did you party much while there?"

"Are you kidding" At U of C the social center of the school is the Regenstein Library...every night."

"Hahahaha...I hear you. That university is very well renowned and has a solid reputation. So, what else is important for the job, you think?"

"I think traveling to all the major countries in Latin America and the Caribbean is important. Don't you?"

"Yes, I think so. You can't beat having extensive regional experience. That's a major requirement...in fact I would say it's a biggy," added Pete.

"I remember that as the G2 of USARSO, I've been invited by the G2's of various countries to help redesign their army's intelligence organizations."

"Really?"

"Yes...seriously. I advised the G2's of Argentina, Bolivia, Ecuador, El Salvador, Honduras, Nicaragua, Paraguay, and Venezuela. Together we crafted new and innovative designs for their intelligence organizations. Can you believe what a privilege that was?"

"That's pretty awesome...even at my age," laughed Pete some more.

"You're making fun of me."

"No, honest, I'm not. It's just so unheard of that I'm baffled and impressed at that same time. Have you got anything else up your sleeve?"

"Let's see...Well, we served as advisors together in El Salvador during the conflict. But I know that basing promotions on combat experience has never been that important to the senior MI leadership today."

"That's right…you had two combat tours. I think that's a qualifier. Not a lot of guys out there have any combat advisory experience, particularly down in the trenches. Not since Vietnam. "You did other stuff in the region too, didn't you?

"Well, I did combat parachute into Torrijos International Airport in Panama with the 82d Airborne Division during the invasion in '89."

"I remember that. That's where you earned your combat jump star on your Master Parachutist wings. That mustard stain on your wings looks nice. Smokin'…"

"But you know, Pete. Jumping in was dangerous and exciting and all that, but the most gratifying and memorable thing for me was to provide translating support and liaison for Father Laboa and the other priests at the Papal Embassy in downtown Panama City. That by far was the center of gravity of that operation and being there to assist in the negotiations for the hand over of Noriega, his Minister of Finance, the Chief of Security, and the three Basque terrorists that were holed up in the Embassy was most gratifying. This will forever be a source of pride and wonderful memories. Remind me to tell you my war story about my encounter with one of the three Basque terrorists while working the front gate of the Papal Embassy."

"Yeah, you'll have to tell me sometime."

"You know as I look back what I take the most pride in is having had articles published in professional military journals. Five of those dealt specifically with Latin America. I've also been quoted in six books and two journals dealing with Latin American insurgencies. Someday I hope to write a book."

"Wow, that's something to be proud of. Do you know that 90% of serving generals have never written anything professionally themselves? Too busy politicking and networking, I guess."

"Well, I don't know that this should be a qualifier for making general. Personally, I just think that every officer should give something back to the profession in the form of professional articles…while still on active duty…The more…the better."

"Yeah, I agree with you. Otherwise, they are nothing more than air-sucking shoe salesmen….hahaha," laughed Pete.

"Hey, don't laugh. I once told a general officer that if leadership were a requirement for making general, half the generals in the Army would be selling shoes,"…I laughed.

"You didn't?"

"I swear to God, I did."

"Actually that's probably a very true statement. I hope for your sake you didn't mean that comment was intended for him?" asked Pete.

"No, of course not…But I did have another self-serving, politicking, egomaniac general in mind when I said this. But you're right. He may have taken it personally."

"Well, if he did, you're dead in the water with this guy. He'll make sure you don't become a shoe salesman like him…hahahaha."

"Yeah…He personified everything that's wrong with MI Branch…the backstabbing… the lack of integrity…the lies…the cheating…all that crap. Hell will have a special place for him and his kind," I added. This discussion was beginning to stir some bitter memories for me.

"Hey, I hear there's an Officer's Club just for MI generals in Hell…hahahaha…It's so large, Satan may have to start charging membership fees to pay for the maintenance and upkeep. It got so bad one day Satan telephoned God asking him to work harder at giving these guys some religion. They have such a track record of deviousness, that Satan gives them honorary membership as his assistants after a three day refresher… hahahaha. Wait… wait…I've got another one. If there's any justice in life, these guys have got to pay their debt to humanity. Kind of like bad Karma, you know? Maybe they'll all reincarnate back to Earth as leeches so that they can spend more time sucking and leeching some more…hahahaha…Boy, I'm on a roll. Somebody, stop me…. hahahaha…"

"Hey, man. I thought this was a serious discussion. Do you want to continue our discussion or do your stand up comedy routine?"

"I'm sorry…I'm sorry…I apologize…" said Pete red faced and tears coming down his face from all the laughing. "Gosh my sides hurt. Give me a second to catch my breath…Whew…Okay, okay, where were we?"

"Well, I thought we were talking about the ideal qualifications for an officer going into a position like J2. You know what's important too…?"

"I think I know where you're going with this next," said Pete interrupting me. "If you're going to put someone in a primary joint staff position for a regional command, you will want someone having previous experience in joint commands…Right?"

"Makes sense to me. I've had three tours in joint billets…all in Latin America…"

"How about G2 time?" asked Pete.

"Obviously, it is critical and essential to have primary intelligence staff officer experience…not the deputy…not the assistant…but the primary. In fact, my friend, the senior MI leadership has always espoused that professional MI officers should always seek positions as the G2…not the deputy…not the assistant…but THE G2. With this as our mandate, I have always sought those hard jobs. In fact to this day the toughest and by far the most challenging in the Army was G2 of the 82d Airborne Division. Not only did I pay my dues as a Division G2, I also served as a G2 Plans Officer of the XVIII Airborne Corps, and am now serving as the G2 of USARSO…the G2 of a MACOM, a major command in the Latin American region. We are the Army Service Component Command for USSOUTHCOM. I've been in that position now for two years and plan to stay on for at least another year. I've got too many projects and initiatives in Latin America to quit now. What more would you want from a J2?"

"I can't think of any. In fact you may be over qualified…in my opinion."

"You know…since you've got me going now…There is no doubt that I could take that job today…hit the ground running… and never skip a beat. There would be zero ramp-up time. I could do it with my eyes closed. It's too bad that you have to be a general officer to get that job. I just thought of something that really bothers me too. Although the MI senior leadership says that an officer should serve as an S2 or G2, the promotion system doesn't reflect this. One retired MI general officer even confided with his young protégé who he was grooming for general that he felt it was too risky for aspiring officers to be G2's because of the many risks and potential failures while serving as one. You see what this translates too? Take the visible high payoff jobs that have minimum risk, spend time in the Pentagon networking, look good, and you get promoted."

"No, I believe you. It certainly sets a bad precedence for the Branch and you have to question the quality of the individuals getting promoted. Based on the available officers in the promotion zone to BG…with any Latin American experience…anyone else selected will probably spend his first year trying to figure out why *Colombia* is not spelled *Columbia* or how Paraguay and Uruguay stack up historically." said Pete jokingly.

"That is exactly what's wrong with the general officer assignment process today. The amount of importance that the Army leadership places in putting highly qualified regional experts into key positions in support of regional commands is atrocious. Most of the serving officers in the region don't have an understanding or appreciation for foreign history and culture. For example just in Latin America these officers don't know and probably don't care who the great Latin American military leaders and liberators were. If you asked them who were *Simón Bolívar, José de San Martín, Bernardo O'Higgins, Antonio José de Sucre, Andrés de Santa Cruz, José Gerasio Artígas, Francisco de Paula Santander, Francisco Morazán, Manuel José Arce, Alvaro Leonel Méndez Estrada,* or *Ignacio Zaragosa*, you'd get a blank stare. In fact I'm willing to bet that the serving general officers in USSOUTHCOM couldn't tell you who any of these famous men were even after having served two to three years in the region. Well, maybe they might know Simon Bolivar, but that would be about it. Our American culture is one of not caring about other foreign cultures…only ours. It's that pervasive attitude and arrogance that will continue to affect American foreign policy around the world. Garbage in…garbage out. The lack of language skills and cultural expertise from the senior officers and generals working regionally will continue to reflect poorly on the nation's performance around the world. I think this is what the Chilean general really meant when he referred to the lack of language skills by our senior officers as being a detriment to security cooperation in the region."

"You're dead on, man. It's a sorry state of affairs indeed," said Pete. "And the sad thing is that it will never get fixed until someone who really cares about this problem is put in a position to influence that. But generals are too busy looking out for their careers to give a shit. That's the bottom line."

For a minute we both paused and reflected…sipping our beers and looking out over the flowing waters of the Orteguaza; slapping at a mosquito or two. Pete began the discussion again.

"Okay, Rick, for your next test…Do you have a Sugar Daddy? You know…a *Padrino*…a godfather?

"Pete, you know I don't play those silly political games."

"Alright, then…Have you been a golfing partner with any of the MI generals that will sit on your BG selection board?"

"Pete, I just picked up golf about two years ago and I'm already planning on quitting."

"Okay, then…Have you done any heavy socializing…schmoozing…you know…gotten in tight with any of these guys…like inviting them over for dinner at your house…things like that?"

"Ahhh…No."

"Has your wife been close to any of the wives of these guys?"

"Ahhh…No."

"Then, my friend, I'm here to tell you that I have some bad news for you. You probably stand zero chance of getting picked up as a BG on the next board."

"Zero…?"

"Zero…"

"But what happened to the pep talk about qualifications and expertise for J2 jobs?" I asked Pete. I was now interested.

"That should be important…essential…probably required, but unfortunately in today's Army, it's not. If it were, we would have better quality leadership in our Army…which of course, we don't. I can't speak for all Army's branches, but making general in MI is so political that it defies common logic…ethics…even integrity. Remember the old adage? It's not who you know, it's who you…"

"Yeah, yeah, yeah, I know all that. But somehow I thought that being technically skilled and branch qualified could overcome all the politics."

"Not on your life, buddy… If only life were that simple. Look, man. It's all about being liked. The MI general officer that selects you…has got to like you. There has to be a previous relationship established there. There has to be an existing strong social bond there."

"What are you really saying, Pete?"

"Rick, what I'm going to tell you now is ugly…very, very ugly. But it's the truth and you have to hear it. It's going to disappoint you. It's going to break that crystal palace of naivety that you live in. It's going to destroy your belief in the American Dream, the Land of Opportunity, Life, Liberty, and the Pursuit of Happiness and all the bumper sticker labels that you're always espousing. Let me take it from the top. Consider this my version of *Clausewitz On War*. Instead of *On War*, it's about Generalship." He paused to let his words sink in. *Carl von Clausewitz was a famous Prussian military officer whose book, On War, was highly read and debated by military professionals.*

"Clausewitz wrote that effective leadership was the essence of military success. He even went on to describe the essential qualities required of an effective leader. Unfortunately, in my opinion, leadership is not an essential quality to becoming an Army general. You see, Army generals in general…and Army MI generals in particular…are part of a big Mafia. They themselves refer to it as "The Club." It's a very exclusive club because to get in you have to have a godfather. No godfather…no club membership. Are you with me?"

"Yeah, go on."

"Now, to ensure that the Mafia has absolute control in the process of membership, the mob bosses in a sense rig the elections. Here's what I mean. You know how the Army's promotion system works. Decisions to promote an officer are made by a board of officers…usually about 20 officers. The impartiality and fairness of the system resides on the fact that as they review officer files, the board officers are not allowed to share personal information about the officers being evaluated between each other. This is because all voting is done secretly. Now here's the kicker. This procedure is true except for what rank?…general officer, of course. Those are the controls that the Mafia puts into place to ensure absolute control. So, these generals set up this kangaroo court like 'board'…and I use the term "board" very loosely…It's really more like President Andrew Jackson's Kitchen Cabinet…

Pass the whiskey bottle around as we vote on policy. These generals, these "good ole boys," get together after having reviewed officer files. Then the general representing MI branch will get up and say, 'I want Colonel Richie Cheese Eater as my pick for general officer because he's my golfing partner on the annual AUSA golf tournament and he can drive a golf ball 300 yards.' Well, since all the officer files are equally competitive, most of the other generals sitting around the card table will simply say, 'Gee, these guys are all good officers...but if General Bobby Shit-for-Brains from MI Branch selects Colonel Richie Cheese Eater by name as someone he wants in HIS branch, who am I to say no?' So, they all agree and go along with the recommended choice from the general representing HIS branch. It's not about OUR branch or OUR Army...It's about HIS branch and HIS Army. But you got to hand it to them... they're ingenuous...they're unstoppable...the Mafia rules. It decides who gets the secret handshake and the Mouseketeer ears and who doesn't. The travesty with this system...the tragedy of this manipulation...this favoritism... is that many...I mean, many great, outstanding, highly qualified officers who could run rings around half the pile of cow manure that we call the Army's general officers today are not promoted because of this highly discriminatory and self serving process. It makes me puke to know that this goes on all the time."

"Wow...not much more I can say," I said rather glumly.

"Really...there is nothing that can be done, as long as the yahoos at the top control the membership. The exclusiveness of this Club then creates a problem for the Army. The problem is that because of the extreme favoritism, the Army is not promoting the most qualified and talented into the ranks of general. How do I know this? Just look around you. You have to look hard to find general officers who deserve to be called generals. A commanding general I once served with complained to his staff that at any given moment, 50% of Army generals are under investigation by inspector generals, equal opportunity representatives, equal employment opportunity investigating officers, or congressional investigators. What for? For abuse of authority, cheating, lying, stealing, womanizing, alcoholism, discrimination, favoritism, verbal abuse, ethics...you name it, they've done it. That's a sad track record for any organization's leadership. What I have the biggest problem with is how general officers freely and openly disobey Army regulations. Have you noticed that? They stop being leadership examples to their subordinates. They stop being role models. They stop doing everything that leadership manuals ask of its leaders. How many generals have you known that do not take their annual PT test? Lot's of them, right? Oh, I know that many generals do take their PT tests, but far too many hide behind busy travel schedules and blow the whole thing off. Generals talk about taking care of soldiers and families, but don't follow through with action. I think this is because they are too busy protecting their careers to care anymore. At some point general officers stop being leaders and become strictly politicians as they campaign for their next star. This is detrimental to unit morale and combat effectiveness. It's truly a sad and sorry state of affairs for an American nation that bestows its national treasure...its sons and daughters...under the care and trust of these incompetents. God help us if we have to go to war against a real and powerful adversary that will put to test the leadership and Army values of these misfits."

"Pete, I agree with you on some of your views, but not all of them. The reason I say this is because I've served with great and inspirational general officers in my career. For example my commanding officers in the 82d Airborne Division come to mind as officers who I thought more than deserved to wear their stars. I will agree with you on one thing, however. Entirely too many generals...whether that number is 50%...greater or less...are wearing stars they don't deserve…and in some cases have no business wearing the Army uniform, period."

"Amen, brother…I can't argue with that logic. I accept," said Pete.

"Pete, I meant to ask you something as you were on your tirade about your contempt for generals," I laughed "You've obviously been burned by the system or have been a victim of some of the abusive behavior of general officers…I'm not sure which. Is this the case?"

"Rick, I don't really know. I see stuff in our Army that I don't like and I'm not sure what it is, to be honest with you. But now that you've asked the question, let me attempt to answer it. Let's call the problem the racial factor, for lack of a better word. Okay? Look, I admire the Blacks of this country. You know why? Because Blacks, God bless them, broke the code years ago. They understand racism, prejudice, and discrimination because it has been a part of their unique Black history and culture. And as a minority group they are united and strong. What do I mean by this? Let me tell you a true story that I'll use as an example. I'm a member of an officer's promotion board…one of about twenty officers. We are reviewing thousands of officer files, right? Then the one black officer, the one Asian-Pacific officer, and me, the one Hispanic officer, are pulled aside and told that we are to review minority officer files to determine if we can detect discrimination. Rick, I ask myself how the hell do I detect something like this in a written evaluation? I don't know. But anyway, we went ahead and conducted our review. Later in the day after we completed the scrub of records, I pulled the black officer aside and asked him, 'Hey, Don, did you detect any discrimination in those minority officer files that we reviewed?' He told me, 'Of course I did. It was absolutely clear to me that many of the black officers suffered from discrimination.' 'But how do you know this?' I asked him. 'I just know, Pete…I can feel it…I can sense it…I can read it in the written evaluations. It has more to do with what is not said, than what is said. The write ups are not glowing…they do not inspire.' Then the light bulb went on. I realized for the first time what the problem is with Hispanics in the Army…probably in the US in general. Our problem is that we think that we as a minority group have somehow been assimilated into the Army. We think that we are an accepted part of the big Army at large. We think that we are an integrated part of them…the white majority of the Army. My friend, I'm here to tell you that this is exactly our problem. Unlike the Blacks who suffered open discrimination for years within many parts of the US and in particular in the southern states at a time when civil rights were only a dream for Martin Luther King Jr., Hispanics have not been openly attacked in a similar fashion. There may be a historical reason for this. While Blacks became an institutionalized component of the American Nation early in its history…primarily beginning in the1700's…Hispanics are just now becoming a large and more prominent minority. I think that the growing number of Latino immigrants may be playing a bigger role now. So, what does this mean? The open and unlawful discrimination of previous years has been replaced by a subtle… finesse… form of discrimination. Of course, helping this discrimination is the fact that most Hispanics haven't got a clue of what's going on. This type of covert discrimination leaves no clues. The culprit hides behind a smiling face. Like the Blacks, Hispanics have got to be more attuned to this hidden form of prejudice and be on the look out for it. Have you ever asked yourself why certain whites don't like you or why you seem to have problems fitting in? You immediately conclude that it's you…or that you have a lousy personality. You grow to accept the cold shoulders or the shunning. But you tell yourself…gee, I'm an alright guy…I'm a nice and decent individual…I'm courteous and respectful…what could be the problem? If this happens more often than naught, you may be a victim of this subtle or hidden form of discrimination. How do these discriminating individuals ultimately sock it to you? Look at your officer evaluation report because it will be less glowing than your white counterparts in your unit. That's what Don meant when he said that he could read the discrimination in the officer evaluations. Discrimination in this country has become harder to detect and identify. This does not mean that it is any less rampant and destructive than ever."

"Wow…Pete, let me fully absorb this for a second," I said.

"Sure, take your time," he said looking at his watch. "Well, don't take too much time."

"Pete, I hear what you're saying about the subtle discrimination and all that, but you know, if you don't shine in your job, you can't expect to get a glowing evaluation. I don't think that has anything to do with discrimination. I've done relatively well in my career. I mean, making full colonel is no fluke. It's quite an accomplishment and I'm quite proud of it."

"Yes, of course and you should feel proud. But understand that you are only a useful statistic for the Army's leadership. The ruling white majority of the Army has to promote minorities to preclude being investigated by Congress. So, they continue to perpetrate the big sham. You are a token…a representation. The fact is that If you look at the stats, Hispanics are not equally represented in the general officer ranks. For being the largest minority in the US…having overtaken the black minority…Hispanics are greatly underrepresented and will continue to be until someone starts to look closely into this. I mean look at the numbers. How may black generals does the Army have?...Probably around twenty or twenty-five. How many Hispanic generals are there?...Probably between five and ten. That, my friend, is an example of under-representation due to discrimination. This is the product of the control and manipulation by the Army's Mafia." Pete paused to sip his beer again and continued.

"You know, some times I feel I'm too hard on the Army's leadership because they are merely a reflection of the ugly nature of the society of our country. I think this is the case because contrary to what you read in history books, the South won the Civil War. What do I mean? The North won the war, but the South won the cause in that discrimination against minorities still rules in this country. 100 years after the end of the Civil War, this country still had Blacks being beaten up in downtown Birmingham, Alabama…simply for being black. What more can you say? And do you think we are rid of racism? Think again. It is rampant. The United States is a country that promotes and advertises the ideals of equality, democracy, and freedom, but whose citizens practice the opposite. I think the rest of the world recognizes this. They recognize hypocrisy when they see it. Americans in general hide behind this façade and don't even know it." Pete paused to get his breath. He was clearly agitated.

"True story, Rick, and I'll get off my soapbox. A friend of mind, a retired navy officer, moved to a new community in a large city in the Midwest. He and his Filipino wife went to their first church service there for the first time. After the service the wife of the minister approached him and said, 'We would prefer if you didn't bring the likes of your wife to our services.' Rick, can you believe this? Mind you…the minister's wife. That's what I mean by the hypocrisy of this country. On the surface everything looks like a scene from the 1965 movie with Julie Andrews, *The Sound of Music*. Underneath, we are victims of the South having truly won the war of ideology. If I were to reincarnate back in my next life, I would want to be a white Irish Catholic. Because in a society that is primarily white, it helps to be white also. Being a white Irish Catholic has its advantages because you have roots to an important part of the massive immigration and labor force that created this nation. The average American will stand up and cheer if you say, 'I'm a red blooded Irish American.' That is considered a truly rooted American. Now see what kind of reaction you get if you say, "I'm a red blooded Chicano or *Puertorriqueño*. My friend you'll get scorned. The sounds of last names like López, Rodríguez, or Jiménez don't ring the same nor are they embraced with the same degree of affection in this country as O'Riley, Harrigan, or Sullivan. We are not all equal, regardless of what you may be told. By nature we are different and weren't part of the massive immigration that came to this country early in its history and whose minority groups became its middle and working class. The majority of whites have no clue. In their white world, they honestly believe that America is the Land of the Free and Home of the Brave. Meanwhile, the ministers' wives, gun toting trailer trash, and rednecks reflect how people in this country really feel. It will take centuries for Hispanics to assimilate as part of the so called American Melting Pot. Until such time, we will be treated like outcasts."

"Pete...I don't know. On one hand there may be some elements of truth to what you say, but on the other hand I see far too many honest, good, and wonderful people in this country. I don't think they all fall into the category of people you're describing. This country is not perfect by any means. It has a lot of bad apples, but I think it is still a beacon of hope to people seeking freedom and equality. Those ideals are still alive today."

"Rick, the ideals are still alive, but the bad apples dominate. Look, I grew up in the streets of El Paso, Texas. I know what I'm talking about. And unlike you, I am dark skinned and I look Hispanic...in a true stereo-typical way. I can't hide my Hispanic heritage. On the other hand, you are a white Hispanic and look kind of Gringo. But don't fool yourself. As soon as you tell people that you're from Puerto Rico...Wow...the defense shields go up. It's sad...It's really sad."

"Well, thanks for the wake up call. I wish I had known this a few years ago where I may have been more on the lookout for all this subtle discrimination you describe."

"It wouldn't have made much difference. It would have just made you cynical and bitter like me over time. There's nothing that you could have done anyway. The problem is too big and you and I are just two specks of dust in this dirty vacuum cleaner bag of an Army and our society."

"Yeah, you're probably right."

"So, to wrap things up, Rick, if I apply my logic to the problem, I predict that the next J2 of USSOUTHCOM will be someone who doesn't speak Spanish, has never served a day in his life in Latin America, may have never served as a primary G2, but will have one big advantage over you. He will be well connected to an MI godfather and he will have a great golf swing."

Narrator's Note: I guess I can step back in now. True to Pete's prediction, I was never selected for promotion to brigadier general. But that's okay. I'm not bitter because I was never in the running and never felt I was as good or as well qualified as some other guys and gals in MI branch. Many more officers who I knew truly deserved this opportunity much more than I did. What bothered me is that the BG promotion board did select another officer to be the J2 of USSOUTHCOM. Like Pete had predicted, the officer selected did not meet any of the regional or job-related qualifications to occupy the position, was not a particularly gifted officer, but he was well connected to an MI godfather...and he was a great golfer, too.

After leaving TQ, Pete did mail me a letter. I'll share it with you:

26 August 2001

Rick,

I know it was a real disappointment for you...I mean about the promotion list and all that...I mean... I tried to warn you...I even explained to you that it wasn't about being well qualified for a job…not about merit… but about being well connected and liked. I know that you weren't convinced and…well… now you understand why I get so emotional about this topic.

What can I say, my friend? The system is as morally corrupt as any criminal organization. It's an institution that doesn't look out for the greater good of the organization. It is run by a bunch of low life's that look only at their personal interests and friendships, rather than doing what's right for the Army.

But you know what's really sad about all this? The Army will lose a fine officer. It will lose an officer and a gentleman who always does what is right for the organization… what is right for his fellow soldier… who never loses sight of the mission. Receive strength and consolation in knowing that regardless of who was selected over you, you are ten times better qualified to do the job. If you had only taken up golf earlier in you career you may have being a more serious contender (hahahaha…I just threw that in to make you laugh).

In retrospect, though, I almost think that it's just as well that you didn't get picked up for BG. I mean, knowing what we know about the unethical selection process, would you really want to be a part of this? No…Probably not. Put it behind you, my friend. You're too honest and decent and life has some bigger and better things in store for you.

You know, I've always believed in the Bible when it states, "As we sow, so shall we reap," or to put it in West Texas parlance, "garbage in…garbage out." Some day the Army will pay a heavy price for its corruption. These scams and charades that continue to promote friends and golfing buddies into the general officer ranks will someday cost the Army dearly. These personal choices will someday come back to haunt these self-serving individuals that have corrupted the institution. Some day… in the not too distant future… our Army will find itself on a foreign battlefield… on a foreign land…far from our Homeland…against an adversary who will test the true mettle of the Army's senior leaders. We will then see what our general officer corps is made of. We will see whether they truly personify the Army Values of leadership, duty, responsibility, selfless service, integrity, and personal sacrifice. Will they be up to the challenge? Will they rally to the call? Will they look out for their soldiers? Will they accept responsibility for their actions? Or will they cower and cover themselves in lies and deceit to protect their all important careers? The true test will come...not on golf courses...but on the plains, mountains, deserts, and urban areas of the future battleground.

May God help us all if we have to entrust these incompetents with the lives of America's young men and women. For the full burden of fighting for the survival of our nation will rest on the shoulders of those least willing to accept responsibility for their actions.

Good luck, my friend. Enjoy the rest of your tour in "Beautiful, downtown Tres Esquinas." May God bless you; keep you safe, and always healthy. Un gran abrazo from your good friend, Pete.

Reflecting back on Pete's rantings and ravings... and that's all they were...Pete just had a lot of pent up anger inside. Although there may be some truth to it, It's much too general of a statement to say it's one thing or another. Certainly, not to the extreme that Pete perceived it. I really don't know. Yeah, the USA is not perfect, but I'll still take it over any other country. As to racial equality...well, I'll let you decide that one for yourself.

What say we get back to our story. We have some major problems heading our way. Things are going to get a little sticky for us soon. Please turn to the next chapter...

Air pollution, revolution, gun control, sound of soul…Shootin' rockets to the moon…kids growin' up too soon…Politicians say more taxes will solve everything…And the band played on… So round 'n' round 'n' round we go…Where the world's headed, nobody knows…Just a Ball of Confusion…Oh yea, that's what the world is today.

The Temptations

CHAPTER THIRTEEN

THE APPROACHING STORM

Everybody's talking about revolution, evolution, masturbation, flagellation, regulations, integrations, meditations, United Nations, congratulations...

All we are saying...is give peace a chance...All we are saying...is give peace a chance...

"Give Peace a Chance"
as recorded by John Lennon
and the Plastic Ono Band

HEADQUARTERS, JOINT TASK FORCE-SOUTH
TRES ESQUINAS, CAQUETA DEPARTMENT, COLOMBIA
0730 HOURS, 5 SEPTEMBER 2001

I carefully folded Pete's letter and placed it back into the left breast pocket of my fatigue shirt. Pete certainly seemed to think more highly of me than I did of myself, but I really didn't have time to worry about all this now. I had work to do. I put on my web harness and pistol belt; slung my document bag with radios over my shoulder, and grabbed my field cap. I was in deep reflection as I drove the Chevy pick-up truck to the COJIC for the 0740 hours morning update.

Pete had returned to his job back in the States a week ago and I really missed our chats. He would come back to TQ to replace me, but we still had no confirmed end date for me. As is usually the case, he would probably show up sometime after I left. That's what usually happens in these cases.

Within minutes I was inside the cavernous COJIC. To my surprise, Colonel Gutiérrez, his deputy, Major Cano, and the chief of imagery interpretation, Lieutenant Díaz, were huddled in front of the large scale map of the JTF-South area of operations. COL Gutiérrez was extremely agitated about something as I walked in.

"Buenos días, Coronel. *Cómo ameneció?*" greeted COL Gutiérrez in the customary Colombian morning greeting.

"Muy bien, gracias, mi Coronel. Qué pasa?"

"We are concerned about the latest series of reports in the last 24 hours indicating suspicious movements in the vicinity of Tres Esquinas. We are evaluating similar reports that have been coming in over the past week that are beginning to establish a pattern of activity. Last night the guards on the east side of the perimeter fired at what they thought was an infiltrator attempting to penetrate the perimeter wire. This morning we sent a patrol out, but we found only small evidence of that. We're trying to evaluate all this before briefing General Montalvo this morning."

"Hmmmm...What time was the sighting?"

"At 0115 hours"

"Did you personally verify this report?" I asked in an attempt to ascertain the validity of the information.

"I personally talked to the officer of the guard last night and the patrol leader that led the patrol this morning."

"You said that they thought there was an attempt at penetrating the perimeter. What made the perimeter guards think this and what evidence do we have that someone in fact had been in the area?" I interrogated further.

"According to the officer of the guard, the perimeter guards observed a dark form walking into the perimeter wire and then loitering there. The individual appeared to act suspiciously. There were also some bare footprints found. This would indicate that a *campesino* may have wandered into our perimeter by accident."

I thought about this for a minute. Although having someone run into the perimeter wire was highly unusual, there had been cases in the past where inebriated farmers, after a night out drinking, had accidentally run into the camp's wire as they walked back to their homes. Although never confirmed, the reports concluded that these cases were simply accidents. I resumed the discussion.

"Bare footprints, did you say?"

"Yes."

"Certainly, that may indicate that it was a disoriented rancher coming back from drinking with his buddies in Solano. But, do campesinos generally walk around barefooted?

"No, not really," COL Gutiérrez answered.

"Hmmm…" I muttered.

"Hmmm...what?"

"No, no, no…just…something popped into my head. But it's not important. Let me see…Do we have any other reports of movements in the vicinity of Tres Esquinas?"

"We have reporting from our volunteer campesino agents that are imbedded among the populace in the surrounding ranches."

"So, we had human eyes on target informing this. Could we get them to elaborate on their reporting?"

"No, I'm afraid not. You see these agents transmit with their SATCOM telephones when the opportunity presents itself… not on scheduled times. So as to not compromise them, we are not allowed to call them or engage them with questions on their reporting. We simply take down the information and wait for them to report again, hopefully with more information. Just for your information, some of these so called intelligence agents are little old ladies that volunteer to put their life on the line in support the government. This is not very sophisticated. They are also not very well trained at all."

"Hmmmm...." My eye brows furrowed as I thought deeply. "What was the nature of the reporting?"

COL Gutiérrez flipped through the stack of papers he held in his hand.

"For example, this one report says, a convoy of six large motor *Cayucos* headed up river...this report states overall boat counts on the Río Caquetá are up from normal levels...Let's see...this one says heavy foot traffic detected along a logistics corridor... this one states that a long convoy of SUV's and trucks moved along another route...irregular population movements to the north...Stuff like that."

"Show me on the map where these movements have been reported," I requested.

COL Gutiérrez took his laser pointer out and pointed to the colored arrows that his analysts had marked on the map. It was difficult to access the nature of these movements because they were along well established routes that the guerrillas used to move drugs and logistics north and south between Colombia, Ecuador, and Peru and east and west within Colombia.

"To the east FARC personnel were active out of the Peña Colorada base camp area along the Río Caguán and Río Sunsiya. Farther east from there, the Río Yari corridor appeared to be quite active also." The bright red dot from COL Gutiérrez' laser pointer traced north and south along this complex of rivers east of TQ.

I looked at the map and traced my index finger along these routes. I nodded affirming the information.

"This would indicate that the 14th Front is active, doesn't it?" At this moment I was the novice analyst being tutored by the local expert.

"Absolutely...That's in the 14th Front's area of operations and main base camps."

"What else do we know?"

"To our north and parallel the Río Ortegezua we have activity reported near La Unión Peneya and San Antonio de Getuchá."

"15th Front?"

"Most definitely."

"What else?"

"To the south of Tres Esquinas movement has been reported from west to east along the Río Mecaya and Río Sensella corridors." COL Gutiérrez ran the laser dot west to east along these two rivers.

I traced my fingers along the routes of the two rivers on the map, contemplating the extent of this information. I whistled in disbelief.

"Wow…Both river corridors were active?"

"Yes."

"48th Front?"

"We think so…this is within their operations area."

"How about the 49th Front…Is it active?"

"We don't know. We've had no reports from their area."

"That's interesting. Usually when these logistics corridors are active they should all light up shouldn't they? What do you think is different about this activity as opposed to just normal logistics or cocaine runs by the guerrillas?" I asked.

"Coronel, I've been working in Tres Esquinas now for almost 11 months," said COL Gutiérrez. "The volume of movement along these trail and river networks doesn't fit the norm. It seems to be much greater in magnitude. Plus, we never pick up much UHF and VHF communications when the guerrillas are running their drugs. That is pretty routine and commonplace for them. Now the National Police Intelligence Directorate in Bogotá detected an increase in these communications. There is an increase in HF communications coordination between cabecillas…and they appear to be moving. That does concern me."

"What is our own monitoring station reporting? Do we have any indicators from them?"

"Our station reported an increase in VHF FM communications on the 2 meter band. As you know, Coronel, any time we intercept radio traffic in this band, we raise our alert levels because that in itself is an indicator that the guerrillas are within tactical transmitting range, which as you know in these jungles is not great on this band."

"Do we know what they're communicating?"

"No, everything is encrypted."

"But we've broken some of their codes with captured code books before."

"Yes, but apparently the FARC has changed over to a new code book. We are clueless right now."

"Are they still using their standard four number code groups?"

"Yes, that has not changed."

"How about their HF communications? What's happening on the 40 and 80 meter bands?" I asked.

"They've confirmed what the National Center is telling us. The monitoring station has detected both AM and SSB communications between the cabecillas of the fronts. Everyone, of course, is using the new encrypted code. Three of the fronts that have been most active are the 14th, 15th, and the 48th. Of these, Fabián Ramírez' and Martín Corena's female radio operators have been most active constantly sending numbered code groups. Yesterday morning, the two cabecillas themselves got on the air and used their talk around communications to pass some information between them. A few words were in our glossary of talk around terms and we think we picked up the words, *gran fiesta*. You can see why I am concerned, Coronel."

"Big party...huh? Well, I understand your concern." I said. "Do we have any aerial photo missions scheduled today?"

"Coronel, the Colombian National Police recon bird is on standby to support us this afternoon, but I'm afraid black and white imagery won't do us any good with the overcast conditions this week and the triple canopy forest around Tres Esquinas."

"How about the FLIR from the AC-47?"

"We could use it with special permission from General Montalvo in the evening, but General Ocasio, the Air Force commander, has prohibited the use of the Fantasma for surveillance missions because we're using it entirely too much for that purpose and it's burning up fuel and air hours. He wants it exclusively flown for close air support missions."

"I can understand his concern about putting too much flight time on those old DC-3 frames."

"Coronel, can we get a special FLIR mission from the Embassy?"

Narrator's Note: This is probably a good time to jump into the middle of this conversation. I didn't want to interrupt the discussion. The FLIR or Forward Looking Infrared is a special imaging device and sensor that picks up the heat signatures of people deep in the jungle. It is particularly effective in detecting personnel movement at night. The advanced cameras used by the US counter-drug surveillance aircraft delivered a very high quality image that was superior to anything the Colombians had. Warm bodied objects on the ground appear as white hot spots to the FLIR operator. Let's get back to the discussion...

"I can call my liaison over there and request it. The Chief of Station will have to decide if the threat here warrants sending the platform in support of us. I certainly think it does. I'll see if we can get priority on rerouting an already scheduled mission for this evening or tomorrow night."

"Gracias, Coronel. I think we have a real problem brewing and I'd hate to get caught with our pants down."

"Believe me, Coronel Gutiérrez. None of us wants to get caught in any kind of surprise attack by the FARC. It's our necks on the line…literally. We won't have any intelligence failures on our watch. That's the ultimate slap in the face for any intelligence organization."

I walked over to the classified CIA phone and inserted the crypto key after removing it from the classified safe in the corner of the COJIC. I then dialed the Embassy air reconnaissance office. The phone on the other end rang and rang with no one answering.

"Blasted civilians," I grumbled while glancing at my watch. "Don't they know there's a war on?"

I estimated the time that the air reconnaissance office might open. I returned to the briefing maps.

"Any luck?" asked COL Gutiérrez.

"No. I'll have to try again in an hour when the Embassy personnel arrive for work. Besides it's almost time for the 0740 hours programa. What are you going to tell General Montalvo during your briefing?

"The truth as we know it," said COL Gutiérrez.

"Well, good luck. Like most combat arms officers, General Montalvo is never satisfied with the intelligence he gets."

"Will you back me up?"

"Count on me, amigo. This is my war too," I smiled.

"Gracias, Coronel. I really appreciate it."

"Look, Coronel Gutiérrez. I've been in your position numerous times. The life of the primary intelligence officer is lonely and unforgiving. You're supposed to divine the future…know what the enemy is doing or thinking. After signal officers, it's the worst job in my Army. It's the worst job in any army."

"Especially during the tough moments," smiled COL Gutiérrez.

"Especially during the tough moments, amigo," I repeated while smiling and placing my hand on my counterparts shoulder.

"Come on. Let's tell the old General what's going on. What's the worst he can do? Send us back to Bogotá?" I laughed.

Together we entered the briefing bunker. I sat down on one of the folding metal chairs at my normal place in the middle row, while COL Gutiérrez went to the front row of chairs where the T3 was already waiting for him. In about a minute the call to attention rang through the bunker as General Montalvo walked to the front of the briefing area. The Chief of Staff waited up front to provide the customary reporting beginning with:

"*Atención...Vista a la izquierda,*"...and all the customs and courtesies of their army.

The briefing commenced with the Staff Duty Officer providing a summary of the overnight activities, including the report on the suspected infiltrator.

"Another disoriented drunk coming back from a night of drinking in Solano?" asked General Montalvo getting up from his chair and turning around to face the assembled officers.

"We think that this may be the case, General," answered the T2.

"Coronel Vallejo, what do you think?" asked General Montalvo in Spanish.

Surprised, I jumped up from my chair. "I concur with the T2 that this may be the most likely explanation, mi General," I answered. "Unless..."

"Unless what?" asked General Montalvo.

"Unless your campesinos typically run back and forth from Solano barefooted."

"Only if this guy lost everything, including his shoes in a poker game," said General Montalvo as the room broke out in laughter. "No...They usually wear sandals, running shoes, or cowboy boots of some type. Why?"

"The report from the patrol that inspected the area of the sighting reported finding bare footprints."

"Bare footprints? Should I be concerned, Coronel?"

"I'm not sure, General. There is something about barefooted infiltrators that does bother me, but I don't think that I can make a solid connection. Let's just say that we will put it in the pot of conjectures and hypotheses for now."

"Muy bien, Coronel. I wouldn't worry too much about it, though…next briefer," he said as he sat back down.

The T2 got up and went to the front of the briefing area. In the next 20 minutes, COL Gutiérrez briefed General Montalvo on all the reporting, as well as voicing his own concerns about what appeared to be going on.

"Coronel, you deliver the reporting…And allow me to voice concerns." General Montalvo was not one to mince his words.

"Yes, General…of course," said COL Gutiérrez.

General Montalvo thought for a moment and then again got up from his chair and moved over to the briefing map of the area of operations. Occasionally he would lean forward to look at areas of the map with more detail. He then called the T3 to join him. They whispered back and forth for the next five minutes or so while looking at the map.

"Coronel Vallejo, can the American Embassy support us with some FLIR tonight?"

"General, as a matter of fact I tried calling the Embassy requesting immediate support, but couldn't raise anyone at the air liaison office. Once I get confirmation, I'll let you know if we are able to get a priority flight."

"Excelente…Gracias. Does anyone else have anything to brief before the net call?"

"No? Muy bien." He began his net call.

"All stations this net, this is Marte 6. Acknowledge when called."

All units assigned to the Task Force gave Marte 6 a summary of activities. General Montalvo was particularly interested in the status report from the commander of the 1ˢᵗ CD Brigade again operating to the west of TQ. Once the last station had checked in, it was then time for Marte 6 to add his comments. The General began with his customary opening slogan:

"*Escúcheme y oígame...escúcheme y oígame. Soldado en la rutina es un muerto caminando.*"

Narrator's Translation Note: Hear me and listen to me. A soldier who establishes a routine or pattern is a dead man walking.

Over the air General Montalvo proceeded to site examples of why it was important for the leadership to not establish repeated patterns and routines by their soldiers in the field. This is something the FARC was good at recognizing and detecting. After detecting these patterns they would mount a surprise attack that generally ended in severe losses to the army. He stressed that it was the leadership who was responsible for ensuring that laziness and complacency did not creep into the operating procedures of units. The leadership at all levels would be held personally responsible for any ambushes or raids by the FARC that killed or wounded Colombian soldiers. He again cited the surprise attack of the 49ᵗʰ Jungle Battalion back in June and then requested that each station on the net comment and acknowledge. Once the units cycled through, he ended with the JTF-South slogan: *Dios concede la victoria a la constancia.*" This was followed by the customary "Marte 6 is QRT."

Narrator's Translation Note: God concedes victory to those that persevere or to perseverance. BG Montalvo's always delivered his favorite customary saying every chance he got. Sorry. Back to the scene...

General Montalvo looked up from his position in front of the HF radios and motioned Colonel Gutiérrez and me over to him. I sensed what was coming up next.

"Coronel Vallejo…Coronel Gutiérrez… rumor has it that the FARC is planning a major attack in the Southern Bloc area. General Dora personally informed me of this. This information allegedly came from a high level source reporting directly to the E2 in Bogotá. Undeniably, Tres Esquinas is the most strategically important base for Tirofijo and his hoodlums. Personally, I don't think the FARC has what it takes to mount a sizeable attack on Tres Esquinas. Our defenses are just too strong. Now Larandia is a different story. I have always been concerned about our heliport there. If I were a betting man I would say that all these guerrilla movements are associated with logistics preparations for possible harassments or attacks on Larandia. What's your assessment?"

I looked at COL Gutiérrez who in turn looked back at me. In situations like this, I always followed my personal advisor rules. Rule #1: Always make your counterpart look good in front of his boss. Rule #2: Your counterpart should always answer directly to his boss, not the advisor. So, I knew that in a situation like this I must take a supporting role to my intelligence counterpart. Advising was about making your counterpart look like a professional officer, not about making the advisor look good in front of the boss. COL Gutiérrez obviously read my mind and commented.

"Well, General, certainly anything is possible in relationship to these movements. Based on what we're observing, the FARC could be staging and preparing for attacks to our north. But, far too many indicators point more to activity focused on Tres Esquinas…Unless the FARC is using us as diversionary attack while they focus their main attack on Larandia."

"Coronel, spoken like a true intelligence officer…You've covered every angle just to be safe," General Montalvo laughed.

The fact of the matter was that Colonel Gutiérrez was not a true intelligence officer, but an engineer officer fulfilling the position of T2. The Colombian Army still placed senior non-intelligence branch officers in intelligence positions.

"Coronel Vallejo, what's *your* assessment?" *Note that Rule #3 applies here. If the boss asks for your assessment, you have no choice but to give it to him. Ideally, you and your counterpart's positions are one and the same.*

"Well, mi General, I agree with Colonel Gutiérrez. What we know is that the FARC is actively using their movement corridors in an unprecedented level. Second, most of the activity is around Tres Esquinas, not Larandia. So, Tres Esquinas plays an important role, probably more as main attack than a supporting one. Thirdly, the 49th Front has not been reported active and since Larandia lies within its area of operations, I think there's a lesser probability that Larandia will be targeted. Bottom line, based on what we know today, both base camps could be targeted simultaneously within the next few weeks or so. However, there are more indicators pointing to Tres Esquinas than Larandia. Still, I would certainly recommend that we move to put all bases on a heightened state of alert for the next few days or until we can obtain a clearer picture of what's going on."

General Montalvo looked at me, winked, and then smiled. He then poked his index finger into my chest.

"Okay, you've convinced me that we cannot assume anything at this time. I want all of you to use every available resource to attempt to get to the bottom of this activity. I will not stand for any sort of surprise attack to a key and vital base. Support from the American Embassy is critical at this time."

"Yes, sir and I'll be working that all day," I reaffirmed.

"Bien," said General Montalvo. "If you don't get any support, I will call the American Ambassador myself requesting that resources be redirected to support us." With this he headed to his office adjacent the COJIC.

"Do you think you can get us that reconnaissance platform tonight, Coronel?" asked COL Gutiérrez.

"I'll give it a shot. In the meantime let's get the collection manager to develop multiple target folders for the crew, if and when we get the imagery bird. I want to ensure that the crew gets a complete briefing of what we're up against. Second, I would recommend that you talk to the T3 and advise him to direct the navy component to begin more active night time patrolling of the rivers adjacent Tres Esquinas. The collection manager can assist in preparing reconnaissance zones for those patrol boats. Third, I would double the number of personnel at the monitoring site and have them do a full court press on intercepting guerrilla communications. Have every radio on and intercepting. Tell them to contact the monitoring stations in Puerto Leguízamo and Larandia to ensure that we are all working in concert. Can we get any kind of patrolling outside the perimeter wire?"

"General Montalvo feels that would be more of a liability than an asset. He prefers to have all personnel inside the wire on alert after curfew than to have patrols outside the perimeter during the evening. We can, however, send out daytime patrols, but we are currently operating at minimum level because the 1st BACNA has most of its personnel available for guard duty involved in its operation around Puerto Asís."

"Yes, I forgot about that. Okay...well, let's get working on the collection plan and target folders while I try contacting the Embassy again."

★ ★ ★

"I'm sorry, Rick, but that will take authorization from the Chief of Station himself," said the voice over the secure phone. "I don't deny that you have strong justification, but you know the Admiral at the JTF in Key West doesn't take too kindly to having his narcotics interdiction platforms diverted for use by an American advisor on the ground."

I knew that Mike Manley on the other end from the air reconnaissance office at the Embassy was a strong supporter of my effort in TQ. He was one reasonable voice in an ocean of bureaucracy and procedures not intended for a shooting war involving American soldiers on the ground. If anyone could convince Dirk Jones, the Chief of Station, it was Mike

"Okay, Mike. I'll leave it in your hands. Call me just as soon as you have an idea of when I can count on the platform, how many sorties I'll get, and for what period of time."

"Wilco, Rick. I got it. In the meantime keep your powder dry and hang in there," said Mike.

"Thanks. I'll try. Talk to you later."

I kept the telephone receiver in my hand as I thought about the phone call. Getting the boys at JTF-South in Key West to hand over their imagery platform to me would be a tall order. They were part of the bigger US counter-drug mission that provided support to the US/Colombian drug interdiction effort. But these were unusual circumstances. They would have to understand that force protection had to momentarily take priority over the drug war, particularly when American advisors lives might be at risk. Well, it will be interesting to see how this all pans out. The boys in the Tactical Analysis Team at the Embassy will be scrambling trying to make the necessary phone calls on behalf of the COS.

"Halcón, Halcón, this is TQ Tower."

"Roger, Tower this is Halcón." It had been five hours and I had not heard from the Embassy. This was the kind of foot dragging that often hurt my credibility with counterparts.

"Halcón, this is TQ Tower. We have an Embassy bird on final approach. Were you expecting visitors?"

"No, not that I know of."

"Well, they've been cleared for landing from the north and will taxi to the ramp adjacent the COJIC."

"Gracias, TQ Tower. I'll drive over to greet them."

Who in the world could this be? No one from the Embassy had contacted me. Well, I would find out soon enough.

Taking the pick-up truck over to the parking apron, I met the twin engine Beechcraft as its left engine was shutting down. I recognized the tail number of the aircraft as being CIA's. From the inside the crew popped the back door and it hinged down.

Exiting the plane first was no other than the dark haired Dirk Jones...his thick and bristling black mustache recognizable at a distance. He wore a khaki-colored bush shirt and black jeans. A black Colombian Army rucksack hung over his left shoulder. Behind him, wearing an Army field cap and dressed in faded camouflaged fatigues was the tall, thin, and lanky Colonel Kent Bernardo, the USMILGP Commander. He also carried a black rucksack. Spotting me, he could not contain the ever radiant smile that showed his front teeth. We all shook hands and walked together toward the COJIC.

"Mr. Jones...Kent...to what do I owe the pleasure of your fine company this afternoon?" I asked, half jokingly.

"We came to get to the bottom of this force protection request that you put in this morning. If the threat looks as grim as you described to Mike, we need you, Stan, and SFC Tirado to pack your things because you're flying back with us to Bogotá," answered Dirk seriously.

"You're kidding, right?" I wished this was just a bad joke.

"No, unfortunately I'm serious as a heart attack. The ambassador is under strict orders to not let any advisors wind up on the losing end of a surprise attack by the FARC. Congress would hammer her if any advisors were to die in combat. It would jeopardize our successes in Plan Colombia, thus far."

"Oh, I see…just like El Salvador during the advisory years. Keep our efforts quiet and don't get shot."

"You know the politics of these wars as well as I do," said Kent, half grinning.

"I understand, gentlemen, I really do. But what kind of signal does this send our Colombian hosts? When the situation gets a might bit heated, the American advisors are sent packing home. How are we to build trust among our counterparts? I don't believe it ever got this bad in El Salvador."

"Well, you know…different times…different places…different administrations…" added Dirk. I'm sorry, but those are the Ambassador's orders."

By this time we had entered the COJIC. I led them over to the planning map that still had all the graphics from this morning's meeting. Colonel Gutiérrez and Major Cano were standing in front of the map talking to one of their analysts. They looked up surprised.

"Coronel…Mayor, you know Mr. Jones and Colonel Bernardo, don't you?" I said in Spanish.

"Oh, yes, of course. We met a few months ago during another of their visits to Tres Esquinas," COL Gutiérrez said in Spanish while shaking their hands.

"Do you mind if Major Cano gives them a complete threat briefing of what we discussed this morning? In the meantime can we get an orderly to inform General Montalvo's office that he has guests here?"

"No problem, Coronel," he answered as he called for an orderly.

Major Cano covered all the details with the two visitors. He pointed to and described all the active corridors and movements associated with the intelligence reports. He also went into detail about the information obtained from the monitoring station. It was a thorough and very professional presentation.

Dirk and Kent conferred in hush tones back and forth as they pointed to different landmarks on the map before them. They both had sufficient time in Colombia to assess the severity of this threat. Finally, Dirk spoke.

"I will contact Mike at the Embassy and have him chop you a surveillance bird for your use tonight. You direct where you want it to fly. It's one of our better FLIRs, so that you can get the kind of resolution that you need for something like this. You'll have it for seven nights, starting tonight. If you need more after that, I'll grant you an extension, but only if it is absolutely necessary."

"Thanks, Mr. Jones, that's great of you to support the effort like this. How about the business of leaving TQ tonight?"

"Kent and I discussed the matter and we think that we will stay overnight with you to better assess the situation for ourselves. After that we'll make a final decision. As for us, don't make any special arrangements. We brought our own MRE's. We'll just bag out on the floor here in the COJIC."

I was envious. I would give anything to have a few MREs to eat in my room. They were certainly more appetizing that the food from the Officer's Club or my cheese spread. I answered appropriately, though.

"Okay, that's great. And I see General Montalvo entering through the door."

General Montalvo broke out in a big smile upon seeing the two American visitors.

"Dirk...Kent...cómo están, amigos?"

"Muy bien," answered Dirk as he vigorously shook hands with the JTF-South Commander.

"So, what brings you to Tres Esquinas?" asked General Montalvo.

"We got the request for aerial imagery support from Rick and I just wanted to see for myself the severity of the threat to Tres

Esquinas," said Dirk. I've agreed to give you priority on the use of our imagery platform."

"Fantástico," said General Montalvo with delight as he put his arm around Dirk. "We graciously accept the support."

"We're also requesting to stay overnight to better appraise the situation and brief the Ambassador. If that's okay, I'll alert John my pilot that he will be remaining overnight too. He'll probably opt to sleep onboard his plane.

"Dirk, mi casa es su casa. Of course you can stay. In fact I'll expect you over to my quarters for some snacks and some Johnny Walker Black Label later this evening…say around 2045 hours after tonight's programa."

"Con mucho gusto, mi General. We'll be there. Gracias," answered Dirk.

"Well, let me get back to my office. I have a lot of work piling up. Good to see you both."

"Likewise, General. Thank you."

General Montalvo departed and returned to his office. Dirk then turned to me.

"Get me a phone so I can call Mike and get the platform lined up for you."

I did so and 15 minutes later we had obtained all the information we needed. The surveillance bird would land at approximately 2200 hours tonight. It would provide four hours of coverage time. Weather permitting, it would then return the following six consecutive nights after that for a total of seven missions. The following nights would be busy for me. But I was up to the challenge.

Dirk and Kent flew back the next morning. I watched their plane until it was out of sight.

★ ★ ★

"Rick, you're getting too old for this," I told myself as I quietly waited adjacent the TQ runway. It was a few minutes before 2200 hours. Overhead, the dark Colombian sky glowed with the light of a thousand twinkling stars, more than I ever knew existed.

I got the call from the TQ tower that the bird was inbound. Soon, the quiet and solitude were interrupted by the distant drone of a single engine aircraft. Staring down the runway, the dark form of the surveillance bird appeared, landing in total blackout conditions. It taxied over to the ramp next to where I stood. The aircraft was an impressive sight with all its sensors, pods, and antennas hanging underneath the aircraft's tail. It was much larger in real life than what I could appreciate from photographs. The large cabin of this upscale Cessna 208 Grand Caravan could hold a good size crew and all its surveillance gear. I slowly walked over to the aircraft as it shut down its large single engine. The main hatch door opened and as it hinged down, the lights from within the aircraft lit up the runway area. I waited at the foot of the hinged door waiting for the crew to disembark.

Within a few minutes, the crew slowly began their descent down the steps. What surprised me was that they were all dressed in casual civilian attire. One by one they greeted me and in turn I shook hands with the four crew members. Then the fifth member, a Colombian NCO, walked down the steps. Unlike the others he was in Colombian camouflaged army fatigues.

"Welcome to Tres Esquinas, gentlemen," I said to the crew.

"Thanks. This is the first time that we have actually landed here," said the younger looking man. He was a tall and lean black gentleman that was nicely attired in dress slacks and a colorful black and gold floral shirt. The way he was dressed, he could have come out of an evening social event anywhere in the US. It turned out that he was the pilot of the aircraft.

"Can you arrange for us to take on some fuel before we go on your support mission?"

"I've already notified the flight operations folks. A refueling technician should be here shortly," I said, having gotten a heads up from the TQ tower prior to their landing.

"I'll leave Sergeant Barrientos, our Colombian intelligence counterpart, and my co-pilot, Josh Anderson, with the aircraft to supervise the refuel operation."

"Fine…Why don't the rest of you accompany me to the COJIC where I'll provide you with the mission profile and target folders."

"Great," said the pilot. By the way, I'm John Jacobs. This is my FLIR systems operator, Derek Scruggs, and my SIGINT operator, Dave Cummings."

"Nice to meet you, gentlemen. I'm Colonel Rick Vallejo, the senior US military advisor in TQ."

Together we walked across the gravel and mud parking apron toward the COJIC. I engaged them with questions about the flying weather and the visibility that evening. As we walked by the parked AC-47, I waved at the security guard guarding the aircraft that evening.

"Talk about a high value target," Dave Cummings said.

"No lie," Josh said in agreement.

Inside the COJIC, I walked the crew over to a large conference table where I had the target folders already laid out for them. Lieutenant Díaz, the imagery chief, was waiting for us with the folders.

"Gentlemen, this is Lieutenant Ángel Díaz, our chief of the imagery section. He prepared your target folders."

The crew nodded their heads at LT Díaz.

For the next 30 minutes, LT Díaz and I went over four target areas that we wanted covered. Each of these areas corresponded to areas associated with the most recent FARC activity. Some were known FARC base camps, others were suspected assembly areas and important transit sites. These target folders represented our best collective guess on areas that might reveal some of the FARC's intentions. It was based on a thorough IPB, intelligence preparation of the battlefield, of the area of operations. The first to speak was the pilot, John Jacobs.

"Colonel, this is really great stuff. This is the first time we've received a mission briefing like this. Generally, we are handed a list of coordinates on a map and told to fly over the area with no knowledge of what we're looking for or why it's important. This type of flight briefing makes a big difference in our ability to support you. I wish we could make it the standard for mission briefings in Colombia."

"Thank you for that comment, gentlemen, but I wouldn't have it any other way. I'm glad it serves a useful purpose for you also."

"It certainly does," John said. "Well, we'll be on our way. If we see anything of value we'll relay the info through our radio operator who will call you via landline from the Joint Operations Center in Bogota. Otherwise, we'll land after completion of our mission and give you a VHS video copy of the take from the FLIR mission for further exploitation by your imagery personnel."

"That will be great. Have a safe flight. I'll be waiting for you on the ramp upon mission completion."

I escorted the crew back to the parking apron where by now the aircraft was fully fueled and ready.

"We'll fly three hours for you and save the last hour for landing back here and returning to Bogota later tonight."

"I looked at my watch. So I'll see you guys back here at say…0200 hours?"

"Yes, that's about right. We'll see you then. Try to take a power nap in between," laughed John. "I know this makes for a long day."

"That's okay. I have plenty to do in the meantime."

With that we shook hands, parted, and I waited from the parking apron as the dark form sped down the runway and lifted heading south. I remained watching as the aircraft's anti-collision and position lights, now turned on, became but one more small and insignificant blinking light in the vastness of the star filled sky.

> *All we are saying...is give peace a chance...All we are saying...is give peace a chance...*
>
> *John Lennon and the Plastic Ono Band*

★ ★ ★

CHAPTER FOURTEEN

THE FARC HAS ITS DAY…AND WE GET OURS

I am the god of hell fire…and I bring you…Fire…
I'll take you to burn. Fire…I'll take you to learn…
I'll see you burn…

"Fire"
as recorded by Arthur Brown

HEADQUARTERS, JOINT TASK FORCE-SOUTH
TRES ESQUINAS, CAQUETA DEPARTMENT, COLOMBIA
0030 HOURS, 11 SEPTEMBER 2001

Over and over again for six consecutive nights the surveillance bird flew. But we still had nothing to show for our efforts. It's as if the jungle had swallowed up the FARC. To complicate matters, no further HUMINT field reports came in and the monitoring station stopped intercepting VHF or UHF traffic. Only the HF bands continued to provide the typical daily passing of four digit number code groups between the FARC front headquarters.

I was ragged from staying up to receive the nightly flights. But I felt that it was my job to ensure that the Embassy missions were supported. Too much was at stake here, especially for the security of the base. Finally, on the seventh and last night the FLIR bird got an important hit. This time they radioed it in to the COJIC. I had coordinated with the Embassy to allow the crew to radio their spot reports directly to the TQ TOC, Tactical Operations Center, in the command bunker, thereby bypassing Bogotá.

I was in the TOC when the call came in at 0035 hours.

"Halcón this is Spirit...We got numerous hot spots just south of...(static)...at grid coordinates...(static). We can make out individuals...definitely combatants in a bivouac site...Over."

The communications link was poor. They would have to resend.

"Spirit this is Halcón. Say again location...Over."

"Roger, I say again location...ten clicks southeast of Currillo at grid coordinates Victor Foxtrot 130410...Over."

"Roger, good copy...Ten clicks southeast of Curillo at grid coordinates Victor Foxtrot 130410. What else can you tell me about the target?...Over."

Narrator's Note: Curillo was a small town about 50 miles northwest of TQ.

"We have approximately 100 personnel setting up what appears to be an overnight camp. Some are already underneath ponchos and blankets. There are a lot of personnel down there... more than we usually see in one location on our missions... Over."

"Roger. Can you stay on target while we get a decision from our hosts?...Over."

"Roger. We have enough fuel to stay on target for another 45 minutes...Over."

"Roger...Out."

I would have to get a decision from the acting commander of TQ because General Montalvo was in Bogotá again for a meeting with the commander of the Colombian Army. He would not be back until tomorrow. The TOC officer on duty got in touch with Colonel Sordo, the Colombian Air Force officer who that evening happened to be the senior officer in charge at TQ. I groaned. Of all people to have to deal with. In about fifteen minutes COL Sordo appeared in the TOC. I did not relish this moment.

"This better be good, Coronel," he said in his usually unpleasing manner.

"It appears to be a good target...operating in the 49th Front's area of operations." I sidestepped his usual 'I hate you attitude' and went on to explain the target sighted by the FLIR.

"How do we know they're not friendly troops?" asked COL Sordo.

"You'll have to confirm with the nearest parent unit. Isn't that in the 12th Brigade's zone?" I asked in return.

"Yes it is."

"Well, can you call them and confirm if they have any units operating in that zone?"

COL Sordo didn't answer. He picked up the telephone directory and began dialing numbers from the TOC land line switch.

After making a series of calls to various elements of the 12th Brigade, the final word was in. The 12th Brigade had no personnel at that location this evening.

"Looks like you have a good target." I stated enthusiastically.

"That decision will be made by a Colombian pilot and not an American advisor, Coronel."

"Right," I answered, a little peeved. "It's the pilot's call."

Precious minutes passed. COL Sordo then called the house where the Fantasma crew bunked out and talked to the pilot. I sent one of the COJIC duty personnel with my pick-up truck over to the crew's house to expedite things. A scant fifteen minutes and after a quick briefing the crew had the AC-47 cranking and on its way to the target. There was no time to send one of our intercept operators with them.

I then called the crew of the FLIR bird to advise them of the host nation response. They would pull away from their target in ten minutes to allow the AC-47 freedom to fly and engage, if need be.

Fifteen minutes later the pilot of the AC-47 radioed in.

"*Urano 5...Urano 5... Satanás 13...*I am vicinity of the grid coordinates near Curillo. I have a large heat signature on my FLIR, but I can't make out the target... Over."

"Satanás this is Urano. Wait…Out," answered COL Sordo.

I should have guessed. The vintage FLIR on board this particular model AC-47 did not have the resolution of the Embassy FLIR bird. The pilot would not be able to confirm the target based on this.

Colonel Sordo looked at me and shook his head. I decided to speak.

"Based on what the crew of the Embassy FLIR reported, that large heat signature is a legitimate target," I said.

"Coronel Vallejo, I can't give that pilot the go ahead to engage that target unless he can personally confirm what's on the ground. For all he knows it could be a bunch of campesinos out partying this evening."

"But the Embassy FLIR confirmed that they were armed and definitely combatants. They reported seeing approximately 100 of them."

"I'm sorry, but it's my ass, not yours," COL Sordo was clearly agitated.

Narrator's Note: I don't remember exactly what he said, but this comes close to his meaning. I think you get the drift of the mood he was in.

COL Sordo continued. "We get beat up enough by your government's human rights officials and I don't want to be charged with a war crime. You don't expect that pilot to pull the trigger of those .50 caliber machineguns simply based on the word of an American Embassy surveillance aircraft operator do you? Where will you or he be during a human rights investigation if we open fire and kill innocent civilians? I'm calling the crew back in."

"I understand, Coronel," I answered disappointed. It's your call, not ours."

COL Sordo radioed the crew and they returned back to TQ.

Ten minutes after the AC-47 landed, the Embassy FLIR also landed. The FLIR system's operator handed me a VHS tape of the target while the engine remained running.

"I've never seen so many FARC in one area," he told me. "In fact that's the most I've seen since I've been flying here. I hope you were able to do something with our information."

I just looked at him and shook my head. He looked back at me and didn't say a word. They immediately taxied and took off back to Bogotá as I silently walked back to the COJIC.

I popped the tape into the VCR player. The proof was undeniable. The Embassy air crew had it right. No question about it. It was FARC. Weapons were clearly visible and the resolution was so precise, you could make out the small details of their uniforms. The AC-47 would have had a field day that evening. But it was not meant to be. Not that night.

Would things have been different if General Montalvo had been on duty that night? It's hard to tell. In this kind of war the danger of collateral damage is always great. I learned a lesson, though, that I'm still coming to grips with. Based on a technical intelligence product like the one obtained by the Embassy FLIR bird, when does one have 100% assurance that the target spotted by the optics is the enemy? You don't. But you can certainly eliminate the risks by doing a little cross checking as we did by contacting the friendly units. It really doesn't matter. This night the FARC got off easy.

On the other hand we did confirm one thing. The FARC was definitely out in force and active. The sighting around Curillo represented a good find and substantiated all the HUMINT reports we were receiving about large FARC movements. The 49th Front had personnel 50 miles from TQ. Something was definitely up. The primary intelligence question still left unanswered was, "Where and when would the FARC attack?"

For one day this question lost its importance. Because later that morning a bigger surprise attack than any of us could ever imagine did hit. But it wasn't in TQ...or anywhere in Colombia for that matter. It was in the USA...

Where were you on 11 September 2001? Will you ever forget? Regardless of your political, ethnic, or cultural outlook you must have felt something. Whether it was shock, anger, sadness, fear, or celebration, if you were anti-American... you must still remember that day. If you are an American, you'll probably remember walking around in a daze...at a loss for words.

Yogi Berra is often quoted as having said, 'It was Déjà Vu all over again.' That was my case for I had felt this same feeling in 1963 when President John F. Kennedy was assassinated. I was only 12, but I still remember that day. In a 7th grade classroom the loudspeaker came on in the middle of a broadcast. We students stared at each other trying to figure out what was going on. Soon we learned. I still remember the shock on the face of my 7th grade teacher, Mrs. Lowry, as she brought her hands to her face when the news hit her.

However, 9/11 hit me harder. I won't forget it either because not only was I in the same state of shock as you, but remember, I was deep in the jungles of Colombia. How will I ever forget where I was on that day?

You know what's really ironic? On that day and for the first time while working in Tres Esquinas, I felt very safe. I don't believe anyone living in the continental United States on that day felt safe. But I felt very safe to be in Tres Esquinas. I think it's because I was so far from New York City and Washington D.C. Physical separation from tragedy may have a cushioning or shock absorbing effect. It certainly did for me.

Next in line to discussing the emotions about 9/11 with someone else comes the discussion on how you learned about the tragedy. Did you hear about it from a neighbor...a friend...a relative? Did you happen to see the events unfolding live on TV?

I remember like it was yesterday. As Stan and I finished the morning update, he got a call on his satellite phone. His face looked pale.

"That was the Embassy. We have to find the nearest television."

"Why what's up?"

"An airplane crashed into the World Trade Center in New York."

"Wow, what a terrible accident. Was it a small Cessna or something like that?"

"They didn't say. Come on let's go to the white house and see what it's all about."

Our thoughts and feelings were suspended as we, like the rest of the world, viewed the unfolding events on the TV in his quarters. The rest, of course, is history.

> *You fought hard and you saved and learned... but all of it's going to burn. And your mind, your tiny mind...you know you've really been so blind...Now it's your time burn your mind. You're falling far too far behind. Oh no, oh no, oh no, you gonna burn. Fire to destroy all you've done. Fire to end all you've become. I'll feel you burn!*
>
> *Arthur Brown*

★ ★ ★

CHAPTER FIFTEEN

★ ★ ★

RIVERINE CONVOY

War, huh, yeah...What is it good for...Absolutely nothing...Uh-huh...War, huh, yeah...What is it good for...Absolutely nothing...Say it again, y'all...War, huh, good God...What is it good for... Absolutely nothing...Listen to me.

"War"
as recorded by Edwin Starr

HEADQUARTERS, JOINT TASK FORCE-SOUTH,
TRES ESQUINAS, CAQUETA DEPARTMENT, COLOMBIA
0530 HOURS, 12 SEPTEMBER 2001

The riverine convoy looked like something out of the 1979 movie, *Mad Max*. It consisted of elements from *Puesto Fluvial Avanzado 93*, Advanced Riverine Post 93 of the *Batallón de Asalto de I.M. No. 90*, 90th Riverine Marine Infantry Assault Battalion. At the center of this unusual configuration were two large barges, called *Bongos* by the Colombians. These would carry 483 tons of gravel and cement bags back from the small river port of Solita, just up river and west of TQ. Each barge would be pushed, not towed, by a river tugboat. The flat blue painted tugboats, like the barges, were sandbagged for protection. The tugboat, *Castro*, mounted two 7.62mm M60 machineguns, while the other one, *Marandúa,* had only one. Each barge had firing positions for the two convoy security platoons of Colombian Marine and Army infantrymen.

The convoy was armed to the teeth. All along the flanks and front, six 22 foot Zodiac-type, rigid hulled inflatable, twin 175 horsepower *Piraña* or Piranha patrol boats swiftly moved around the convoy. Each mounted one .50 caliber MG, four side mounted 7.62mm M60 MGs, and a 40 mm MK-19 grenade launcher.

Between the two tugboats and barges was a 32 foot, fiberglass hull, PBR MK-II riverine patrol boat carrying twin .50 caliber MGs, a single pedestal .50 cal MG, two side mounted M60 MGs, and a MK-19 grenade launcher. A second PBR MK-II with the same weapons' configuration provided rear security for the convoy. Bottom line, the extreme threat from the FARC necessitated that any convoys traversing TQ's waterways should be well armed. They took their unit motto, "Victory from the Rivers," quite seriously.

Well before dawn, this unusual looking flotilla floated south down the Río Orteguaza and then turned west up the Río Caquetá, passing the neighboring town of Solano along the way. Circling overhead, a single engine Embraer T-27 Tucano aircraft provided early warning and close air support, if needed. It would fly over the convoy until reaching the final destination of Solita. A second Tucano was on standby strip alert at TQ. The cement bags were transported to Solita because unlike TQ, its roadways linked it with other towns in Caquetá Department. This roadway allowed gravel and cement laden trucks to drive to the port. Once loaded, the barges would turn around and head back to TQ. The gravel and cement were being used to extend the concrete runway at TQ to 10,000 feet.

Colombian Marine Infantry Lieutenant Colonel José Suárez, the short and muscular convoy commander onboard the lead tugboat Marandúa, carefully scanned the river from side to side… scrutinizing every detail…as he searched for any possible hint of a FARC ambush. However, the veteran riverine Marine knew that there was less probability that the trip upriver would end up with their convoy being hit. On the return trip…well, that was a different story. Moving downstream, the barges would be a more formidable target because they would be weighed down by the heavy cement bags and gravel almost to the point of taking in water. The cement bags were the precious cargo and everything humanly possible would be done to keep that cargo from going overboard, if the FARC made any attempts to intercept them. The FARC would like nothing more than to sink a barge or two, thereby blocking the river and further delaying any future trips to deliver cement for the runway extension at TQ.

By late morning, the slow moving convoy reported arriving at the sleepy river port town of Solita. Many heavily laden trucks had already dropped off their cargo. The loading of the barges began immediately. As soon as this was completed, the convoy would then head back to TQ. It would be several days, however, before the task of loading the 483 tons of gravel and cement bags would be completed.

"They're headed back."

The call was relayed over the command bunker's radio in the early morning hours. The heavily laden riverine convoy was returning to TQ. The adventure would soon begin.

LTC Suárez' dark brown eyes scanned back and forth between the dense jungle vegetation and the shoreline. The light falling rain made his job more difficult because it provided a constantly shifting and distracting panorama. However, many years of experience operating on Colombia's jungle rivers gave him an edge on knowing what to look for. If you were to ask him what he was looking for, he would simply say, "Anything different...

anything out of place...I let the jungle speak to me." LTC Suárez was confident that his years of training and experience navigating along Colombia's inner waterways would not let him down.

This was his third time on convoy duty. When he got the call that he was going on another one of these highly despised missions, he asked to review the duty roster. How could he be back on another one of these when he had just completed a similar mission a scant three weeks ago? No one liked being a sitting duck. And this very much described the nature of convoy duty. The barges were so overloaded with the heavy cement bags that they could barely maneuver in the river. The captains that pushed the barges along in their tug boats would tell you that it is challenging to navigate the river while pushing a multi-ton cargo like this. Just up ahead the river narrowed. The sand bars were everywhere. Then there was the ever present threat from the FARC...

The tall, thin, and sickly-looking guerrilla, Comandante *Manco,* and his platoon from the FARC's 49th Front occupied their ambush position on the north bank of the Río Caquetá three days ago. He was rain soaked, cold, and tired of waiting. They were low on provisions and this morning he ate his last plastic sandwich bag of *arroz, plátanos*, and *chicharrón.*

Narrator's Note: Rice, plantains, and pork rind...Were you expecting maybe caviar, truffles, and Cabernet?...hahaha...Back to the story...

Earlier that morning he received a radio call from *Lagarto,* his jefe from the 49th Front, that the convoy had departed Solita at first light. He carefully gazed upriver, but there was still nothing in sight. The overcast day reflected his mood, but everyone in his group was ready. They just wanted to get this mission completed so that they could get back to some hot food and shelter. His jungle base camp along the Río Solita seemed like the Taj Majal compared to the water-filled trench he had been standing in.

On his right and left were Lázaro and María with their Russian-made RPG-7 rocket propelled grenade launchers. He had placed them near him because the ambush would commence with their firing. With these, Manco hoped to destroy the bridges of the two tugboats pushing the barges. Without the tugs, the barges could not maneuver and they would run aground.

On the right and left flanks of his trench, Manco had positioned one US made Browning .50 caliber machinegun and four 7.62mm M60 machineguns. The .50 cal would engage the Colombian Marine infantry and soldiers on board the barges. The four M60's would attempt to engage the Marine infantrymen and sailors on board the Piranhas. He hoped the PBRs would not have time to join the fight. The success of this operation depended on the element of surprise to quickly take out the bridges on the tugboats.

About fifty meters to his rear were two IRA-made propane gas tank mortar launchers. Although highly inaccurate, a well-placed hit from one of these could disrupt the entire convoy. They would launch their two rounds as soon as the RPG's commenced firing.

The one unknown was the disposition of the Piranhas. Highly maneuverable and heavily armed, these boats could not be accurately targeted because of their speed. Plus, the gunners onboard were highly trained and deadly in laying down suppressing fire. Manco knew first hand how accurate this fire was. He lost his left hand as a result of a direct hit from a .50 caliber machinegun round fired from one of these…hence his alias Manco. His left stump was a reminder of the deadliness of the firepower.

Suddenly, the early morning stillness and the soft sound of falling rain were shattered by the noise of two speeding boats. Two Colombian Navy Piranhas headed toward his position. They were in the lead providing forward security to the tugs and barges. The main convoy would be coming into view shortly. Manco anxiously watched the Piranhas speed by him and circle back toward the main convoy. This action would probably repeat itself one more time before the tugs and barges moved into the ambush kill zone. Overhead, he heard the drone of the dreaded Tucano close air support aircraft. Manco and his platoon would have to act quickly before the Tucano had time to join the fight. He did not want to feel the effect of those twin .50 caliber machineguns or the four 250 pound bombs it was probably carrying. This mission would not be easy. It depended on surprise and precise timing. Any mistakes could prove costly or deadly.

LTC Suárez temporarily looked away from the river bank as he leaned back against the railing and sipped his mug of hot coffee outside the bridge of the tugboat Marandúa. The steady rain was now falling harder and his olive drab poncho provided only partial protection from the elements. A Kevlar helmet kept his head dry.

His tight jaw muscles momentarily relaxed and a little color returned to his tanned and weather beaten face. "At least coffee is something military men can live on when they have very little time for eating," he told himself. A small coffee pot, a ceramic mug, and a bag of Sello Rojo coffee were part of the essentials in his duffel bag.

He glanced at his watch. It was only 0630. The morning was still gray and overcast and the sun had not yet broken through the clouds. The rain would probably be with them for their entire trip. The good news was that he was headed back to Tres Esquinas and, a much needed rest after this convoy mission. In the times that he had pulled convoy duty he had never been attacked. He hoped that he could maintain his perfect record. His thoughts were interrupted by the voice of his experienced tug captain, Jacobo Aponte.

"Coronel, the going is very slow this morning. My barge is taking in water because of the extra weight from those additional bags of cement you asked me to load. If we don't slow down, the foundering could become a bigger problem."

"I know, Jacobo, but we had to do it. As you know we lost a lot of time this month because the water level has been so low. General Montalvo directed me to max out our carrying capacity."

"Well, we have done that and are now paying the price. I hope we successfully negotiate the turn around the sandbar that's on our starboard side right now. If we don't, we could be held up here for awhile. I don't relish the thought of being a sitting duck for the FARC."

"Okay, I'll alert the Piranhas and we will decrease speed to allow us to..." He never finished the sentence. The explosion from the RPG round blew him out of the bridge and onto the deck below. Lying in a pool of blood, broken glass, splintered wood, and twisted metal, the barely conscious Marine infantryman passed out just after he heard the second explosion from a FARC gas cylinder mortar round exploding in the middle of the river.

Colombian Army Captain David Gaitán, a second generation soldier commissioned through the Colombian Military Cadet School, and a seasoned ten year veteran of the war, was the company commander in charge of convoy security. As soon as the bridge of the tugboat Marandúa exploded, he knew he was in a FARC ambush. He was in the barge directly in front of the tugboat that was now on fire and moving without its pilot along the river. In a few minutes the barge would run aground on the north bank of the Río Caquetá. From his sandbagged position at the rear of the barge, he attempted to assess the situation, but was precluded doing so by the intense heavy machinegun fire raking his barge and the obscuring thick smoke from the tug. He immediately got on the radio and called his boss, LTC Suárez, but received no answer. His call to Calamar 6 was answered instead by Calamar 15, Colombian Marine Infantry Captain Jairo Quintero, Piranha Combat Element Commander.

"Astuto 11 this is Calamar 15. We are in contact and receiving enemy machinegun and small arms fire from the high ground on the northern bank...Over."

"Calamar 15 this is Astuto 11. Our heads are down at this moment and we are unable to return fire. Can you increase your fire on the objective?...Over."

"Astuto this is Calamar...Wilco."

Although the rapid movement looked seemingly confused and agitated, the six Piranhas immediately executed their ambush reaction drill and blasted away at the river bank with every available automatic weapon firing at full cyclic rate. The black boats powered at full speed while J-turning and dodging to avoid the relentless FARC enemy fire. They circled the tugs and barges...bows flying out of the water...splashing, spraying, and crossing their own wakes in controlled chaos.

The overpowering pungent smell of expended ammunition was slowly beginning to cover and spread over this watery hell as it mixed with the choking heavy black smoke from the burning tugboat, Marandúa.

In the meantime the PBR on rear convoy security was too far back in the extended convoy to get into the fight and the crew of the center PBR had its hands full attempting to pull out of the convoy to avoid hitting the Marandúa.

Perceiving a lull in the incoming fire, CPT Gaitán was finally able to observe that the more mobile Piranhas appeared to be concentrating on one particular point along the northern bank.

He directed one of his men to fire a smoke grenade round from his 40mm M79 grenade launcher at this spot. This would mark the location for not only the 1st platoon that was with him on the barge, but also for the Tucano aircraft flying overhead. When they had fired the smoke round, he called the Tucano on the radio to establish contact with the crew.

"Matador 2 this is Astuto 11. I've placed smoke on the target. Can you identify?...Over." Onboard the Tucano, Captain Gabriel Jiménez answered the call.

"Astuto 11 this is Matador 2. Roger, visibility is low, but I see your purple smoke...Looks like an enemy trench line with about twenty-five combatants. I'll make a first pass with 250 lb. bombs... Over."

"Roger...Astuto standing-by...Out"

An RPG round whizzed past the bridge of Castro, the second tugboat. In the bridge, tug captain Diego Miranda immediately gunned his engine in reverse in an effort to get out of the ambush kill zone. He also needed to avoid colliding with the barge and burning tugboat to his front The thick black smoke from the burning Marandúa, obscured his vision and fortunately for him, probably that of the enemy gunners as another RPG round went flying past his window. He managed to stop the forward progress and his tugboat began to slowly move in reverse. Unfortunately, this would preclude the 2d infantry platoon from getting into the fight, but at this point the battle was being waged primarily by the Piranhas. The best he could do was to save his tugboat and its precious cargo.

When his barge ran aground on the north bank, CPT Gaitán and his men quickly dismounted, apparently unobserved by the FARC guerrillas. He looked overhead and spotted the Tucano coming out of the east and making its first run. It dropped two bombs which hit wide of the target. This wouldn't cut it, he surmised. He got back on the radio.

"Matador this is Astuto…your bombs landed wide and off target. The trench line was not hit. Recommend you make a second pass with machineguns…*Déles plomo a los pelados, hombre…déles plomo*…give the enemy lead, man…Over."

"*Puta*…this is Matador…Wilco…Out."

As the Tucano made its second pass, CPT Gaitán kept his men in position. There was no sense endangering them further with potential fratricide from the Tucano.

However, the second pass was more effective as CPT Gaitán radioed the crew back.

"Matador…Berraco…Buenísimo. Your fire got right down into that trench line. Give me another one like that as we start to advance toward the objective…Over."

"Wilco…rolling hot…Matador…Out"

Slowly, CPT Gaitán and the platoon maneuvered forward through very dense jungle vegetation along the river bank. The covered and concealed route prevented the FARC guerrillas from observing his movement on their right flank. Since the Piranhas were still pounding the FARC position, he was able to quickly move up from the shoreline and could now see the guerrillas themselves. He again radioed the convoy commander, but got no answer. In the intense heat of battle, it still had not dawned on him that LTC Suárez was lying dead onboard the Marandúa. The Piranha element commander came back up on the net.

"Astuto 11 this is Calamar 15. We are receiving less fire. We see you on the river bank. Can you assess the situation on the objective…over?"

"Calamar this is Astuto…I can see a handful of FARC to my front firing from a trench. I would estimate there are about twenty of them there. If you can lay down some more fire, I will move and take the objective with the 1st Platoon…Over."

"Astuto, Calamar…Wilco…Out."

The Piranhas, now joined by the two PBRs, concentrated their fire on the objective while CPT Gaitán and his men slowly maneuvered forward. They would advance a few steps and then hit the ground. Using their fire and movement technique, they got to within 50 meters of the main trench. They waited for the Tucano that was now making its third and probably final run since it would soon run short of fuel. It initiated its run coming out of the west with twin .50 cal MG's blazing. As it pulled up from its run, a stream of thick black smoke poured out of the engine compartment.

"Astuto…Matador…we've been hit! Oil pressure is dropping! We will try to get back to Tres Esquinas. I'll radio Matador 1 to relieve us. Good luck on the objective…over."

"Roger, thanks for your support. Good luck getting back. Astuto…Out."

CPT Gaitán and his platoon began placing fire on the FARC position before the guerrillas realized they had been outflanked. They were so surprised to see the Colombian infantrymen that they ran out of their trench in fear, despite the intensive fire from the Piranhas. The 1st platoon fired and killed at least five guerrillas from the first two groups exiting the trench, while the Piranhas mowed down another eight.

By the time CPT Gaitán and his men reached their objective, he counted seventeen dead FARC guerrillas in and out of their fighting positions. Barely alive and clutching an AK-47 assault rifle, one wounded guerrilla who was missing a hand lay on the wet and muddy ground. Rain drops fell and mixed with the blood on his face. CPT Gaitán kicked the weapon out of the guerrilla's hand. The fame of the FARC commander was well-known to him.

"Manco," he said to the guerrilla in Spanish. "You fought one battle too many. Obviously, the situation got a little bit out of hand," he said while laughing at his own joke.

"*Vete al carajo, pelado...*" the guerrilla managed to say, while coughing and spitting blood. These were his last words as he succumbed to his mortal wounds.

"Better you in Hell than me," CPT Gaitán said to the already dead guerrilla.

He ordered his men to secure the objective and to bring up some additional ammo from the grounded barge. He knew that once they had secured and consolidated the area, his next mission would be to see how to best secure the barge with the gravel and cement bags. Hopefully, there were no more FARC in the area.

By now the fate of LTC Suárez was known. Captain Gaitán was now in charge of the convoy. He met with the two security platoon leaders to assess overall damage and to devise a plan for their new mission. All six Piranhas had been hit by machinegun fire, but only two received damage serious enough to affect their operational capability. Basically, the security platoon would divide forces between the one remaining operational tug and barge and the one barge that had run aground. Two of the more damaged Piranhas, a PBR, and one operational Piranha would stay with the 2d Platoon to secure the grounded barge and its cargo. The three less damaged Piranhas, the other PBR, the tug-boat Castro, and its barge would continue on to Tres Esquinas. The wounded...14 Marines...and the dead...5 Marines onboard the Piranhas were placed on the tugboat Castro. The bodies of LTC Suárez and tug captain Jacobo Aponte would take the slow ride back to Tres Esquinas on their tugboat funeral hearse.

Overhead, the drone of an aircraft signaled that the relief Tucano from TQ was now on station and ready to provide air support. As he looked back from the bridge of the Castro at the still burning and now sinking tugboat Marandúa, Captain Gaitán shook his head in disbelief. "What a wasteful war," he said to himself..."What a wasteful war."

War, it ain't nothing but a heartbreaker...War, friend only to the undertaker...Ooooh, war... It's an enemy to all mankind...the point of war blows my mind...War has caused unrest within the younger generation...induction then destruction...who wants to die...ahhhh, war-huh...good God y'all...what is it good for... absolutely nothing.

Edwin Starr

CHAPTER SIXTEEN

STAN...SOCCER...AND SUSANA

If I fell in love with you...would you promise to be true...and help me understand...'Cause I've been in love before...and I know that love is more...than just holding hands...

"If I Fell"
as recorded by the Beatles

HEADQUARTERS, JOINT TASK FORCE-SOUTH
TRES ESQUINAS, CAQUETA DEPARTMENT, COLOMBIA
1400 HOURS, 13 SEPTEMBER 2001

Following the deadly ambush of the riverine convoy, a sense of gloom and foreboding hung over TQ like the dark storm clouds that shrouded the base daily. The gravel and cement bags on the barge from the stricken Marandúa were all miraculously recovered despite extensive combat damage to many of the cement bags. The Tucano crew managed to land their crippled aircraft safely back at TQ. General Montalvo was fit to be tied and incensed that the FARC had been so brazen. But despite all this, the big news was that young and quick thinking Colombian Army Captain David Gaitán, call sign Astuto 11, Colombian Marine Infantry Captain Jairo Quintero, call sign Calamar 15, and Colombian Air Force Captain Gabriel Jiménez, call sign Matador 2, were cited for their quick, brave, and heroic actions in reaction to the enemy ambush. Their exceptional leadership probably prevented a major catastrophe. Everyone was thankful for that.

But let's pause for a moment. In fact let's take a breather from all this combat and move to another side of life in TQ. Then we'll get back to more action…I promise.

While writing this book, it dawned on me that I really hadn't talked much about my fellow intelligence officer, Stan Luna. And I suppose the reason for this is that I was initially hesitant to discuss anything that Stan did while assigned to TQ. After all, he worked for the CIA…not the Culinary Institute of America, but the Central Intelligence Agency. After thinking about it, I realized that what he did was not secret at all. Everyone there, especially our Colombian hosts, knew and understood what Stan's job was. His job was to win over the hearts and minds of our counterparts and later pump them for information of value to the American Embassy, the CIA, and presumably, other US intelligence agencies. Please understand that the information that Stan sought was not high level classified intelligence. I would categorize it as incidental tidbits about just about anything happening at TQ. Some of it may have been hearsay. Some of it may have been information about upcoming operations. And some of it was just nice to know stuff. He really didn't ask our counterparts for information that would compromise their positions or standings within their military, nor did he ask them for information that would violate anything on a strictly need to know basis. I wanted to clarify this upfront because the nature of his work was very different from the cloak and dagger activities of intelligence operatives that you read about. Sure, there are agents that do the highly covert stuff. But Stan did not operate at this level in TQ. The officers he approached all knew who they were talking to and could decide for themselves what they wanted to talk to him about. In a sense he was like a military attaché. Attachés are accepted for what they do and their overt reporting on behalf of their countries is traditionally tolerated and accepted.

Addditionally, Stan was also a good friend. He and I did many things together professionally and socially, and he never failed to invite me to the white house to relax. I in turn would go out of my way to help him in whatever way I could. His house was called the White House by our counterparts for two reasons. They said it represented an official US presence on the base, hence, "The White House," and more to the point, it was painted white. Across the street there was a house used by the Colombians that was called "La Casa Roja" or the red house, but in this case it was named after Colombian general officer of the army and president of Colombia, Gustavo Rojas Pinilla. But that's another story... and it wasn't red in color. At least that I remember.

From my perspective, a more appropriate name would have been the Party House because that's what it became on weekends...the party place of the base. Well, that's not exactly true. The real party place on base was at the house adjacent the radar facility that was being hosted by a US government contractor and that included the unauthorized ladies that stepped off the Antonov that I wrote about earlier.

So, what happened at Stan's party house? Well, dear friend, I will explain. True to classy CIA form, Stan had a nice budget that helped him set the setting for his work. When the Agency bird made its supply run from Bogotá, I would help Stan take provisions to his house. We're talking cans and plastic bottles of soft drinks, beer, steaks for barbecuing, and last but not least, booze... and plenty of it. Bacardi Rum, Smirnoff Vodka, Tanqueray Gin, Johnny Walker Scotch whiskey, Bailey's Irish Cream, assorted wines, wine coolers...you name it. Stan had it.

I had to remind Stan of something Pete had taught me in El Salvador too. I learned from him that if you just want to entertain your guests, you serve them Johnny Walker Red Label

Scotch whiskey. If you want to make them feel super special, then you serve them Johnny Walker Black Label. Of course there were also JW Gold and Blue Labels, but we won't go there. After all, there were limits to the operational budget.

The simple fact is that although alcohol helped relax our Colombian counterparts and loosened their tongues, thus, making Stan's job easier. I would have to say that the center of "Party Central" was the barbecue. I can remember one day standing in front of the grill that sat on the concrete pad in his backyard with the Río Orteguaza running just a few yards behind the house. The smell of the charbroiled rib eye steaks...as they sizzled on the grill...was truly heaven. I thought to myself, how nice to have a party here in the middle of the Colombian jungle with delicious steaks on the grill. I mean I have to admit, this was a great morale and welfare operation that really benefited everyone at TQ, including the US personnel. Understand that there was nowhere for us to go on weekends. You kind of just hung around your work site or in your room. Stan's parties were the place to be on those afternoons or evenings.

So, I think you get the idea. This was the perfect setting... the perfect cocktail party environment...for Stan to talk shop with our counterparts and for him to engage them on issues involving operations and the like. It worked. Heck, I was probably telling Stan things about my work without realizing that I may have been a target too! Hahahaha...just kidding...at least I hope so.

Oh, did I say that we had a wide assortment of music CD's to play on his stereo and even picked up some FM radio stations from Florencia to our north? I mean what's a party without music? Right? Let's see, so we had the drinks, the food, the music, and our Colombian military counterparts. What do you suppose was missing? Take a guess. Give up? Let me help you. Women! We had no women! What's a party without women? But wait a minute, readers, I've been holding out on you. We did have women at our parties. And yes they were legitimate. Stan had it all figured out. I'll explain.

The Colombian government had a neat program that I wish our government would copy. Students with special medical skills, such as psychologists, nurses, and medical technicians, were given college supplemental payment by the government to help them with their studies. In return these students would serve for a period of one year in isolated bases like TQ in support of the military after they graduated. The program had a name. But for the life of me, I can't remember it. Theses student ladies helped Captain Nickey run the base clinic.

One day they just showed up. I'm not sure how we found out, but as soon as Stan got wind of it, he gave them personal invitations to his parties. If I recall correctly, we had four of these auxiliary nurses assigned to the base. It seems to me that they were all very attractive and more than willing to join us at these parties. Remember, they were confined to the base too with very little to do from a social standpoint. Before you get the wrong idea, let me assure you that these ladies behaved correctly, like true ladies, and there was no hanky panky involved. At least from the part of the US advisors and I think, generally, most of our counterparts, except, maybe Colombian Air Force Major Espinoza. But Eduardo was incorrigible and obsessed with women. I describe him this way so as not to categorize him with the popular slang label that describes someone with an insatiable sexual appetite. I already discussed his obsession with our Agency pilot. But getting back to our lady friends, they were very nice, serious, and decent girls. In fact one of the ladies was married and the others were engaged or had boyfriends back in Bogotá.

On many weekends I attended Stan's parties still in uniform, as did most of my Colombian counterparts. I don't know that we were ever in civilian attire, except if Stan threw his party on Sunday when we were technically off duty. My memory isn't too clear on this. But the parties generally followed the same routine. Stan would announce the party and we would all show up to eat barbecue steaks. Man, were they delicious. We drank a little... remember we were in uniform...enjoyed good conversation...and then we headed back to our quarters. At one party, I believe there was actually dancing. At least the ladies were asked to dance by the Colombian officers...some Latin dancing, such as *salsa, merengue, cumbia, vallenato,* and on one occasion, American rock music. But it seems to me that this was far and in between.

There you have it...entertainment, TQ style. But let's not forget that the purpose of these parties was for Stan to set the stage to engage with counterparts. I must say that every time I saw him, he did just that...and quite effectively. Stan was a gentleman, a great asset to his profession, and his organization. He was also an excellent host, a great cook, and professional socializer.

Speaking of socializing, let me list the other things we did in TQ. At least twice, the 1st BACNA threw a barbecue party for everyone on base. The meat wasn't as good and top quality as Stan's, but hey, it was free and plentiful. It seems to me that beer was available at these functions and there was even a mariachi band with members from the unit. General Montalvo was big on attendance to these by everyone as a morale and welfare activity for the troops, and he encouraged all of us to partake of his hosting. These activities took place in open areas near the soldiers' barracks. Overall, these events along with Stan's removed some of the stress from work and isolation out of our lives.

General Montalvo would also host small, by invitation only, get-togethers at his quarters from time to time. These were attended by the senior officers of his staff and me. An event of this nature normally included a light dinner of Colombian finger food and alcoholic drinks. For the life of me I can't remember what I had there, other than I do remember that one plate consisted of fried rice with bite-size pieces of fried pork. Another plate had sliced frankfurters accompanied with rice. During these get-togethers we generally just sat around a table, ate and drank beer, rum or Scotch, and challenged each other to a round of joke telling. Because of General Montalvo's curfew at 2300 hours, these get-togethers didn't run late at all.

The last type of social event was soccer...or rather watching professional national soccer teams competing in the Latin American *Copa de Oro* or Gold Cup. All I remember was a meeting room full of uniformed soldiers all yelling, screaming, or cursing the Colombian national team that didn't particularly do very well during that year's competition. It's true that foreign countries treat their soccer or *fútbol* with the passion of a religion...and with probably more devotion and reverence to it.

Fútbol matches between members of the military units would also be played in the afternoon in a large field in front of the COJIC. I never participated in these for two reasons. One, I can't play worth a hoot and two, suffering a broken leg at one of these would not go over well at the Embassy or back in my parent unit. I mean, can you imagine the reactions if I had hurt myself during these matches? It would probably be more like: "He got hurt doing what?" or "He's supposed to be fighting the enemy, not his counterparts" or "What was he thinking?" Anyway, although it would have helped my standing among the Colombians if I had participated, my sense of good judgment kept me from engaging them on the soccer field.

I mentioned earlier that I did play tennis with some of the members of the staff on a few occasions....nothing regular. There was one tennis court with a net at TQ, but it was surrounded by a muddy field. This meant our one tennis ball became covered and encrusted with wet mud as we played. By the end of a match, it weighed as much as a softball and it felt like you were swinging a tennis racket at a softball too. With that kind of abuse it's a wonder that the tennis rackets donated by Stan's morale and welfare fund stood up to the constant abuse. I use to play tennis after classes while in college and a little bit while on active duty, but that's about it. I don't remember having played very well and my hitting was challenged even more by the absence of court lights when we played in the early evenings at the TQ court. Half the time I couldn't even see the ball. My eyesight at that time was progressively worsening as a result of cataracts in both eyes. So, add this to my tennis challenges and you have a poor tennis player. Regardless, we had fun chasing the ball around the court. I don't precisely remember, but I think I was in BDU's when I played. I may have worn tennis shoes...don't remember.

Speaking of chasing balls...while in Colombia, I was still in a phase of my life where I considered myself an avid golfer. This is no longer the case, but then...yes. Notice that I didn't say good or proficient...just avid. Along with my military gear I had brought a couple of short irons along...a sand wedge and a 9 iron to be exact...for you golfers out there. For you non-golfers the irons I brought are called short irons because they are physically shorter in length than other irons, have higher loft when swung, and are used for shorter distances and approach shots to the green. Just like the confusion of scoring in a game that gives a golfer having a negative score a higher score than one with a plus score, the higher the number an iron is, the shorter the distance. So, an 8 or a 9 iron will propel a golf ball a shorter distance than say, a 4 or 5 iron. Makes sense, right? Hahahaha....you gotta love it.

Anyway, getting back to my story, one afternoon on a slow day and before the 1940 hours evening update briefing, I decided to practice hitting a few golf balls on the open field that was used for soccer matches. Unexpectedly, General Montalvo drove up in his Humvee along with his Executive Officer, COL de la Barca. Little did I know that both of them were also *avid* golfers and enjoyed taking a swing or two at golf balls. I let them use my clubs and they swung away hitting the balls beyond the extension of the soccer field. What was particularly interesting about this little impromptu practice and what most sticks out in my mind, was the extra help we had on this makeshift golf driving range. You all know that caddies walk along with a golfer and carry the golf clubs. That afternoon we had ball caddies. These were soldiers assigned to General Montalvo's security detachment that were given the duty of retrieving the golf balls that the General and his Executive Officer hit. The soldiers ran after the balls and retrieved them wherever they landed. At one point I worried that in everyone's zeal, someone would get hit on the head with a golf ball. Fortunately, that was not the case that afternoon. But I still remember those soldiers running around downrange chasing those golf balls.

If I hesitated to write about Stan, I had more reason not to write the following. You see it involves...a woman....a woman I met in Bogotá. Yep, I got involved with a woman. But before you jump to conclusions...because I know you're thinking the very worst...sex, drugs, and videotapes...please allow me to allay your suspicions. Or would you prefer to hear about a sizzling, steamy love affair?...hahaha. Let me see what I can do to satisfy every category of reader by simply telling the story and letting you decide for yourself.

I first met Susana Marie...and I'll call her that, although that is not her real name...during one of my routine trips to Bogotá prior to my deployment to TQ. It all happened very casually and unexpectedly. Don't these things always happen along similar lines?

Anyway, during my first trip to Colombia, I told COL Bernardo, the USMILGP commander, that I wanted to buy some emerald jewelry for my wife. He linked me up with his wife, Amelia, and we arranged for a meeting with her friend, Susana, to show me some of her jewelry. The meeting was to be in my hotel room.

That evening Amelia showed up with Susana. Immediately, I was struck by Susana's beauty. She was an elegant lady in her late 40's or early 50's. Susana was of medium height, light-skinned with dark long hair, and beautiful dark brown eyes...and a knock out body. She had a certain aristocratic air of self confidence about her that was intoxicating. That evening she was dressed in a tailored business suit...beautiful dark gray skirt, matching coat, white blouse, and black patent leather high heels. Imagine an impeccably dressed business woman and you will visualize Susana. In addition to her self confidence, she also had a certain grace and sophistication about her that captivated me. During this first meeting, my mind wondered back and forth between staring at her and her emerald collection. As her hands moved around her jewelry display box, I couldn't help but notice the beautiful diamond engagement ring and wedding band on her left hand. I don't remember what I purchased from her, but I'm sure it was more than I had originally planned on spending.

To make a short story long, this first encounter with Susana developed into a long term friendship. Every time I flew to Bogotá, she made it a point to meet me in the lobby of my hotel and on occasion, even in my hotel room. This went on for about three or four years. These meetings were never intimate or sexual, although I sensed that she would have liked to have turned it into something a little more intimate. I could feel it when I stared into her eyes. Plus, the fact that she always made it a point to visit me when I was in Bogotá made me believe that she was definitely interested in me. After all, why would she risk her reputation and social standing to see me?

As I've hinted to you already, Susana was a married woman and despite problems between her and her husband, she was faithful to her husband. That was our dilemma. Interestingly enough, though, when we were together we managed to put aside any personal frustrated desires and spent our time talking about her business, her future plans, dreams, and her children. She was a workaholic with unlimited energy, and true to her astrological sign, multi-tasked as well as any Gemini that I knew. Her energy reserves had no limits. We always parted by hugging in customary Hispanic fashion...no long embraces or kisses... just a good bye hug.

During one of her visits, Susana told me that she had decided to divorce her husband. As is sometimes the case in marriages, her husband had been seeing another woman for some time now and was never around. Her successful business also put additional strains on an already shaky relationship because her busy schedule with customers also kept her always on the go. She stressed that I had nothing to do with her decision. Then things took an unexpected turn.

The last time I saw Susana in Bogotá she called me in my hotel room and said she wanted to stop by and see me before her next appointment with a customer. As usual she was prompt and impeccably dressed in business attire. If I remember, she was wearing a tailored light grey business jacket with matching skirt. I believed she was also wearing a pink blouse with that. As she entered the room, the combined essences of vanilla, citrus, jasmine, and rose made for a fragrantly subtle, but firm and well defined presence.

There was something different about her that afternoon. When she saw me, she gave me the customary hug...nothing particularly noteworthy about it, other than she seemed to hold on a little longer than usual. Hmmm...I thought to myself...I wonder what's up?

After we sat down together on the sofa, we immediately began our conversation with Susana telling me about her new enterprise. She was expanding her client base to the States and had some prospective buyers and sales representatives already lined up.

Then things started to happen very quickly. As we talked, she began moving a little closer to me. I put my arm around her and she placed her head on my shoulder. We just sat in silence for awhile.

Then, I began lightly kissing her on the side of her face… slowly and yes, my readers, passionately. The musky and spicy fragrance on her neck simply enhanced the moment. She responded with gentle whispers…light moans of approval…and moved her head up and down and from side to side to better accommodate my warm and gentle kisses…all in a very slow and natural way. You know what? Even as I write these lines, I am reliving this moment. It was a wonderfully tender moment of affection…very innocent…and very taboo at the same time. Life and upbringing certainly create guilt trips that overshadow passionate moments like this. But, I put all this aside and decided to just accept the overpowering feelings of the moment.

Then it happened. As I gently nibbled and played with her right ear, Susana turned her head to the side and her warm, wet, and voluptuous lips met mine. This was a fireworks moment for me…and her. We kissed, kissed, and then kissed some more. Boy, did we kiss…long and passionate…French kissing like none that I had ever experienced. Our tongues playfully met each other as our breathing became heavier. Body temperatures began to rise. Time seemed to stop as our lips locked in feelings of fire and passion. These years together heightened the mutual feelings of curiosity, love, lust, and passion.

But I've got to hand it to her and also respect her. Susana never relinquished control as my right hand slowly ran up and down her leg… adding to the increased intensity of the moment. Twice she moved my mischievously roving hand away from its curious intentions. But I took it all in stride. Your lustful Lothario wasn't frustrated, angry, or upset with her. After all, this was the most intimacy that we had ever shared. It was nice to be sharing this moment of tenderness together.

We finally stopped to come up for air. She leaned back in the sofa with her eyes closed...relishing the feelings surging through her body. All she could say to me was, "If this is any indication of what making love to you is like, I don't think I could stand it." And all I could manage to say was, "Well, we will just never know, will we?" She thought about this for a moment and then just shook her head. "No, I don't think so."

Rising from the sofa, Susana straightened her skirt and reached for a small spray bottle of Coco perfume that she kept in her Chanel-emblazoned black and white leather purse. She lightly sprayed her neck and wrists and then glanced at her Rolex.

"I'm sorry, but I have to meet an American customer from the Embassy in less than fifteen minutes. Thanks for sharing this wonderful moment with me."

"No thanks required. I was quite surprised by how you opened yourself up to me," I said.

She laughed. "Don't tell me you never suspected how I felt about you."

"I did suspect. It's just that you were always so proper that I never imagined that you would ever give in to your true feelings."

She looked down at the floor and then looked at me. "I'm sorry. I hope you don't think less of me."

"Are you kidding? You were wonderful. And you know what? In the grand scheme of things, we really didn't do anything bad. We never totally succumbed to our sexual urges. Clothes stayed on. It was pure and innocent teen-age kissing."

Come on now, ladies. Isn't it great how guys can explain away intimate, but wrongful moments and put them into proper and noble context? Give us some credit. I certainly didn't want her to begin having second thoughts and guilt about what had just happened. What we did was morally wrong, but you know? It happened and it just felt good.

With purse in hand Susana gave me a nice hug and kissed me on the lips one more time. As the emotions started to build up again, she backed away, shook her head, and simply said, "No, I don't want to start those feelings again." While turning in direction of the door, I took her by the hand and walked with her to the hotel parking garage where her car was parked.

Although Susana and I talked on the phone one more time during my deployment to TQ, we never saw each other again. Conflicts in schedules precluded further meetings. We parted as friends and not lovers, with the joy of having shared a brief moment of intimacy and the curiosity of never really knowing the 'what if' of future contact. Memories of that brief moment together will last a lifetime and will linger in my mind like the subtle and sweet fragrance of vanilla, citrus, jasmine, and rose.

> *If I give... my... heart... to you...I must be sure...*
> *from the very... start...that you...will love me*
> *more than her...*

> **The Beatles**

CHAPTER SEVENTEEN

"POST ONE...AMERICAN EMBASSY...WE ARE UNDER ATTACK!"

Well, come on generals, let's move fast...Your big chance has come at last. Now you can go out and get those reds...'Cause the only good commie is the one who's dead...And you know that peace can only be won...When we've blown 'em all to kingdom come.

"I Feel like I'm Fixin to Die Rag"
as recorded by Country Joe and the Fish

FARC MILITARY OPERATION, RIO ORTEGUAZA,
TRES ESQUINAS, CAQUETA DEPARTMENT, COLOMBIA
0030 HOURS, 15 SEPTEMBER 2001

As Corporal Hudson in the classic 1986 movie, *Aliens,* said, "Stop your grinnin' and drop your linen." Let's move on from that last chapter. I told you I almost didn't include it, especially Susana's story. But now that I did, I hope you are a good sport about it and recognize that your dear narrator also has a foible or two. However, If you wanted more action, then I'm sorry. Write your own book and make this stuff up. The only real action is the ongoing drug war...hahahaha...just messing with you...

Speaking of which, let's resume our story for things are really going to get a lot hotter now than that hotel room scene. We are now going to observe a FARC operation in progress. Dim the lights...grab the popcorn...pop a beer...and let's roll it...

★ ★ ★

The partially-submerged, dark brown Styrofoam and composite wood log floated down the Río Orteguaza ...too natural looking an object to raise much attention or interest for that matter. Underneath its hollow frame, Tiburón held on to the leather handles that had been affixed to the structure. In a small compartment to his front was his GPS...the only instrument and the only way that he would know when he was at his objective.

Tiburón was accompanied by his two team members, *El Cachaco*, the best foreign trained sapper and demolitions expert in the Teófilo Forero Mobile Column and *El Primo*, Cachaco's young protégé. They had been at the mercy of the south flowing river current for a couple of hours now. Earlier that night, they had entered the dark and muddy waters of the Río Orteguaza at a secret location a few miles south of Larandia or approximately forty miles up stream from Tres Esquinas. Despite the fact that they were wearing scuba wet suits, the tight quarters and cool water were already causing cramping in their legs.

"Tiburón, you're getting too old for this," he thought. "Special operations are a young man's sport." He promised himself that after this operation he would hang it up. He would simply be a special ops advisor to the FARC. That would allow him to spend his weekends in Barranquilla with his wife, son, and mistress. It was time for him to enjoy a little bit of the good life of a retired guerrilla. He was past due.

The GPS indicated that they were floating past the town of San Antonio de Getuchá, which would be on his left. Tiburón had no way of knowing or verifying this other than putting faith in his navigational instrument. However, he thought he heard music playing off to the distance from a small cantina in the town. The owner had promised to play the music louder than usual tonight, not really knowing why the high paying FARC guerrilla that had visited him was willing to pay big money for this request. Tiburón assumed that this music was in fact coming from the *Estrella Azul* Bar in San Antonio de Getuchá. The GPS seemed to confirm this.

Occasionally, their feet scraped the sandy bottom and they had to push their floating vehicle off the many sand bars in the Río Orteguaza. On another occasion a large fish or something brushed against his leg. Try as he might, he could not forget the fact that the Río Orteguaza was part of the Amazon river basin and had all the living creatures that corresponded to this...*Bagre*, large prehistoric-like catfish that weighed anywhere from 100 to 150 lbs...electric eels...and of course *cahamas,* the piranha-like predators. "What a place to be dangling legs and feet from," he laughed out loud.

"Did you say something, Jefe?*"* Cachaco who was behind him whispered. It was the first words that they had exchanged since they entered the river.

"No, just thinking out loud what a privilege it is to lead this glorious attack tonight," he whispered back.

"Yes, of course," said Cachaco.

"Viva las FARC," said the young Primo. Primo was on only his third mission with Tiburón.

I woke up to the sound of the TV remote control hitting the floor. The television show I had been watching before falling asleep was already long over. Picking up the remote, I instinctively began flipping through channels, not really quite sure what to look for. Not finding anything worth watching, I turned the TV off. Glancing at my watch, I groaned when I realized it was only 0035 hours. I got up from my bunk and opened the small refrigerator, poured some cold bottled water into a cup, and added some Tang orange powder mix. I then looked around the dimly lit room, checked that my flack vest was hanging from the door knob, the load bearing equipment was still hanging from the back of the single wooden chair, the M4 carbine was on the small dining table, and my 9 mm pistol was under my pillow. Satisfied, I plopped back into bed and I was soon sound asleep.

Cabo Segundo Tomás Figueroa shifted the weight of his body from the right foot to the left. The trench he occupied had water up to his ankles and his feet inside his jungle boots were already soaked from all the rain that evening. His poncho glistened as the moon occasionally showed through the thick rain clouds over Tres Esquinas. This promised to be a long night of guard duty. At least the rain had eliminated the cloud of mosquitoes that constantly hung over him and the other soldiers of his platoon in Company B of the permanent TQ guard force. Well, he could do nothing for now but hope that his shift would go quickly. It was only 0040 hours.

Cabo Primero Luís Vega swatted the pesky moth flying around the desk lamp with his patrol cap. He then propped both his feet back on top of the radio intercept monitoring table. To his right, two suites each with three vertically stacked VHF radios were on automatic scan searching for any FARC communications. On his left, one radio scanned the FARC HF frequencies. Meanwhile his right index finger slowly spun the tuning knob of another VHF radio in front of him. He looked up at the clock on the wall and shook his head…the lonely and routinely boring life of a signals intercept operator. It was 0045 hours.

★ ★ ★

The map coordinates on the GPS told Tiburón he should now be going past the small town of Agua Negra. He strained his ears to catch some hint of manmade sounds possibly from the town, but was disappointed that none could be detected. He fought off the desire to stick his head out of the small hatch on top of the log to confirm his location.

"Too early for that," he thought. "Total stealth and secrecy were imperatives for now. I wonder how the other moving parts of this operation are unfolding?" The complexity of this operation was beyond the scope of comprehension. "Too complex... too much room for error," his boss, El Paisa had told Mono Jojoy at the planning conference in La Macarena back in June of this year. Even now Tiburón started to have doubts of its success. He knew that he could count on his special operations team to do its job, but he was a little uneasy about having so many other Southern Bloc elements involved in this operation. Many of the guerrillas in these units were only kids and not professional and experienced combatants like the members of the Teófilo Forrero Column. But he also accepted the fact that because of the number of Colombian Army soldiers there, any successful attack on Tres Esquinas would require total surprise on his part and overwhelming diversionary supporting fire from the Southern Bloc units. The ability of the Colombian soldiers to detect his operation and quickly mount a counterattack could easily destroy any chance of his escape. The fires from the supporting FARC columns would have to effectively draw fire and attention away from his infiltration.

Yes, this was by far the most ambitious and complex waterborne infiltration that Tiburón had ever devised. But Tiburón was also the waterborne infiltrations expert of the Teófilo Forero Column. In fact he was probably the most highly trained special ops member in the FARC... period. His alias, El Tiburón, was formally bestowed on him by Tirofijo himself after observing one of Tiburon's river infiltration demonstrations.

"The man swims like a shark and is probably more dangerous than one," he was overheard to have said. The nick name stuck.

Tiburón's legacy among the FARC was the stuff of legend. Particularly remarkable was that Tiburón was not a young man, but was already in his early 50's...quite an accomplishment for any guerrilla. It was in his blood...derived from his father who was also a Latin American freedom fighter. Where there was revolution, his father had volunteered his services to guerrilla organizations...a year here...a year there...first with the Montoneros in Argentina, the PCB in Brazil, the MIR in Chile, and the Tupamaros in Uruguay.

Tiburón had followed suit. He spent some time with the ORPA in Guatemala, the Chinchoneros in Honduras, the FMLN in El Salvador, and the FSLN in Nicaragua. His last assignment was providing security for the commander in hiding of the FALN *Macheteros* in Puerto Rico. Now with the FARC, he was back in his native Colombia after a break and a short stint with M-19 before they politicized. Although as a special operations expert his reputation within Latin America was not widely known, his expertise was second to none.

The use of the Styrofoam and composite wood log was his idea. It was also his least preferred course of action. Two previous reconnaissance and probing actions of the base at Tres Esquinas had been unsuccessful. The first probe from the Río Orteguaza using a small three man *Cayuco* had shown that the quick reaction force in Tres Esquinas was quite adept. This probe along the river ended with one member of the infiltration team being killed by .50 caliber fire from a Tucano that provided close air support after the alarm was sounded by some alert guards. Fortunately, the other two team members of the team managed to return back to base, otherwise the entire operation might have ended in total disaster. Infiltrating from the landward side of Tres Esquinas was out of the question too, even when using locals from the nearby town of Solano as probes. All those attempts had to be cut short. His last personal attempt at cutting the perimeter wire at Tres Esquinas almost cost him his life. They just couldn't afford to make more mistakes. The perimeter guards at Tres Esquinas were on their toes. A large composite log floating downstream…? Well, he would certainly find out tonight.

Success hinged on his ability to reach the enemy base camp. He had one chance to get it right. If he missed and floated past his infiltration point along the west bank of the compound, he and his team would not be able to move back upstream for a second attempt.

Tiburón knew that the 15th Front had completed its movement into positions along the northeast sides of Tres Esquinas earlier in the evening prior to his departure down the Río Orteguaza. Additionally, elements of the 49th Fronts had been authorized to cross the Orteguaza to reinforce the 15th Front's area. They should have also completed their movement by late evening. Elements of the 48th Front were to execute a supporting attack on the southeast side of the perimeter. Finally, elements of the 14th Front had departed the area of Peña Colorada days before and would act as reserve for the 15th Front.

The GPS informed Tiburón they were slowly approaching Tres Esquinas…about thirty minutes out. The rain outside was so heavy, he could now hear it hitting the artificial log. For a minute he panicked. He hadn't thought about what the sound of rain hitting the composite materials of the artificial log might sound like outside.

"Would the hollowness of the log accentuate the sound?" he thought. "Would it catch the attention of the sentries along the shore of Tres Esquinas?" "It's too late, my friend," he thought. "It's now show time. Besides, consider the fact that a heavy rain will aid the infiltration. It will reduce visibility and, more importantly, cause the guards to huddle in the bottom of their trenches and bunkers attempting to stay warm…the perfect scenario. Now, would his guide be in place?"

The white haired and 60's something José Restrepo had slowly walked out of Cilantro's, the small night club in the small town of Mandalay early that evening, an hour before the 2300 hours daily curfew imposed on everyone in Tres Esquinas and the adjacent town of Mandalay. The town had become incorporated into Tres Esquinas and many of the civilians that worked on the base lived there. Dressed in faded jeans, worn out Nike running shoes, a faded blue and silver Dallas Cowboys T-shirt, and carrying a small backpack, the slow moving José casually walked down the muddy road past the COJIC. He tipped his dilapidated black umbrella and waved to the guard on duty at the entrance of the building and continued on his trek up the road trying to look as normal as possible. Although rare for someone from the town to be out on the streets in the evening, it was not totally uncommon. If stopped or questioned, his excuse was that he had a sick relative in Florencia and had to make a long distance call from the central telephone office phone booths.

He then reached a point where a small dirt road cut to the right from the main road. He followed this dirt road past the aluminum trailer-like buildings which housed the American advisors and Colombian army company grade officers that worked in the COJIC. He prayed that no one would see him. Walking around this area would definitely create suspicion.

Behind the aluminum barracks was an earthen bunker…long abandoned and totally overrun by grass and weeds. Triple strand concertina wire that surrounded the entire compound ran along the front of this bunker. Looking to his right and left, José stooped and secretly entered the dark interior.

This bunker was truly a stroke of good luck. He had discovered its entrance while on a grass cutting work detail for the installation. The soldiers of the base did not know that inside and opposite the entrance of this dark, wet, and dingy bunker was a canvas tarp that concealed a tunnel. This tunnel ran underneath the perimeter wire and out to an abandoned observation position. Apparently, for years this tunnel connected the observation point with the bunker, so that guards could move freely underneath the wire. Now it was strictly his and Tiburón's secret.

José waited in silence inside the bunker. Occasionally, he turned on a penlight flashlight to check his watch. He thought about the $25,000 in American dollars that he was getting for assisting the FARC on this mission. This would pay his debts and get him out of the servitude that was the story of his poor life. He had been contacted through a relative in Florencia a year after beginning work as a laborer in Tres Esquinas. Although he had never sympathized with the FARC cause, the offer of money was too tempting, despite the risk involved. He had already received a small partial payment and he was anxious to get the rest. He had never imagined getting involved with this guerrilla organization... until now. He passed away the hours by taking short naps.

He finally woke up abruptly and looked at his watch and figured that Tiburón should be arriving in about twenty minutes. Hopefully, Tiburón's cruise down the river was moving as planned.

José slid the canvas tarp aside and shined the penetrating beam of the penlight into the dark tunnel. He was immediately met by a number of bats that came fluttering out.

After a minute or two to compose himself, he figured it was then safe to enter the tunnel. This time he moved threw the tunnel in total darkness and hoped that there were no other creepy crawlers or animals still in there. The idea of running into a snake... and there were many in Tres Esquinas...did not appeal to him. Once outside the tunnel and in the observation point...a small foxhole…he was not visible to anyone inside the compound. Even the powerful perimeter floodlights that illuminated the river did not cover this spot. Except for the rain that soaked his skin and his running shoes, it was the perfect location. Through the darkness and the rain he peered out across the dark waters of the Río Orteguaza looking for some sign of Tiburón. He reached into his backpack, turned on a small infrared marking light that he had been passed to him from a relative visiting Mandalay, and set it to blink three times in succession. Invisible to anyone not wearing night vision goggles or NVG's, this would be Tiburón's signal.

With GPS telling him that it was time, Tiburón popped the small hatch on top of the artificial log and stuck his head out. With his NVG's, he saw the three flashes from the infrared signal from his guide about 100 meters away.

Then he saw a dark silhouette in front of him. A Colombian Marine Infantry Piranha boat was tied to a tree on the bank of the river. About four personnel appeared to be onboard. Tiburón quickly closed the hatch and prayed. The artificial log bumped and grazed the Zodiac. "This is it," he thought…"Compromise of the mission." He held his breath…but nothing happened. They continued to flow downstream. Could they have outwitted the patrol boat?

He hesitated for a moment. Then he slowly popped the hatch again. Looking back at the Piranha through his NVG's, he noted that the boat was still tied to the bank. Then he realized what had happened. The lifeless figures on board were apparently fast asleep!! "Whew"…he thought. "What a stroke of luck." He would have hated for those M60's or the single .50 Cal MG to have opened up on him. It would have been ugly.

Tiburón then turned his head and looked forward. There was the infrared signal again, flashing to his left front. He whispered to Cachaco and Primo to kick with their scuba fins as they steered the log to the shore. Slowly they edged closer and closer, scraping the river bank. Then in unison, Tiburón and Cachaco, removed their NVGs, took deep breaths, slipped from underneath the log, came up, and tried to grab anything they could along the river bank.

Tiburón's efforts were met by the outstretched hands of José Restrepo who heaved with all his might to help the two commandos. Tiburón held on to José's left hand while fighting the swift river current. The bulkiness of his slung 9mm MP5 submachine gun and the canvas bag around his neck that carried demolitions created additional drag, but not nearly as much as the weight of Cachaco who held on to him by his utility belt.

Laboring and almost out of breath, Tiburón stepped unto the slippery muddy bank on his hands and knees. Once he felt he was on the edge of more solid, grassy ground, Tiburón turned to help Cachaco.

Cachaco had already let go of the log which slowly moved downstream again with Primo still onboard. Fully on shore and lying on their backs, the two commandos could only breathe heavily…feeling the heavy rain falling on their faces.

"Hombre…that was painful," Tiburón whispered to Cachaco.

"Sin duda"…no question…"I'm glad we rehearsed the dismount procedure. Can you imagine if we hadn't?" Cachaco softly commented. For a moment it almost seemed they had forgotten that the more important work of the mission was still ahead of them. José Restrepo interrupted their moment of peace.

"Señor Tiburón," he interrupted in a hushed tone. "Is there anything more I can do to help?"

"You've been a tremendous help, José. I don't believe we could have made it without you."

"Thank you, señores," he beamed. "When you finish catching your breath, I will escort you to the bunker."

"We're ready, José. Show us the way."

"Listo, señores...please follow me."

With that they followed José through the tunnel into the bunker. Once inside, Tiburón was the first to speak.

"Do you have our water?" he asked.

"Yes, here are your bottles." José reached into his backpack and produced four plastic bottles of the thirst quenching liquid.

The two commandos drank a quart of water each...which went down in a matter of seconds.

Tiburón spoke. "We need to inventory our equipment now. Let's see...do you still have your individual NVG's?"

"Check," Cachaco answered.

"Canvas bag with three charges and timers?"

"Check."

"Individual 9mm MP5SD3 submachine gun with suppressor?

"Check."

"Individual 9mm Glock 19 pistol with suppressor?

"Check."

"Pistol belt and harness with three magazine pouches?"

"Check."

"Nine MP5 thirty round magazines?

"Check."

"Two M67 fragmentation grenades?"

"Check."

"Knife?"

"Check."

"Good. We've got everything," affirmed Tiburón. Let's leave our scuba fins in the bunker. With the heavy rain still coming down, we'll proceed in our wet suits and booties."

Before exiting the bunker, Tiburón paused. He looked at José, patted him on the shoulder and said. "Here's the rest of your payment. You've earned it." With that he pulled his 9mm Glock 19 pistol with suppressor from out of his satchel bag and fired it at the unsuspecting man, who fell backward on the muddy floor in dead silence. Without batting an eyelash, Tiburón then looked at Cachaco and said, "Well, hermano, it's show time."

"Listo," Cachaco said with a big grin.

Cabo Segundo César Ospina's head bobbed up and down as he unsuccessfully fought off the heavy slumber that night. Sitting in a metal folding chair, he huddled underneath his poncho. Earlier he had tried to stay dry by sitting underneath the left wing of the AC-47, but the strong wind and horizontal rain off set any advantages coming from that. He had been on guard duty at the AC-47 parking area located on the south side of the COJIC since 2000 hours and the rain had not subsided. He was cold, tired, and wet. Despite the inclement weather his vision again began to fade as he slowly succumbed to the ever present slumber. It was just as well. That was the last thing he would remember as the sharp knife from the commando slit his throat. Cachaco dragged the limp body over to a wooden maintenance shed and dropped it behind a stack of metal cargo pallets.

He then placed his first demolition charge up near the left landing gear well of the AC-47. Next, he entered the side gate of the chain linked fence surrounding the COJIC which their sources had reported was never locked at night. His next priority was to place a demolition charge near the south entrance door of the COJIC and next to the two primary SATCOM satellite communications antennas sitting on the ground. Both charges were programmed to explode in fourteen and fifteen minutes, respectively. Demolition charges with timers in place, Cachaco quietly left the area and waited behind the discarded pile of pallets for Tiburón to emerge from the COJIC.

Once Cachaco had disposed the guard's body on the AC-47 side of the COJIC, Tiburón entered the side gate unseen. He slowly walked toward the front of the COJIC, hugging the side of the canvas building. He found the guard at the entrance of the facility snoring in his chair. He didn't even bother with a knife. A quick twist and snap of the neck was all it took to eliminate the sleeping guard. Tiburón dragged the body away from the front gate and left it behind the sentry box. He walked over to the command bunker and placed his first demolition charge at its entrance which was located on the north side of the COJIC. He then placed the second charge at the west side of the COJIC near the guard entrance. Because of the additional distance from Cachaco, his timers were set for ten and eleven minutes, respectively. Once set, he stealthily left the COJIC and headed back out the side gate, linking up with Cachaco. Together they quietly began their walk back toward their earthen bunker...the heavy rain and darkness helping conceal their movement. Their third and last charges would be placed at the doors of the senior American advisor and his force protection NCO. Because of the small size of the building, two charges would be enough to destroy the barracks and kill the Colombian intelligence officers that also slept there.

Sargento Primero Miguel González, Sergeant of the Guard, walked down the main Tres Esquinas road from the guard house. He was accompanied by his two relief guards for the COJIC.

Because one of his relief guards had reported sick that evening, he had delayed the relief time as he looked for a substitute.

SGT González strained his eyes to clearly see through the rain, but he thought he saw two dark figures walking from direction of the COJIC and headed toward the officers' barracks in what appeared to him to be a suspicious manner.

He called out in Spanish, "Halt, who goes there?"

He got no answer.

"I say again…who goes there?"

Another short pause and one of the two mysterious figures answered, "Nobody

…we're just two soldiers coming back from the club in Mandalay."

"Advance and be recognized," SGT González shouted.

The two figures did not move. The situation soon took the appearance of a stand off.

SGT González decided to carefully walk toward the two, accompanied by his two relief guards, and still not sure what was going on.

"What about curfew?" He shouted as he got closer. "You're both in violation of curfew."

"It's not a problem. We have permission from General Montalvo to be out here."

Walking a little closer towards the two, the still confused sergeant stated, "General Montalvo? I don't think so. General Montalvo never grants exceptions to his own curfew policy."

Then he froze in place. It took but a split second for SGT González to realize the two figures were dressed in black rubber wet suits and were aiming sub machineguns at him. But it was too late. In a flash the two dark figures each fired a three round burst from their silenced MP5's and it was all over. All three soldiers fell dead on the spot.

Precious time having passed, Tiburón and Cachaco quickly turned in direction of the bunker as the demolition charges went off almost simultaneously. The unexpected encounter with the Sergeant of the Guard had delayed their egress back to the bunker just enough to catch them in the open as the loud explosions created a blaze that illuminated the sky. However, much to their surprise, the AC-47 was still intact. Apparently, the charge that Cachaco had placed underneath it failed to detonate. The main explosions, however, were the signal for the main FARC attack. At that moment all the FARC fronts positioned for the attack opened fire.

The explosions and automatic weapons fire were enough to make me jump out of bed. Without turning on the lights, I slipped into my jungle boots without lacing and automatically grabbed my web gear and M4 carbine. Already dressed in BDU's, I grabbed my patrol cap, opened the door of the hootch, and peered out into the rainy night. Carefully, stepping outside, I was joined by two Colombian officers who had assembled outside my room.

"What's going on, Coronel?" one of them asked.

"I don't know, but it sounds like the perimeter is under attack from at least two sides and loud explosions came from vicinity the COJIC. Let's go check it out."

As we three headed toward the COJIC, we were joined by SFC Tirado and more Colombian army officers leaving their rooms. We finally grew to about eight personnel, counting me. Then over my Saber radio I heard Stan calling me.

"Halcón, this is Condor…what the hell is going on?" he queried at the top of his voice.

"Stan"…*I dispensed with correct radio procedures…*" The COJIC got hit and we are under attack. I recommend you stay in your house and don't come out until things settle down. It's dangerous for you to come our way right now. I gotta go."

"Wilco…got it…I'll be standing-by. Condor…Out."

Suddenly, two of the young Colombian officers with me were hit and fell to the ground. Their buddies immediately went to their aid.

The fire came from two dark figures that were running and firing past us about fifty yards away.

The Colombian officers and I fired back at the two, but we were immediately met by hand grenade explosions.

"Damn," I thought. These guys are good!!" From prone positions we all returned fired and saw one of the two stumble and fall to the ground. The other stopped to help his comrade, while continuing to fire.

I got a good bead on that other one and fired. Down went the second one that was carrying his wounded comrade right to the entrance of a bunker behind our sleeping quarters.

Very carefully, two officers and I slowly approached the two fallen black wet-suited figures.

By the time we reached them, both were dead, trigger fingers still in place in their weapons. Each also had a satchel charge strapped around their bodies.

"Search them," I ordered.

The young lieutenant and captain accompanying me quickly checked the bodies.

"There's an explosive charge with timer in each bag. Other than that, they have nothing on them. The older one who was carrying his wounded friend had these military identification tags and a crucifix around his neck. That's it."

"Let me have those," I said placing the tags and crucifix in the left cargo pocket of my fatigue pants. "We'll check them later. Leave the bodies here for now. Let's go to our rallying point at the COJIC."

Before we left, however, we walked over to the wounded Colombian officers to check on their condition. A young army captain had taken a round through his right leg, but seemed stable. The other army officer had been hit through the left arm and was not seriously hurt. Both were able to walk with assistance. I gave them the keys to my pick-up truck so they could drive to the base clinic. The on call medic would be able to further stabilize the patients, at least for now.

While in the heat of our own battle, the bigger battle for the defense of TQ was still ongoing. Based on the intensity of explosions, automatic weapons fire, and the flashes illuminating the dark Colombian sky, the northeast corner of our perimeter appeared to be under most pressure. Lighter, but still intense fire seemed to be emanating from the south perimeter.

At that moment I heard our Colombian Air Force AC-47 gunship fire up its engines. It rolled out of the parking area precariously fast at almost full throttle and careened dangerously to the left onto the main runway. I could not believe what I was seeing. The aircraft then rapidly taxied partway down to the north end of the runway and returned while lifting into the air only half way down the concrete airstrip. It took off under full black out conditions.

As the AC-47 gunship cleared the south end of the runway, the dark sky exploded with the intense brilliance of multiple blazing streams of bright green and red tracer rounds that reached to heaven like fiery tentacles of death.

Suddenly, the aircraft veered sharply to the left with its port engine on fire. Quick work by the pilot avoided a tragedy as he pushed heavily on his right rudder while increasing power to the starboard engine to compensate for the loss of thrust. He then feathered the port engine propeller and extinguished the engine fire.

The heavily damaged aircraft changed its directional heading and made a wide turn to the left to return to TQ. Flying slowly in a counterclockwise direction, it began dropping sun dazzling white illumination flares to help the base defenders see their targets.

When the AC-47 flew around a second time, the illumination flares had already burned out, so the aircraft opened fire with its three .50 caliber machineguns, aided by its FLIR. The three streams of intensely bright green tracers spewing from its guns looked like a flaming fountain of mint colored molten steel falling on targets below. The aircraft's .50 caliber machinegun fire joined the 60 and 81mm mortars from TQ that were already pounding the FARC guerrillas. The battle for TQ was on.

By this time we had made it to the COJIC, I was shocked with what I saw. The canvas siding and roofing were on fire and there didn't appear to be much that we could do. It was a sad sight to see. By the time we arrived, Colombian soldiers were attempting to put out the fire and rescue teams were moving among the blackened interior searching for wounded or dead personnel. We moved past the COJIC and attempted to enter the command bunker where perhaps some communications equipment might be available. Part of the bunker entrance had been destroyed, but luckily it appeared to have been only slightly damaged. The reinforced concrete and sandbags had helped keep it from caving in. Despite the smoke and lack of lights, I could hear General Montalvo yelling over a VHF radio from his Humvee parked next to the command bunker. From what I was able to ascertain, it sounded as if he was in contact with the security guard personnel on the perimeter, as well as the AC-47 crew.

As I came within earshot, I could hear General Montalvo fuming. His talk over the radio was pretty much one sided at this point and only punctuated by a few seconds of silence as the unfortunate officer on the other end of the radio attempted to give the General a satisfactory answer. The radio monologue sounded like this:

"*Pero qué vaina es está?*"...(a momentary pause)...*"No me saque la rabia, hombre!!!"*...(another momentary pause)... *"Dejen de mamar gallo"*... (a longer pause). He then yelled into the mike, "*No me vale queso,*" and ended the radio call by throwing the microphone down on the table.

Narrator's Note: Euphemistically and loosely translated, General Montalvo said, "What's going on?...Don't get me angry, man...and I don't care." Trust me...it was not pretty...but realize the extreme stress and urgency of the moment...we were fighting for our lives...It's tough not to get excited...Let' get back to the scene...

He then looked up at me with an intensity in his eyes that could have blow torched a hole through a solid steel door.

Deciding it was not the best time to talk to him since he was trying to I get updates from his commanders, I momentarily walked away from the bunker and pulled out my own portable Global Star satellite phone. Talking to SFC Tirado as I impatiently waited for the indicator to show that at least three satellites were within range, I punched the phone number to Post One at the Embassy. The voice on the other end identified itself with "Post One, American Embassy, Corporal Harris speaking, Sir or Ma'am."

"Post One, this is Colonel Rick Vallejo, senior US military advisor in Tres Esquinas. We are under attack...I say again... We are under attack. Call the Ambassador, the COS, and the USMILGP Commander immediately."

"Roger, Colonel. Are any US personnel hurt? Do you need immediate assistance?" asked the sharp USMC corporal.

"Negative. All US personnel are accounted for. The base appears to be holding its own at this time. However, the COJIC has been totally destroyed. I'm not sure how many Colombian military personnel were on duty inside at the time of the attack and might be dead or wounded."

"Roger, Colonel. I'm dialing phone numbers as we speak. Sir, can you stay on the line while I contact key personnel? They may have some questions for you."

"Roger...Standing by."

From the entrance of the command post, I could see that in the meantime, General Montalvo had been joined by the T2 and T3. All three officers were now standing with flashlights in front of a map board of the base camp. I walked back and interrupted their discussion.

"General Montalvo, I have the Embassy on the line. Do you have a situation report I can pass to them?"

"Tell them that we have 11 friendly KIA and 5 WIA in the COJIC, including two guards KIA. I'm still getting status reports from the perimeter security commanders, but we have approximately 3 friendly KIA and 18 friendly WIA on the northeast side of the perimeter. The southeast side is also under attack, but I don't have a status report yet. I've already contacted the 12th Brigade commander in Florencia and 1st CN Brigade commander in Larandia. They are prepared to send reinforcements, but I've told them that it is currently too dangerous to reinforce by air."

"General Montalvo, we got 2 confirmed enemy KIA. From the looks of them they were commandos that infiltrated the COJIC."

"*Hijo de puta,*" General Montalvo said angrily. He got back on the radio and advised his commanders to be on the look out for potentially more enemy infiltrators.

The other radio, on UHF, crackled with the voice of the AC-47 pilot.

"Marte 6 this is Satanás 13. We are out of ammo and proceeding on to Larandia to repair our port engine, reload, and attempt to return...Over."

Roger, Satanás…great support. Let us know if you are able to come back. What did it look like from up there?…Over."

"Marte this is Satanás. A lot of bad guys…I would estimate you have at least 300 on the northeast side of the perimeter. We flew over the southeast side and spotted another hundred or so… We hit them pretty good, however. I think they'll think twice before attacking again…Over."

"Great…Thanks for the report. Good luck on your flight to Larandia. Remember. Just as I always tell you…*Dios concede victoria a la constancia*…*Marte 6*…*Fuera.*"

By that time Corporal Harris from Post One was back on the line.

"Colonel, I have the Ambassador on the line. I'm patching you through to her."

A pause…and then I heard a familiar woman's voice.

"Rick, this is Ambassador Masterson. How are you doing?"

"Mrs. Ambassador, I've had better days, but we are all safe and the situation here is still developing. Other than a couple of infiltrators, as far as we know the compound has not been penetrated. General Montalvo is firmly in control and executing his base defense plan."

"That's good. Well, this is no time for heroics, you know. Ensure you let the Colombians do all the fighting. Don't forget, you gentlemen are just little helpers."

"Yes, ma'am, I won't forget. Count on us not to embarrass you."

"Oh, I'm not so much worried about that as I am about your safety."

"Thank you ma'am, but everything is in the hands of the Colombians. General Montalvo is on top of things. At that moment the blast from an enemy mortar round shook the command post.

"Yes, sounds like you are all on top of things," repeated the Ambassador rather weakly.

"Don't worry, ma'am. I'll call Post One back if the situation changes."

"Well...God bless you Rick. We're very proud of you all... Good luck and thank you."

"Thank you, ma'am."

The conversation ended. As I reflected on the conversation with the Ambassador, the telephone again came to life with Corporal Harris' voice.

"Colonel Vallejo, are you still there?"

"Yes, I'm here."

"Sir, I have Colonel Bernardo on the line. I'll patch you through to him."

A few seconds and then I heard the all too familiar voice.

"Rick, my man...Kent here. I hear things may be a little sticky for you there. How's it going?"

"Things are not too bad, Kent. General Montalvo reports 14 friendly KIA and approximately 23 friendly WIA. We have 2 confirmed enemy KIA...commandos, mind you. Those are our preliminary estimates. Our AC-47 managed to take off and laid into them. Unfortunately, he got shot up, but the crew's okay and on their way to Larandia for repairs and possible return depending on the extent of damage. The COJIC is pretty much gone. Apparently, the work of the 2 FARC commandos with demolition charges."

"Wow...the FARC sure has *cojones*. What's your assessment and prognosis?"

"I'm not really sure. The main attack appears to be coming from the northeast side. That's where the AC-47 crew reported the largest concentration of bad guys. And apparently there's a supporting attack on our southeast side. Nothing reported along the river or the adjacent river bank. If I had to guess, I would say this is more a harassment than a full up attack...They don't seem to be putting a lot of pressure or effort on us. I'm not really sure why they would risk it."

"You said you have two confirmed enemy commando KIA? Could that be the main effort itself? I mean, could the enemy fire along the perimeter be simply covering fire to allow the commandos to escape?"

"You know that's quite possible. I hadn't thought of that... Yeah, that makes sense...Must have been some pretty important guys."

"Like most special ops, those guys are highly trained. The FARC can't afford to lose strategic assets like that."

"Well, they are minus two right now. My concern is that there may be more hanging around here."

"That's possible, but highly unlikely. They operate on speed, stealth, and surprise. If any more were involved in the attack, they are probably long gone."

"Yeah, you're probably right. Hey, I'll let you know if anything changes here. Other than an occasional mortar round, things are not too bad right now."

"Okay, great. I'll inform Dirk Jones. When everything settles down, we'll try to fly down to get you out of there, if necessary. Let us know when it's safe."

"That sounds like a plan. Anything else I can do for you, Kent?"

"No, just stay safe and don't be a John Wayne. Congress would go ballistic if any of you guys are killed or wounded."

"Yeah, I know, I know...just like El Salvador. We're here, but we're not really here. Just get the job done. Don't risk your life. Don't get shot. And then leave. We've been through this before."

"Well...don't worry about that now. Let's focus on the real important events today. We can worry about the politics later."

"I know, I know, I know…I'm just venting," I said with a laugh. "I'll call you back if anything changes."

"Roger…talk to you later…Out."

Primo was getting fidgety. Forty-five minutes had elapsed and still there was no sign of his team members. After Tiburón and Cachaco disembarked, he had stayed with the composite log on the bank of the river, a short distance downriver from the infiltration entry point. He had thrown a small anchor-like grappling hook on an overhanging branch along the river bank to stop the movement of the log. He now waited from a concealed position on the river bank.

But things didn't make sense. According to the plan, the loud explosions he heard were from his comrade's demolitions. Then he was to wait exactly twenty minutes for his two team members to join him. This was more than enough time for them to link up. Then, inside the log, all three would allow the current to take them downstream for approximately thirty miles to a location where the Río Sencella flowed into the Río Caquetá. Members of his unit would provide security, warm clothes, and food at this designated rallying point.

His dilemma was that if he stayed longer then the agreed upon time, he risked being discovered by enemy Piranha boats that would soon get on the river on patrol from Tres Esquinas. He knew there was already one boat in the water that they had passed earlier that night. But if his comrades encountered any unforeseen delays, he risked leaving them stranded. What should he do? He pondered and thought. "What would his supervisors do in a situation like this?" "Follow the plan," he could mentally hear Tiburón's voice…"Follow the plan." Primo had no choice. He untied the knot that secured the grappling hook on shore to the composite log and slid back into the dark waters of the river. He quietly floated away, down the Orteguaza in total silence.

Before first light the fighting had tapered off as the FARC guerrillas dispersed and faded back into the jungle. By sunrise all was quiet outside the perimeter line. Patrols from TQ went out later that morning and recovered additional enemy dead around the base. At least 75 enemy bodies were recovered. Most died at the hands of the AC-47. Numerous blood trails pointed to an even higher body count. Overall, the Colombian Army suffered 23 FKIA and 41 FWIA. Many of the KIA were inside the COJIC when the charges detonated. A battalion from the 12th Infantry Brigade in Florencia flew into TQ by UH-1N helicopters early that same morning and immediately set off in hot pursuit of the retreating FARC. The 3rd BACNA flew from its base in Larandia to set up blocking positions along suspected FARC egress routes to the north and east of TQ. The AC-47 made it safely to Larandia, but had been damaged too severely to return to rejoin the battle. The brave AC-47 crew, particularly the pilot, Major Miguel "Mike" Sanz, call sign Satanás 13, was cited for bravery above and beyond the call of duty. That morning, soldiers found the body of José Restrepo with a bullet wound in his head inside the bunker that the two dead FARC commandos had attempted to reach. To my knowledge no further contact occurred between the FARC and our forces that day. The battle of TQ was officially over.

Come on mothers throughout the land...Pack your boys off to Vietnam...Come on fathers, and don't hesitate...To send your sons off before it's too late...And you can be the first ones in your block...to have your boy come home in a box.

And it's one, two, three…what are we fighting for? Don't ask me, I don't give a damn…next stop is Vietnam…And it's five, six, seven…open up the pearly gates…Well, there ain't no time to wonder why…whoopee, were all gonna die.

Country Joe and the Fish

CHAPTER EIGHTEEN

HELLO, LIFE...GOOD-BYE COLOMBIA

Is this the real life? Is this just fantasy? Caught in a landslide...no escape from reality. Open your eyes...look up to the skies and see. I'm just a poor boy, I need no sympathy. Because I'm easy come, easy go, little high, little low...Anyway the wind blows doesn't really matter to me...to me.

Mama...I just killed a man...put a gun against his head...pulled my trigger...now he's dead. Mama, life had just begun...but now I've gone and thrown it all away...

"Bohemian Rhapsody"
as recorded by Queen

HEADQUARTERS, JOINT TASK FORTH-SOUTH
TRES ESQUINAS, CAQUETA DEPARTMENT, COLOMBIA
1400 HOURS, 4 OCTOBER 2001

I stared at the bent military dog tags still in my hand. Looking away from them again, I pondered their significance. What were SSG Fred Grogan's dog tags doing in Colombia? Fred had been killed in the FMLN attack of El Paraiso, El Salvador in 1987.

After the attack on TQ, the Colombian Army determined that the infiltration of TQ was led by FARC commando, Luís Enrique Azriel Uribe, alias El Tiburón. Tiburón was a high ranking FARC commander and second in command of the Teófilo Forrero Mobile Column. The other dead commando was Bernabé Hernández, alias, El Cachaco.

I thought and thought. On a hunch, I asked the USMILGP to investigate Tiburon's affiliations prior to Colombia. Could he have served in El Salvador?

Tiburón was old enough. He appeared to be in his early to mid-fifties. He was about my age when he was killed in TQ. For a moment my mind traveled back to the fateful night in 1987 when I had been caught in an attack similar to the one at TQ a week ago. A sudden chill made me briefly shudder as I shook off those unpleasant thoughts.

"Yes, we got a positive match," said the voice on the phone.

"You're sure...100%?" I queried.

"*Sin duda*...no doubt about it," said Colonel Kent Bernardo over the phone. "The USMILGP Commander in San Salvador requested that the Salvadoran military get permission from the FMLN political party to review their old rosters from the war. The rosters showed that a Luís Enrique Azriel Uribe, native of Colombia, served in the ranks as an FES Comandante with the FPL faction of the FMLN. His alias was Comandante Quique. And get this," Kent's voice got more serious. "This guy led the attack on El Paraiso in 1987."

I felt a cold tightness grip my stomach.

"Thanks...thanks, Kent," I mumbled.

"Sure, glad to be of help. Friend of yours?" he asked jokingly.

"No...but I'll tell you a story over a cold Águila beer in Bogotá next time I see you.

"Okay, well...you know where to reach me. Hey, how's your packing coming? I just left General Valencia at the military ramp of El Dorado. His US Army Gulf Stream should be on its way to your location as we speak."

"Roger, thanks. I'm finishing up."

"Okay, well...again Rick, thanks for the outstanding support. I know the Ambassador has had only praise for your dedication to the effort. I hope the ceremony and presentation of your award last week reflects her sincere appreciation for your work."

"Yes, by all means," I said. "I did not expect it. Thanks for arranging the flight up to Bogotá for that event."

"Hey, think nothing of it. You deserve it. You did a great job there in TQ. Have a safe flight back home. See you around the region."

"Thanks, Kent. It had its moments. Take care." And the phone clicked.

I was still stunned. I was so caught up in thought that I continued to stuff my duffle bag with clothes without even thinking. The robotic action continued until I had all my personal items packed. I glanced at my watch. I probably still had forty-five minutes before General Valencia's plane arrived. Already tending to business in Bogotá, the Commander of US Army South had promised to pick me up in his Gulf Stream after his official meetings.

But my mind went back to ponder the news. After all these years I surmised that life comes around in a full circle. To think that the same guerrilla that killed Fred ended up dying in Colombia at the hands of the same advisor that had him in his sights fourteen years prior.

I carefully placed the military dog tags in the left breast pocket of my BDU shirt. I had already promised myself that I would personally present those dog tags to SSG Grogan's widow in Fayetteville, North Carolina upon return to the States to tell her that her husband's death had been avenged in Colombia.

It took awhile, but eventually we got things cleaned up in the COJIC and a new structure was already being built by the personnel from the Army Corps of Engineers within weeks after the attack. It would be operational by the time Pete arrived to take on my duties as senior American military advisor.

As the US Army Gulf Stream aircraft lifted from the TQ runway, I felt a lump in my throat. It is hard to believe that as much as I had detested duty at TQ, I was actually sad that my tour was over. I peered out the aircraft's right window looking at all the familiar sites that I had come to know…and yes, to love. Breaking through the first layer of low lying clouds, I strained my neck attempting to get the last glimpse of the aircraft runway and old buildings of the base below me through my window. I wondered if I would ever return to TQ. In the Army you never know. It is better to say, "Until next time," because life has a way of bringing one back at the most unexpected time.

The soft bump of the runway in Isla Grande regional airport in San Juan woke me up as the pilot put the jet engines in reverse thrust. We were back in Puerto Rico and my unit's headquarters… the place were my journey had begun. My mission to TQ had officially ended.

> *Too late, my time has come, send shivers down my spine…Body's aching all the time…Goodbye everybody, I've got to go…Gotta leave you all behind and face the truth…*
>
> *Queen*

EPILOGUE

LIFE'S FULL CIRCLE

Many times I've been alone and many times I've cried...Anyway you'll never know the many times I've tried...And still they lead me back... to the long, winding road...You left me standing here...a long, long time ago...Don't leave me standing here...lead me to your door...

**"The Long and Winding Road"
as recorded by The Beatles**

**LOCATION, ANYWHERE
TIME...YESTERDAY...TODAY...TOMORROW...**

I've thought, pondered, and reflected on my tour at Tres Esquinas and my support to the Colombian Armed Forces many times since my return. I will say this. Starting with the American Embassy, the ambassador, and her staff, I couldn't have served with a more professional group of civilian and military officers than those that worked in Bogotá. I saw the cream of the crop tirelessly working to solve the many problems that they faced daily. The Chief of Station, Dirk Jones, was a dye in the wool career CIA officer and, you know what? He was a solid operator and he supported me without question. After I got to know him, I saw that he was just a little gruff from having a lot of responsibility and an overall tough assignment in Colombia. I will always be indebted to him and his operators for making my tour at TQ as successful as it was. My old friend Kent Bernardo and his USMILGP staff gave me everything I needed in terms of solid country knowledge, moral support, and encouragement. Kent will always be one of my heroes and life long friends.

Last, but not least, and probably the most important protagonists of this war are the Colombian Armed Forces. These guys and gals are well trained, proficient in the art and science of war, and they are brave soldiers. I admire them for being at war in defense of their country for so many years. When Colombia eventually defeats the FARC and the country achieves peace, it will be a result of its professional military corps and the fine officers and enlisted men that are at the heart of Colombian military successes.

God bless them all and may God bless their devotion and dedication to the fight. I couldn't have been assigned to advise a better bunch of professional soldiers and jungle fighters. They are truly among some of Latin America's best. I propose a toast to them out of respect and admiration, for as General Montalvo was fond of saying, only through their hard work and perseverance will God concede victory to them in the Colombian war on drugs.

I've also reflected on this episode in my life. As I see it, my contribution to the war on drugs was but a drop in the bucket of many initiatives that the US military made and continued to make in support of our Colombian allies. Whose war is it?...theirs or ours? It really doesn't matter. What matters most is that we are all in this together...working to bring this situation to some kind of resolution.

There were days at TQ that I felt overwhelmed by the magnitude of the mission. Other days I really felt that we were making a difference and having an impact on defeating the threat. I guess we can attribute that to the US Army's can do attitude. We are the consummate optimists because like the Colombians, we also know that God will concede victory to those that persevere. We in the military must never give up the fight.

A war of this nature is like a war on crime. You have to stay the course...improve security...maintain vigilance...strike at the warlords and the gang leaders...destroy the infrastructure. If we give up, then the criminals will simply have free reign to do as they please. We have no choice but to pursue our national and security interests to the best of our ability.

My Colombian counterparts were always fond of reminding me that until we in the US reduce demand for cocaine, cocaine will continue to be produced in Colombia or other countries of the region. Perhaps, we need to look at our drug education program and see how we can make it more effective. When I talk to friends about how cocaine is made, they are usually dumbfounded. Does the drug consuming population understand the long term effects of snorting or shooting up a product that is made from Drano, sulfuric acid, hydrochloric acid, nail polish remover, cement, gasoline, liquid ammonia solvent, slaked lime, and even urine? Is it not surprising that drug users get nose bleeds as the inner linings of their sinuses get eaten away by these caustic and cor-rosive chemicals? The deterioration of the body may be as much a result of the long term effects of consuming a coca-based nar-cotic as it is from injecting one's body with lethal chemicals. We need to do better in informing and getting the word out. Perhaps videos shown in schools of how cocaine is made might prove effective in letting present and future cocaine users know more of what is at stake in their decision. Seems to me that it's worth a try. We can at least say that we are fully engaged in fighting the war on drugs, not only through police enforcement, military surveil-lance and interdiction, military operations that target the cocaine producing infrastructure in Colombia, but also doing our share in better educating and informing the cocaine consumer. I suppose like everything else in life, time will tell.

Despite the passing of time, however, I'm sorry to say that I never saw TQ again... except in my memories and dreams which would serve as my photo mosaic of a hundred and one sights and emotions.

Eventually the day that all professional officers know will arrive, did. Three years after returning from TQ, I retired from active duty, and like many former soldiers, I could not totally get away from the military. I accepted a job as a military contractor and continued to serve in support of the US Army. I eventually even purchased a grand piano...one of my lifelong dreams.

As to the others, Pete also retired from service and we continued to stay in contact, just like old times...always sharing views and opinions on life, politics, and our military institution, that despite its flaws and shortcomings, we still loved. In time we lost touch with each other as other interests and demands created a thousand and one excuses for not writing or e-mailing.

General Montalvo did very well in his career. He went on to eventually lead his country's armed forces. He was an outstanding officer and a great leader. When I close my eyes, I can still see him...especially the morning of the attack on TQ when he was on the radio shouting instructions and orders to his soldiers.

Most of the officers that served in TQ went on to also have successful careers. Even the US Army NCOs that supported me continued to serve for many more years to come. As to be expected, I never heard from Stan again since I was no longer linked to the national intelligence system. Someone did tell me that he returned to the CIA's academy as an instructor and later retired. My buddy Kent Bernardo also retired from active duty in

Colombia and as far as I know, remained working as a civilian contractor in support of the Colombian military.

With every passing year our lives just seem to fade away into the twilight of time. I guess as the saying goes, "Old soldiers never die...they just fade away."

I too felt my life fading away. After being in the limelight for so many years, we withdraw somewhere into the background of life. But even though we may be in the background, it is important to stay engaged, to stay involved, whether it is in a new profession, involvement in the community, or being active in your church. Volunteering fills our need to help others and to stay connected to something bigger than us. Otherwise, life becomes a meaningless transition.

In his book, *American Caesar*, the author, William Manchester, captured the words of General Douglas MacArthur regarding this subject. Let me share these words with you for I feel that they best reflect this view:

People grow old only by deserting their ideals...Years may wrinkle the skin, but to give up interest wrinkles the soul...You are as young as your faith, as old as your doubt; as young as your self-confidence, as old as your fear; as young as your hope, as old as your despair. In the central place of every heart there is a recording chamber; so long as it receives messages of beauty, hope, cheer and courage, so long are you young. When...your heart is covered with the snows of pessimism and the ice of cynicism, then and then only are you grown old—and then, indeed, as the ballad says, you just fade away.

Many years later, I got an e-mail from a friend who informed me that Pete passed away in his sleep. I was saddened by the news, but in my heart I felt that he had lived a full life and had done more than his share to make it a better place for all.

Some of the military personnel that I worked with professionally in Colombia passed away too. I got the e-mails or read the obituaries. I even stood over some of their headstones or attended their funerals.

The world revolves, pages turn, and so do our lives. After many years, even being a 'Mister' became acceptable to me, except when I would be reminded while standing in line at the local Walmart department store waiting for the cashier to tally up my order. Her voice interrupted my deep thought and the daze I was in.

"Thank you for shopping at Walmart, Mr. Vallejo."

"You're very welcome."

THE END

Rick's last day also finally arrived. It is ironic that it was just as he had envisioned. He was playing his grand piano in the family room one crisp and cool autumn morning. Outside his window and in full view, the oak, elm, maple, and sweet gum trees were in full autumn splendor. The vivid palette of bright red, yellow, and orange served as a colorful inspiration to him. But that splendor and vivid palette were but a brief moment in time. I'm sorry to say that the heart attack came quickly. Rick didn't finish the song he was playing on the piano…but he was close. Somewhere at the end of the Beatles' *The Long and Winding Road*, his life ended on a fine note.

Ruthie Vallejo

But still they lead me back...to the long, winding road. You left me standing here...a long, long time ago...Don't leave me waiting here... lead me to your door...

The Beatles

★ ★ ★

Made in the USA
Lexington, KY
01 July 2012